PINE RIVER

SPECIAL EDITION COVER

TIJAN

Edited by Jessica Royer Ocken
Developmental Editor: Becca Mysoor
Proofread by Paige Smith, AW Editing, Amy English, Kimberley Holm,
Michele Ficht, & Chris O'Neil Parece

For my readers and for any that feel they've been broken at some point in their life.

1

RAMSAY

Creak!

I opened my eyes to the sound of someone sneaking into the house.

I rolled over and checked the clock. Seven twenty-eight in the morning.

I knew who was sneaking in. It usually wasn't the parent creeping in at this time of day. I sighed and sat up. My mom was coming home from a double shift at Pine River Nursing Center. She was being the adult, doing all sorts of adult things the way she always did. She'd made the hard decision that what we'd had back in Cedra Valley was dunzo, and since we were in a situation where we needed family, off we went to Pine River. The population here was barely three thousand, which was the opposite of everything we were used to. My last school had that number of people just in my grade.

I got up, not fighting a yawn, and headed to the bathroom.

Washing. Putting on makeup—the whole ordeal.

Then came choosing my clothes, and since it was my first day at Pine River High School, I knew I needed to be smart about it. Clothes were important. Clothes made the first impression, and I didn't want too flashy. That was another lesson learned from this last year: Don't be flashy. Don't stick out. Don't be a target. But I wasn't a wallflower either. I wasn't a pushover.

Hmmm...

I went with tight black jeans, a textured gray short-sleeve tank that tied in the front with a red flannel shirt over it to cover my arms. My light gray high tops rounded out the outfit—oh, and long, black feather earrings.

There.

I was preppy, edgy, and cutesy, but also nothing on me stood out to put me in the pretty-girl clique. I was pushing toward fashionable tomboy, and that was more me than I'd ever been back in Cedra Valley.

It felt good.

It felt right.

I could pull this uniform off for a year—my last year, then it was off to college and WTFK (who the fuck knew).

I sighed and took one last look in the mirror.

I had dark brown hair, but my highlights gave me a tawny brown look. I kept it shoulder length so I could sweep it back and not worry about it.

Not that I had to since it never got flat. It never got frizzy. There was always a slight curl to it, and when it dried, it looked healthy and shiny. I had fan-fucking-tastic hair. That also meant I stayed away from product. I wasn't a dummy. I splurged with what money I had and bought the good stuff for shampoo. No conditioner. That was it. I kept it simple, but it worked for me.

I had almond-shaped dark eyes and a heart-shaped face—symmetrical. I'd been told that meant it was appealing to the eye. No bullshit, I had a face I could do almost anything with. Being confident in my looks wasn't my problem. I was confident, but not arrogant. There was a difference. My mama taught me to love my body, love my mind, and love my soul. I did all three, but that didn't mean everyone else did. Because of that, I was on a mission for no drama, no fighting, no targeting, no jealousy. *Blend* but not let anyone target me either.

Okay. My pep talk done, I nabbed my backpack and headed to the kitchen.

"Hey, sweetie," my mom called.

I left my bag in the hallway and rounded the corner. She was at the toaster, and I stopped for a moment and took her in. She was tired. She had the same hair as me, but she'd put hers up into a clip. She also didn't believe in makeup because, what was the purpose anymore? Her scrubs were baggy on her because she'd gone to the thrift store for those. She had good sneakers, though. She needed them since she was on her feet for sixteen hour shifts.

"Morning. Did you eat?" I asked as I helped myself to the coffee, knowing she'd brewed this pot for me.

"I did on my last break." She set my toast on a plate and put it on the counter.

After grabbing some creamer, I went over and sat, but I didn't stop eyeing my mom.

We were in an odd situation.

We had money, or we were supposed to have money. My dad's family was fighting for what he'd left us, so what money we had, we might just lose to the lawyers. Mom and I understood that, while we might have some nice things from our previous life, those could be the only nice things we'd have for the foreseeable future.

My mom had gotten an education, but she had never used her degree. She married my dad and did whatever housewives did. Back in Cedra Valley, that was a lot of volunteering, a lot of luncheons, a lot of shindig parties in the evening, and a lot of gossiping. To Mom's credit, she didn't partake in the gossip, but she was friends with those ladies because usually the bigger the gossip, the bigger the purse. My mom cared about giving back, so being friends with those types was a requirement.

Sucks that they turned on her after my dad died, but not only had my mom taught me to love my body, mind, and spirit but also she taught me to believe in karma. One day those hypocritical, self-righteous bitches would be ousted when their husbands wanted an upgrade that came in the form of a newer and younger version of them.

"Ramsay, are you ready for your first day?" Mom leaned back against the counter.

I had to grin. She was more nervous than I was. I took a bite of my toast and gestured to her. "You can chill, Mom. I'll be fine."

She let out a sigh. "A part of me knows you'll be fine. Your cousins are there, but the other part of me . . ." She gave me a sad smile. "You know I worry, honey."

Yeah. Because the last year almost took the life out of us.

I got real and lowered the mask a little. "I'll be fine, Mom. I mean it."

She eyed me for a moment and then nodded. I could see the relief come over her. Her head lifted, and the worry lines eased. They were replaced by exhausted lines instead, but one small victory at a time. Reassuring my mom so she could get some much-needed sleep? That was a victory I'd carry with me all day. Score one for myself.

She crossed the room. "Okay, sweetie." Cupping the back of my head, she pressed a kiss to my forehead. "I love you very much. Don't let Clint get you in trouble today, and I'll see you after school. Want me to pick you up?"

I shook my head, giving her a hug. "I'll be good, Mom. I promise. I might bike, give the car a rest."

She frowned, taking in my coffee and the piece of toast I still had left. "You're going to bike and carry your coffee?"

"I'm super talented. I can do many things at once."

She groaned, but chuckled. "I have no doubt. Just . . . be okay, okay?"

Be okay. The other mission I had for this year.

"I will." The words slipped out on a whisper. I hadn't meant for that to happen, but she looked even more relieved.

"Safe and smart." That was my motto.

Biking in Cedra Valley wouldn't have been safe and smart— too many interstates and bad neighborhoods. But Pine River? Totally safe. I'd visited my cousins so many times and they'd driven me through the town. If there were a bad part of town, it was isolated to one or two blocks. For the most part, this town seemed like the quintessential small town—everyone knew everyone. Everyone looked out for everyone.

Right?

I'd have to wait and see. I only knew my cousins here.

After pouring my coffee into a to-go cup, I finished my last slice of toast in four bites and took it with me. My mom was already upstairs, and she'd be out within a few minutes, or so I hoped. I locked the door behind me, making sure my phone was in my bag.

I grabbed my bike and headed out.

2

RAMSAY

I'd been to my cousins' high school before, but not the new one. According to my cousins, they tore down the old one and built a brand spanking new one over the spring and summer, and this was the first year for everyone to use it. Riding up to the parking lot, I was surprised. The building was gorgeous. Huge columns extended from over the doors to the roof, up probably three stories. The rest of the front was all glass windows, floor to ceiling, and there was some kind of walkway on the second level. As I went in through the metal detectors on the first level, I spotted the cafeteria. There were tables and booths everywhere.

Looking into the middle of the school, there was an open-air atrium with some serious skylights. It gave the school a very cool feeling—like we were outside, but not. Vitamin D must've been an issue in this part of the country.

"You done gawking?" A security guard waited for me to move forward.

I shot him a look, picked up my bag, and headed to the office. There were a few other students inside. I could tell a few were underclassmen because they looked tiny. There was another guy in a chair with a seriously pissed-off look on his face. He had tattoos all over him and his hair in a crew-Mohawk, which was kinda cool. It fit him.

He glanced at me, his eyes sparking in interest, but before he or I could say something, a girl stepped aside and the receptionist held out her hand. "Sweetie, come here." She wiggled her fingers to me, and I stepped forward.

"You have papers?" She peered over the top of her reading glasses, squinting. "You're new, right? I don't recognize you."

"Yes. Ramsay Williams."

"No papers?" She pursed her lips together, looking me over before making a clicking sound in her throat and going back to her computer screen.

I frowned. "I didn't know I was supposed to bring papers. What papers?"

She was paused in her typing and leaned closer to her screen. "Nope. You're good. You were registered last week." Those very no-nonsense eyes pinned me in place. "What are you in here for?"

I shifted on my feet. This lady was unnerving. I adjusted my bag over my shoulder. "I was told to stop in for my locker and class schedule. That stuff."

"Gotcha." She went back to typing, and a curse left her before the printer started up behind her. Wheeling back, she grabbed the paper, scribbled something on the back, and handed it over. She pointed to the top corner. "Locker number. Code is here. And your schedule. We're not doing student IDs this morning, but stop in anytime this afternoon and we'll get that settled for you as well. Now, you'll need an ID for lunch. You got money on you? Know anyone here?"

Fud-ruckers. I did, but I'd been hoping to keep my connection to my cousins on the down-low. They were the opposite of *blending in.*

"Uh . . ."

"I'll spot you." The tattoo guy stood, giving me the head jerk. It was something cool people gave other cool people, so I guessed I was officially part of that group.

Just then, an older guy wearing a tie, dress shirt, and slacks came out from a back hallway and stopped, looking over the waiting room.

"Macon?" He made a motion to follow him. "Why are you already in my office?" he added with a sigh. "School hasn't even started."

The guy smirked, grabbing his backpack and circling around me. "Macon Rice," he said under his breath as he passed. "Find me at lunch." He gave me a once-over before whistling to himself. "No problem at all."

Maybe I needed to rethink my outfit choices? The once-over was too in-my-face. I didn't like it.

"Thanks, but I know people." My tone was cool, the chilly kind this time.

He paused and assessed me again. Then he tipped his head. "See you around."

I was a dick.

I'd thrown back his invite, and he'd noted it, and I knew—I was overthinking this. I just hoped he wasn't some school dictator because those did exist.

The receptionist cleared her throat, and I looked back to find her giving me a suspicious look. "Come this afternoon for your ID. Do you, in fact, actually know people here?"

I nodded. "I do."

"Good, and word of advice"—she gestured down the hallway where Macon Rice and the older man had gone—"stay away from that one." Then she pasted on a smile. "Have a nice day, dear." She leaned to the side. "Next!"

On my way out the door, a girl came up beside me. "Hi."

She had blonde hair pulled back into a low bun, and her face was covered in freckles. She beamed at me. "I'm Gem, and

I overheard everything. I've decided that you and I are going to be friends."

I raised an eyebrow. "We are?"

Her head bobbed up and down. "Oh yeah. Anyone who can give Macon Rice the toss is already a goddess in my mind."

Oh great. "Is he a big deal around here?"

She shrugged, then nodded to my paper. "I'll tell you on the way to your locker. What's your number?" I told her, and we headed down a hallway. "He's not a nobody, if that's what you mean. He goes through girls, like, one a week. It's kinda gross, when you think about it, but all the girls know. They still end up in his bed, and then they fight about it when the next girl is chosen. He got two girls pregnant last year, so it's a good sign that you read him right and didn't take him up on his offer. You'd be labeled as the first-week girl, and I don't think that's what you want. Also, don't get freaked about the security guards. They're only here on certain days." She veered through a group of people, nodding to a locker. "Here's yours. Mine's over there." She pointed across the hallway. "Give me two seconds. I'll grab my stuff and be back to show you to your first class."

It took two tries before I got my code to work.

I had my bag in and was pulling out my phone when it buzzed.

Alex: Hey!! You here? Where are you?

Crap.

Me: Here, but you guys are supposed to act like you don't know me.

Gem was heading back, a notebook and laptop in hand, when I felt the mood in the hallway shift.

The crowds parted, and a group of guys sauntered down the hallway.

Gem sighed, falling against my neighbor's locker, and jerked her chin toward the group. "Wanna know who are at the top? Those guys are." Her eyes narrowed. "Or most of them are there. But, see those triplets?"

My heart sank because I did see them. I saw them very well.

"Gorgeous, blond gods," Gem narrated. "Triplets. All jocks too, by the way, but interestingly, different sports. And again, can I say triplets? That's Trenton talking to the dark-haired guy. The dark-haired guy who isn't a triplet is Cohen Rodriguez. The middle triplet is Clint, and he's the troublemaker of the three. The last triplet is Alex, and—"

Her hand clamped on my arm, and I winced as she whisper-shrieked in my ear, "OMG! Alex is looking right at us." A pause. "At you. He's looking at you! OMG!"

Her voice gave me a nails-on-the-chalkboard vibe. I gave Alex a dirty look and turned my back to my locker because Trenton and Clint hadn't seen me. She wasn't exaggerating when she said Clint was the troublemaker of the three. I didn't want to start the first five minutes of my new high school career by getting into a fight with him, but I would if I had to because those triplets were my cousins.

She sucked in her breath. I could hear her hyperventilating next to me as another presence appeared on my other side.

I waited.

He didn't go away.

After a little bit, I said, "Go away."

Alex started laughing, falling against the locker next to me and facing the hallway. He rested one foot on the wall behind him, doing the jock-cool-lounge thing, like he didn't give a rat's ass who was watching. The nice thing about Alex? He truly didn't care.

Or he didn't pay attention.

He poked me on the arm. "Come on. This is ridiculous. It's going to come out. Some guy is going to hit on you or talk dirty about you, and we all know how that'll go over. Embrace the cousin love, Rams. We're here, and we're not the ones embarrassed to tell people who we care about." He leaned around me, and I could hear his smile. "Hey, Gem." His arm fell around my shoulders and he turned me around, pulling me back against him, and resting his chin on my shoulder. "Have you met my cousin, Ramsay? She's pretty awesome, if you want a cool friend."

I groaned, closing my eyes.

I could feel the attention from the girls in the hallway watching us.

Gem looked as if she were about to fall over. "You know my name."

Alex laughed again, shifting to stand beside me with his arm still around my shoulders. "Our school isn't that big." He nudged me. "What's your first class?"

I held up my schedule.

He smirked. "Yeah, that whole plan of yours would've died a quick death anyway." He gave me a look. "Clint's in your first class."

I groaned again. "Seriously?"

"What class do you have?" Gem asked, her cheeks flushed.

"AP chem."

I showed her my schedule, and her eyes got big. "These are mostly AP classes. Fourth-year Spanish?"

"*Si.* I moved from Texas. Knowing Spanish down there is just smart."

"We have sixth period together, though."

Alex reached over and took my schedule. "Uh . . . I'm in your third period and your fifth period. Trent's in your fourth. Clint will show you where your second class is."

I took it back. "When's lunch?"

"Between fourth and fifth. You have study hall seventh period?" He shot me a grin. "You do that on purpose?"

I was smiling on the inside, but only shrugged. "Maybe."

He gave me a knowing look. "They take attendance here for study hall. It's not a skip class."

Well, fuck. "I'm new. Maybe if I don't show up the first week, I don't *ever* have to show up."

Alex burst out laughing. "Yeah, that right there tells me there's no way you can blend in here." He shook his head, his eyes amused. "I'm excited to have you here."

The first bell rang, and Alex took off, telling me to find him for lunch.

Gem faced me, her eyes back to bulging. "I cannot believe you know Alex Maroney. That means you know Clint and Trenton too, and I claimed you first as a friend." She pivoted on her heels, her hands shooting up in the air. "Go me!" She rounded right back, dropping her arms. "I'm just kidding. Not really. I'm excited, that's all, but please remember I wanted to be your friend before I knew you were related to Pine River royalty."

"Royalty?"

A second bell rang.

She groaned. "Okay. We have to go. I'll show you your first class."

We took off, and she dropped me at a classroom down the hall.

She gave another wave. "See you at lunch!"

3

RAMSAY

I walked into the class and saw two empty seats. One was in the front, and another was in the back next to the cool guy in the group, my cousin. He was laughing at what two guys in front of him were saying, but once he saw me, his laughter died down and he straightened in his seat.

Here was my dilemma.

Yes, Alex was right. The whole keeping-the-cousins-quiet thing had been dumb, and it was already shot. Alex hugging me and putting his arm around my shoulders had cemented that. If our relationship weren't already around school, it would be by lunch. My cousins were seniors and they were top shelf. But Clint and I? That was a whole other dynamic.

He got me in trouble.

I got him in trouble.

We got each other in trouble. We were the trouble twins.

But today, right now, I didn't want trouble.

So I hugged my laptop tighter and headed for the seat in the front.

He harrumphed as I passed. "Chicken shit?"

The guys all choked. "Dude. Why?" one asked.

I swung around because, goddamn it, he'd already lit the fuse attached to my Clint bomb. It was permanently inside of me. "Excuse me, dipshit?"

The room went silent.

"Damn!" The same guy laughed.

Clint rotated on his stool so he was facing me, the same height as me standing. The tables were high-top chemistry tables.

He smirked. "You're new. Why the fuck are you going to sit up front? Sit here. We're the cool guys."

I smirked right back. "Funny. When you have to explain that you're cool, it makes you not cool."

His eyes darkened, but I saw the flash. Clint loved this, loved when we fought. He leaned forward, placing a hand on the empty stool between us. "You're scared. Don't think you can handle hanging with us?"

The class was silent, listening. I had no doubt we were the new entertainment. Alex had been so right it wasn't even funny.

I glared. "I can hang, *honey*. I just don't want to."

To our credit, the words weren't really controversial or particularly mean for us. If we wanted to, we could really go at it. We had a complicated relationship, but everything was more dramatic since Clint was popular and no one knew who I was. If they knew this was a family dispute, half the people would've already gone back to their daily programmed conversations.

Just then, the teacher entered the room and sighed. "Clint, this is the new girl. Are you already flirting with her?"

Clint's face screwed up in disgust.

I whirled around. "Don't. Please. I don't want to vomit in my first class here."

A few kids gasped, but Clint snickered.

His friends laughed too. One whispered, "She's sassy. I like it."

"Don't go there." Clint's voice cut off on a growl.

"What?" The guy was confused.

"Miss . . ." The teacher looked at his attendance sheet. "Williams?" He looked up for confirmation.

I gave a quick nod.

"I'm Mr. Leonard," he said. He looked behind me and scanned the room. Then his eyebrows pulled together, and he went over the list again. "Where is Mr. Raiden?"

No one said a word.

"Clint, where is Mr. Raiden?"

Clint glanced at me. "I don't know. He had a fight last night, so he might not be in today."

The teacher let out a frustrated sound before returning to his current problem: me.

"You can have a seat with Miss Harthorne in the front."

"What?" the girl in front protested. "I sit alone, Mr. Leonard. You know I have claustrophobia. I don't know her. I'll be claustrophobic if a stranger sits next to me."

Another frustrated sound gurgled from Mr. Leonard's throat. His eyes went flat. "Then sit with someone who won't give you claustrophobia because you won't be claiming an entire table to yourself and forcing three other students to share. Choose."

Her mouth fell open, but when the teacher didn't change his mind, she squeaked, shoved up from her seat, and looked over the class. She looked at Clint.

I looked at Clint.

He looked at me, a plea in his eyes. He *did not* want her to sit with him.

Just then, the door swung open, and I wasn't prepared.

Someone should've told me because the guy who walked in was the most gorgeous specimen I'd ever seen, on or off screen. I got a little light-headed.

He was tall and lean, with a strong jawline. His shirt was kinda tight, but not embarrassingly so. More like tight in all the right places. His biceps were delicious. He had a tribal tattoo running around his arm, and when he raked his hand through his hair, I could see the same line on the underside as well. There was a peak of it under his sleeve.

His chin had a dimple in the middle, and his cheekbones were high, shaping his face so his lips were fucking mesmerizing.

Golden.

That was the best word to describe him.

A golden god.

I'd thought my cousins were golden, blond triplets, but not like this guy.

His eyes were dark and piercing, his hair a dirty blond and the kind of messed up that showed he didn't give a fuck, and it worked because it made everyone want him. Like, *immediately*.

I felt punched in the face, followed by another hit to my chest, a third to my stomach, and a knee to the vagina. It was . . . not a reaction I wanted, and because of that, I hated this guy.

I shouldn't be scowling, but I was.

I couldn't help it.

He also had a decent black eye, and the right part of his face was banged up. The side of his mouth was cut and swollen as well.

"Ah, Mr. Raiden," the teacher said. "You have graced our school with your presence this morning."

I waited for the teacher to comment on his bruised face. He didn't.

"We have found ourselves in a dilemma here. We have two empty seats. You and Miss Williams both need to claim one of them, but we also have Miss Harthorne who claims she'll be claustrophobic if she sits with someone she doesn't know." He looked at me. "Please don't take this personally. You're new. Miss Harthorne is having a temper tantrum. This is common—"

"It is not!"

As the teacher spoke to me, I felt Mr. Raiden's gaze come my way. Most times, I wouldn't have been affected by such a casual glance, but this guy's eyes trailing over me flooded me with feelings and sensations and shivers I did not want to experience. It only made me more pissed, and by the time he got to my face, he checked my lips, then checked my hostility. His eyes flew to mine, and his blatant interest was masked as he scowled back.

I relaxed. Good. As long as we'd gotten that settled—I didn't like him, and considering the fuck-you look in his eyes, it seemed he didn't like me either.

I really only had one option because no way I was letting the Harthorne girl take Clint's seat and force me to sit with this guy.

"I'll sit with Clint," I announced and dropped abruptly onto the stool behind him.

Or I would've.

Clint pulled the stool away.

IT HAPPENED IN SLOW MOTION.

I heard the class gasp and then the laughter.

I locked eyes with my cousin and saw him smirking at me.

And as I was falling, I grabbed him. If I was going down, he was going with me. Once we both hit the floor, he shoved upright, but I twisted and kicked his feet out from under him. He fell back down, and then I was up, and I took his stool instead.

He jumped to his feet. "Get off my stool, Rams," he growled.

My answer? I kicked out the one on the floor and said, "Go fetch."

He glared at me but didn't make a move to take me off his

stool. He knew better. I'd grown up with this kid. We didn't spend our time playing with stuffed animals, like I had wanted. We wrestled. We played football. Foosball. We did everything the boys wanted because they were the majority. I didn't love it, but I'd learned to hold my own.

Clint knew this. He and I had tangled the most, but we weren't in one of our backyards right now. We were in his school, and he had a reputation to uphold.

I raised an eyebrow, and he grabbed my stool, slammed it back in place, and then scooped me up as if I weighed nothing. I made some sort of sound, and then he deposited me back on my stool. He returned to his with a huff.

I'd forgotten how strong he was, and—I noted to myself— how strong Alex and Trenton would be too. We weren't little kids scrapping anymore.

Everyone was gaping at us. Even the teacher. I didn't look at Mr. Raiden. I already knew I'd be ignoring him forever and ever, but then Clint announced, "We're cousins. It may not look like it, but I love this piece of shit."

I found a good chunk of his underarm and twisted. He cried out before squashing my hand and wrenched his arm back.

"Don't call me that," I said hotly.

He sighed.

Tit for tat.

This time he gave in. "Fine. Sorry."

The teacher had the last word. "Detention for both of you."

4

RAMSAY

Word had gotten out about me.

Clint showed me where my second class was, and Alex was waiting for me after that one to walk me to our third. Trent was in my fourth period, and with each class, I caught more and more people shooting me looks. The conversations and whispers went quiet when I got close.

I wasn't expecting this much attention. I knew the triplets were popular, but this much focus was a lot. I found Gem in the cafeteria, and mentioned this when she asked how my morning had gone.

"Yeah." She moved forward in line, grabbing a salad and a water. "That's because we're outside the city. There are a ton of smaller towns surrounding us, but they aren't big enough to have their own schools so everyone congregates here. Plus, Pine Valley is across the river. Pine Val is way bigger than us."

"With the distance, that's allowed?"

"They aren't that far away. District boundary lines are broad here. Really broad."

"Wow."

At the register, Gem glanced at me. "You don't have your ID yet, do you?"

I shook my head. "I was going to ask one of my cousins to cover me."

"Not a problem." She handed her card to the lady. "It's not like this is the only time we'll be eating together." She gave me a wink as she took her card back, and then we scanned the cafeteria.

It was bustling with people. Almost every table was full, and the door was opening and closing constantly. People were in the hallway, and I could see a store that had a whole line of people waiting to get food from there.

"I could've paid for my own food there."

Gem shook her head. "That's all junk food. This line has some healthy choices. It's all good." She nodded toward a table in the far corner. "Look. That one's mostly empty. I know the girls sitting there."

But as we approached, those girls got up and headed out, heads bent together, laughing and talking. They hadn't seen us coming, so I didn't take it as a sign of my social status.

Gem grinned at me. "Even better." She went around to the far side, and I sat with my back to the room. She looked beyond me. "I don't know if your cousins will come in. The elite crowd don't usually eat in here. They get their food and go outside, or to a fast food place." She went to take a bite of her salad but paused and straightened upright. "Oh. Whoa."

I turned, feeling my phone buzz.

Alex: Where r u?

Clint calling.

I answered while trying to see what Gem was looking at. "Hey."

"Where are you?" he barked into the phone.

There was a crowd gathering in the middle of the cafeteria, and Gem was on her feet.

Everyone was on their feet. People started running to see what was going on.

"In the café—

He hung up, but as I swung my head around, I found him over by the door. He nodded to me as both Alex and Trenton appeared. Seeing I was okay, they ran forward. Clint held up a hand to me, yelling, "Stay there!"

Gem heard him and grabbed my arm. "Fuck that." She pulled me with her.

Clint angled through the crowd, coming to my side. "You should go somewhere else."

Gem frowned at him and tugged me around. We hopped up onto a table to see better. In the middle of the crowd were three guys I recognized, which shocked me. I shouldn't recognize anyone. I barely knew enough people to recognize someone, but I did.

And it wasn't my cousins, which *also* shocked me.

Macon Rice, tattoo guy from the front office, was trading punches with the dark-haired guy that'd been talking to my cousins, and standing directly behind that guy was Mr. Raiden from first period. I still didn't know his first name.

"Fight! Fight! Fight!"

The crowd was chanting, egging them on, and Macon and the other guy seemed evenly matched. One would punch, and the other would counter. Then the one guy got in a couple of roundhouse kicks to Macon's face, and that pushed him back, but teachers and security were running in. They pushed through, but Macon and the other guy wouldn't stop hitting each other.

Clint growled and jumped off the table, pushing into the crowd.

By then, Alex and Trenton had moved forward as well. Clint grabbed the dark-haired guy, wrapping his arms around his arms and yanked him back. Trenton did the same with Macon

Rice, and Alex stood in the middle, his arms held out between them. All three of them were yelling for the other to stand down.

I couldn't stop myself as my gaze trailed toward Mr. Raiden, who I found staring at me with an intensity that made me jump back in surprise.

Glowering hatred came at me, and as I readied myself and stared back with a good fuck-you look, his jaw clenched and he swung his gaze back to his buddy. Macon and his friend were yelling at each other, and he kept trying to swing around my cousins.

Then Mr. Raiden stepped up.

He said something I couldn't hear, but it was short and simple, and as if he'd flipped a switch, the guys stopped fighting. My cousins dropped their arms. The guards grabbed the two fighters as the teachers started waving for the crowd to disperse.

"Fuck you, Scout!" Macon yelled.

Scout? That was his first name?

Raiden started for him, and Macon melted backward. Almost literally. It was somewhat comical to watch.

My eyebrows shot up. "If that dude had the power to stop the fight like that, why didn't he step in right away?"

"Oh." Gem looked at me, biting her lip. "I can see the job of filling you in on all the school gossip has fallen to my shoulders. I suppose your cousins aren't going to tell you the hierarchy here."

I frowned at her.

"Come, my child. You have much to learn."

Most everyone was sitting back down now, but a group still lingered in the middle of the room—a few guys and a bunch of girls. They were talking with my cousins.

I followed Gem to our table.

"Okay." Gem dropped into her seat, giving me a shrewd

look. "First off, I have a feeling your cousins are going to head over here any second, so I gotta start at the top. The top being Scout Raiden."

Scout. That *was* his first name.

Why'd he have to have a hot name too?

Figures.

"And the reason he didn't fight is because he can't."

"What do you mean? The dude was in a fight last night, Clint said in class."

She nodded. "Like a sanctioned fight, as in a fight in a league where people can bet and make money off him."

"Like a pro?"

"That's the rumor. He's too young for the UFC to give him a contract, but he's on his way. He moved here a year ago when he was starting to really get noticed. I guess his uncle is some big guy in the UFC world and has been training him. Miles something. I don't think they have the same last name. I don't really know, but his uncle's loaded. I do know that. He has a gym on the river. Other guys pay to work out there, but Scout was the reason it was built. All I know is that the guy can fight. Like, for real fight."

"What if he has to fight?"

She shook her head. "It can't happen—or, I don't think it can. I'm kinda fuzzy on the rules myself. Self-defense might be one thing, but even there, it's frowned on. But if you want to know someone who's going to end up famous, he's it. He's getting a name in the fighting world right now, and he's probably going to get a contract when he turns nineteen. The UFC has only signed two other nineteen year olds. He'll be the third."

I glanced over and saw he was grinning at something Clint said.

His face was normally locked down. Guarded. But when he grinned, it made me do a double take. He wasn't just stunning.

The guy deserved to be on a runway or a magazine cover at the very least.

Ugh. Why'd he have to be so hot?

"What's he like?"

"Like?"

"His personality. He's friends with my cousins, but they've never mentioned him."

Gem shrugged, eating her salad again. "He's okay, I guess. He doesn't talk to anyone except for Cohen and your cousins. I guess you'll get to know what he's like."

"Cohen was the guy fighting Macon? You mentioned him earlier."

"Yeah. Cohen Rodriguez. He and Scout have been tight since the first day. I think they knew each other before he moved here, but he's gotten close to your cousin too."

I looked over again, unable to stop myself.

As if hearing our conversation, Scout stopped grinning and turned. His eyes found mine, and his amusement fled. The same hatred as before simmered there as he glared back at me. Then I realized I'd been glaring first.

I turned my back, frustrated. What was my problem?

No. Wait. I knew.

I wanted to fuck Scout, but I wasn't going to because of the last guy I slept with.

And thinking of *him*, a wave of emotion swept through me, threatening to choke me. No, no, no.

The panic was coming in.

I wasn't going there. I couldn't, unless I was okay going comatose for a full week. But, damn, that feeling in me was rising, building. Spreading. It was too fast, too strong. I knew what was happening, and I couldn't stop it. I was already too far gone.

The attack was here.

I knew what I needed to do to handle it. I shoved up out of my seat, muttering, "I gotta go."

So dramatic, but . . . gah.

I thought I'd dealt with this stuff. I thought I had pushed these emotions out of me, destroyed them, but they were still there, and they were taking over. They always took over.

I'd be paralyzed if I didn't do something soon.

I passed the hall with my locker and sailed out of school. I was on my bike within a minute, and I was leaving the parking lot when the tears started falling. I couldn't hold them back any longer.

Shit, shit, shit.

Talk about teenager tragedy.

It was the first day, and I was skipping lunch with a sobfest choking my insides, but damn. Damn!

I couldn't go there.

I didn't know Scout.

I hadn't even spoken a word to him.

He reminded me of *him*. That was why. That was all.

When I thought of *him*, I also thought of my dad . . . and I *could not go there.*

I wouldn't.

This was old crap that hadn't been counseled out of me.

That was it.

That was all.

I'd be fine.

I could take a day.

My mom would understand.

Just one day.

5

SCOUT

I 'd just gotten to the gym when my uncle found me. He was coming out of his office and jerked his chin up. "I need to talk to you."

I didn't stop, just headed into the locker room and opened my locker. I dropped my bag and began going through it, pulling out everything I'd need to work my ass off for the next few hours. He followed me and leaned against the wall. A few other guys were in there, so my uncle raised his voice, "Can we have the room, fellas?"

"Yeah, man."

"No problem."

Once they were gone, he went over, hitting the door shut and locking it. Word would spread that we were having a meet, so if anyone needed in, they'd deal with it. The guys liked my uncle, really liked that he built this gym. Half the guys were hoping for a fighting career because of this opportunity. Having the right place to train was vital.

"What's up?" I stripped off my shirt, pulling on a tank.

"I know you just did a fight, but I got a call."

"No," I said it quick and firm because no fucking way was I

fighting so soon after I just had one. And the way he was approaching me about it, told me it was going to be soon. Otherwise, he would've waited and hit me up at the house or after training.

"It's good money. Good exposure."

"No."

"It's next Thursday." He kept on as if I hadn't said a word. "Way I see it, you pretend as if the last fight never happened and we've just extended training by a week. That's all."

I rounded on him. "I said no!"

He didn't care. That was obvious as he leaned forward, still resting against the wall, his arms folded over his chest. "It's Brandon Nelson's kid."

That made me pause.

Brandon Nelson was a bigwig in the MMA world. If they were asking for his son to fight me, that was a big deal.

I straightened. "I'm going to wipe the floor with his kid."

My uncle sighed, pushing off from the wall and coming closer to me. "I know. He knows it. The kid knows it. Neither of you are signed yet, and everyone is aware of your skill level. I think you fight his kid and he sees how it goes, how you handle yourself. If he likes what he sees, he'll approach for a fight against him. Think about it. The PR spin is already written. You beat the kid, he wants to beat you for his kid once you're signed. The money could be really good—the best you've gotten yet. This could set you up *big* time."

He was right, but hell. A fucking fight in a week. We usually trained for months.

"I don't know."

"Look, normally I'd never recommend you do this fight. But this one, just this one, I think you should."

My phone started buzzing, and after checking the screen and seeing it was family, I turned it off.

"Was that your mom?"

He saw the screen. Jesus. I knew why I came out here. The reasons. I knew the rumors, and the rumors were so far from the truth, and my uncle knew it all too, but I did not want to have this conversation. Still. He asked, and that was his sister.

I kicked off my shoes and socks, then finished changing. "Yeah."

"What's she want?"

"I don't know. World fucking peace?"

"Hey," he barked at me, shutting my locker and getting in my face. Once there, he got a good look at me, and he backed up. "Sorry. I—it's your mom. She's not the bad guy."

A hard laugh ripped from me as I sat on the bench and grabbed the tape for my feet. "You're right. That's Grandpops and everyone else."

"Not your mom. Not me. She sent you out here, and you know I'm not part of that group."

He was speaking truth, which I appreciated, but the whole thing still pissed me off. "Look, I don't want to talk about it."

He was watching me, in a knowing way, more knowing than I would've liked. He took a whole step back, his tone changing, softening. "He can't do anything to you."

Another hard laugh from me. This one came from my gut. "That's not the truth, and you know it." I finished the taping and put it back on the bench beside me.

I stood. I was ready to train. Fuck. I *needed* to train to get this conversation out of my head.

He went and picked up the tape. "I'll call your mom and tell her to back off you for a bit."

I didn't respond, but that'd be nice. He saw it on my face, and I knew he saw it.

He nodded, starting for the door. "Let me know by tonight about the fight."

"Yeah."

"Stretch, then hit the mats. I want you to work on leg whips first. And remember to keep your head down."

My fucking family. But even though he and I didn't have a 'share our feelings' kind of a bond, I was like the other guys. I was grateful for him too, just in a whole different way.

6

RAMSAY

The house was big and creepy when it was dark and my mom wasn't here. But it was the closest place to my cousins that we could find for rent. And we had a backyard. If we got a dog, bonus for the furry baby. I liked the house because of the space—lots of space in the kitchen and living room. There was a back patio, and the backyard had a sidewalk that connected to a back alley. The public beach for the river wasn't far. I'd heard from my cousins that the river was *the* place to have a home.

The only con was that the house was old, but I figured maybe there would be ghosts, and I'd try to befriend them in my head. Maybe not so creepy then?

Creak!

Nope.

Still so creepy!

Also, we needed better curtains. The ones we had were ragged and thin, with holes in them and the ends frayed. Since the house was set back from the road a little, I wasn't too worried about someone being able to see inside. Still, though—

ten o'clock at night, and I was locked in my room because the creaks wouldn't stop.

I was starting to think my whole ghost theory wasn't just a theory.

Knock! Knock!

I screamed, a full-body, hair-raising, bloodcurdling scream.

Gasping, I saw a hand at the window, then a wave.

I knew that hand.

Cursing, I lunged for the curtain, whisked it back, and glared at Clint. "Are you serious?"

He only grinned and nodded to the window. His voice came through muffled. "Let me in."

"How are you—" I cut myself off, unlocking the window and trying to push it up.

Oofta. The frame was made of solid wood, and I didn't think anyone had tried sneaking out of it since it'd been made. I got it up an inch, and that was it.

Clint watched me, an eyebrow raised and a sneer on his face. "You serious? You used to be tough. When'd you get weaksauce?"

Well . . . I sent him a withering glare, reached forward, and slammed the window right back down. "Thanks for stopping by."

His mouth fell open. "Are *you* serious? Come on!"

I threw the curtains closed again, but he could still see me because they were hella thin.

He snorted, and I heard that loud and clear. "You weren't answering downstairs, and you took off all day. I came over because I was worried."

Oh.

Man.

Now I felt stupid.

Standing, I motioned for the door. "Can you get back down? You won't fall and break your legs?"

Now he glared at me. "Such weaksauce."

I taunted him, grinning, "I'm not the one who broke his nose because he turned and ran smack dab into the telephone post right behind him."

He growled, but he'd already turned, and I knew he'd get down just fine.

I went to meet him, turning on all the lights because it was still creepy. I unlocked the back door and Clint came in, brushing off some paint chips that had fallen on his shirt. He stopped just inside, looking all around. "Where's Aunt Chris?"

"Working. Double shift. Ailes knows you're here?"

Ailes was Aunt Aileen, my mom's sister.

"No clue. She'll call if she realizes I'm gone." Clint shrugged. He followed me to the kitchen. "You get in trouble for ditching?"

I shook my head. "She understood." I was downplaying it because, while she did understand, she also mentioned finding another counselor for me to talk to. I almost regretted ditching when she said that, but I was hoping to convince her I didn't need to talk to someone.

I'd handle it. I'd have to.

Clint gestured around the place. "I've never been in this house. An old guy used to live here." He grinned at me. "I heard he bit it in here too. You had any ghostly encounters?"

"Shut up." I shoved him to the side. "That's not even funny."

"Even? Don't know why you added that word. I wasn't trying to be funny. I was going for scary since you're scared of the supernatural stuff."

I growled low in my throat, before going to the freezer, grabbing a pizza, and turning on the oven.

"You're making pizza?"

I stifled a laugh and pulled out a pan.

Clint looked through the cupboards and pulled out two glasses. "You got soda in this bitch? Or we drinking wine?"

I was cutting off the packaging but paused and gave him the side-eye.

He was waiting, a small grin on his face, and I just sighed.

He knew the answer.

"Right on!" Clint continued his search through the cupboards until he found the wine. Grabbing the sweet stuff, the one with the twist-off cap, he laughed. "You and Aunt Chris have the coolest and weirdest relationship ever. She doesn't drink this shit, you do, and she buys it for you. My mom would flip a lid if we asked her to do something like that."

I glared as I put the pizza in the oven. "You're a douche."

"What?"

"She buys that for friends and guests—you know, like your mom who likes wine. And she's okay with me sipping it at times because, I mean . . ." I got quiet, shrugging. "You know, this last year sucked major baggage."

Clint got quiet, and I moved around the kitchen.

We'd need plates.

Paper towels.

A pizza cutter.

An oven mitt to pull the pan out.

What else?

I could feel Clint watching me. This time, I felt the heaviness, the concern. I'd brought up the last year. We didn't talk about that. My mom and I referenced it, but there'd been no in-depth discussion.

I couldn't even think about it now.

But I *couldn't* stop because I had already started. Now that was all I was thinking about.

And the pressure was building. The heaviness.

I was crumbling.

Dad . . .

Oh God.

Dad.

"Hey."

I didn't . . . What was I doing?

Getting ready for the pizza. I had to do that.

"Ramsay." Clint was behind me.

I couldn't deal.

I was crumbling.

My dad . . .

"Stop," I told him.

Clint's arms circled around me, and he pulled me back. He held me tight, almost bent over me at the same time. His forehead resting on my shoulder.

"No—"

His arms tightened. "Shhh. Just stop, Rams. Stop."

My knees crumpled. I was going down.

Clint guided my fall, lowering me to the floor and sitting with me. I scooted away from him, flattening myself against one of the cupboards. If I could've opened it, crawled in, and hid forever, I would've. If I could've gone to sleep and never woken up? Yes, please. Here. Right now.

"Rams." Clint's voice was strained. "You're fucking bawling."

I was? I touched my cheek. I was.

Clint was sitting across from me, his knees up, his arms hanging over them, and his face lowered. He was pale. Worried.

I did that to him. "I'm sorry," I rasped.

He flinched. "That's what happens to you?" Forget strained. His voice dipped to being hoarse.

My neck was stiff, but I managed a jerky nod. "Yeah."

He swore under his breath. His Adam's apple bobbed and his hands balled into fists. He smoothed them out, but it was in a rough motion. "I'm sorry. I didn't know."

I closed my eyes. *I'm sorry.* That phrase haunted me.

I swallowed over a knot. "It's kinda a lot, you know?"

"I figured. I mean, we all wondered. We knew how much you loved Cedra, and then you moved here. Had to be bad."

"Yeah," I whispered.

The panic attack was lifting. This was the time when I felt drunk. All my senses were jumbled together. I'd slur my speech. Clint had seen me in a panic attack before, but that was when I was little. I'd gotten better, knew how to recognize them, knew how to prevent them, and then . . . last year happened. Now they were back with a vengeance.

"You wanna talk about it?" He clasped his hands together and let them hang over his knees. "You can think of me like a captive therapist. If you want to, you know, talk about what happened. And all. You know." His Adam's apple moved up and down again before he glanced away. He was blinking a bunch.

"Captive?"

"Yeah." He looked back and smirked. This time, he relaxed, his head resting against the counter behind him, and he stretched out one of his legs. His hands lowered to his lap, but they were still clasped together. "You're making pizza. No high school guy is leaving when he's getting pizza." He gave a slow grin as he watched me, and when he saw my lip quiver in a laugh, the rest of the tension left him. His other leg stretched out, touching mine. "I'm still hoping we'll light into that wine. Wine and pizza? I'm thinking cousin sleepover."

"Wine and pizza? And you'll let me unburden all my trauma on you?"

He rolled his shoulders. "Well, I figure the more wine in me, the better my therapist skills will be. So there's that."

I barked out a laugh.

Another was right behind it.

And a third.

I couldn't stop laughing, and after a bit, I stopped trying. I hadn't laughed in so long.

Clint laughed with me. "Not sure what's so funny about me drinking wine, but I'm rolling with you. See how good my skills are? I'm meeting my client where they are."

That made me laugh harder. "You're such a dumbass," I breathed out, my sides hurting. A good hurting, though, and finally, the last of my panic easing away. "And I love your dumb ass."

He chuckled. "Look at that. Therapist be damned. Next panic attack, we're booting up some Leslie Jones."

That sent me laughing all over again, and soon Clint had his phone out and we were listening to a comedian playlist.

After the first set, the pizza was done.

Clint didn't pause the show, just raised his phone up. He remained on the floor.

I brought the pizza down. The wine and two giant plastic cups came down too. It was that kind of night.

He went to a second set, and I scooted over next to him, the pizza in front of us. By the third set, I was lying on the floor in one direction, and he was lying down, facing the other way. He put the phone between us.

During the fifth set, I opened my eyes to find the pizza was gone. The wine cups were too. I had a pillow under my head, a blanket over me. Clint had the same.

I yawned and mumbled, "I can sleep in my bed."

"Okay."

He got up first, taking the blankets and pillows, and when I looked back, he'd wiped the counter clean.

The back door was locked, and he'd put out all the lights except the one above the oven and the one in the stairway. He'd found the old air mattress he used when we were little, and it was filled with air. Everything was ready.

I'd forgotten what this felt like.

I used the bathroom, brushed my teeth, and crawled into bed.

He came in from using the other bathroom, and he'd turned off the stairway light, but another light farther down the hallway was on. I was guessing the guest bathroom. He kept the door propped open as he got onto the air mattress.

I was almost asleep when I heard him say, "Nothing's going to hurt you. Not here. You gotta know that."

That. That was the feeling I'd forgotten about, forgotten what it felt like.

"I know," I whispered.

I just wasn't sure if I believed it.

7

RAMSAY

"**Y**ou ditched yesterday afternoon, and your cousins went bananas."

Gem informed me of this as soon as I arrived at school the next morning. I hadn't even gotten off my bike. I did that now and pulled the bike to the rack, taking my lock out. I looped it and clicked it shut, then regarded my new friend.

She was giving me a beady-eyed look, holding on to her backpack's straps with one foot resting against the other. It was an awkward stance, but somehow she was pulling it off.

I blinked a few times. "You actually like me." It wasn't a new experience. I'd been blessed in Cedra until I wasn't so blessed, but for the first time, someone who'd only met me for one day actually liked me. That was new. Family didn't count in this category.

Now she was the one to blink a few times. "Well, yeah. You're cool. A Gem can always tell."

My eyebrows went up. Third person?

"Incoming!" A baritone yell came from behind me, and a second later, I was lifted off my feet and twirled around. I reached down, guessing it was one of my cousins, and when I

got a glimpse of Clint and Alex with Cohen and Scout, I
decided it must be Trenton holding me up.

"Put me down, Trent."

He did, tripping back but managing to keep both of us off
the ground. "You rolled yesterday," he said. "What the fuck? We
were going to hit up Louie's." Alex, Cohen, and Scout joined
the group. Trenton threw his arms around Alex's shoulders and
motioned to the other two with his thumb. "You haven't officially met the rest of our group. This is Cohen and Scout."

I was not making eye contact with Scout. I felt singed
enough from yesterday's glaring sessions, and seriously, I had
enough on my plate. Cohen gave me a guy up-nod and a half-
smirk, generally used to convey, "I think you're cool and I'm
cool, so what's up?"

"Hi." Both got the same polite wave, and for appearance's
sake, I looked at Scout's chin. The only one who knew I wasn't
totally making eye contact would be him, and let's see him try
to call that out.

Cohen gave me another cool-guy chin-up. Scout did nothing. No greeting. His chin did not move.

Fine. I mean, I wasn't making eye contact for a reason.

"Clint said you guys had a pizza and wine-out last night."

I tensed, registering Alex's not-happy tone. Alex was always
happy, always kind.

Then he grinned. "Why the fuck weren't we invited?"

"Yeah. What the fuck?" Trenton joined in.

Another arm came over my shoulder. Clint's. I sagged into
his side, already knowing what he would say.

"Back off, assholes. It's her second day at school. Jesus."

His tone was teasing, but there was another hint of something there. Both his brothers straightened. They'd gotten the
message.

Alex redirected immediately. "Scout, you already got a
fight?"

Topic changed. I relaxed a bit even though we were talking about Scout and his upcoming fight.

Different sensations were manifesting in my body, farther south, and it was uncomfortable. I squirmed out from under Clint's arm but tapped his side with a fist to let him know I was fine. Moving around the group, I gave a small wave and headed inside.

Gem walked right next to me, but instead of the questions I thought would come, she kept quiet. She stuck to my side until we got to my locker. "I'm going to toss my bag in my locker," she told me. "One second."

I gave her a nod. But as I was putting my bag away and pulling out my phone and what I needed for my first class, I felt another presence at my side.

It was Alex. "You okay?" he asked. "For real? We wigged yesterday when you took off."

I sighed softly and stepped back, closing my locker. "Clint didn't say anything?"

He shook his head, his hands on his backpack straps.

I motioned forward, and we started for his locker. "He got home around five this morning," he said. "I only knew because I'd gotten up for the bathroom, but this morning, we were all in a rush. Trent was interrogating him, and he said the pizza and wine part to shut him up. You know T. He's worried."

We got to his locker, or I assumed it was because he'd stopped there, but he wasn't opening it. He also wasn't looking at me. He let a deep breath out. "Just . . . that shit's not going to happen here. You gotta know that." When he finally looked at me, his eyes were fierce. "No way in hell. Okay?"

My throat swelled up, and I had to push down a huge lump. I nodded. "I know. I just . . . I have some lingering aftereffects, if that makes sense? I'll work it out."

He nodded. "We're here for that too."

The lump was back in place and getting larger. It was a

good lump, an emotional lump, but I needed to handle this. Fast. I moved closer to him, dropping my voice. "Listen. What happened last year was a freak tragedy. I know it won't happen here, and I am not going to start burdening you guys with the shit in my head. We're in high school. You have your own shit to deal with, and no offense, but you guys aren't therapists. I appreciate you being there—Clint last night and you this morning. And trust me, knowing you guys are here and you give a fuck is helping. But that's all you need to do. The heavy stuff? That's on me to handle, and I will. I'm not going to fuck you up by releasing my damage on you. I'd hate myself more for doing that."

"You hate yourself?" he hissed. "After what that piece of shit did? You hate you? Hate that guy!"

His voice had risen.

People were looking.

I was going to try to deflate the situation when a fist hit the locker right next to Alex.

"Dude," Clint said in passing. That was it. He hit the locker and kept on walking. Trenton and Cohen were with him. Both gave us a look as they passed by.

Alex seemed to remember where we were and cursed under his breath. He straightened up. "Sorry." His eyes moved past me, and he stepped back, giving the same Cohen cool-guy chin-lift to someone. "Hey, man."

I looked and wished I hadn't.

Scout Raiden was standing a few feet back.

I glanced up and caught his gaze, but unlike yesterday, the frostiness wasn't there. His eyes were dark. There were emotions there, but they were stuffed down, and I got the feeling I wasn't supposed to see them. My whole body snapped to attention. I jerked my gaze away, flustered.

"I gotta find Gem," I told Alex.

I started forward, but a hand caught my elbow and turned

me the other way. "Locker six seventy-eight," Alex said. "But she went to class. I saw her."

"Oh."

I heard a low whistle.

Clint was standing outside our classroom.

I moved toward him, and he lowered his head. "What was that about?"

"Nothing." I sailed right past, going to our table and taking my stool.

Clint took longer to come sit next to me. His friends took their seats.

Then the teacher came in and announced, "We've had a few changes."

That was all he said because I guess the details weren't our business? I'd agree with that, but this affected me because I heard from behind me, "Mike, take Hector's spot."

Mike, the friend on the other side of Clint, grabbed his stuff and moved to the seat in front of me. Scout Raiden took Mike's old seat.

The other adjustment?

Macon Rice took the seat where Scout had been yesterday.

Macon sat and wheeled all the way around and looked at me with a full, even stare before his gaze moved to Scout's. Then, he smirked before turning back to face the front.

Scout ducked his head down, but I could hear him say, "He needs to get fucked up."

Clint grunted. "We'll help set that up."

I turned to stare at him because, *what?*

What was I missing here?

8

RAMSAY

I asked Gem about it at lunch. We'd decided to go outside after we got our food.

She pushed open the door with her back, rotating with it and leading the way to an empty picnic table by the basketball court. "I'm assuming your cousins don't know about your exchange with him in the office?"

I gave her a look.

She laughed, sitting down.

I sat across from her.

She leaned forward. "I told you before that Macon Rice always has a girl?" She had, and she kept on. "He does, and that annoys most guys—not your cousins, not Scout or Cohen. Those guys are the top and generally not in competition with Macon. He crossed paths against Cohen a while back when Macon started dating Cohen's little sister. Issue was that Macon is a senior and Cohen's sister is a freshman. They had words with him, i.e., I think they threatened him and by *they*, I don't really know who. I'm guessing Cohen, you know? Anyway, Macon ended things, until last Friday. I guess he and Amalia are back on. There was a party, and they were talking. People saw, and everyone flipped out. At least, that's what I'm assuming the fight was about yesterday."

"Why's Scout Raiden so invested?"

She'd been cutting her apple, and paused. "What do you mean?"

If it were just Raiden, I'd tell her in a heartbeat, but Clint might be involved as well. I shrugged. "He was in the fight yesterday, but he wasn't *in* the fight. That's all."

"Oh." She continued cutting her apple. "He's loyal to Cohen and your cousins. I'm sure that'll extend to you now, since, you know, family."

Right.

That made me uncomfortable.

We sat and ate as Gem filled me in on the rest of the school's hierarchy, including the popular girls. We were nearing the end of lunch when I realized my cousins hadn't checked on me. They hadn't texted or called, and they hadn't found me at lunch.

Which meant . . . Crap.

I was eating a piece of bread and dropped it. It landed on my plate with a *thud*.

Gem gave me a look, laughing. "Don't spill or anything—"

"It's happening now."

"Huh?" She bit into a piece of her bread.

"Now. Right now." I pushed up from the table, scanning the area. There was nothing amiss. I mean, people were looking over. I knew that would happen. People were probably still curious about me, but I saw none of my cousins. Or Scout. Or Cohen.

Or Macon.

I knew it in my gut.

Whatever they were doing, it was going on right now.

I was moving before I could stop myself. If they were doing something, it wouldn't be outside. Someone would see or hear.

Where could they be? The bathroom? No. The locker room.

The jock code was real. No one would say anything if they saw something happening in there. That was where they were.

Locker rooms were usually near the gym, or at the end of a hallway.

My mind raced. *Don't get involved*, I tried to tell myself. *Let it go.*

My cousins knew what they were doing. This was their school.

I was new. I was a girl.

And then also, *fuck that.*

Gem yelled my name, but it came from a distance, far away. I pushed through the doors, going inside.

There were people at their lockers. Some leaving the cafeteria, going into the cafeteria. Going in and out of the library. Going around me. A group of girls had congregated by some lockers. They turned to look at me and grew quiet as I passed them.

I needed to leave it alone.

I couldn't.

I moved down the hallway, and as I approached Alex's locker, I saw a guy slip into a room at the end of the hallway. It didn't look like a classroom. There were a couple guys set up halfway down the hallway. I assumed they were keeping people from getting near that door.

I knew it. I was right. I started toward them.

One got in front of me, his hands up. "Hey, listen. You shouldn't—"

I gave him a look, one of my don't-fuck-with-me looks, and it worked. He stepped back, his hands lowering.

I heard the other guy say, "They're going to skin you alive, man."

He sighed. "Did you see that look? I'm not messing with her."

Once I got to the door, I could hear muffled shouting and the sound of something getting hit—someone getting hit.

I pushed open the door, and there was a second door. I could hear the voices more clearly.

"Fucking piece of shit."

Thud.

"Told you to stay away from my sister. You should've listened."

Thud. Thud. Thud!

Moaning.

A gasp. "Help me, guys."

I pushed open the second door.

There was a set of lockers immediately in front of me. My steps faltered when I heard Alex's voice. "She's fifteen, you piece of shit."

"Fifteen."

That was Clint, and shivers moved down my spine. I'd only heard that cold tone from him once in my life.

I rounded the end of the lockers.

They didn't see me at first.

Scout was holding Macon back, all by himself. He had an arm twisted around Macon's arm and under his neck and his leg positioned around one of Macon's legs from behind. Macon couldn't fight back, except to strain to get away, but it was useless.

I felt sorry for him. A pang went through me, and then I was in a bathroom.

Someone held me down, a hand at my throat. Fists hitting my stomach.

"Ramsay!"

I jerked out of that memory.

Cohen was lining up for another punch. My cousins stood in a circle behind him, and all six heads turned my way.

I looked, but I didn't see the guy I'd followed in.

"There's another guy."

Trenton, who had started for me, pulled to a stop. "What?"

"I saw a guy duck in here." I looked around. "It wasn't one of you guys."

Clint and Alex both came for me.

Alex's face was darkening. "You're saying there's someone else in here?"

I nodded.

Clint cursed, pushing past me. He pointed the other way. "Trent."

"On it."

My cousins separated, fanning out.

I stayed rooted, and my gaze went right to Scout's.

His face was like granite. He tightened his hold and barked at Cohen, "Finish it."

"She said—"

"We'll handle him too. Finish this one while we got him."

I couldn't look at Macon's face. It was swollen, covered in blood, and he went back to struggling to get free from Scout. I focused on his feet instead. They were useless for him, not supporting him, not doing anything. He was trying to kick out Scout's leg, but he wasn't moving. His legs seemed rooted into the ground, and then I heard the thudding again.

Cohen went back to hitting.

"You thought you could get away from me?" That hand tightened on my throat.

"Max," I gasped, tears almost suffocating me. "Please."

His arm was like cement. I couldn't do anything.

He raised his fist, and I closed my eyes.

I knew what was coming.

"You're going to leave my sister alone." *Hit.* "You're going to lose her number." *Punch.* "You're never going to take her calls, answer any DMs from her. You're not going to retweet any shit from her. You hear me?" *Thud. Thud. Thud.*

Someone gasped.

There was moaning.

"You're never going to get away from me."

"Max." I couldn't speak. He was crushing my throat.

The lights started swimming then, moving around me.

My back arched, my toes leaving the floor. I rose up from the floor, but his hand kept me pinned in place.

Something crashed into a locker, and I jumped at the sound. Then I was moving, almost blind in my need. "Stop." I rushed in.

I got between Cohen and Macon and shoved him back.

"What the fuck?" he yelled.

I turned, pulling Macon from Scout's hold and shoving him back—not toward the door, but toward Cohen. My chest heaved. "Give him a fighting chance. It's not right, the way you're doing it."

I heard movement, and someone else ran into a locker. Trent was herding a guy forward. Alex next to him.

Clint came around the other way. "Found him." Then his dark smirk fell flat. "What's going on?"

Scout growled from behind me, "Your cousin got involved."

I ignored him because Macon saw his chance. He started to run, but not for the door. He tried going the opposite direction. Cohen was on him, grabbing his shoulders and throwing him into the lockers and onto the floor. Macon tried fighting back, but it was pointless. Cohen had him down, and he rained punch after punch on him.

From behind me, Scout growled, "That's why I was holding him. Now I gotta pull my friend off the guy so he doesn't kill him. The other way, he was getting his hits in and Rice could still walk." He brushed past me, knocking into my arm as he reached for Cohen. Clint was there too. They lifted Cohen off Rice, and I thought Macon would get up and make a run for it, but he didn't. He was unconscious.

Cohen spun around to me, wiping his arm over his mouth. "Don't get involved in shit you don't know."

Shit I didn't know? I didn't give a fuck what he thought. "He preferred that beating to the first one," I stated clearly. "He had a chance to fight back, and I can tell you that's something I do know."

With that, I turned and left.

I didn't make eye contact with any of my cousins.

They'd know. If that shit happened to them, they'd know.

Rice probably deserved that beating, but he should get it when he could fight back.

I WANTED to ditch school again. Every cell in my body was telling me to run, but it was my second day. I couldn't do that. What I did instead was go to the library until the fifth period bell rang. Alex was with me for that class, so it went okay. Gem waved me over to the seat beside her in sixth period.

I slipped in, hunching forward. "Hey."

"Hey." She frowned, watching the door as everyone else came in. "What happened? Did you find your cousins?"

I looked up to answer and saw Scout coming into the room.

He paused, seeing me. A hard look came over his face as he sat in the chair behind Gem. The fucker knew what he was doing. Every time I would look or talk to Gem, he'd be in my line of sight.

His eyes were dark as he watched me.

Gem's eyebrows rose as she noticed who was sitting behind her.

"I was wrong and felt like a dumbass, so I went to the library," I told her.

There was a flicker in Scout's gaze, but he didn't say anything.

"You were in the library this whole time?" Gem asked.

I nodded.

"I thought something was seriously wrong, the way you took off. I got rid of your tray."

Crap. I'd forgotten that. "I'm sorry, and thank you for the tray. I thought something was wrong, but it was fine."

"But why didn't you come back? I was waiting for you."

That was when I tuned into something else, something that had completely escaped my awareness yesterday. Did Gem not have any other friends? That didn't make sense.

As if reading my mind, she scoffed. "I mean, it was fine. I hung out with some peeps, but not cool just taking off for a second day in a row. Text a girl, would ya? Let me know if you're hiding so I won't feel like a dumbass if I have to cover for you."

Some of my tension faded, and I managed a smile. "Sorry. I'll tell you next time I need to hide."

"Good." She rolled her eyes, grinning back. Someone sat in the seat behind me, and she shot upright. "Switch with me."

"What?" I looked back.

A girl gave me a wide, but closed smile. "Heya. I'm Theresa."

She had dark hair and dark eyes. Looked Latina. She was also freaking gorgeous.

She added, "I'm Gem's cousin."

"Yeah. Switch with me." Gem shoved my arm. "Hurry."

She already had her stuff in her arms, so I grabbed mine. As soon as I stood, Gem slid into my seat. I locked eyes with Scout before rounding the desk and coming up behind him. He leaned back, resting his arm over his chair as I slid into Gem's vacant seat.

"Don't say shit," he murmured so quietly I knew only I could hear.

My whole body locked down, but screw that. "Don't threaten me."

His eyes flashed. "Or what?"

Or what? Seriously?

Then *my* eyes flashed, and I leaned closer to him. "You have no idea the PTSD shit going on in my head. You don't want to fuck with a crazy person. There's no rationality. No reasoning. Why do you think my cousins are worried about me? They know how messed up I am. Threaten me again, and you'll find out the first step I'm willing to take. Guarantee you have more to lose than I do here, buddy."

I ignored the sensations building under my skin, making me heated, making my neck feel flushed, my face hot.

He stared at me. I stared right back. We were back to the glaring fest from yesterday. Whatever unspoken truce we might've had earlier was all gone.

He smirked, but his eyes were still hard. "If you're that crazy, maybe you're a danger to the students here? Maybe you need to be in a mental hospital?"

I heard his threat, and it boiled my stomach. "You'd exploit me like that?"

Pure hatred replaced his smirk. "You say anything that'll come back on Cohen, and yeah. You bet your ass I will."

New emotions flooded me, ones I didn't want to identify. "I bet Cohen's little sister could use a friend. From what I overheard, you were telling him to stay away from her. That means she's not done with him. I'm older. She probably knows who my cousins are, probably thinks they're cool. Maybe has a crush on one of them." I ignored how still he went. I kept on, my voice so soft. "She'd like me, I bet. I could use all of that to get in with her. I could be a friend she'd look up to. I know how to spin that, and once I had her ear, I could say anything to her. You wouldn't want me to tell her how overbearing and controlling her brother is. It's easy to say what people want to hear."

A new darkness came over him, a dangerous sort of darkness.

Goddamn.

The throb was back, smack between my legs. I was more messed up than I thought.

"You even talk to her, I'll fuck your cousin up," he warned, his voice like ice. "Trenton or Clint. You got me? Cohen and Amalia are off-limits."

"I could tell my cousins you threatened one of them."

"Go ahead. Cohen's ride or die for me. They know that."

Right. We were at an impasse.

I didn't mean what I'd threatened, but as I turned back around, I knew both of us stepped over a line that didn't feel right.

This was my first real conversation with him.

I shuddered to think what the next one might be like.

9

SCOUT

"**H**ey guys!" Kira skipped her way over to us, linking arms with Alex.

We were heading out for food, our usual thing to do before Alex went to football and I went to training. Normally I didn't mind when Kira and her group tagged along. But that was only because they left me alone. She'd been after the triplets more this year, finally letting go of her target on me. Which I was down for.

Kira liked boyfriends. If she didn't have one, she was freaking, and when she did have one, she was already looking for the next one. Just how she was.

"We're heading for food. You want to come?"

Kira's gaze jumped to me.

We were going to Carby's, a popular fast food franchise in town, and going there was never my choice. I hated the place, but everyone else fucking loved it. I lied, "We're going to Cohen's for tacos."

Her eyes went flat.

Not because of the tacos or because she thought we were going to Cohen's but because Kira and her friends did not get along with Cohen's mom. Maybe it was because Cohen was friendly with Theresa Garcia. Theresa and Kira did not mix, and if we were at Cohen's, damned sure Theresa would show up with her friends, who really didn't like Kira. It was almost like a turf war.

But again, I was lying and wasn't surprised when Kira let loose of Alex's arm and gave a smile before waving. "I think I'm going to catch up to the girls, see if they want to hang." She caught Alex's hand just before we were out of arm's length and pressed up against him, smiling. "Call me later, okay?"

Alex nodded, and then she was off, making sure we were watching as she went. And Cohen and Alex were, so she walked slower, swinging her ass a little more than normal.

"Damn. I want to hit that. Badly." Cohen whistled under his breath, shaking his head.

Alex laughed before frowning my way. "We're going to Carby's."

We were at my truck and I swung in, tossing my bag in the back. The guys followed suit. Alex took the front. Cohen liked the back when someone else was riding with us, and as I reversed, I shrugged. "Can't talk if she's there."

That got Cohen's attention. His head lifted, and he leaned forward. "You talking about this afternoon?"

I was eyeing Alex, who was watching the other students leaving as we drove past them.

I answered, "Your cousin."

Alex looked my way, settling back in his seat. He got more grim, more guarded. "What about her?"

"She knew what we did. Girls have big mouths."

"Not Ramsay."

"She's your family."

He wasn't liking where I was taking this. "I already told you. Ramsay won't say shit. I get what you think of chicks, but she's not like that. She's one of us."

I met Cohen's gaze in the rearview mirror. He was slowly sitting back again, and I knew we were thinking the same thing. No chick was a part of us. And they all talked.

It was a matter of time.

But I dropped it, and we went to Carby's. Since I had a fight coming, I had chicken and broccoli.

10

RAMSAY

My cousins lied to me. Fully and outright lied to me.

Clint called me, said they'd pick me up for food, and nope. We were outside a warehouse in the neighboring town, standing in the middle of a crowd of people. These people weren't normal we're-going-to-a-concert or we're-going-to-watch-a-movie type of people. These were heavily muscled, heavily tattooed, heavily scary type of guys and girls who were barely wearing any clothes. Bikini tops with underwear was not that uncommon among some of the women. Some at least had tank tops and miniskirts on, but that didn't help with how seriously underdressed I was. Throwing on a hoodie, jeans, and sneakers sounded appropriate to wear to grab some food with my cousins.

Because that was what I was wearing, and by the time we hit the front doors, I knew where we were going.

I smacked Clint on the arm. "You lied!"

He laughed, putting an arm around my shoulders and jerking me to his side. "Come on. I didn't really."

Alex laughed, angling his head to see me. "Yeah. He said food and we're planning on getting food inside for you."

Trenton had to put his two cents in, bumping his arm into mine. "Clint just didn't say where we were getting food. No lie."

"Assholes. All of you." We were at Scout's fight, and I didn't know if I was ready to watch him get all hot and sweaty and dirty and rough—good Lord, the sweatshirt needed to go. Plus, this place was heated with the amount of bodies inside along with heaters set up in the corner.

"My man. My men. Hello!" Cohen approached us, giving Alex a fist bump before pulling him into one of those half-hugs guys do. He did this with my other two cousins before stepping back and giving me a reserved nod. "Female Maroney. How's it going?"

Clint laughed. "Ramsay. Do us a favor and call her Ramsay or she'll skin our dicks off."

Cohen's eyebrows shot up, but he gave a tight nod, also reassessing me. "Noted."

They talked more, and we headed to the concessions first. Clint made a big deal out of buying me my food and saying, "Promise fulfilled." Alex and Trenton were laughing. Cohen looked confused. No one explained to him that the joke was on me.

Once the guys grabbed their food, we headed off.

Cohen led the way to a section elevated above the others. We climbed up.

It was weird, I thought as I looked around.

Girls were walking around, wearing Scout's name on their shirts. Some had his name spelled out on their faces or cleavage. A lot of guys were drinking, all talking, laughing loud, and pointing to the ring, which was smack dab in the middle of the entire warehouse. The place just kept getting fuller and fuller, which made me thankful to be standing where we were. A few people tried climbing up, but Trenton and Clint weren't letting them. A few shared words with them, but knowing Clint liked to get into trouble and Trenton had a little bit of a crazy switch in his head, I figured neither boy cared. They were welcoming it. There was one situation that I thought would come to blows, until another guy pushed in, tapped one of the men on the shoulders, and said something to them. Whatever he said worked wonders because the other guy shared with his buddies, and then he yelled up, "You're Raiden's friends?"

Clint smirked. "My brother's his best friend."

That settled them and they moved along.

When the announcer climbed into the arena and grabbed a microphone, Clint got close. "You okay with this?"

I glanced at him, then did a double take because there was serious concern there. "Are *you* okay?"

"It's—" His mouth got tight, and his shoulders hunched forward. "I didn't think. *We* didn't think. It's violent . . ."

I shook my head, touching his arm. "I'm good. I promise."

"We just didn't think, then I realized maybe this isn't a situation you want to be in."

"It's fine."

When the announcer finished announcing and a guy got into the ring, I stopped thinking altogether.

This guy was huge. I knew they did the same weight classes, but no way was he the same weight as Scout. Fear trickled through me, but that shifted quickly to something else. Something way more distracting because Scout had gotten into the ring too.

He wasn't wearing anything but shorts, and oh my God, the tats. The tattoos. They were everywhere on him. Not in a bad way, but in a very-hot and so-not-legal hot way. The crowd was going nuts, but I was dumbstruck.

On both arms, there were tattoos of wings, and as he turned and lifted his arms, they *were* wings. The detail was incredible, even from where I was standing, I could see it, and down the middle of his back was an eagle. When his arms were up, the wings were stretched out, intertwining with his tribal tattoo on his one arm. When they were down, it looked like a normal tattoo of an eagle. He had other tattoos on him. They were perfect.

My heart was pounding.

Good gracious, this attraction to him was going to kill me. Maybe literally. It was annoying, and distracting, and I wanted it to go away. Seeing him like this was like lust had been injected with three shots of adrenaline.

His eyes were dark, stormy. His face was fierce. The other guy was jeering at him, trying to get a reaction, but not Scout. He wasn't there to put on a show. He *was* the show, and everyone knew it. The crowd's volume was incredible when they said Scout's name, and then—they rang the bell.

The match was on.

I totally understood why people thought violence was hot. Because it was. If it was controlled. If it was a spectator sport. If the guys looked like Scout and his giant opponent as they swung on each other. Jabbing. Dodging. Kicking.

The guy tried to kick at Scout's head, but he took the opening to tackle him. It was a takedown, his arms and legs wrapped around the guy, and the other guy was trying to twist free. He was struggling, struggling, until a whistle sounded.

I didn't know what happened, but they were going again. This time, the guy came straight at Scout. He was pissed and sloppy. Even I could tell.

Scout capitalized, ducking and then bam! He gave him an uppercut, then another, and another. He had the guy against the ring's cage and was pummeling him.

Scout knew how to move. He did it effortlessly. With perfect precision. He darted when he needed, danced back when it worked, and then moved in for the kill ruthlessly. He did it over and over again, and the crowd was loving it. They were eating it up.

They wanted more.

He was going to win. That was obvious from the first big move, and the opponent's giant size no longer worried me.

My pulse was racing. I was breathing fast.

I lost time because I was locked in on watching Scout.

They went three rounds before Scout delivered a hit that the guy didn't get up from. He was declared the winner, and everyone went nuts.

The guys were yelling next to me. Cohen was clapping and then turning and high-fiving my cousins and me. I stepped away from the intensity because it was overwhelming, and jarring, but it was also a reminder where I was. At a fight. Watching a fight. With strangers, and my cousins, and I'd completely forgotten everything else until that moment. I'd been so enthralled with Scout, and my gaze went back to him.

His eyes were on me.

They were piercing.

He wanted me in that moment. I knew it, like his eyes darkened at seeing me because he knew I wanted him as well.

Fuck.

Fuck!

The ache was there, right where he'd thrust inside. Him moving in me. Him touching me. Tasting me. I *wanted* to feel his arms around me, his sleek muscles holding me in place as he pounded me, and I wanted it bad.

God.

I ripped my gaze away, physically aching. Aching from looking away from him, from seeing what I was feeling reflecting in him, and aching from the total and complete throbbing that was going through my entire body.

"You ready?"

I startled, rounding on my cousin. "What?"

Trenton was the one who asked, and I looked around for everyone else. Clint in the corner, talking to some girls, but Alex and Cohen were gone. After another second, I spotted them winding their way to the cage to talk to Scout. I couldn't endure that, standing there, listening to the guys talk to Scout, not being able to touch him. And knowing he would know the torment that'd be on me. It was humiliating in a way because I had no doubt he'd have his needs checked by then.

Or hell, he'd literally have them fulfilled by someone else. Someone not me.

No matter how much my wanton body wanted to do it, I couldn't. No way. He was Alex's best friend. He and Cohen were friends with Clint and Trenton. I was their cousin.

It'd be wrong.

I coughed, my voice coming out hoarse, "Could we leave? Like now?"

Trenton blinked, his grin fading. "Are you okay?"

"Could Alex get a ride back with Cohen? This whole situation was a lot for me. I thought I could handle it . . ." I was lying. I needed to stop and just let it be where I left it because my cousins could tell when I lied. They'd always been able to tell. They were human Ramsay lie detectors, but Trenton's gaze had darkened. He nodded quickly. "Yeah. Yeah. We can go."

Relief hit me hard.

We started down, and I heard him yelling at Clint, "Gotta go, doofus."

"Don't call me doofus, doofus. Hey, wait. What's going on? Is something wrong with Ramsay?" He caught up, zeroing in on me and getting a good look at my face. I let him see how bothered I was, masking the other emotions. He cursed under his breath. "I'm sorry, Rams. I thought—"

I shook my head. "Let's just get home. I had fun, but it got to be a lot by the end."

"Yeah. Yeah." He ran a hand over his face, sharing a look with Trenton. "We'll head home."

Right before we stepped outside, I glanced back and saw Scout watching us as if he knew the truth.

His gaze was almost mocking as I ducked my head and kept going.

Kept running from him.

11

RAMSAY

"CANNONBALL!!!!!!"

The next day, I went home from school excited to spend the afternoon with my mom, only to find her packing our cooler because we were *not* going to be spending the day alone. Instead, we were spending the day on the river with my cousins, my aunt, and my uncle since it was a hot day. So here we were, or here I was, lying out on the front of the boat when Clint jumped over me. His knees were tucked to his chest as he crashed into the water. It splashed up and over me.

The guys had been cool after the fight. At school, Cohen asked if I'd been okay and that made me feel guilty. He knew the guys took me home right after the fight for a reason.

The only person who hadn't seemed to care was Scout, and well, he knew the real reason.

Then Gem found out I'd gone to one of Scout's fights without her and that took precedent over everything else. Even my cousins started avoiding us if they saw I was with her because, by the end of the day, I was offering a blood promise to invite her the next time I went to one of Scout's fights with my cousins. Especially with my cousins. That was a big part of it for her.

And so here we were, and Clint wasn't alone in cannon-balling me.

Alex followed Clint's cannonball with one of his own. Trenton came next.

I glared at the fourth guy in line to jump, but Cohen only laughed, held his hands up in mock surrender, and jumped over me anyway. He just didn't cannonball.

When he'd shown up, I'd been nervous that Scout was coming too. Turned out, I had nothing to worry about.

He'd given me a chin raise and a "What's up?" before he followed Alex to the back of the boat. My uncle and aunt's pontoon was huge with a whole sitting area in the back. The middle had a table, a couple chairs, and a couch, and then the front had another seating area. There was a gate in front of me that blocked a small standing area. But the guys didn't launch themselves from there. They stepped on my bench and sailed over me.

"Douches," I yelled after Cohen jumped in.

Clint laughed as he swam back. "Don't be dumb. Jump in. You like swimming."

"Not today."

He shook his head.

Trenton hit the water with his hand and a good wave jumped up to splash me once again.

"Trent!"

"Come on! You've never been lame before. Don't start today."

No way. No effin' way. I knew my cousins, and they were going to gang up on me—pulling me under or jumping on me, and I'd barely have time to take a breath before someone else yanked me by the ankle back down. They were wound up, but I didn't know why. Maybe from Scout's fight last night?

Alex and Cohen swam over to the front end of the boat and climbed up. They grabbed towels from a pile and began drying off. Stepping over the gate, Alex sat across from me, tossing his towel back on the floor. Cohen plopped down at the end of my bench, both guys eyeing the adults.

My uncle had dropped the anchor twenty minutes ago so the guys could swim and was sitting at the table with Aunt Ailes and my mom. All had coffee thermoses, which I knew didn't have coffee in any of them. They were laughing and didn't look like they were paying us much attention.

Cohen said to Alex, leaning forward, "Think we could sneak some booze?"

Alex shot me a grin, also leaning forward. "Thinking there's a good chance. Your mom's drinking? I didn't think she normally did."

I shrugged. "She doesn't. Maybe she wanted to blow off some steam."

Cohen laughed, sitting back and kicking his leg out. "I don't blame her. It's been a week, huh?"

He watched me as the boat dipped and Clint and Trenton climbed back up. They walked through the gate holding towels.

I got all cautious, not sure what Cohen was referencing or if he was testing me, seeing if I'd say anything or not. He'd been fine at Scout's fight. I chose to play dumb. "I guess. It's my first week here. It's a lot in general."

Cohen kept watching me, solidifying my suspicion that he was testing me. Something flickered in his eyes, and he eased back.

Clint dropped to the floor on the other side of where I was sitting. Trenton took a seat next to Alex. He hit the side of Alex's knee, watching the adults. "Go grab the cooler."

"Like that's not obvious." Alex frowned.

Clint shrugged. "I put water in there. If he says something

or if he's watching, just grab the water first. It's not like you don't know how to sneak, dude."

Alex shrugged and stood, going to grab the cooler.

"Grabbing water, Pops," he explained over his shoulder

My uncle kept watching for another second as Alex lifted a water bottle. What he didn't see was that Alex shifted, his front half blocking his dad's view as Trenton grabbed the rum. As soon as that was hidden on the other side of Trent, Clint leaned forward and nabbed a soda.

With that, my uncle returned to the conversation.

"Rams?" Alex held out a soda for me.

But Clint snagged it, opened it, and drank a third of it. He handed it to Trent, who filled it back up with rum before holding it out to me. "You're welcome."

I glared at him but took it.

A part of me was digging this. I felt like a normal teenager, sneaking booze. And I was with my family, so it was safe. That was like a double bonus.

Trent went back to filling the rest of the sodas.

We kept sneaking drinks over the next hour, and I finally joined them swimming. Another hour after that, my aunt and mom brought out the food. While we were eating, I noticed Cohen checking his phone. He nudged Alex. "Where are we? We far from Eagle Peak?"

"Oh, yeah! What time is it?"

"He's finishing up now. It's eight."

My chest sank because I hadn't realized that much time had gone by and I also knew who *he* was.

Before I could think of something to say, Alex scrambled up. "Dad! Can we swing by Eagle Peak and pick up Scout? He's done at the gym."

"I'm surprised he trained today. Didn't he have a fight last night?"

"He helps out his uncle sometimes," Cohen responded.

My uncle checked our location and his clock and nodded. "We're not too far. Tell him ten minutes."

"Has he eaten yet?" my aunt asked.

Alex gave her a look. "Mom, when would a fighter ever turn down food even if he had eaten?"

"When he's trying to make weight."

He shrugged, going back to his seat. "He's not doing that today, so we're all good. Bring out the food!"

Clint had gone back to pull up the anchor.

Cohen returned to his seat beside me. "You okay with this?" he asked, his voice low.

I gave him a surprised look.

He ducked his head, a little flush on his cheeks—but that might've been from the sun or rum. "He told me. He tells me everything, just so you know. And you left the fight last night so fast."

I said quickly, "I just needed to get back." But I looked over at Alex because, if he'd told Cohen what he'd said to me, had he . . .

"He didn't tell him. It's different with me and Scout. I knew him before he came out here. I'm part of the reason he came here, but he doesn't need to know I told you that, right?"

I studied him. "Right."

He gave a nod and relaxed, his leg touching mine. I didn't think he registered that. "He told me what he said to you, about what he'd do." He shook his head. "He'd never do that, you know. I want you to know that. Never. He felt bad about what he said."

"He told you that?"

"Not in so many words, but he's like my brother. That's why he's so protective of my sister too—thinks of her as his little sister. I'm sure you can relate, the way you are with your cousins and all."

I grunted. "Uh-huh."

Cohen chuckled. "Your cousins are right. You're not like normal girls. You're like a dude."

"What?"

"Nothing." He leaned forward, patting my knee. "Glad we had this talk."

I wasn't sure *talk* was a good descriptor for it, but okay.

We moved quickly over the water, the waves splashing. A cool wind had kicked up too, and as we sped forward, I felt Clint watching me. Looking over, I tried to give him a smile. His eyes were dark, suspicious, and he glanced between Cohen and me.

My chest got tight. I did not need to be the cause of any situation between my cousins and Cohen, so I shook my head and mouthed, *It's fine.*

His eyebrows only drew closer, and he got a stubborn look on his face.

I sighed internally because I recognized that look. Clint would be cornering me later to find out what Cohen had said to me, so I needed to figure out what I wanted to tell him. I knew a couple things. One, I wasn't going to lie to my cousins for Cohen or Scout, and two, this was going to suck.

Cohen was ride or die for Scout. I was ride or die for my cousins and them for me.

Drama was coming.

12

RAMSAY

Scout was waiting for us on a dock outside the most magnificent log building I'd ever seen. There were punching bags outside and weights, so I figured this was the gym his uncle had built for him. There were a bunch of cars in a small parking lot and some guys outside jumping rope, but Scout looked freshly showered in swim shorts, a muscle tee, and a bag over his shoulder.

Another man was walking toward the building, and when we pulled up, I got another surprise.

My uncle and aunt loved him—like, *loved,* loved him. Each hugged him as if he were a lost-long son. Uncle Nick was asking how his fight went the night before and looking as if he were a teenager. I'd never seen him like that.

My mom shot me a look, her eyebrows up, and I only shrugged. She didn't need to know this guy reminded me of Max and that was what had sent me home from school early on my first day. I knew my mom. The mama bear claws would come out, and she'd make my aunt choose: her niece or her sons's friend.

After the year we had, Mom didn't bullshit around anymore.

"Scout, you hungry, honey?" My aunt had returned to the table and was unwrapping some of the food.

He grinned an almost lopsided grin, stepping toward her. "I mean, I did eat, but ..."

She laughed. "Okay. You sit. I'm assuming you've met my niece. And this is my sister, Christina. We'll get some food for you."

He shot me a look, his face blank and his eyes guarded. When he turned to my mom, he gave her an almost shy nod with a small smile. "Hello, Mrs. Williams."

"Oh goodness. Just Chris, how about?"

The shy look had worked on my mom. I could see her melting, and she stepped forward, giving him a small hug before indicating their couches. "Sit, sit, sit. You want a sandwich?" She raised her voice. "Anyone else want a sandwich?"

"Uh ..." Trenton stepped over to his dad, throwing his arm around my uncle's shoulders. "Pops, Mom." He gave them a disarming smile. "I know we ate, but we were thinking since we've been swimming and being active and—"

Alex stepped forward. "Pike's Pizza is like five miles from here."

"What's Pike's Pizza?" I asked Cohen, my voice low.

"It's a local pizza and barbeque spot on the river," he explained. "A lot of boaters like stopping by. They bring the food out to you. Also great for bathroom breaks."

I nodded. Score. I was sold. I shot my hand up. "I gotta pee."

There was a smattering of choked laughter, and my uncle blinked, gripping the steering wheel for a second. *Jesus.* He was weirded out by that?

I snorted. "Be thankful you don't have a daughter or that I'm not bleeding right now."

"Ramsay!" came swiftly from my mother, but she was grinning.

My aunt was laughing.

My uncle looked like he wished a wormhole would open and swallow him, but he nodded. "We can make a stop. That's fine."

Trenton shot a fist in the air. "Yes! Score one for the Pussy Republic." He winked and snapped his fingers at me.

I didn't care. I really did have to go to the bathroom.

Alex and Trenton got up to sit in the back section with Scout.

Cohen seemed to be dozing off next to me, so I moved over to where Alex had been sitting.

Clint turned my way. "What was that about before?"

I'd been hoping to put this off and have no drama until—I didn't know, when I wasn't around? But that was the coward's way out.

I sighed and told him. Everything.

"Are you kidding me?" His eyes were stormy and dark, violence seeping from them. He glared toward the back of the boat. "I'm going to fuck him up."

"Cohen said Scout felt bad about what he said, that he'd never do it. What I said was messed up too. I mean, think about it, Clint. I was going to toy with Cohen's sister. You know me. I'd never do that either."

"That dickhead needs to stay away from you. How about that? That's what I'm thinking."

"What's going on?"

Cohen had woken up. He turned to me, and those eyes went on alert. "What'd you do?"

I sat up because screw him if he was going to blame me for this. "*You* talked to *me* and my cousin noticed. Just like you're not going to lie for your 'brother', I'm not going to lie to my cousin."

He scowled, scooting forward, his arms loose at his sides. "You told him? Everything?"

"Yep."

"He was going to fuck me up or one of my brothers?" Clint asked Cohen, slowly standing though our boat was still moving over the water.

Cohen stood too, his hands flexing into fists. "It wasn't like that. He was talking shit."

"He was talking shit to my cousin about me and my brothers. How's that okay with you?"

Cohen lowered his head, a flush working its way up his neck. This one wasn't from the sun or the rum.

"He was nervous. She saw what I did—"

"And my telling both of you that she was cool wasn't good enough? That's where he messed up. He didn't need to go to her or say what he did. He started this, not her."

"What's going on?"

Lovely. Stupendous. Scout had joined the conversation.

The pontoon slowed. We were nearing a bank, but all eyes and ears were on Clint, who didn't waste his words. "You threatened my cousin, and when she didn't fall in line, you doubled down and threatened me and Trent. That's what's going on."

"What the fuck?" Alex joined the conversation, coming up from behind Scout. He moved to stand next to Clint. "That true?"

Scout opened his mouth.

My cousin beat him to it. "I said it. You know it's true."

Scout closed his mouth, but his dark gaze found me.

I felt punched by his look. The anger made his eyes glitter.

Then Alex moved forward, blocking his view. "You don't need to look her way. Ever."

"It's not like that."

"Fuck, it's not like that. I saw the way you looked at her," Alex countered.

"Come on, guys," Cohen pleaded.

"He threatened her, and then he threatened us. How are you okay with that?"

"She threatened my sister."

I jumped to my feet.

"I told him she was cool," Clint argued. "It didn't need to go there. He fucked that up, not her."

"What are you all talking about?"

That was my uncle.

We had parked at a dock, and it was obvious something was going down.

Alex spoke up, his voice sounding strained and unnatural, "It's nothing. Just . . . high school friendship shit."

"It sounds like more than that," my mother said.

"It's really stupid petty high school stuff, Aunt Chris," Trenton said. "Let us all sort it out and everything will be fine."

"Off the boat," Clint added, through gritted teeth.

Scout led the way, brushing past me, his gaze ominous as he caught the side of the boat and launched himself over. I ignored the shiver that went down my spine and moved to follow because I wasn't going to get blamed for this whole thing. Clint stopped me with a hand on my stomach so he could go next. Instead of jumping over the side, he went through the gate and stepped off the boat like a normal person.

Alex was next, giving me a look. "Let us handle this."

I opened my mouth, but Trenton cut me off. "This is more between us because we're all friends. That's all."

I closed my mouth.

Cohen brought up the rear, and all five guys headed down the dock and up a small hill, disappearing behind a row of trees.

"Ramsay?" My uncle's voice was serious.

I turned slowly.

He glanced to where the guys had gone. "Is that a situation I need to interrupt?"

Oh man. That'd be the icing on the cake—my sending an adult. I shook my head quickly. "No. It's not like that. They'll figure it out. It's just a situation where someone should've listened and they didn't. That's all."

I tried to tell myself that was all it was.

My aunt and mom shared a look, and my mom came toward me, her arms open. I went to her side and burrowed into her. She nuzzled my ear. "How about us girls go get a table? And I'm going to ignore how I know you kids have been sneaking drinks. That sound like a plan?"

That sounded wonderful. I could do with some aunt-and-mother-daughter bonding time, at least until I saw the fallout from what was going on behind those trees. I wrapped an arm around my mom's waist and hugged her tight. "That sounds great, Mom."

I felt her lips move up in a smile as she pressed a kiss to my forehead. "I love you, honey. Don't ever forget that."

I wouldn't. "I love you too."

Aunt Aileen joined the hug, coming up from behind to put an arm around both of us. "Don't leave the only other girl out here. I need some sisterly-niece lovey times too."

We laughed and opened up. Aunt Ailes snuggled right into the middle. As we walked up the dock, my mom's hand found mine. She gave me a gentle smile.

In a way, this was a perfect ending right here.

Then we walked into Pike's Pizza, and that moment came to an abrupt stop.

MY AUNT AILEEN froze as we stepped inside. "Oh no."

"What?" My mom took a small step backward. "Oh no."

This sent alarm signals through my body, but there wasn't anyone or anything out of the ordinary that I could see . . . families sitting and eating. Some little kids running around. There were other teenagers in the back, and I frowned, wondering if I knew them from school?

Aunt Ailes whispered, almost to herself, "I can't believe she's here."

She? What?

My mom glanced my way but spoke to her sister. "Ailes, Ramsay."

My aunt sucked in a breath, blinking back sudden tears. She reached up, pressing her fingers to the corner of her eyes and nodding. "Yes. You're right, but Chris . . ." Her whisper was agonizing to hear. "I can't be here. I can't . . . see her. I can't. Oh God. Nick is coming in too. This is going to be a disaster."

The door opened at the end of her statement. Nick came inside, and the door shut behind him.

In the back was a woman at a table with a man who was probably her husband. They had a teenage girl with them and two little boys. No one but the older woman reacted when they saw Nick. She froze, her eyes getting big, and the blood drained from her face. Her husband was laughing at something one of the little boys said when he noticed his wife's reaction.

His gaze followed hers, and in seeing Nick, he jerked upright in his chair.

The girl noticed her parents and frowned, confused. She started looking around. Seeing us at the door, she said something to her mom.

Mom's hand touched my arm. "Honey, let's go to the back patio."

I didn't move. "What's going on?" I pulled my gaze away from the family and focused on my mom, then my aunt and uncle.

Uncle Nick's eyes were riveted to that table, and he cursed, stepping back.

The husband was coming toward us.

Uncle Nick growled, "I don't need this right now. Get her out of here."

My mom and I stiffened, but neither of us responded to the order.

But the guy was on us now, and Nick held up a hand. "My family is here—"

The guy's voice was harsh, almost shrill. "So's mine. We were here first. You leave."

"What?" Uncle Nick looked ready to stand his ground.

The guy swung his gaze around, skimming over my mom and me, and landed on my aunt. "How can you be okay with this? What he did—"

My uncle surged forward. "I said I have family with me."

The husband jerked back, getting right in his face. "And I said so do I. We were here first."

"So you can finish and leave early. Makes more sense than my turning around and telling my three teenage sons and their two friends that suddenly we're not getting pizza here."

"Okay." Aunt Aileen stepped between them. She touched my uncle's stomach, though she was mostly turned toward the husband. "If we leave, it'll raise questions. We'll go to the back patio. Let's all try to ignore each other, okay?"

Uncle Nick shook his head and cursed once more before swinging around. "I can't do this." He went back outside.

The wife came to a stop just short of our group.

Aunt Aileen paled and her mouth trembled.

My mom took charge, grabbing my arm in a firm hold and reaching for her sister as well. "Okay. Enough of this. I've got a very curious and intelligent daughter, so prepare for this to get out. In the meantime, you guys go to your table. We'll go outside, and let's all pretend none of us is here."

The husband seemed flustered, his chest rising. "We were here fir—"

My mom whirled on him. "Your wife cheated too. There are guilty parties on both sides, and hurt parties right next to them. Play your part and ignore us. We'll do the same."

My mom ushered my aunt and me past the hostess and out to the patio. I felt the floor tilting under me as I walked. *What?* There was a large empty table on the patio, so that was where we went. A waitress tried to intervene, but my mom had words with her. Aunt Aileen took my hand and led me the rest of the way to the table.

There were still dishes on it, so my aunt started clearing them.

Two girls hurried over and began cleaning around us.

"You guys didn't totally come out here because of what happened to your father," she told me. "It was for me too." She watched the back door of the restaurant, a haunted look in her eyes. "Nick had an affair. I found out six months ago, and that woman isn't even supposed to be here. She and her husband live in the city. They work together, she and Nick. I thought . . . Why is she here? This is where we live. Why?"

I reached over, taking her hand and holding it tight.

She moved her other hand on top of mine, grasping like I was a lifeline. Tears filled her eyes and she shook her head, talking to herself. "It doesn't make sense that she'd be here. Unless . . . Oh God, unless she was hoping to see him again. But . . ." Suddenly, she jerked and went stiff. She looked me in the eyes. "The boys don't know."

My stomach tightened, and so did my hand between hers.

She shook her head, patting my hand. "Don't worry. You've had too much to shoulder over the last year. I won't ask you to keep this from them. I think it's time it got out anyway. The boys have started noticing things. Clint asked the other day why his father was sleeping in the guest house. I told him it was because he snored, but he's too smart of a boy. I'm sure he has suspicions." Her voice broke, and she took a deep breath. "My boys. They're going to be so angry. They always rally. They're going to rally all over again. They shouldn't have to. I was hoping this wouldn't get out, and they go to college next year."

I was speechless, but my hand in hers seemed to be helping more than any words possibly could. She stopped crying. They finished cleaning the table around us, and I wasn't even going to think about what they thought or might have overheard. My mom came to the table with a pitcher of margaritas. The waitress she'd been talking to followed with water and a basket of something. Bread, maybe?

Mom put the pitcher down and sat directly across from us. Her eyes questioned me, wondering how I was. I gave her a small smile because, what else was there to do? "We need to do this more," I told them.

Both my aunt and mom frowned at me.

"Us three ladies," I explained. "I think we need some girls' nights."

My aunt started laughing, and my mom grinned back at me. "We'll do it next Saturday night at our house. The boys can fend for themselves for a night."

"I'm not going to say anything today." I looked at both of them. "There's enough drama going on."

They both nodded, seeming relieved.

We sat and sipped our drinks, but Uncle Nick never came to the table. No one asked where he went. The guys joined us thirty minutes later. They sat at the end of the table, and I didn't look at them. After finding out about my uncle's affair, Scout's hatred seemed petty.

Everything seemed petty.

A family was almost ripped apart.

Just like mine.

13

RAMSAY

I was getting ready for bed when my phone's alert sounded.

Unknown: What's your damage?

I lay down on bed and texted back.

Me: Who is this?

Unknown: Fucking guess. You cost me three friends today.

Oh.

Me: You owe me an apology. It's your fault you were a bitch and not trusting Clint. He said he vouched for me.

I programmed his name in.

The Dick: I've never known a chick to be cool. I didn't believe him.

Me: That's your bad. How it went down today isn't on me. That's on Cohen.

As I waited, my heart started to pound.

I didn't understand Scout Raiden. That was obvious. When he came to the table at Pike's, everyone was subdued. My cousins were fake polite, and only Clint said he'd tell me later what happened. He wouldn't. Whatever had happened, none of my cousins would tell me.

So, I decided to ask Scout.

Me: What happened today?

The Dick calling.

I yelped, almost dropping the phone, but I hit accept and lay back, firmly ignoring how the flutters in my tummy moved up to my chest.

His voice came through, sounding more mystified than anything. "They didn't tell you?"

I swallowed, my throat feeling scratchy. "Clint said he'd tell me later, but I don't think he will."

He grunted. "Your cousins said their piece. I said mine. Everyone knows where we stand now, but I texted you because shit's going to come out about Amalia. People are going to talk, and I gotta know if you're going to feel a certain way in a weak moment and share with your new friend Gem what you saw and heard in that locker room. None of this is about me or you or whatever fucking issue you have with me. It's about Amalia. She's fifteen."

A pang shot through me, splitting me in half. Old demons and haunts rose up. "I had a boyfriend who used to . . ." My heart picked up. What was I doing? I never talked about him, ever. But I heard myself adding, "He hurt me . . . a lot. The reason I'm sharing is because I started dating him when I was fifteen. So no, I'm not going to say shit."

With that, I hung up.

Me: Don't call me again.

Me: Also, I saved you in my phone as The Dick. Just so you know. #themoreyouknow

---

THE DICK WAS RIGHT. But also not because nothing came out about Amalia.

The friendship breakdown between the Maroney triplets

and the other two stud muffins sitting at the top of the social ladder, Scout Raiden and Cohen Rodriguez, was the biggest highlight.

Then the gossip started about me. I was being blamed for it.

"So . . ." Gem chewed her lip, and I knew she was wondering if we were good enough friends yet for her to pull a friend card and demand to be in the know.

I had no idea what to say, so when I saw my cousins leaving school, I grabbed my stuff. "I gotta go."

We were in one of the classes where the teacher liked to use worksheets. He'd come in, give us notes in a lecture, and then pass out the worksheets. We were supposed to use the rest of the class to fill them out and hand them in. I thrust mine at Gem. "Fill it out for me? Hand it in? I gotta go."

"But—"

I was out the door.

To be honest, I didn't care whether she did the worksheet for me or not. If she didn't, I'd deal. If she did, then awesome.

My cousins were in the parking lot by the time I grabbed my stuff from my locker and got outside. "Hey!"

They were waiting by Trenton's truck.

"What are you guys doing?"

Alex folded his arms over his chest, tipping his chin toward the school. "We're ditching early, going to our house. Wanna come?"

"Don't you guys have football practice?"

"Not till four today."

I glanced back at my bike, and Clint shoved off from Alex's truck. I unlocked it, and he put it in the back, before hopping up and extending a hand my way. I didn't need it, but I grabbed ahold of it anyway and climbed up and over. Alex got in the front, and Trenton was pulling us out of the parking lot when I saw Scout and Cohen leaving early too.

"He asked for your number, said he was going to apologize," Clint told me. "He call you?"

Well, shitters. He'd texted. He'd called. But he hadn't apologize. I didn't want to cause any more waves.

"He did."

Clint nodded and settled back as we drove past Scout and Cohen.

Feeling an itch I didn't like, I took my phone out of my bag.

Me: You need to apologize.

The Dick: "For what," said The Dick.

Me: So funny. Apologize, now.

The Dick: Gonna shock you, but . . .

I waited, expecting a middle finger emoji.

The Dick: I'm sorry for threatening you and your cousins.

Well. That was surprising, and I didn't feel so bad for lying to Clint.

I sent him the middle finger emoji instead.

The Dick: I just apologized. Wtf?

Me: I owe that to you for all this mess. You should've just believed my cousin.

I waited, holding my phone, but he didn't respond.

THE RESPONSE CAME LATER that night after the guys were back from football practice. I was still at their house. My phone buzzed at the end of *Captain America*, our first movie.

The Dick: I'm not that bad of a guy.

I replied right away. I blamed my hormones.

Me: You've given me death stares since day one. Then you threatened me and my cousins.

Me: Credit to you for apologizing after I demanded one. Most assholes would try to blame me somehow.

The Dick: Again, I'm not that bad of a guy.

Me: Jury's out. I only trust my cousins.

The Dick: Fair enough. How are the guys?

Me: Ask them.

The Dick: Jesus. Give me a break.

Me: Nothing came out today about Amalia, not that I heard.

The Dick: Yeah. Everyone's worked up about the friendship split. Everyone's blaming you.

Me: I should tell everyone it's your fault, but right. The girl gets blamed.

The Dick: If anyone asks me, I'll tell them it was my fault.

That made me pause.

Me: Why would you do that?

The Dick: The truth. Also aware you're taking the brunt of some attention that might've gone Amalia's way.

Me: What happened? Can I ask?

The Dick: We're enemies who text. Not telling you.

I huffed, but that was fair.

Me: Is she a nice girl?

The Dick: Yeah. Sweet. Idolizes her brother.

Me: And you?

The Dick: I don't know.

The Dick: That guy you mentioned before? He's the one who held you down?

Oh man. I couldn't breathe. But I typed back, my fingers feeling wooden.

Me: We're still enemies who text. Not telling you.

The Dick: He the reason you moved here?

A fist squeezed my chest, taking hold of my organs. It was slowly circling, pulling everything tight with it, twisting it all up.

Me: Same answer, see above.

What am I doing?

My phone buzzed, but I didn't look at it. We were starting *The Winter Soldier*, and I didn't look at my phone for the rest of my night.

He was right. We were enemies. I needed to remember that.

14

RAMSAY

I was at my locker a week after I'd last texted Scout when Gem bounced up to me. Literally bounced up to me. Her cheeks were flushed. Her hands were holding on to her bag's straps, and her hair was in pigtails. I had a total flashback to myself when I was six and got my first stuffed animal instead of a doll. I'd been so excited.

Gem huffed out, almost out of breath, "I figured out how you can make it up to me."

I frowned, shutting my locker. "Make what up to you?"

"You going to Scout's fight without me."

"Gem," I started because that wasn't my fault.

She waved a hand in the air. "I get it. They said you were going for food, but you could've called when you got there. My cousin fights too. I know people who go to those fights. I could've got a ride."

I opened my mouth, feeling like I needed to defend myself.

She kept on, "Anyway, you can totally make it up to me by . . . ." She pretended to do a drum roll, complete with sounds, and then she said, "By joining the Homecoming committee with me!" She finished with her hands doing a ta-da motion, sparkle fingers in the air, and her legs kicked out so her body formed an X. "How exciting is that?"

It was the end of the day. I had plans to find Clint and make him take me for snacks. I was in desperate need for some sugar.

"What?" I gutted out.

"Awesome!" She perked up, linking her elbow with mine, and she dragged me with her.

We went past Clint, who was standing with some other guys, and he started laughing at me.

Past Alex and Trenton, who were heading out for the after-school dinner before practice. They paused, saw me, frowned, and then started laughing.

I harrumphed, a sarcastic comment on the tip of my tongue, but I didn't get the chance. Gem was moving too fast.

And also past Scout and Cohen, who had locked not-happy gazes on me.

I gulped, but rethought that and glared instead. He was the enemy. Not Cohen because he was only being a ride or die, but *also* Cohen because *I* was a ride or die too.

She got me to the cafeteria before my wits got back to me, and I was starting to put the brakes on right as she whisked us in and announced, "Ramsay and I will help, Mrs. Charlotte." Gem was back to beaming at the teacher who had a clipboard. She took one look at us, and said, "Lovely. Thank you, Gem and Ramsay."

"I—" But she was already writing our names down and then I got the growl out, "What?"

Mrs. Charlotte smiled and motioned to the side. "Kira, welcome these two girls to the committee and help them get situated?"

The girl who turned to me had her hair in braids, and she was wearing black leggings and a pink sweater that hugged her whole frame. Two more girls joined her, both in similar clothing except instead of a pink sweater, one wore a vintage-looking green T-shirt with white letters on the front. It was tied in a knot over her stomach, and her hair was sleek, swept back so it almost looked like something from The Matrix.

"Hi. I'm Kira." The first girl gave a wave and a friendly smile. "I know who you are. We're friends with your cousins." She indicated the other two. "This is Ciara and Leanne."

Both waved. I had no idea who was who.

Kira focused on Gem. "And you're Theresa's cousin."

Gem started to answer.

Kira cut her off, her eyes growing more chilly. "I wasn't asking. I know who you are. We're not friends with Theresa, so is this going to be a problem?"

Gem's mouth snapped shut, and she wavered back on her feet.

I frowned, stepping forward. "I don't know the history—"

Kira swung my way. "You're right. You don't, and no offense, but I don't want to start by being enemies with you. The history you need to know is that her cousin and us don't get along, at all." She looked back to Gem, thawing a little. "I have no problem with you helping, as long as it's genuine. If you're here to start a problem, then we can't have you helping us."

A door shut behind us, and I glanced back to see Scout standing there. His hard stare landed on me before he went to the vending machines.

Okay. I couldn't do anything about that situation, so I focused back on Kira. Before Gem could say anything, I got in there. "Listen."

Her face locked down.

I didn't care. "She dragged me in here and got our names written down before I could even say yes to this. I've met her cousin once, and it was super brief, so you're right. I don't know the history, but I don't need to because I know Gem. She obviously wants to be here. I've done this at my old school and getting good volunteers is hard. My advice is, don't be stupid and scare away two new volunteers. If you knew Gem, you'd never be saying any of that shit."

There you go. I waded in, not sticking to being under the radar which was my first plan of action. I sighed because I couldn't do anything about it now. I knew who Kira and her friends were. They were the popular girls. I knew who I was—the Maroney triplets' cousin, but I was also a loyal friend. And Gem was my friend.

I'd be loyal to her no matter what bridge I had to burn down for that to happen.

Which, again, was so stupid of me, but here I was, being *stupid*.

Kira drew in a sharp breath, and her chest puffed out, and I was ready for a blast from her.

"They're cool, Huerl."

Kira and her friends both snapped around to where Scout was standing, a water in his hand.

Her entire demeanor changed after that. "If you vouch for them, then . . ." She looked back, reassessing me. "Right now, we need help going to stores and seeing what they'd be willing to donate. You can go with Ciara, if you're up for that?"

The other girl wearing a pink sweater stepped forward.

"What about me?" Gem asked.

The green T-shirt girl said, "You can help me with some lists we need to do."

"Awesome," Gem whispered, her eyes big and shining at me.

Gem wanted to do this, and I got it then. I got why, too, because she wanted to be popular. Though, no disrespect to her because so many wanted the same thing. But a part of me crumbled inside because I didn't want that.

I wanted the opposite.

Kira moved in closer, dropping her voice. "I'm not trying to start anything. I really meant that. Just. Gem's cousin and I have been fighting for so long, you know? But also, that's super cool that Scout waded in for you. He doesn't do that, ever."

She seemed more friendly, so I nodded. "Yeah. That's cool, but Gem is a sweetheart."

"I know." She also seemed genuine. "Hey, uh. Instead of going with Ciara, you can go with me? I need to run some errands, and there's one store that loves your cousins. I think we could get a bigger donation if you're with me."

At this point, I was just going where I would cause the least amount of trouble, so I nodded.

She smiled widely at me. "So lit! Okay. Give me ten minutes, and let's meet by the main office. I need to run to my locker, and if I come back in here, I'll never be able to leave again."

She headed off, and I looked, but Scout was gone.

He'd vouched for me.

I pulled my phone out and texted.

Me: Why did you do that?

His answer came twenty minutes later when I was in Kira's very expensive-looking Mercedes-Benz SUV after we'd stopped for lattes.

The Dick: Didn't do shit.

Right.

But he had.

15

SCOUT

"That was surprising."

Cohen and I were heading out to grab something to eat. "Shut it." I knew I was going to get shit. Williams already texted me a thank you. We didn't need to talk anymore about it. It was a momentary lapse in judgment. To be honest, I didn't know why the fuck I vouched for her. "I did it for Alex."

"Right." Cohen was laughing under his breath, right before his phone buzzed. "Shit."

"What?"

"Amalia." He was reading his screen. "She's saying she's having a bad day. Could do with a pick-me-up." He glanced my way. "What do you think?"

"Tell her we're on our way to pick her up."

He sent off the text, then we were heading out to my truck.

When we picked her up, she didn't run from their aunt's place. She walked with her bag half dragging behind her. Cohen and I shared a look. Despite all the shit happening in her life, Amalia didn't let it show how it got to her. She was infectious, usually all smiles. Happy. That normal spark from her was gone, and I wanted to wring a guy's neck not for the first time. My hands tightened around the steering wheel right before she got in the back seat.

"Heya, bug."

She gave me a small smile, and a little giggle slipped out as she got in. She tossed her bag to the other seat and closed the door.

Cohen turned his head to watch her. "You going to say hi?"

"Hi guys." It was a mumble from her. She crossed her arms over her chest and slid down in the seat. Her face looked out the window.

Cohen and I shared another look.

She had a situation going on with a guy she liked and thought she was dating, but he was, in fact, a prick and a predator. We knew what was going on, or what had gone on, but if we talked too much about it, both Cohen and I started having murderous thoughts. Amalia tended to get even more upset when that happened, so for her mental well-being, it was the topic we didn't cover.

"We were thinking pizza and arcade?" Cohen spoke.

She groaned. "Uh. Cringe. Carby's and a trip to Arts n Cats!"

She wanted to go to her favorite crafting store in Pine River.

"Amalia," Cohen started.

"Come on. Thirty minutes. Not even."

I hated that damn store, but Cohen was already giving in. I saw it as he gave me a pleading look, and I grunted. "Fifteen fucking minutes and we're doing the drive-thru at Carby's."

Cohen chuckled.

"Suh-weet! Thank you, Scout."

COHEN GOT A BURGER AND FRIES, Amalia got her chicken strips and coleslaw, and I ordered a salad with chicken. The store's manager handed me the food with a wide smile. "It's on us, Mr. R—"

"I can fucking pay." I tossed him a twenty, hoping that covered it, and sped off.

Cohen was grinning, looking through the bag. "They never make you pay, and you always act all pissed about it. You're a local celebrity with your fighting. Just deal with it. More of that shit is going to happen the further you progress in your career."

I had stiffened, so I forced my hands to peel from the steering wheel. "Right."

"How are you going to eat your salad?"

I was pulling out of the lot and headed for the craft place. "I can eat while you two go in and buy crafts."

"What? No fair. You gotta come in too." Amalia's little hand lifted over the seat, taking her tenders. "I like going in there, but it's more fun to see how annoyed you get with Mrs. Meomeuooux."

Jesus. That name. Only Amalia knew how to say it. It sounded like a mix-up of meow and Sioux.

"I'll eat my salad. You go and get whatever new stamp you need."

"But—"

"We went to Carby's for you, Mals. Scout and I wanted pizza. Give this to him, huh?" Cohen gave her a wink. "Besides, you know Mr. Raiden here can't handle how a grown middle-aged woman has a crush on him."

I rolled my eyes. "It's the fucking cats. She's got like nineteen in there. It's weird."

Amalia was back to giggling, which helped ease some of the tension. "It's only six cats."

"And twelve kittens," Cohen added. "I'm with Scout. It's weird. She's a cat hoarder."

"She's a *craft* hoarder!" Amalia exclaimed. "And it's amazing. I'm going to open up my own Etsy store and sell enough where I can actually get a store."

"Right. Mom and Dad will love that."

She only laughed. "You just wait and see. I've got plans. Big plans for the future."

That was a relief to hear. I offered, "How about we hit up a movie after the store?"

Cohen's eyes snapped to me. He knew I was offering to postpone training for the day.

Amalia's eyes widened in the rearview mirror. "Ooh! Can we do the river screen? Uncle Angel bought that new paddleboat." She was scrambling higher up in her seat, her feet curling under her. "We can pack a cooler and put that on a tube next to us. Let's do it!"

As we were putting the boat in the river, and after Amalia had already gone back for the cooler in the truck, Cohen asked under his breath, "Do you even know what movie they have on this screen?" Pine River's movie theater had six screens inside and one outside that faced the river. They had an area roped off where people could lounge in paddle boats, canoes, kayaks, or in tubes when it was warm enough. "Also, we could've just used one of their boats."

I half-laughed and half-grunted. "Not a damn clue, but Amalia wanted this one."

He laughed before she came back, and we were paddling out.

We were of the same mind. It didn't matter, as long as Amalia was happy and distracted from everything else. That was all that mattered.

16

RAMSAY

The Homecoming planning went well. In fact, though I wasn't going to let Gem know, I was kinda glad she dragged me into doing it. Literally.

I'd forgotten how I used to enjoy doing stuff like this at Cedra. It'd been so long ago. Before—yeah. Before life happened.

Even Kira wasn't bad. She wasn't the typical mean girl, though I'm sure she had it in her, but for now her, Ciara, Leanne, and some others had been cool to myself and Gem.

That was why I was considering going to Kira's house for a shindig on Thursday night. It was supposed to be low-key and Gem was salivating over going.

I was torn.

A part of me wanted to say no to all parties or anything like it, but then I had to stop myself. Because why not?

This wasn't Cedra.

This was a new start. A new life. And hello, I was still in high school.

Socializing was normal and healthy.

Another part of me was automatically going to say no

unless my cousins were going, which is what I started to say when I found out the triplets had to stay home. Clint said a family meeting was called, which by itself wasn't worrying but considering I'd found out about my uncle's affair and hadn't told my cousins yet . . . I was worried.

I'd been waiting for the right time to tell them to present itself, but then Aunt Aileen called me and asked me not to say anything. She wanted the boys to hear it from her. I couldn't argue with that so I was kinda wondering if that was going to happen Thursday night because my cousins were not known for missing parties.

That left me at the same place I was at: to go or not to go.

Then Gem dropped the mic when she said, "Theresa's mortal enemies with those guys, but I'm not. And I've always wanted to go to one of Kira's parties. It doesn't matter if it's a small thing or a rager. I just want to go. Once. And before you, I've never had a friend outside of Theresa's group. They all do what she wants, but not in a bad way. They're just showing respect, but that's the thing. Theresa was friends with Kira in elementary school and she always talked about how fun Kira can be. I want to go. I know it's stupid and silly, and probably something you'd never understand but—"

"I'll go." I gave in. Totally just bent my knees, put my hands in front of me, and I dove into my capitulation. If that was a thing? If not, I was making it because that was how fast I surrendered.

And so, there I was, attending a Thursday night party, which was easy because my mom was working the evening shift.

We got a ride from another of Gem's cousins.

Kira's house was big, gated, and metallic. Everything looked as if it were made out of metal or cement, and I was sure it would've looked great in a magazine. For me, I preferred our house with a yard, and one day I was hoping to talk my mom into getting a dog. Everyone had different tastes. To each their own, but when we went in, no way was this a small event.

Thirty people were inside, with music blaring.

"Hey! Hi! You're here." Kira ran over wearing a swimsuit and a see-through wrap. She had large hoop earrings, her hair pulled back, and her makeup looked professionally done. "Guess what? Omg. Scout came. I can't believe it. He never comes to these things. Hi, Gem." She squeezed my arm, then reached to squeeze Gem's.

When she leaned over to hug Gem, that was when I smelled the booze. It was also when I saw all the alcohol on the kitchen island. The entire counter was covered in alcohol, mixers, glasses, and anything needed to go with it like salt or limes. I frowned at the skittles.

A burst of laughter sounded from a sitting room where people were standing and sitting on a bunch of couches. Or no, there was a television mounted on the wall above. They were playing a video game.

"Scout's here?" Gem asked breathlessly, taking everything in as Kira stepped back.

"Yep. He showed up ten minutes ago with Cohen, but I don't know where they went. Probably downstairs. I think an MMA fight is on the television, so everyone who wants to be cool with Scout is down there with him."

Cool with Scout. That was a thing?

"Come." She grabbed Gem's hand, pulling her to the kitchen.

Ciara and Leanne were there, both looking a little buzzed. "Hi!" Ciara waved.

Leanne started laughing and had to turn away to keep it under control.

Gem's grin slipped, and yeah. Here I was, being stupid again because I laughed, "You know those movies with the mean girls and how they're all nice and buttering you up before they embarrass you but you always get the revenge in the end?" My smile went flat as all three stared at me. "This is feeling like the beginning of one of those scenes, but that would be so cliche and lame. Right? You guys aren't lame, are you?"

Leanne choked on her drink while Ciara's eyes bulged out.

Kira forced out a laugh. "Why would we do that? You're cousins with our friends."

I eased back. "Right. That's true." And that was it. I held their gazes then, letting my slight threat, which was vague but still totally a threat, hang in the air between us.

"Jesus, Williams." Scout moved in behind me, and I sucked in my breath because damn it, I hadn't felt him at all. I'd started to be able to feel him lately. He went to reach for the bourbon. His gaze was cold and mocking as he poured it into his glass. "Maybe wait a full month of being here before making more enemies? Just a thought."

Kira brightened. "Scout! When's your next fight? I want to make sure I go."

He ignored her, sipping his drink and heading past me. His arm brushed against mine.

A wave of tingles spread through me from that touch, and I had to inhale slowly before exhaling to let those sensations ease out of me. He had too much power over me, way too much.

Another laugh sounded behind me, but this one didn't send my alarms going.

Kira snapped, "What, Cohen?"

He moved so he was standing next to me, his drink still mostly full, and he swirled it around. "You know, I came to get into your pants tonight, but I'm thinking maybe I should focus elsewhere." He sidled closer but didn't touch me. He didn't need to. The whole movement was an insinuation, and that was when I saw the mean girl in Kira. She'd been veiling it the whole week on the committee, but I'd felt it sidling earlier, and

I saw it now. She cocked her head to the side, her tone nasty, "Don't even, Cohen. She's the Maroney triplets' cousin. They'll ice you out in a heartbeat if you touch her."

Well. I didn't know how I felt about that, but I was kinda enjoying hearing the insecurity in her tone.

I decided to let it play out. I wasn't going to wade in or say anything. I wanted to see what else would be said about me, in front of me.

My surprise? It was Gem who took care of it.

"Forget Clint, Trenton, and Alex." Gem picked up a glass of something that I was hoping was okay to drink and took a sip. She didn't make a disgusted face, so I figured it was fine, but she did smile, almost cockily at Cohen. "You touch my new friend, and you'll have me to deal with. Don't forget. I have your mother on speed dial."

He swore in Spanish, before breaking out in a laugh. "And you'd totally call her. But don't worry, little Gem. I've got no plans to hit on your friend. Too many people would mess me up." He went over to her, hooking an arm around her neck, and pretended to mess her hair up. As he did, he gave me a wink, and I knew then that the whole thing was a charade. I just didn't know why. Either way, I relaxed enough and took a drink when Kira offered me one.

———

"We're not that bad."

I was on a couch in the living room, buzzed, and Gem was flirting with a guy in the corner. I liked seeing that. It made me happy that we'd come, but I shifted a little as Kira sat by me.

Half the people had already left, but there was still a good amount partying. And I'd been too paranoid earlier because nothing mean or bad happened. It'd been truly a party with people drinking, laughing, talking, and flirting. No humiliation scene had happened.

I said as much to Kira, then added, "I'm sorry for thinking that."

Her eyes grew thoughtful. "Alex wouldn't say why you left your last school or really anything. I'm guessing something happened back there?"

I nodded, my neck stiffening. "Yeah. Something."

"You don't need to worry about me."

I was beginning to believe her. "How long have you known my cousins?"

She glanced over her shoulder, and I knew where she was looking. She'd been looking there all night long. It's where Scout was sitting, talking with Cohen and a girl, who was obviously into Scout. Kira had been over there half the night too, but both guys were ignoring her and I wouldn't stick around if that was my treatment either. "Can we talk about Scout instead?"

I was back to being tense. Guarded. "Sure. Though, I don't know the kid so I can't say much."

Her eyes locked on mine, studying me. "He vouched for you in the cafeteria. That's big for Scout. He only vouches for Cohen, Cohen's sister, and Alex. That's it."

I shook my head. "I don't know what to tell you. He's not my friend."

Her eyes narrowed. She sat back, and it was as if she released whatever she'd been looking for. She sighed, crossing her arms over her chest. "I don't get him. He moved here last year, and I had such a massive crush on him, but it's like I'm nothing to him. I usually get what I want, you know?" She grimaced. "That made me sound cocky. I'm not like that, but I just don't understand. Cohen wants me or he did until something I said tonight pissed him off, now he wants nothing to do with me."

"Are you after Cohen or Scout?"

"Scout is first preference, but he's become unattainable. He doesn't mess with any girls in school. It's girls in his fighting world. I know a few of them from Pine Valley who he's hooked up with. There's one that's more regular than the others, and she's a massive bitch. No one in our school. But, yes, Cohen too. I mean, Cohen's hot. I thought he was coming here for me tonight. Now look at him, he's all over that girl."

I looked without wanting to, but I still felt pulled because I felt the prickling on the back of my neck. I was right. Scout was watching me, and he wasn't hiding it. And while he was watching us, the girl who was almost sitting on Cohen's lap was watching him. The wistfulness was there. I saw it in her eyes before she masked it, smiling at something Cohen said to her.

"She's so stupid. Cohen just wants in her pants, and because of that look she just gave his best friend, he'll fuck her and then dump her." Kira huffed, turning around and settling back into the couch. She rolled her eyes. "Guys are all the same. Just wanting sex."

I frowned, hearing her bitterness seep out.

My phone started buzzing, and I stood, saying, "It's probably my mom."

Kira nodded, pouting and not giving me another look as I left.

I headed down the hallway, pulling the phone out.

I was right. It was a number from her nursing home.

I answered it right as I got to the back bedroom. People had been going upstairs or downstairs to hook up, so I was certain it was empty.

My hand found the doorknob when I realized it wasn't a call. The screen switched and I saw a picture of my dad there.

He was on the ground. His face swollen. Blood all over him. His eyes were so beaten that I could barely see them, and his skin was an unhealthy pallor.

Pain sliced through me. The room began to swim around me, and I tried to grab hold of the doorknob, but then I didn't care because it was my dad. I was seeing my dad. I was seeing him—I was choking.

I was going down.

My knees shook. I saw flashing lights. It had happened enough to me over the last year. I knew the precursors, and this time, I couldn't stop it.

Then firm arms came around me and carried me down a hallway.

"What?"

"Relax. Not going to do shit to you."

That was Scout. Scout was carrying me.

A door opened. Someone else was there.

"Cohen, cover us," I heard Scout tell Cohen.

"Got it."

A door was being opened, then shut. Then water was on.

"Wha—"

He didn't answer, plucking my phone out of my hands. He ran his hands down my pants.

"What are you doing?"

I got that question out right before he straightened and placed a hand on my chest. He pushed me back, right under the shower spray. It was freezing cold, and I gasped, surging toward him. "What are you doing?"

He shoved me back, adjusting the water so it'd get warm.

"You dick!"

He held me against the shower wall until the water started warming.

I stilled, letting it drench me, only then realizing he'd been checking to see if I had anything in my pockets.

My shoes—no. I had sandals. They were fine.

My clothes were drenched. My hair.

My makeup would be wiped away.

When he saw I wasn't struggling anymore, he removed his hand and raised it to lean against the top of the sliding door. "It's the only thing that stops you from going into shock. You gotta think clearly if you're going to handle whatever was on your phone."

I grimaced, feeling slapped. But he was right.

I hated that.

"What do you know about this shit?"

His eyes cooled. "More than you might think." His eyes narrowed. "You thinking more clearly?"

Damn him, but I was.

The result was a good one, a needed one, but I didn't appreciate his delivery. I shared this sentiment with him as he reached for the door handle.

He chuckled, leaving. "I'll keep that in consideration for the next time you're about to have a freak out at fucking Kira Huerl's party." He opened the door. "I'll be out here while you do whatever you need to."

He shut the door.

God.

My dad.

The picture.

Scout was right.

I couldn't think about it, remember it, though—goddamn it. It was burned in my head.

This was serious.

Max had texted me. The number was local, and I had no idea how he did that, but he did. It was from him. I'd have to tell my mom—no. I wouldn't. She handled this for me last year. I knew the ropes. I knew the channels. I'd handle it myself this time.

I'd call the police, let the detective know, and go from there, but I already knew what would happen. Nothing. Max would lie, say it wasn't him, but he and I both knew the truth.

Dad.

God.

I missed him so much.

No, no, no. Searing pain and shame and guilt and—it was all mixing together, rising, threatening to choke me.

Scout. I'd focus on him.

I could do that.

He'd push it away. He'd make me forget.

Scout Raiden.

I hated him, but fuck, I *wanted* him.

And he'd put me here. Soaking wet.

I gritted my teeth, turned off the shower, and stepped out. Reaching for a towel, I grabbed it right as the door opened. Scout was inside before I could do anything. The music from the party was blasting behind him.

"Wha—"

He was in. The door shut, and he turned to face me.

The room shrank.

The air electrified.

It was him, glaring at me. I was remembering how he looked at his fight. How he'd looked *at* me as I'd looked *back* at him. All hot and sultry, and I had to gulp to deal with the need rippling through me. He'd be a perfect distraction. Push everything away. The bad feelings. The trauma. The hate. The guilt. The sadness. The feeling that I should be the one—I licked my lips, moving toward him, when he said, "Give me your clothes."

"What?"

His teeth were bared. His eyes were so hard. "Your clothes. Strip."

I clutched the towel tighter. "Why?"

"Cohen's covering for us, but your friend is outside. She'll throw your clothes in a dryer before we take off."

"Can't she find me new clothes? Dry clothes?"

"Kira's room is busy."

Oh. OH! "I thought Cohen wanted to hook up with her."

"He changed his mind. Her feelings got hurt. She found another guy to make her feel better." The way he said it, so casual and careless, made it clear he didn't give one shit about Kira.

I tucked my chin down. "Why are you doing this for me?"

He didn't answer.

I looked back.

Those eyes were still on me, looking so harsh. "Alex is still one of my best friends. Don't get a big head. Doing this for him."

Right. Yeah. That made sense.

I shivered from the coldness of his tone.

"Your clothes, Ramsay," he growled again, impatient.

"Turn around."

He made another grunt, but turned.

I took my clothes off as fast as I could and wrapped the towel back around me. Balling the clothes up, I pressed them to Scout's hand. He took them, opened the door, and handed them through. "Make it fast," he said to whoever was out there, probably Gem.

He took my arm and dragged me from the bathroom and into the bedroom he'd been in before.

"What—"

"Chill." He walked to the bed, flicking a look over his shoulder to me. Everything about him was tight and controlled, almost annoyed. He sank down, his phone in his hand. "Not going to jump you or interrogate you. Do not give one fuck why you were going catatonic." And with that, he turned his attention to his phone.

I was frozen just inside the door, holding my towel together. A few minutes later, I realized he meant what he said. My body started to relax, just a little, and the text came back to my mind.

I couldn't shake it.

I'd fallen apart before. I'd been strong, then I'd fallen apart, and I couldn't keep falling apart. Not here. Not in a new school. Not where my cousins went to school. I had family here. I wasn't alone.

I closed my eyes a moment.

"I can't believe you're doing this to Max. You're such a slut."

"Waste of space."

"I'd fuck her, but I ain't going to trial for that piece."

Male laughter.

Female laughter.

The whispers.

The snide comments.

The openly asshole comments.

Then the threats.

The names written on my locker.

The letters. The notes. The spit wads. The shoving. The tripping. The elbows in my body as I walked by, as they walked by, as I was just standing there. The tweets. The DMs. All the ways to get at me, they'd done it.

Max Prestige came from a long line of Prestiges who ran Cedra Valley. I'd learned the hard way how untouchable my boyfriend was.

I'd thought I'd left that behind, but here it came again.

Take two, motherfucker.

"The clothes will be a bit. You should sit."

I jerked out of my thoughts, seeing Scout watching me. He'd put his phone away, but the coldness from before was fading. A darker, warmer look was coming over him as his eyes tracked my body. All the way down. All the way up. Going slow.

Finding my mouth.

Staying there.

The need from earlier washed over me again. I knew my body. Knew it was only reacting to him because he could give me what I was craving, those moments where I felt good, where I could escape the past.

Moments hidden.

But, God, what an asshole to be the one who could give that to me.

I clenched my teeth before moving to the far corner of the room. I sank down, keeping the towel around me and all the important bits covered.

"Thanks for helping me."

He didn't reply.

"I'm surprised you did," I added.

He rolled his eyes. "Already told you, did it for Alex. Don't make it a thing." His eyes narrowed on me. "Though, full cards on the table. I don't like you. You know I don't like you."

I laughed because, *damn.* "I don't like you either."

He grunted, a faint grin on his lips. "I'm aware. You wanted to tear me apart on the first day."

That was true.

"But you're hot," he added, matter-of-factly. "I'm laying it out right here, right now. If the chance popped up, I'd pound you. I'd be down for that. Full on. I'd do it rough, and I'd do you in a way that'd have you screaming for release."

I shook my head, my insides a full inferno.

I started to say something, a retort, but he stopped me. "Don't. You want me too. I can tell. Could tell at the fight. All the fake shit that happens, I'm not fake. I like that we're honest with each other. I don't like you, but I want to fuck you. You know where I stand. I'm not trying to hit on you or be crude in any way. I just felt you should get some straight-up truth."

I didn't question him or claim otherwise. With his looks, where he was, where he was going, he wasn't dumb. He knew when a girl was hot for him.

I remarked, "Nice knowing where we both stand."

17

RAMSAY

My clothes were dry, and my hair was almost dry. I'd been given a proposition in the most matter-of-fact way I could've imagined.

I wanted to go home.

But we needed to call Gem's cousin, and we also needed to get past Kira and her friends, who were sitting in the kitchen.

Scout had left when Gem gave me my clothes so I could dress.

I was dressed.

I still hadn't left the room.

I didn't know why.

There was a sudden knock, the door opened, and Scout's head pushed in. He frowned at me. "What are you doing?"

Suddenly, I was exasperated and threw my hands in the air. "I have no idea! No clue. Not one fucking clue, Scout." I said his name.

He got a weird look on his face.

I'd never said his name before.

I turned, starting to pace, and when I looked back, Scout had come into the room. The door was shut. His back was leaning against it, and he tilted his head to the side, a hand going into his pocket. Scout was the image of badass, cool, and hot all rolled into one.

I was suddenly sick of that too.

"You're annoying."

His head moved back, his eyebrows rising. "What?"

"Annoying. You say all this shit when I'm wearing nothing but a towel, and you do it here, in a house where I'm not friends with this girl. I don't know if I even want to be friends with this girl, but here you are. Why did you come tonight? Kira said you never come to these things."

"Cohen wanted to fuck her. He doesn't now." He shrugged. "We won't be coming again."

That made so much sense. Perfect sense.

I threw my hands in the air again and paced in a circle.

The phone. The text.

The picture.

My dad.

God. My dad. How he looked . . .

I knew when that picture was taken, and I knew who took it. There was only one person who could've—"Did Alex tell you why I moved here? My mom and I."

The confusion left him, and something more serious took its place. Darker. He leaned forward slightly, slowly. "Something happened with your ex. There was a bully situation. Something like that."

"My dad? Did he say anything about him?" My voice was hurting. Rasping. I felt as if I were choking from the inside out.

He shook his head, his eyes never leaving mine. "Just that he's not in the picture anymore. I assumed there was a nasty divorce."

Divorce.

Right.

"My dad was assaulted, and the night that happened,

someone took a picture of him. That's what got sent to me tonight."

He jerked forward. "Are you serious?" He started for me.

I stepped back from his intensity, from the moment, from what I was feeling twisting inside me. "Yeah."

"That's fucked up, Ramsay."

Ramsay. He said my name.

I didn't know why I was fixating on that right now, why that was important to me, but it was.

I liked hearing him say my name.

"Will you give us a ride home?" My voice was so soft I almost didn't hear myself.

I felt so small in that moment.

Tiny.

Like I didn't want to exist.

I wasn't looking at him, but I heard his rough, "Yeah." He coughed, speaking more clearly, "Yeah. I can do that."

I still didn't look at him. I didn't know why. Another item on the list of things that didn't make sense to me, but I nodded in response to him, and he opened the door.

I went through it.

He followed for a step or two before going around me and saying to Cohen, "We're taking off."

I blinked a few times, trying clear my vision. Cohen was leaning against a counter in the kitchen, his arms crossed. His legs too. Kira was next to him, her hands behind her on the counter, as if she were doing reverse push-ups. Ciara was on the island, her legs swinging. Gem was behind her, sitting on a stool, a guy next to her, and their heads were bent together. Gem was giggling.

I let that wash over me. I liked hearing that.

But at Scout's no-nonsense bark, Gem's head jerked up. The laughter died when she saw me, concern filling it. Cohen didn't react except nod and push up from the counter.

Ciara chirped, waving a hand, "Nice seeing you tonight!"

Kira cast her a frown before coming over. "You okay?"

I nodded, not quite staring at her. I focused between her eyes, and she seemed appeased by that because her shoulders lowered and she nodded to herself before bending and whispering, "Did you guys . . . you know . . . do it?"

Jesus.

Of course that was what they'd think.

I swallowed tightly and shook my head. "No. We were talking about Alex."

She angled her head back, getting a better look at me. "Serious?"

Of course she didn't believe me. I nodded, trying to let her see I was telling the truth. "Yeah. Sorry."

"Your hair is wet."

Shit again. "I kinda had a freak out. It's—family stuff. Scout knows cause of Alex, but no one else."

Understanding clicked, and I saw the relief flash in her eyes. "Gotcha. I'm so sorry."

"Williams." Cohen made a motion before turning and gently pushing Gem out the door. Scout had already gone out. I picked up my pace because when they said they were leaving, they meant they were leaving. There was no lingering behind for goodbyes. Good to know.

Gem waited for me outside, hitting my side and staying there. "You okay?" she whispered, her hand finding mine and squeezing it.

I didn't have the heart to lie, but I didn't want to tell her the truth. "I'm okay." That was all I could manage.

"You sure?"

I nodded, giving her a smile. "Some family stuff just popped up for me. I'll be okay, though. I mean it."

"You can talk to me, you know."

"I know." I really did. I felt it in that moment. Maybe it

would pass. Maybe I'd go back to not trusting anyone but family, but in that moment, I really did feel like I could tell Gem everything. I just didn't because I didn't want to crumble. Not tonight, not more than I already had. "Thank you."

She stopped and wrapped her arms around me, hugging me tight. "I'm here for you."

I stood, surprised, until slowly, my arms lifted and I hugged her back. "Thank you."

Gah. I was a mess.

Who was I? I didn't remember this Ramsay. I used to be like Kira, top girl in the grade. No sad emotions like this, and here I was, choking back some tears because a girl who liked me, declared we were friends was now hugging me, telling me she had my back.

Seriously. I needed Clint time. I needed to remember the thrill of getting in trouble again. I needed to toughen up again.

A high-pitched whistle sounded. Scout was there in his truck, his window down, his arm resting outside and he was not amused. "Let's go!"

Cohen was in the back, and he was grinning from behind Scout.

Gem giggled, skipping over to them and she climbed into the back by Cohen.

I got in the front, sitting stiffly, but he didn't seem to care as he took off.

We dropped Gem off first, and Cohen was right after. Almost literally because he climbed out behind Gem, after the two had been shoving each other in the back the whole ride over. Both were laughing, and if I'd been questioning if they knew each other, that would have been put to rest. The two were giving off siblings-who-were-crazy-about-each-other vibes. Gem had pinched Cohen in the chest and he recipro-cated by tickling her, which had her shrieking, but still laughing shrieking.

It was contagious. By the time they left, I was pulled out of my mood until the door closed behind Cohen, and yeah.

I remembered.

Everything else left me because I was choking again, but choking from the past. Choking from the future. Choking from what brought me here. Choking from what could come and get me. "You live in the old Catering house, right?"

I had no idea what that meant, but nodded. "Sure. Yeah."

I was quiet on the way to my place, and when he pulled into my driveway, the house was dark. I'd not checked my phone, but it was past midnight by now. My mom had probably stayed for a double shift.

"Your mom's asleep?"

I laughed, an ugly laugh. "She's working."

He glanced my way.

I felt his question, though he didn't say a word.

And somehow, for some reason, that unfolded me. I wanted to tell him.

I wanted to tell someone.

But why him?

Why him?

"You're living with your uncle?" The words gutted out of me. Abrupt. I didn't know I was going to say them until I said them.

"Yeah."

"Why? What happened with your family?" I looked his way and found him slightly frowning at me. There were dark shadows over his face, but it was night. Dark. The moon was out. The shadows made sense. Still. It seemed more with him, like he was *supposed* to be in the shadow. That thought made something want to crinkle up inside me and disappear. He was hiding when I didn't want to, when I was tired of hiding.

But it was momentary.

I'd have a clear head tomorrow.

"Daydream" from Lily Meola came on the radio at that

moment, and I almost laughed because how appropriate. He reached forward, turning it down, and how appropriate was that gesture too?

"Not really getting why you're bringing up my family?"

Of course that was his response.

I nodded, facing forward, still not moving to reach for the door, to leave the vehicle.

I couldn't for some reason.

But that was a lie. I knew the reason.

"Is your dad alive?"

"Not your business, Williams."

"Your mom?" I didn't care. I kept asking. I needed to know.

I had to know before I could say mine. A tit for a tat. It only made sense to me.

I needed him to give a little, and then I could say.

And I needed to say. I needed to share.

It was killing me.

"Also none of your business."

"Why are you living with your uncle?"

"Still none of your fucking business—" He was growling.

I didn't care. "My ex beat me."

He quieted.

I added into the silence, "He beat me. He stalked me. He did everything a controlling abusive asshole does, and I stayed with him." Another beat.

My heart felt like it was breaking.

I kept on. "I lied for him. I made excuses for him. I told myself he'd change. I told myself it was a phase and that I needed to love him through it. I was lying to myself."

There was no radio on.

He didn't say a word.

I didn't either.

He'd be the first person outside of my mom or the police

who I told. I hadn't even told my cousins. Mom did that deed for me.

"His family owned Cedra Valley. They owned the police. They owned everyone and everything, and still, there I was. In the police station. Beaten. Bloody. And making a report to try to keep him away from me. Guess how much good that did for me?"

I looked now, still seeing his face in shadow and *really* hating it.

I was stepping forward. The least he could do was look at me, let me see he was looking at me, but then he did.

He moved forward, shifting so I could see him, and he was right there.

He was watching me.

There was no sadness in him.

No anger.

No disbelief.

Not even resignation. It was as if he'd heard this story before—or, at least, a version of this story with different characters.

He was watching me like he always did. Waiting.

"He broke me. I still feel that. He did that to me, and here you are, not caring what I'm about to say to you. I think that's the only reason I want to say it, to say it to *someone*. Someone who doesn't care. Someone I can unburden myself to, and it won't matter to them." A tear broke free, the first of so many that I'd never let fall. This one fell. This one, I *let* fall. "My ex beat me. I already told you that, but I didn't tell you what else he took from me. One night I couldn't hide what he did. Guess what my father did? Because he was a good man. Not everyone gets a good dad. I did. I got a *great* dad, and because he was a great dad . . . because I couldn't hide the bruises from him anymore, he went there. To my ex's place. He knocked on the door. He told Max to stay away from me. He told him to stay out of my life, that I would be nothing to him. Do you know what my ex did?"

Another tear. This one ran down the side of my face, all on its own volition.

"He shot my dad."

I stared forward, just reciting.

"On his home's doorstep, he took out a gun, shot my dad, and beat him. When my dad stopped breathing, *that* was when he called 911. He knew it was too late. He took away my father because he was told that he couldn't keep kicking a toy that he liked to kick. That's why I lost my father. That's why we moved here."

There. It was done. It was out.

I'd told someone else.

Wasn't I supposed to feel better?

18

RAMSAY

I was getting looks the next day. Lots of them.

During first period, I just thought word got out about the time I spent with Scout last night. Like what Kira thought, that others thought the same thing. Then a girl in my second period started to say something, but she choked on her words as soon as I looked at her. She wouldn't turn to me the rest of the class.

There were looks in the hallways. People turned away, their heads almost bumping against each other in their haste not to make eye contact with me.

Something was up. Something way bad.

Between classes? Looks.

In classes? Looks.

I was starting to think this wasn't about Scout and me.

Lunch came around, and as soon as I stepped into the cafeteria, Trenton appeared behind me and ran into my back when I stopped short.

"Okay. What's going on?" There was too much weirdness happening.

He grabbed my arms, his mouth in a flat line. "We have to talk."

My heart sank. "Okay." He didn't wait to hear me. He was walking me out of the lunch room, out the door, into the hallway, and through to an empty classroom. My other cousins were there, looking grim and pissed.

Clint was glaring at the door, his arms crossed tight over his chest.

Alex gazed at me, pity in his eyes.

Oh, boy. My heart dropped all the way to my toes.

"What's going on?"

There was a brief knock. Trenton exploded in a curse, "Finally."

He wrenched open the door. Cohen and Scout came in. Cohen had the same look as Alex, while Scout had—nothing. His gaze flicked to mine but passed to Alex's, which had the two of them sharing a look.

"What's going on? You guys are talking again?"

"This takes precedence," Alex said.

As if it were decided, everyone turned to Clint, who was back to watching me. His anger was there, but it was banked. Just slightly. He started for me. "You've not checked your phone today?"

I frowned, looking at my phone. "What?" The answer was no because I had an emotional hangover from last night. The party. The photo. Coming clean to Scout, who I looked at, and still, his eyes were so unreadable.

"Why?" I started to open my phone.

"Don't!" Alex reached forward.

Trenton jumped. "Jesus, stop!"

"What?" I was getting really scared.

I scrambled, opening it. I'd turned my notifications off last night. I hadn't thought of it, I'd just did it in case a new number sent me another picture of my dad. I'd not told my mom about what happened.

I ignored the guys and saw.

I saw everything.

Gem: Holy shit. Call me! ASAP!

Unknown: U crazy cunt. Leave our school or we gonna make you leave.

Unknown: psycho bitch

Unknown: U shld die, thanx

They'd sent me screenshots, and each one had my stomach shrinking. I'd seen the headlines. I'd already lived through them. I knew what each article was about.

Boyfriend Murders Father, Daughter Blamed!

Love Gone Murder?

She Told Me To Do It!

She's To Blame?

High School Boyfriend Tragedy.

Each headline was wrong and twisted. Sick.

They were as hard to read as the first time I'd seen them. I felt punched with each one, right back to that night when Max had held me down.

My phone was ringing.

Gem was calling me. I answered because she'd not been in school yet. "Hello?" My voice was shaky.

"Oh. My. God! Where are you?" She stopped, her voice coming back calmer. "Sorry. I was panicking. Of all the days for me to have a dentist appointment, but I'm here and you weren't answering your phone and I saw everything. Where are you? Theresa said she saw one of your cousins take you out of the cafeteria."

"I'm—" I looked around, to five guys giving me not-happy looks. "I'm . . ." What did I do? I turned toward Clint.

He read my unspoken plea and took the phone from me. "Hello?"

I could hear Gem's voice from the other end.

He nodded. "Let us have her for a bit. We'll let you know when we're done. She'll need you."

She was talking again, until he said, his voice soft, "Yeah. I know. Bye."

He didn't hand my phone over, going through it instead, sitting on the teacher's desk.

"Clint?"

He was shaking his head, his eyes burning. His anger was surfacing again. "This shit—this fucker. He doesn't get this attention anymore. He doesn't get to do this shit to our cousin."

"Clint." Trenton's entire body was vibrating. His tone was low.

Clint's eyes flicked up, cold. "I'm not doing shit, but I'm going through here and clearing out the crap she doesn't need to—" His finger clicked, and he froze.

I knew it then. Felt it because the room took on a whole new suffocating level of anger. It was sweltering. His eyes locked on me. "The fuck? He sent you this shit?"

It was the picture.

I nodded, feeling faint. "Last night."

He was off the desk and coming at me.

I jerked from the abruptness.

The rest of the guys startled too, but Scout got between Cint and me. "Calm it, Maroney."

He had a hand to Clint's chest, and Clint looked at it, looked at Scout, and growled, "I don't give a fuck how good you hit. You get between me and my cousin, we're going to have problems."

Scout was two inches taller than my cousins, but the way Clint was looking, none of that mattered.

Scout didn't move back, but his hand dropped. "You're coming at her pissed. How's that going to make her feel?"

Clint's eyes were narrowed, and his tone sent chills down my spine. "Don't forget she took the brunt of the school gossip

last week because of our fallout, and we all know that was coin-
cidental timing because you didn't want that other shit to come
out about Amalia."

"Clint." Cohen entered the exchange.

Clint swung his gaze his way, but his head was lowered and
locked. He wasn't chilling. "Don't fucking start, Rodriguez."

Cohen's eyes narrowed to slits too.

Alex coughed. "Okay. Stop. Scout called me this morning
because he knew about the text Ramsay got sent last night."

Trenton and Clint both exploded.

"What?"

"Are you kidding me? You say this shit now?" That was from
Clint.

"We were at the party together." Scout started, but I tuned
him out.

People knew. It was out.

It hadn't been before.

It was now.

I'd told him.

I'd told *only* him.

"You piece of shit," I said it quietly, but it got their attention.

They'd still been arguing.

I was standing behind them.

They all turned to face me.

Now my body was vibrating. Anger. Rage. It was filling me
up, and filling me fast, and I needed an outlet for it. Scout was
my outlet. "You goddamn piece of fucking shit. You told? You
did this. You let it out—"

"I didn't."

"Bullshit. I tell you and the *very* next day it comes out?"

His face had been unreadable, masked, but then it
switched, and white-hot rage was staring back at me. He took a
step toward me, "I didn't! That's the whole fucking reason I'm
here. I called Alex this morning to let him know about the text

because you don't seem rational half the *fucking* time. The other reason I called him was to apologize and to let him know that I knew. That you told me. I'm tired of not talking to three of my best friends, and with what you laid on me last night, I really didn't want to *keep* not talking to them." He stopped after that, his nostrils flared.

He was in his emotions.

I was in my emotions. "You're lying."

Those nostrils flared again. "I don't fucking lie."

"He doesn't lie!" Cohen growled from the side.

I needed to take a minute, one minute. I needed to think clearly, and as soon as I made that decision, I could see everyone in the room wasn't thinking clearly either. Alex was warring, going between his friends and his family. Clint had moved so he was standing at my side, now ready to get between Scout and me.

And Trenton...

"Where's Trenton?"

He was gone.

"Fuck," from Alex.

This wasn't good.

He said, "Oh no."

This was bad. Really bad.

Trenton was a wildcard. With what was said in here, who knew what he would do?

"What's going on?" Cohen asked.

Scout was still seething.

I needed to put my trauma aside because this was so very, *very* not good.

"We need to find Trenton."

19

SCOUT

"Dude. This is insane," Cohen said under his breath as we were going through the hallways.

"I'm aware."

People knew shit was going down. The Maroney triplets were on the warpath, and Cohen and I weren't far behind. Whoever leaked this was going to be in a world of hurt.

"Who do you think leaked it?"

I shrugged. "A piece of shit."

He cursed. "That's for sure."

We were turning down the senior hallway when we heard the shouting, followed by someone hitting the lockers. We took off.

We didn't need to push through the crowd because, with one look, everyone scattered. We could see in the clearing Trenton pushing a guy up against the locker, and he was about to do it again when Clint and Alex got there, pulling him back.

Trenton tried to reach for the guy, climbing over his brothers. His hand in the air, he yelled, "I wasn't going to touch her, dickwad. I was asking her a question."

Whoa. What?

A girl—I saw who it was, and it was making sense. Trenton went to the school gossip.

"Stop!" Alex took over, stepping between the two.

Trenton went at him again, but Alex slammed him back before standing in the middle again. He had two arms up, stretched toward both guys.

"What is going on here?" he asked again.

Trenton was beyond reasoning, and Clint was having a hard time holding him back.

Cohen stepped in, and I got ready in case Trenton shoved him off, but he didn't. He was letting them hold him back, calming a little, but he was still shouting. "I asked Mallory where the information came from about Ramsay. I was all nice about it—"

She snorted, coming out from behind her friend, holding a bag in front of her. "You were not. You were an asshole, accusing me of stuff I didn't do. I wouldn't *dare*."

Now I got involved, stepping into the middle and giving her a hard look.

She saw it and gulped. "I mean, I didn't start it. Okay?"

"I wasn't asking if you started it. I was asking who told you," Trenton snapped back, now calming enough that the guys didn't need to hold him back.

Cohen pulled his phone out, his head bending down. He shifted back a little.

I felt the prick then.

It was like a little trickling sensation on the inside of my skin, but I'd started to recognize it as feeling her. Ramsay. She was near, but I couldn't see her.

"This is getting us nowhere," Alex said. "Just answer the question."

Clint added, "You don't start talking, I got no problem doing something about it."

Her eyes widened. "What does that mean?"

His words were cold. "You got a brand new pink car, didn't you? Your daddy bought it for you." He paused for effect. "Hate to see something bad happen to it, and again, and again, and— you get my drift?"

She gaped at him. "You would never!"

He snorted. "Fuck that, I would. I have no problem fucking shit up. Just give me an excuse, and for your information, you'd never be able to prove I had anything to do with it."

She held her bag even tighter, getting red in the face. "Except for your threat just now."

He shrugged, stepping back. All calm-like now. "Words are words. Start sharing and nothing's going to happen to your little pink car."

Her mouth snapped shut, but she looked my way.

I frowned, not liking that look.

"Uh ..." Cohen started behind me, moving beside me.

I said to her, "What?"

She bit her bottom lip.

Now I was pissed. "What?" I barked.

She jumped back.

No one had heard that from me, but I was getting sick of this. She was wasting time. We needed to handle this. Handle Ramsay and whatever she needed. Then I wanted to handle my friends, get us all back on the same team. I hadn't enjoyed not talking to Alex for a whole fucking week. The apology over the phone this morning went well, but now everything had been stirred up.

"Dude," Cohen whispered, shoving his phone at me.

I looked at it, then looked at it again because it wasn't making sense.

Then it did, and a new feeling went through me. Not a good one.

Shit.

The school's gossip sidled closer, moving around her friend.
She told me, but she didn't need to. I knew.
This was on me.
Fuck.

20

RAMSAY

The look on Scout's face said everything. I didn't need to hear the words, the explanation, because I knew I was right. No matter how it happened, he brought this here. To me.

I was back by the lockers, but he turned, as if knowing exactly where I was, and he knew that I knew.

He did this.

My phone was buzzing in my hand, and I didn't care about who was calling me, texting me, sending me death threats. I followed my cousins, heard everything, every single word that was said, and that school gossip, she knew too.

Everyone did.

She was guilty for spreading it.

I was going to remember her, and I was going to shatter her. I didn't know how, but it was going to happen.

Fuck Scout.

Fuck everyone.

I couldn't hold back anymore. I was past the hurt, the pain, the threats having any effect on me. I was ready to *destroy* people.

I shoved past the few people standing in front of me and stopped right in front of Scout.

His gaze was locked on mine, and we both knew the truth. Both of us. I didn't know how that happened, or when it happened, but we were synced, so I used that connection.

"You did this."

The people quieted, but everyone heard me.

I felt a presence next to me, knew it was Clint, knew he was there to back me up in any way I needed. It was the same way I knew the presence on my other side was Trenton, and he was barely containing the need to hurt someone for this happening to me. And then there was Alex. He had a different energy. More calm. More smooth. Alex was the peacemaker and he was going to say something to make this better.

I snapped at him, "Not this time, Alex."

The vibrations shot through the crowd. I could feel it, could feel people reassessing me, stepping back because they knew this had reached a whole new level of pressure.

Alex surprised me. "I know. Not what I'm about to say, *cousin*."

Cousin.

That word washed over me, reminding me of our connection, our blood. That he loved me, which I knew because all of them went so hard for me just now.

He stepped closer, lowering his voice, "Just saying we should have this talk somewhere without so many eyes? Can really say what needs to be said then." He indicated Scout in the last statement, whose eyes flickered once.

His jaw clenched, and he jerked his head in a tight nod. "Locker room."

"Gladly," Clint seethed, leading the way.

The crowd scrambled back.

Two guys were outside the door, and Clint ordered, "Get lost."

One guy started to argue.

Trenton growled, right next to me.

Scout clipped out, "Now, Hastings."

They scrambled.

It was the same thing inside. A few guys were changing, and Clint ordered them to disappear. He went to the office in the corner, but no teacher or coach was in there so once the guys were gone, the door was locked from the inside.

"Cohen will guard the door for us."

"Don't you need backup?" My tone was taunting.

His gaze latched to me, and I felt singed from the ice.

His eyes narrowed. "I can handle myself *just* fine."

I was sure he could. A memory of his fight flashed in my mind.

"You told!" I didn't care how well he could fight. That didn't scare me, and it was because somewhere inside me, I knew he wasn't like Max. It was the same connection we had where I was starting to just know when he was around, the same knowledge that we could read each other's minds from a look. It was that feeling that, no matter how fast he could use his fists, his body, his speed, his power, he'd never hurt me physically. And because of that, I unleashed everything inside me. "Fuck you for doing that! I told you because, for *once*, you weren't such an asshole. You helped me out, but were you just manipulating me? Hit me when I was weak? When I let it out to someone because I needed to get it out of me because, if I didn't, he'd always be in there? He's like cancer. I can't get him out of me. He's inside me, under my skin, controlling my thoughts, my emotions, and for one second, I let it out to someone. I'd not even talked to them about him. So *fuck* you, Scout Raiden. Fuck you."

There was a moment of shocked silence.

Not from Scout. His eyes were sparking from his restraint, and then he spoke, through clenched teeth, "Maybe if you'd fucking wait a beat, I could explain what happened?" He moved in, his head bending down as he was towering over me. His voice went soft, which made it more dangerous, "The only person I talked about it with was your cousin." His head bent even lower. "Because *again*, I was calling to apologize to him, to make things right, and to let him know that I knew. I was trying to do that for you." Even lower. He was just a few inches away. "How fucking stupid am I, that I thought my best friend might need one more ally in the group."

I didn't move back even though I could feel his breath. "You told."

"I told your cousin. That's it."

I shook my head. "No. I saw the look on your face. It got out because of you."

He didn't comment.

Triumph flared in me. "Right?"

A brief wince flashed over his face before he lifted his gaze, taking in my cousins behind me. He went to one and stayed there. I knew without looking that it was Alex.

But his next words weren't what I expected to hear.

"I didn't sleep at my place. I went back to Cohen's after I dropped her off. I called you from their place. Amalia overheard me. She called a friend asking about who Ramsay was."

I waited.

He didn't say anything else.

I jerked my head up. "And?"

His gaze went back to mine, stark.

"And what? What happened then?"

Clint asked, more calm than I would've imagined, "Who was the friend?"

Scout closed his eyes, regret tightening his face before it was gone and the wall came back down. "Gabby Real."

I twisted around. "Who is Gabby Real?"

But Trenton was gone. *Again.*

Mad déjà vu was happening all over again, but this time, we went after him immediately.

"What? Again?" Cohen was taking us all in, his head following each of us as we passed until he fell in step next to Scout. "What's going on?"

"Trenton's going after Gabby."

"Not good."

Scout didn't reply, and I got it then. He wasn't going to stop us.

He was going *with* us.

We went to the cafeteria, and Trenton led us right to a table where Gem was sitting with her cousin and eight other people. "What the fuck, Real?" Trenton growled at one girl in particular who was sitting on the corner.

Gem jumped up. "Ramsay! Are you okay?"

I ignored her, focusing on Gabby, who showed no emotion as she blinked a few times and then leaned against the table behind her. One of her curls fell forward over her face. She reached up and twirled it around her finger before stretching it and letting it pop back up again. Dark brown hair. Puffy cheeks. Freckles.

Gem's cousin leaned forward so she could see better. She didn't seem to give a crap about whatever was about to happen, but she did have some mild curiosity.

"Rams—" Trenton started.

I didn't look at him as I said, "I got this." Then I asked, "Why'd you blast my shit out to everyone?"

Her eyes widened, and she sucked in her breath. Fear built in her gaze.

There. That was the reaction I was looking for. She didn't think I knew.

"Who told you that?"

"Does it matter? You did it."

Gabby flinched as if she'd been slapped.

Theresa stood and stepped away from the table, a hand on her hip. Her eyes moved from me to Gabby. "Is that the truth?"

Gabby's eyes closed, and she seemed to be saying something under her breath before she pushed up from her seat. When her eyes opened, they were blazing. Fiery. "You're lying."

"You're calling my cousin a liar?" Clint stepped to my side.

Alex moved to my other side. "She's not a liar. Neither are we."

The blood drained from Gabby's face as Alex spoke. "I didn't—I mean—"

"You spread that stuff?" Theresa asked her.

Gabby seemed to shrink. "No. I mean, yeah, but I didn't mean for it to get out like it did. I mean, it's messed up what happened to her."

Theresa looked at me. "Who told you?"

I was prepared to give the same answer when Scout spoke up, "I did."

The fact that he said it, that it came from him, that he was standing with my cousins and I had an impact. Everyone shut up except Clint, who snorted.

Gabby opened her mouth, but nothing came out of it. She closed it, and I could see the wheels turning in her head before she stood taller and squared her shoulders. Her bag fell to the floor, and she held it by the straps, letting it sit there. "I was curious, that was all, and I made a mistake of sharing it with a few friends. It's my mess. I'm sorry." She looked at each of my cousins. At Scout. "I'm sorry. I really am."

Gem moved forward, looking at her phone. "You didn't share it with a few friends. You posted it on your TikTok! WTF, Gabby?"

Gabby's eyes closed.

Clint growled, "That's so fucked up. You did this shit. You spread it—"

Theresa's eyes narrowed when Clint started going off. She moved forward.

I didn't know the dynamics going on here, but I knew one thing: a guy could not go off on a girl. There were rules, and I had to make a decision. My cousins had confronted her, but continuing was a whole different dynamic.

I stepped in, my back to Gabby, and put a hand to Clint's chest. "Stop."

"Rams—"

"I said stop." I looked at Trenton. "I'll handle this."

His gaze was stormy, and when he didn't respond, Alex moved forward. He took Clint by the arm, pulling him back. "Come on."

"*No—*"

"Clint!" I got in his face. "I got this."

"But—"

"Trenton."

Trenton rolled his eyes before giving in and moving to help his brother. Both herded Clint out of the cafeteria.

Once they were in the hallway, I turned back. There was a whole audience now, but I didn't care. No way in hell was I going to let this stand. If I did, they'd keep doing shit. I wasn't certain who *they* were, but there was always a they.

"Listen—" Gabby began.

I waved her off and ignored the vibes Theresa was sending. Her energy was biting. I focused only on Gabby. "I don't know you. I don't know this school or the dynamics here, but you blasted my shit on your social media. You fully fucking knew what that would do." She started to say something, but I got even closer to her. "Save your shit, but you and me? I now give a fuck about you. I give a whole lot of fucks about you. Are you getting what I'm saying here? I've been through hell, literal hell, and I'm standing here. If you think I didn't grow some tough-ass skin going through my ordeal, you'd better educate yourself. Here's my warning for you: I'm going to hurt you. And it's not going to be today, tomorrow, the next day, but I'm the type of bitch who's going to wait for the perfect shot, the one that'll hurt you the most, and that's when I'm going to make my move. Trust and believe, your shit's coming back to bite your ass."

I stepped back, sweeping my gaze over the table.

Scout had remained, and he ordered, "Take that shit off your social media. Now."

It was gone within the minute. Gem told me later.

21

RAMSAY

"You feel good about your showdown?"

I was in seventh period, study hall in the cafeteria when someone tossed two books onto the table beside me. Scout folded down in the seat, an eyebrow raised for me to respond to his question.

I bristled, hearing his judgment. I rolled my eyes. "Spare me your condemnation."

"I didn't tell you that shit for you to go off on her. I told you so you'd stop and think before you did."

"What'd you think was going to happen? You told my cousins. You were there with us. You followed us to the cafeteria."

"I told you as my apology for my part in it. I never meant for it to get out how it did."

That was his apology, and it went a long way. "Don't think Amalia's getting a pass. I don't know your relationship with her, but she had a hand in it."

His gaze sharpened. "She didn't mean to do what she did. She doesn't know you. Stay the fuck away from Amalia."

I didn't respond, and he knew that was my way of telling him to fuck off.

"Ramsay," he warned in a growl.

I changed the subject because we'd be at an impasse, but Amalia was a delicate topic between us. "Are you good with my cousins now? Also, what are you doing here? Have you been skipping this whole time?"

"Your cousins and I are getting there." He opened one of his books. "And I switched so I can take off for training an hour early if I need to."

"I was told that this wasn't a skip hour."

He motioned to the table where the teacher had been, but wasn't anymore. "Jeffries never comes back after roll call, and he's friends with my uncle. I get special privileges."

He was totally serious as he said that, and suddenly I'd had enough—enough of him and enough of this day and its roller-coaster of emotions. I grabbed my books and stood.

"Where are you going?"

"Not here," I said. "I'm done with this day." I wanted to say I was done with the place, but I couldn't because I wasn't. No matter what, my cousins were here, and I'd felt the first remnants of happiness these last few weeks. I hadn't felt that emotion in so long.

It wouldn't last. I knew this as I went into the hallway and to my locker. I opened it and began pulling out what I needed.

A shadow fell over me as Scout leaned against my neighbor's locker.

I stifled a slight scream as I glared at him. "What are you doing?"

He shrugged, watching me put things into my backpack. "This is more entertaining than studying, I guess. And I don't want to go to training yet."

"We're not friends. Remember?"

"I'm aware." His eyes darkened, looking me up and down

before meeting my gaze. He smirked. "Wanna do what I offered last night?"

"Are you kidding me?"

The smirk transformed his face again. It was a whole different vibe than when he'd smiled at lunch, but again, I wasn't ready for the way my body reacted. Did I want to indulge in him? *Yes*. Lots and lots of yesses, but I squashed that.

"I can't." I shut my locker, swinging my backpack on.

"Why not?"

"Besides how many times we cursed at each other today? Or threatened each other? Right. I can't think of one good reason why not?" Sarcasm. I was laying it on as I began walking out the door.

"Our version of foreplay." He pushed off, coming with me.

I stopped, my mouth almost falling down at his response. "Are you for real?"

He stopped and shrugged. "I'm hot for you, Williams. No matter how much I dislike you, I want that body."

"Fine. Want another reason?" I retorted before turning and walking again. "How about because the last guy whose dick was in me beat me up and killed my dad. You want to be the rebound dick after that sort of baggage?"

He had stopped at my words, his face darkening.

"Guess I'll have to find someone else to fulfill that need for me," I told him. "Thanks for the offer, though." I gave him a two-finger salute before shoving out the door. It was only then that I remembered that my bike was in front of the school because, for some reason, I had the great idea to park it there instead of in the back.

Talk about a bomb deflating after what I thought was an epic drop-the-mic comment.

The door opened behind me a minute later, and I heard his laughter. "Come on. I'll give you a ride. You can't grab your bike from in front of the office. They'll know you're ditching." He strolled around me, whistling all cocky-like as he tossed his keys in the air and caught them on the way to his truck.

Walk? That'd take forever. Or stay? Wait for my cousins?

Gah. I went with Scout.

I climbed into the passenger side and ignored the cocky chuckle. "Shut up."

He laughed again before he raised an eyebrow, reversing and heading for the road. "Back to your place?"

I was restless. If I went home, I'd sit there and feel all my emotions. I'd try to study, but it wouldn't work, and I didn't want to think about what I'd do *not* to feel those emotions. I sighed. "What do you usually do after leaving school and not wanting to go train right away?"

"I usually get food at Carby's with Alex and Cohen."

We had a Carby's back at Cedra Valley. It was one of my favorite places to go with my friends. "I heard about Louie's? What's that place like?"

He stared at me for a moment before hitting his turn signal and wheeling down a side road. "You don't want to go to Louie's."

"Why not?"

"It's a social scene. Garcia and Kira both hold court there every day."

"Who's Garcia?"

He slid his eyes my way. "Her cousin is your only female friend here."

Theresa Garcia. Got it. "What's she like?"

"Your friend?"

"Are you trying to be annoying?"

He laughed. "Kinda. I'm finding it's fun to piss you off. You get hotter."

Oh, good God. I ignored how that affected me. "What's Theresa Garcia like?" I asked again. "She's the leader of that group?"

He shrugged. "I don't know her really. She keeps to her friends. Cohen knows her and said she's okay."

"Super helpful of you."

He cracked another grin. "You being bitchy just makes me want to fuck you more. What's your favorite position? Reverse cowgirl? I can see you getting off on that."

My body was getting heated at just the image in my head. I let out another frustrated growl. "You're twisted"

"When it comes to sex, fuck yes. When it's everything else, I'm just enjoying your attitude."

"Agh!"

He laughed again. "It's making *you* hot too. Don't think I don't know that. You like being able to express your inner bitch. You also like me."

"I don't. I don't like you at all."

"Your body does. Everything else, no. Again, we're on the same page. Also, you know we've got this weird annoying-as-fuck connection between us."

I fell silent.

He snorted. "Can't even acknowledge it."

"I should've waited for my cousins."

He sighed. "No, you shouldn't have, and you know it. If you had, who knows the trouble your cousins would've gotten into. Clint's going to get in trouble. It's what he does, it's what he'll do with or without you, but Trenton's different. The sight of you would've reminded him of what happened, and he hates that your mess got here—they all do. You not being there will give Alex time to talk Trenton out of doing something stupid and going to their football game tonight instead. He will be able to take his anger out there instead of in the back of a squad car. That's why you're here with me, and we both know it."

"His game. I forgot that's tonight."

"You want to go?"

I thought about it, then shook my head. "Not after today. Next week, though."

He turned onto a side street that went up a hill. We'd gone through the houses in town and were moving up and away from the town center. My phone buzzed so I settled back, responding to texts as Scout drove.

Clint: Where are you?

Me: Honestly, I don't know. I'm with Scout.

Clint calling.

I silenced it and texted back.

Me: Don't make it weird. He's in the truck with me. I skipped out, and he came with. I didn't want to go home because I knew you'd come over and we'd get in trouble.

Clint: Not cool.

Alex: You're okay?

Me: Yes. I'm with your bestie right now, steering clear of Clint.

Alex: With Scout?

Me: Yes. Are you guys good?

Alex: I think so. What he did today said a lot. He's on our side, and he feels bad at his part. Are you okay being with him? That's weird af, Rams.

Me: I know. I needed to get out of school and get away. Do me a favor? Make sure Trenton goes to his game and doesn't do something stupid with Clint? I know he's in the mood.

Alex: Yeah. I'm already working on both of them. Not sure about Clint, but Trenton is starting to see reason.

Alex: It's weird that you're with Scout. We all saw how you both were in the locker room. Is there something going on between you two?

Me: No. Just . . . he's brutally honest, and right now I need that around me. The Max stuff makes me have trust issues with people.

Alex: Kinda feel you're lying to me, but Gem's worked up about you. Are you not responding to her texts?

Her texts? I checked my phone, and saw thirty-eight of them.

I cursed, but went back to Alex's number.

Me: I'll text her now. If you see her, can you cover for me?

Alex: Yeah, but for real, is something going on between you and Scout? He's my best friend.

Me: Nothing is going on. I mean it.

Alex: If you're lying to me, that's not cool. You're in his truck. Scout does not befriend girls unless he wants to fuck them. I know him. I know this.

Shit, shit, shit.

Me: I don't like him. He doesn't like me.

Clint: What the fuck is going on? Alex just took off and said he's texting you.

I cursed, and Scout glanced my way.

"What's going on?"

I ignored his question.

Me: Alex, don't go down this rabbit hole. Please. I can't handle it.

Alex: He hurts you, and I'm going to have to fuck him up. I'm sending him texts too. You and him, fuck no. I'm telling my brothers.

"No!" I jerked forward, hitting the call button until Alex answered. "Don't say anything!"

"Put him on the phone."

"Alex—"

"He's not answering his phone, so you put him on your phone instead."

"Alex, come on."

"Hit speaker, now!"

My head fell back against the headrest, but I hit the speaker button.

"Scout!" Alex barked.

He cursed. "What?"

"Do not fuck my cousin."

There was a slight pause before, "Are you kidding me?"

"I know you. I know my cousin. My guess is that both of you have been aware of this from day one. Am I right?"

I sighed. "You're making this really uncomfortable."

"I don't care. I'm not saying this just to Scout. I'm saying this to both of you because I know you, Ramsay. You do what you want to do, but don't do *this*. He's my friend. You've just been through the wringer. I—if he hurts you. If you hurt her, Scout!"

"Jesus." Scout plucked the phone from my hand and brought it to his mouth, speaking into it as he continued driving. He didn't look my way. "She's been through hell today. She was taking off, and she couldn't get to her bike. She and I have a weird thing going on. I enjoy pissing her off, and she likes it. It takes her mind off her normal shit going on. Relax, bro. We're going to my house until I have to go to training."

Well, when he put it like that . . . Alex had to be rethinking things now, but he wasn't wrong.

"Oh."

"I'm not going to fuck her at my house. You don't have to worry."

I locked eyes with Scout as we got to the top of the hill and he turned into the very last driveway. He was lying to my cousin. Or was he? He seemed angry now, so maybe not.

"Bring her back when she wants to come back," Alex said.

"On it." He ended the call, tossing my phone back to me. "Was that necessary?"

I flushed, anger flaring bright in me. "You're blaming me? For my cousin knowing us? Are you jerking *me* around now?"

"I wasn't jerking him around."

We pulled up to a seriously nice house. It looked like three stories with brick all over. I was speechless as he parked and turned the engine off.

"I like your cousin, but I thought they'd be cool with a casual arrangement," he said. "Learning you all are fond of emotions and shit, that's annoying. Not touching you now." He got out on his side of the truck, and I got out on mine.

He stalked off, going inside the now-opened garage.

He was right. Riling up the other person just made them hotter.

This wasn't good. Not good at all.

When I got to his garage, he had his shirt off and was wrapping his hands. A punching bag hung in the middle with a mat spread out on the floor. He'd kicked off his shoes. He nodded to me, chucking the roll of tape my way. "Get comfortable and wrap your knuckles. Wrap your whole hand, and go around your fingers and thumb. I'll be right back."

"What are we doing here?"

He paused at the door to the house, nodding to the punching bag. "What do you think? You're going to work off some steam."

I dropped my backpack to the floor and rolled up my sleeves, but that was all I could do to get comfortable. I had a tank under, but I wasn't stripping down to that. He came out in sweatpants, and I let out a myriad of curses because that wasn't fair. The guy was ripped *all over*, and he even had the penis muscles, the V that went down under his sweats.

Plus there was a tattoo of an octopus on his left side. A skull was in the place of its head. The tentacles dipped down so I couldn't see under his shorts, but it stretched to his other side.

Holy shit, what that must look like with those shorts gone?

I was salivating.

"Put clothes back on." I pointed at him.

His eyes flashed. "No."

"Yes."

He got behind the punching bag and held it against his chest. "You need to warm up?"

My mouth dried. He was serious. "I don't want to work out."

"Sweetheart." He straightened.

I didn't like the way he said that. I didn't like how I reacted to it.

"You're hitting a bag," he said. "If you want to work out, that's a whole other ordeal and not something you can handle. Trust me."

I glowered at him. "You're a dick."

"And you being a bitch right now is making me hard, so hit the bag."

I hit the bag. Then I hit it again and again.

Pretty soon, I couldn't stop.

Scout held it for me the whole time.

22

RAMSAY

The house was dark when Scout pulled into our driveway.

The boxing thing had been an emotional release for me. The first time he'd offered to take me back home, I shook my head and moved to the smaller punching bag. He watched me for a long time before I heard him go pick up a jump rope.

He worked out. I saw him on his phone, so maybe he told his uncle he'd train at his house. I didn't know. I never asked. I just moved around his garage. He had weights. Other punching bags. A post sticking up with sticks pointing out at odd angles. There were exercise balls and other things I didn't know how to use. After an hour, I got my phone and headphones out. I turned on the music, and eventually, as my body got tired and my mind went numb, I settled in the corner. There were a couple of couches, so I curled up and pulled out my homework.

I studied as Scout continued working out.

He only stopped a few times to grab food—or, fuel, as he called it.

My stomach had growled, as I hadn't eaten anything at lunch, so I grabbed one of his sports drinks from the fridge set up in the garage. I only went into his house to use the bathroom, and that was just inside the door. Each time, I went directly back to the garage. I could've snooped. I didn't think Scout would've cared, but I didn't.

I continued my homework until I was able to read ahead in two of my classes.

When Scout pulled up to my place, I reached for the door and got out. I didn't say a word. Neither did he. He left, and I went inside, already knowing my mom was working a double tonight. She'd sent me a text on her break, informing me, but I still hated seeing the note she'd left on the counter. It was next to some money for me to order food.

I left the note and cash where they were and headed upstairs. I knew my plans for the night.

I got ready for bed, but grabbed my blankets and pillows and took them all downstairs. I locked the doors and went through the house, double checking that all the windows and the back doors were locked too. Then, with a bottle of wine and a bag of chips in hand, I curled up on the couch. The TV was turned on.

I set my alarm for the morning and watched *The Fallen Crest Diaries*, popping open the wine and taking a big slurp of it.

I was halfway through episode five, season one, when a loud knock sounded at my back door.

I screamed, launching myself off the couch.

The pounding continued.

"Who is it?!" I yelled.

"It's Clint!"

I groaned, willing my heartbeat to return to normal as I made my way to the back door.

"And me!"

I stopped right before I got there. That was Alex.

If he was here . . . "And me!" That was Trenton. All three had showed up.

I lifted the curtain so I could see them, and moved around, trying to see who else was with them.

Clint frowned. "What are you doing?"

"Checking to see if you brought my aunt and uncle too."

He snorted, rolling his eyes. "Let us in. We brought pizza."

Just the mention of that had my stomach growling again. I opened the door and grabbed the box Alex held.

"Hey!"

I took it into the kitchen, and Trenton shut the door, locking it.

They each had their bookbags and some other grocery bags, and when Clint dropped one on the counter, I saw he had a change of clothes in there. "You guys think you're spending the night?"

"We know we are." Alex passed me, grabbed a slice, and went to the fridge.

"Uh . . ." Trenton was at the couch, and he held up my bottle of wine. "We need to talk about this, Rams?"

Clint snorted. "Right on." He went to the cabinet and grabbed another, taking the top off. "We each get our own."

Alex's eyes widened, but he took the wine from Clint and took a drink. Wincing, he handed it back as Trenton came over, reaching for it.

"How was the game?"

Trenton shrugged. "We won, but not by as much as we should've."

"You're coming next time?"

I nodded at Alex. "I couldn't, not today, after . . ."

"We get it." Clint gave me a look and a small nod. He understood.

"Scout said you hit the bag for an hour straight," Alex said. "How are your arms?"

"Like jelly. I'm going to hurt tomorrow."

"Dude." Clint reached over, took my wine from Trenton, and slid it back to me. "What do you think that's for?"

He was right. I took another drink. My stomach was swishing around. Wine. Numbness. My body was beyond tired, and now there was pizza. Best night ever. My cousins deciding we were doing a sleepover? That was the cherry on top.

"No party for you guys tonight?"

All three threw me looks. Clint rolled his eyes. "Right. After today? When our cousin needs us?"

That warmed me up. "Thanks guys."

"Topic change. What are we watching?" Clint eyed the television. "Oh. No. No, no, no. We're not watching that soap-opera, teen-drama shit. No way. We're watching a horror movie or something—anything but that stuff. Seriously."

Alex laughed. "We're aware you've already binged the whole first season."

"Wha—I did not."

Trenton picked up the pizza box and carried it to the couch. "It was either you or Dad, and I don't think Dad even knows what that show is, so you're caught, Clint. 'Fess up to it."

Alex brought the wine over.

Clint's mouth was hanging open, his pizza forgotten in his hand. "I—I'd never—"

"You did!" Alex yelled, disappearing into the hallway. He came back carrying a bunch of blankets.

Trenton looked around, frowning. "Where are your pillows?"

I pointed to where Alex had just come from. "In the closet."

"I got 'em." Alex went back and returned with his arms full of pillows.

Clint still hadn't moved.

Alex dropped the pillows on the floor, and then he and Trenton moved the coffee table to the side. They'd begun spreading out the pillows when I had an idea. "Wait."

I darted upstairs to the guest room and pulled out two air mattresses.

"Oh, sweet." Alex had followed me. He picked one up and gestured to the top corner of the closet. "We can line those up on the floor for anyone who wants extra space."

I grabbed the foam mattresses he'd pointed out and followed him back down.

"Oh yeah. That's what I'm talking about." Trenton came over, all smiles, and grabbed one of the air mattresses. He took it over, plugged it in, and spread it out as the air pumped in. "These are perfect."

"I call couch." Clint was about to sit when a pillow whacked him in the face.

Alex glared. "Help set up."

"Yeah, douche." Trenton added.

Clint motioned. "You guys got it covered. Besides, everyone knows my real job is to be emotional therapist for Ramsay."

I started laughing as I took the wine out of his hands.

"Hey."

I pointed at the blankets and the foam mattresses. "Help, then drink."

He growled, but it was all an act. He was fighting a grin as he spread the mattresses out.

By the end, we had a whole mecca of blankets from the couch to the television. The mattresses raised everything up, so the couch just seemed like one end of a giant bed.

It was glorious. I loved it, and I curled up in the corner of the couch with my favorite blanket over me. I kept my wine on the corner of the coffee table within arm's reach. My phone was quiet, I'd eaten three delicious slices of pizza, and was already half asleep when Clint won the battle and pulled up the latest horror movie.

Alex and Trenton stretched out on the mattresses, their feet toward the TV and heads propped up by pillows. Clint was on the other end of the couch. When Alex switched positions so he was on his stomach, his head toward the TV, I knew he'd be sleeping within minutes.

And he was, his soft snoring filling the room.

Clint moved his foot, getting my attention.

I raised my eyebrows at him.

He held up his phone, and I saw him texting.

My phone lit up a second later.

Trenton moved to his side, letting out a loud yawn, and pulled his blanket tighter. He'd be next to fall asleep.

Clint: You and Scout hung out tonight? What was that about?

Me: Nothing.

He kicked my foot, glaring at me.

Me: I mean . . . there's a weird attraction between us, but we also hate each other.

Clint: Are you serious?

Me: I don't like it either, but I think tonight was just about distracting me. I really can't explain it.

Clint: What did you guys do?

Me: I punched his bag for a long time. He trained, and then I studied on his couch in the garage. We didn't even talk.

Clint: Really?

Me: Yeah.

Clint: Alex is worried about you and S. I am too. Trenton too.

Me: You don't have to be. For real.

Clint: We don't want you to get hurt again. It feels like we just got you back, you know?

I sent him a smile because my chest warmed.

Me: Thank you. Love you guys for coming over and doing this.

He grunted, and Trenton lifted his head to look at him.

"Sorry," Clint said softly.

Trenton closed his eyes and curled into a ball.

Clint: The consensus is that we don't like you and Scout, but we can't make you do anything you don't want to do. I know Alex is going to talk to Scout privately, which he said is none of anyone's business, but you know what that'll be about. Could you let me know if things change with you and Scout? Not that I want to know—because I don't, but I love you and feel like we should know. So we're aware. Is that cool?

Clint: That was a fucking long text.

I grinned, laughing softly.

Me: I will.

Me: What'd you do after school?

He frowned.

Clint: ?

Me: You know what I mean. There's no question if you did something. I know you did something. What'd you do?

His mouth went into a flatline.

Clint: Better if you don't know.

Me: Clint . . .

Clint: Leave it alone, at least for now.

I frowned.

Me: Tell me if I need to know, okay?

He didn't reply right away. I kicked his leg.

He grunted, but texted.

Clint: I will.

Me: Good. LOVE YOU

He grunted and flashed me a slight grin before he tossed his phone to the floor and settled back down.

A girl was about to get butchered on the television, and I had a moment because I realized that between my cousins, the drama of finding out who did what at school, and Scout, I hadn't thought that much about my dad or Max today.

All that warmth had firmly settled in my chest. It wasn't moving.

The horror movie was so bad that it was making me laugh. The guy was butchering the girl with a rubber chicken. Who used a rubber chicken to commit murder?

Clint kicked my foot, rolling his eyes. "Shut up. It's not that bad."

"It's pretty bad."

He started laughing, covering his mouth so he wouldn't wake his brothers, but he agreed with me.

It'd been the perfect fit for the night.

23

RAMSAY

My phone buzzed in my pocket, and as I took it out, I glanced over my shoulder. Then I sighed.

Gem: Hi! What are you doing? How are you?

Gem: Are you okay? It was crazy pants yesterday and you took off, which I get, but also—I need to know you're okay and if you're not, give me a clue. Like send me a single emoji and I'll make a plan to figure out where you are and how to get to you and how to get you out of wherever you are. Okay? Okay. Proceed.

That made me laugh.

Me: I'm currently watching Kira and her friends hanging all over my cousins, and I'm trying not to puke.

Gem: WHAT? Where are you? Do you need me to call in the Red Cross?

Me: I'm pretty sure you're getting your emergency people wrong, but no. I'm okay. At my cousins' for a BBQ. I'm in the backyard at the campfire because I'm avoiding the inside where my aunt and mom are. But I'm also avoiding the base-ment where my cousins and Kira's group were flirting, but they just moved to the backyard. They're pretending to play basketball.

Gem: Oh. Got you. I'm handing you a Kleenex in sympathy right now.

Me: Thanks. I'm taking it.

And oh, boy, but this needed to be handled as well. My chest got tighter.

Me: Also, going to be honest. I don't want to talk about my ex or my dad. I'm sorry I didn't say this to you until today.

Gem: No. That sounds realistic. I'd probably hide for a full month.

Me: No, you wouldn't. You'd go to your cousin and your family, and they'd be there for you. You'd also probably think of me before I thought of you, and I'm sorry for that. I really am.

She didn't respond for a bit.

Gem: That means a lot. A whole lot. Like, I'm totally happy that I picked you as a friend and I'm really happy that I've not let you knock me off.

Gem: Wanna hang tomorrow?

Me: Yes, so much. But something normal and almost boring. Like studying.

Gem: Totally doable. I'm also very boring as a friend. I'm aware that you've not been given the chance to realize that because I've been busy with my secret superpower life, but you'll see tomorrow how boring I can be. School nerd is my disguise. I do it well.

The back of my neck prickled as someone sat in the chair beside me.

I felt him first, so I knew it was Scout before I looked.

Then, once I did, I got all warm.

He was giving the look, the same he gave me as he said, *"I'd do it rough, and I'd do you in a way where you'd be screaming for release."*

A release.

I squirmed, feeling that need in me. I could literally feel him sliding inside, and he'd only just looked at me.

I sent a quick text to Gem.

Me: Gotta go. Call you later.

The phone buzzed almost right away, but I put it away and raised an eyebrow. "What are you doing here?"

He flashed me a smile, but it didn't extend to his eyes. Those were still flat. "Got back on the invite list. That your doing?"

"No. I had nothing to do with that."

He shrugged, lounging back, his feet going up on the edge of the brick circle around the bonfire. His hands went into his pockets, and I kept looking at those hands.

How they'd feel on me.

"I'd do it rough..."

"Not going to fuck you at your cousins'."

My eyes jerked to his, and he raised an eyebrow, but I saw his eyes starting to smolder.

I snapped, though my pulse was speeding, "Didn't ask you to do that. That's your role."

He ignored my last comment, saying, "It was in the look. I can feel when you want me to fuck you."

That took some air from me. "You cannot."

His gaze was knowing. "I can. You can't read me as well, but you'll get there, which is not something I'm excited about, by the way."

I opened my mouth and then shut it. I had absolutely no idea how to respond to any of this, but he was right.

I wanted him, and my body was heating up because of it.

I huffed. "This is so annoying."

He snorted. "Get in line."

We shared a look until one of the girls shrieked from the basketball court. It broke the spell.

"There's something messed up about you hitting on me with my cousins just over there."

"I wasn't hitting on you, just stating facts." He shifted suddenly, jerking forward and moving so his feet were facing me. He bent forward, his hands still in his pockets, and his eyes were piercing. "Want the truth? I didn't know you were here. Alex called me, invited me, and I jumped at the chance. I miss my best friend, and then I walked back here, saw you sitting here with a smile on your face and your legs crossed, and my dick got hard."

He leaned closer.

His voice lowered. "And I got pissed because I don't want you here. I don't want you to be messing up my friendships with your cousins, but I can't give them up, and my dick isn't giving you up. So, you figure out the dilemma. Me? We need to do something to get you out of my system because the reason my hands are in my pockets is because I can't take them out. If I do, they'll be on you, and I'll be carrying you to the back of that garage so I can put them somewhere else on you. *That's* the truth."

"Carrying you to the back of that garage so I can put them somewhere else on you ..."

A guttural sound escaped me, and I had to bite my lip to keep a groan from leaving them.

My whole body was ablaze.

He dropped his voice lower, almost whispering, and he scooted even closer. "I know you're wet because I can smell it. You have your own aroma, and I'm the only one who can pick it up because it's meant just for me. I know that, and you're sitting here, looking all cool and hot, and it's driving me crazy because I want to make you look messed and rode hard."

"Stop," I choked out, thrusting a hand out.

He caught it, one of his hands ripping from his pocket.

The touch sizzled. Hand to hand. Skin to skin.

Our eyes caught and held, and we both knew we just fucked up.

A huge mistake.

He was touching me. I was touching him, and that throb got more demanding. I felt it through my whole body, and images of him touching me more, kissing me, and bending me over flooded my mind.

Knowing how good it'd feel because just his hand holding mine was sending tendrils of pleasure shooting through me, coating my insides.

His voice was rough "Look up. Tell me no one can see this."

I looked and had to refocus to actually see. My cousins were involved in their game.

I looked to the house. Nick was at the grill, his attention there and on his phone.

I looked more, through the window. My mom and aunt had moved to the kitchen table. Glasses of wine in front of them, and they were deep in some conversation.

"No one's looking."

As soon as I said it, a long finger rubbed the inside of my palm—slow, measured, purposeful.

My eyes went back to his, and his were burning into me. Then he shifted, putting my hand down and over his jeans. I felt him, felt how hard he was, how he was straining against his pants. My hand turned, cupping him, and he sucked in some air, but he leaned down and his nostrils flared.

"Yeah. You'd be all ready for me."

"Scout!" someone yelled.

I jerked my hand away, but he didn't move. His eyes held mine for a second before he turned around.

Kira was heading our way, almost skipping. "Hey, guys." She collapsed in one of the other chairs, her feet going up on the brick bonfire circle like Scout had first sat. "What's up?" But she was distracted, her face glowing and perspiring a little as she watched the rest of the group slowly coming our way.

They filtered in. Her friends, Ciara and Leanne holding back. They waited for my cousins to choose their seats and then perched on the arms of their chairs. The wooden chairs were sturdy enough and the arms were flat enough so they could almost sit normally. It was one reason I loved bonfires at Aunt Aileen's house.

I shot up, knowing Clint would see something on my face that I didn't want him to see.

He shouted behind me, "Where are you going?"

I held a hand up, saying over my shoulder, "Bathroom."

Trenton yelled, "Bring back drinks! Booze preferably."

"Trenton," came from his dad.

"I mean, soda preferably."

Uncle Nick grunted, but I glanced over just as I opened their sliding glass doors. He was staring at my cousins before his phone beeped and his attention went back to that. I frowned, just slightly, but my head was a mess. A lust-filled mess.

I needed time alone and time to cool down.

"I want to make you look messed and rode hard."

Sensations broke out all over me, and I cursed softly. I needed to get a handle on whatever this was between Scout and me. It wasn't good. It wasn't right.

I still hated him.

"Hey, sweetie." My mom smiled at me as I came inside.

I coughed, willing my pulse to slow down. "Hey, Mom."

"Wanna come and talk to us? Tell us how school is going?"

That made me pause because I still hadn't told her about the picture.

My stomach dropped.

This would be the perfect place. Perfect time.

Aunt Ailes was here. There were others here.

She couldn't go off the deep end, which was what she'd do. It was part of the reason I didn't want to tell her.

God.

Dread filled me, but I needed to get it over and done.

My mouth dried up.

My mom frowned, seeing the change. "Sweetie?"

Fear clamped down on my insides, shooting all of the *other* stuff out of the way.

My chest grew tight again. "Uh, Mom ..."

24

SCOUT

Me: Come to the Maroney house. Kira and her group are here.

Cohen: I don't want to get with Kira anymore.

Me: Who cares? I need some backup.

Cohen: On my way.

A hand touched my leg as Kira leaned in. She took Ramsay's seat almost the second Ram's ass left, and she'd been breathing on me since. "Who are you texting?"

I gave her hand a pointed look. "Get your fucking hand off me."

She snatched it back but leaned away and arched her back, making a show of it. She licked her lips, a sultry smile stretching her mouth. "Come on, Scout. Let's be real. You're a teenager. Yes, you're eighteen and you always feel like you're in a different place than us, but you still have a dick. I know you use it."

I shot her a look. "You don't know shit about shit, which means you know shit."

She laughed, her voice dipping low. Her shoulders shook a little. "I know a couple of the girls you bang on the regular. I know your deal. No strings. Just the sex and maybe you'll do it again at your next fight."

"Do me a favor. Stop talking."

She laughed again, her voice rising. "Who'd you text?"

"Who do you think?"

"Cohen, huh? Your ride or die." She leaned forward again, her head hanging between our seats. "How does that work? You're best friends with Alex and Cohen? Who's on top? Is there any jealousy between them? You know, for who gets you the most?" She gave me a once-over. "I know I'd be jealous. And I am. You want to fuck Williams, don't you?"

Shit got real with that one. I leaned in, and she jerked back from how fast I moved before she blinked. Her smug grin slipped a little before returning.

I said, "You breathe a word of that anywhere and you will be destroyed."

Her smile slipped again. "That's a little petty of you, isn't it? Going after one girl because you want to fuck another one?"

"You want to know your future?" I didn't wait for her response. "I don't know who fucked you up. If it was your pops who never wants to be around you, your mom who wants to be your friend and doesn't give a shit about being your parent, or someone else."

Her smile was all the way wiped clean.

"Or if it was some creep uncle. I don't know, and I don't care, but whatever made you this twisted will keep you twisted all your life. Your girls don't care about you. You have them because of where you are in the social ladder, but if someone else took your place, they'd go to her instead, and you know it. You go through guys, looking for whoever's willing to fill you because, what? It makes you feel good? Is that why? You get one guy, he gets a feel for you, and he drops you because he doesn't like the feel of you. You're like cotton candy. Sweet taste at first and then nothing. Pure emptiness. How many people want *only* cotton candy all their lives? No one, and that's what you're going to end up with later in life. No one except maybe a rich fat guy who likes cotton candy because while he's eating you, he's got others on the side. Other chicks who are their steak, who they can savor eating and who make them drool for the next time they can have that. That's not you, never will be. Want to know why I don't want to fuck you?" I leaned down. "Because I hate cotton candy."

The blood had drained from her face. Her eyes were wide, stricken. A tear slid down her cheek, and seeing it, I should've felt bad about putting that there. I didn't. That made me an asshole? I also didn't care about that.

Yelling sounded from the house.

"What the fuck?" Clint tore out of his seat.

Trenton and Alex were right behind him.

The door opened, and that yelling got a lot clearer, but I was staring hard at Kira.

She gulped, her throat visibly swallowing. "Wouldn't think you'd want me as an enemy."

"That's another thing about cotton candy." I stood. "Only use for it is to *be* eaten once, and I know you still want to be eaten by any of the triplets. You don't even care which one it'll be." I turned, now sounding bored. "No one will believe a fucking word you say, so have at it."

Maybe it was stupid what I just did, but shit was what it was. Kira saw—or, she would see.

Ramsay was hot, way hotter than anyone else in school, and eventually, someone would see I wanted to fuck her. No matter how long it'll take before we fuck, and we would because she wanted it as bad as me, and Ramsay was the female equivalent of me, so that was a guarantee.

When was the issue, and not losing my friends was the other issue.

As I got to the house, I stopped thinking about all of that

because as soon as I stepped inside, all eyes were on me. And I meant, *all* eyes.

Ramsay's. Her mom's. Mama Maroney's. Their dad's. My friends'.

"What?"

Alex clipped out, "You didn't tell me about the pic she got."

I tensed.

Ramsay jumped in, "Because he didn't know."

Alex turned to her. "He told me you got a text that upset you."

"But I didn't tell him what it was."

She was lying for me. I frowned at that.

Her mom threw her hands in the air. "It doesn't matter!" She rounded on her daughter. "We're calling Detective Edgeley right now. You need to report this." She had Ramsay's phone in her hand.

"Mom."

"Don't!" Her hand was out, and she was shaking her head. "This happened two nights ago. You had two nights to tell me, and I know you waited until we were here because you thought I wouldn't go off the rails. Well, sweetie, I'm going off the rails anyway."

Ramsay shot her aunt a pleading look, who stepped close to Ramsay's mom and murmured softly, "Chris, the kids."

Ramsay's mom was rubbing at her forehead, but her hand dropped. She looked around and winced. Pain flashed over her face. "Maybe you guys could head back outside? Ramsay and I have to make a phone call."

The guys started.

Their mom said sharply, "Not a word to anyone else outside of this room." She looked at every one of her boys one at a time, ending on me. "Do you all understand? Not one word."

I nodded.

I'd always liked Alex's mom. She'd been nice, smelled nice,

liked to make cookies or whatever the guys wanted, but I also knew that making Kira an enemy? Totally fine. I wasn't going to sweat that, but Mama Maroney? No way. She terrified me.

Ramsay wasn't looking my way. She was focused on her mom, the expression on her face was as if she'd just been ripped open, but she was trying to administer aid to the person bleeding out right next to her.

No matter if she was my enemy or my next fuck, I didn't want her to feel that way.

Alex bumped my arm. "Cohen's coming?"

"I texted him."

He started off. I moved to follow, but Clint got in my way.

His eyes were narrowed on me, suspicious.

I got ready. Trenton was the wildcard, but Clint liked trouble. "What?"

His head cocked to the side. "I don't want to think about why my cousin just lied for you, but I know she did. You kept that shit from Alex on purpose?"

I hesitated before shrugging. "Figured it was hers to share."

"That's part of the reason you called Alex that morning?"

There was no hesitation this time. "I called because I meant what I said. I meant my apology for my part, and I was wrong. I should've believed you, and I shouldn't have threatened you guys or Ramsay. And"—this was beyond what he asked, but I was showing him respect by offering him this—"I wanted Alex, and now you, to know that if that guy comes anywhere near her, I'll rip his head off."

His eyes lit with surprise, but I moved past him.

Whatever he took from that, well, he'd take from that.

I didn't care about that *either*.

25

RAMSAY

Mom went off the rails, but it wasn't as bad as I thought. We made the call to the detective, and I was instructed to leave the room after. I knew my mom would have a more in-depth talk with him. And after that, hanging out with everyone wasn't so bad. The guys voted to send the girls home, but I vetoed them, which they totally saw right through. I'd done it so they couldn't be all about me. If Kira, Ciara, and Leanne were there, then there'd be no talk about my stuff. And score, it worked.

It also worked further because Cohen showed up and he had no clue anything had happened. The guy was oblivious to tension. And double score because I invited Gem to the house.

She freaked, in a good way, not in a bad way, and the night ended up being in the basement. Movies were watched. The guys horsed around. Video games were played. We snuck booze, then we got snacks. And Gem and the girls totally planned stuff for Homecoming.

I was a reluctant participant, but I was backed into a corner.

I was scared to leave Gem's side or any of the girls, who took it the wrong way. They now thought I genuinely liked them, which for the record, I still wasn't sure if I did. I wished I could've gone against my gut and let myself befriend them more, but my gut was sending the alarms to keep them at a distance. So, that was what I did, but I also didn't want them to know that I was doing that so I was faking it at times. I must've done it successfully.

Kira gave me a tight hug at the end. Ciara and Leanne followed suit.

"Girl, you don't need to worry about a thing. We'll put out the word that everyone needs to shut up about your situation." Kira gave me an exaggerated look before glancing in Scout's way. Her mouth tightened, but she and the girls left after that.

That was odd, but okay then.

Any help was appreciated because I did not want a take-two from my old school, not that I expected that to happen considering my cousins were top tier.

The rest of the week was interesting too.

Gem hung out at my locker when my cousins weren't there, though that wasn't a lot, and we went back to having lunch together. Cohen and Scout were scarce. I saw them a few times at Alex's locker, but that was it. Scout kept to himself in our classes, and I didn't see him in study hall again.

Now it was Friday, and besides a few nasty comments, almost everyone had moved on from talking about my situation.

I was thankful.

Also, they were talking about the football game instead, which I was down for. Yay football. Yay for not gossiping about me. But I wasn't stupid. I knew it wasn't going away. It was just a matter of time before someone came at me about it.

Until then, only football, please. I was fully planning on making up for missing last week.

"What's your plan for the game?" Gem asked in sixth period.

I shrugged. "I'm guessing Clint will sit in our section. Are you going?"

She nodded, scooting her chair closer. "That's why I'm asking. My cousin wanted to see if you wanted to go with us? We'd pick you up, and we usually grab food before. Mexican food. Would you be interested? We'd go to the game and wherever everyone goes afterward. That's usually the plan. Theresa wants to make it up to you because of what Gabby did."

I gave her a look. The girl who'd been the mouthpiece to spread my stuff on social media.

"Is Gabby in your cousin's group?"

"Kinda, but kinda not. She's been trying to get in with Kira's group lately more. She won't be there. You don't have to worry about Theresa. She's not about what Gabby did, and when you confronted her and Scout and everyone was *right there*, Theresa stopped a lot of what people might've been saying. She put it out there that it wasn't cool."

Seemed I was getting help from all sorts of people.

It meant a lot that Theresa had squashed the gossip, at least for her group of friends.

At the end of the day, I told Clint my plans for the night.

He gave me an unreadable look before nodding. "Okay. You want me to go with my friends?"

I opened my mouth to respond, then realized I didn't know what to say. I shrugged. "I don't know. Do you want to come with us?"

He frowned at me.

I frowned back.

His eyebrows furrowed.

So did mine.

"You're just mirroring everything I do," he said.

"You're parroting me."

"I'm parroting you? I'm a parrot now? You're calling me a bird?"

"Yes."

"I'm not a parrot."

"I never said you were."

"You just did."

Scout walked up. "What are you guys talking about?"

Clint pointed to me. "She called me a bird."

"A parrot."

"You just said you weren't doing that."

"I said you were parroting me."

"That's a bird. A parrot. You're repeating what I do."

I shook my head. "That's not me calling you a parrot."

Clint and I were doing our usual thing, but the underlying issue was that neither of us knew whether he should come with me and Gem and her friends or not. Neither of us wanted to make the decision because, what if it was the wrong one?

We were stalling.

"You guys are weird."

Clint ignored that. "What do you think Rams should do? Should I go with them or not?"

I smothered a grin. Scout hadn't been here for that part of the conversation.

He shook his head. "What are you talking about?"

"Theresa extended an invitation to me via Gem," I explained. "To eat with them and go to the football game. Should Clint go with me or not?"

"Shit no." Scout's eyebrows pinched together. "Who are you people that you have to be joined at the hip all the time?"

"We're not—" Clint started to say.

"Don't think Alex didn't tell me about your sleepover," Scout said.

I nodded. "That was an amazing sleepover, and we all got drunk."

Clint shoved me. "That doesn't help."

"Next time, I'm hoping for forts and margaritas."

"What?" Scout was still confused.

Clint laughed. "I think it's time we let our little Ramsay spread her wings a little." He took a dramatic step away. "It's time, Rams. It's time you fly alone. You be the parrot now."

Scout muttered a curse and headed down the hall.

I gave Clint a slow nod. This energy between us couldn't be ignored. "We're going to do something stupid tonight, aren't we? After the football game."

"Oh, fuck yeah." He held up a fist.

I met it with one of mine.

Gem came over with her backpack. "Uh, do you need a ride home or anything? Theresa said we could give you a ride to your place and wait if you wanted to change or something before heading to Mario's."

"You're going to Mario's?" Clint exclaimed. "I love Mario's."

Gem faltered back a step and dropped her phone. Cursing, she grabbed it and blinked a bunch of times before looking at me. "You can't come." She shook her head at Clint. "Not that you're not invited to Mario's since it's a restaurant and I work there sometimes so of course, any and all customers are welcome, but . . . this is our thing with Ramsay." She spoke faster and faster. "If you come, you'll change the whole dynamic, and Theresa might not get to know Ramsay. I want her to get to know Ramsay."

I frowned. "Wait. Did Theresa invite me, or did you invite me?"

"What's the difference?"

"One is where I'm wanted, and the other is where she thinks she's doing me a favor by allowing me to tag along. Two totally different scenarios."

"Thinking I'll be seeing you at Mario's," Clint said.

Gem let out a growl of frustration. "No! It's—no. It's nothing like that. I swear. Theresa invited you, and I'm glad because I think you guys could be good friends, and I don't want Alex to come because he'll change the dynamic. You've hung out with Kira and her clique more than my own group. You and Theresa will hit it off. I swear."

"Clint."

"What?" She threw him a frazzled look.

"I'm Clint. Not Alex."

"Oh. Then that's even more of a reason you can't come. Sorry. Alex likes Mario's, that's why I thought you were Alex."

"Why is it even more that I can't come?"

"Because . . ." She waved between him and me. "You know."

We did. He winked at me, flashing a grin before pretending to pout. "My feelings are hurt. You're her best female friend right now, and you just hurt one of her cousins. How dare you? What kind of a friend are you?"

She sputtered, "Uh, wh–uh–what's going on?"

"He's messing with you."

"Not about Mario's," he insisted. "I'm coming to Mario's. Me and all my baseball friends who aren't on the football team."

Her mouth dropped. Clint sounded serious, and he looked serious too. I needed to do something. Gem couldn't handle him. Tapping her on the arm, I said, "I'll be right out, and I'd appreciate a ride."

"Okay." She still looked unsure, but she edged forward and headed toward the parking lot.

"Are you really coming?" I asked him.

He jerked up a shoulder. "Thinking about it now."

I shook my head. "I'll be fine. I'll call if I need something, but for real, don't worry about me. See you at the game."

"And we'll do something after."

I shot him a grin. "Nothing too bad, though."

He rolled his eyes. "Please."

I had absolutely no idea how to take his last statement, but I'd find out later tonight. Until then, I might make a new friend.

Hoping Clint and I didn't get into too much trouble was probably a better goal.

26

RAMSAY

"T his is a cool house," Theresa said.

I let us in and found another note from my mom on the counter.

HEY, *honey. They offered double time, so I took it. I know you're going to the football game. Ailes will be there if you want to sit with her or your friends? Be safe.*

You're to sleep at their house tonight.

Love you, honey! - Mom

I PUT the note in a drawer and glanced back as Theresa, Gem, and their friend Alred came in behind me. Alred had been introduced as another one of Gem's cousins, and he'd informed me he had "super duper" crushes on all of my cousins, so I needed to give him the inside dish.

I liked Alred already. He was skinny with thick, full, dark hair and somewhat bushy eyebrows, but he kept his face smooth and clear. He had a pretty face and wore pink eyeshadow that matched his hoodie and jeans, which had white frills on the end. As he walked, they sashayed with him. He'd caught me watching him on the way to the car after school and laughed. "They give me a little extra bounce back there, if you know what I mean."

"Thanks," I responded to Theresa now. "It's a bit big for us, but we like it so far."

She nodded, going to the kitchen island. "You guys rent, right?"

I nodded. "Uh, yeah." I gestured to the television. "I can turn that on, or do you guys want something to eat or drink real quick? I'll just run up to change."

Alred raised his hand, a big smile on his face, but Theresa said, "We're good. Go and change."

He lowered his hand, glowering at his cousin's back and then giving me a wide smile and a thumbs-up. Gem tried not to laugh, watching the whole thing.

I ran upstairs to change into a sweatshirt and switch out my shoes for some sneakers. The black leggings could stay. I knew it'd be cold tonight at the game. In the bathroom, I brushed my hair and put on some makeup. The school colors were orange and white, so I put a small dusting of orange glitter on my eyes. Then I put my hair in two braids, weaving in a white ribbon and dashing some glitter over my hair too. I felt festive and good to go.

I wore a sweatshirt. Underneath I had a black ribbed racer-back tank. I was leaving when I noticed a necklace my dad gave me.

I hadn't worn it in so long, and I didn't even know it had been unpacked. I realized my mom must've gotten it out for me. My throat swelled, but I put it on, a simple silver necklace with a white stone.

I hesitated, but then I put it under my shirt. It felt better against my skin.

When I went back downstairs, Theresa, Alred, and Gem were all huddled together, talking in hushed tones.

I paused and eased back a step.

"I like her!" Alred wasn't being so quiet. "No. I love her. There. I said it. *Boom*. Burn me at the stake, witches."

"You're so dramatic."

"I luuuuh-ve her. How's that for being dramatic?" he snapped back at Theresa. "What's your problem, anyway? You've had a stick up your ass this whole time. She's good people. You can tell."

"She laughed at your joke. That's why you think she's good people."

"It's a test. Anyone who laughs at my jokes *is* good people."

"Guys. Come on. Theresa, you said you'd give her a chance. That's why we invited her tonight."

"I am! God. Both of you just back off. I'm in her house, sitting at her table. What more do you want from me? Can I remind you that I'm not the one who needs friends? Please check yourselves."

"She's new." Gem's voice was quiet.

Theresa sighed. "Her cousins run the school, and she seems not to have a problem with Cohen and Scout. I think she's doing just fine. Plus, she's friendly with Kira."

"No, she's not. That's just Homecoming committee stuff. She did that for me."

Alred sighed. "But can you imagine being around all those guys? All the time? Scout. Good Gad all glorious. I just want to pull down those sweats an inch. Just an inch. Can you imagine? No. Seriously. Let's all imagine together. We'll orgasm."

"I don't just meet someone and become instant friends," Theresa insisted. "That stuff takes time for me."

"We know, but you said you'd give her a chance," Gem countered. "Plus, you've met her a few times."

"In class and during a verbal smackdown doesn't

count. And I am trying. I invited her to Mario's. That's a family place. Not just anyone gets an invite from me, you know."

"I know. Just, be nice."

"I *am*. She's upstairs still. Back off, you guys."

"I *luh-ve* how feisty you are."

Theresa started laughing, but I stopped listening.

I reached in, pulled out the necklace from my dad and kissed it, taking a deep breath. For a moment I could imagine my dad standing next to me, giving me a hug and telling me, *"Get out there and kick ass."*

I blinked away a tear, put my necklace back under my shirt, and plastered on a fake smile. "I'm ready."

ALRED *LUH-VED* my hair and promptly asked if I could do small braids in his hair too. With ribbon. With glitter. He was almost a walking ball of glitter. It was everywhere. His face. Neck. Chest. He didn't care that it got all over his sweatshirt and pants.

After leaving my place, we went to Theresa's for them to get ready where Gem asked me to do her hair.

Theresa's mom came up when we were almost done and gasped, taking everyone in. *"Muy bonita!"*

That was when I saw a different side to Theresa. She softened and was all smiles as her mom gave her a hug. Gem and Alred got hugs. When she came to me, she got quiet. Theresa spoke in Spanish to her. She responded before she got a little misty-eyed. It was too fast for me.

"She'd like to give you a hug," Theresa told me. "Is that okay?"

Gem sidled closer. "We're a huggy family."

"Yes. I'd love a hug."

I stood, and Mrs. Garcia came over and hugged me. For a split second, I pretended I was getting a hug from my dad.

She and Theresa spoke again in Spanish.

I caught most of the words, but Gem translated. That was helpful.

"She's asking about dinner and our plans," Gem said. "Theresa's telling her about Mario's, the football game, and that we'll probably go to Kunz's after."

"Who's Kunz?"

"Someone we know. He has a lot of parties at his place."

Mrs. Garcia's voice rose.

"She doesn't approve of Kunz," Gem explained. "He's got some friends who drag race and do drugs, but we'll probably still go. Theresa and he have an on-and-off thing going. She likes bad boys."

Theresa stopped talking to her mom and said sharply to Gem, "Just tell her all my business."

Gem shrugged. "She'll find out anyway when you're on his lap all night."

Alred held up a hand to Gem. "Word."

Gem laughed and slapped it with hers.

Theresa rolled her eyes, but went back to talking with her mom. A moment later, they were hugging. I got a hug again. When we went downstairs, an older man gave Theresa money from his wallet, murmured something to her, and kissed her on the forehead.

My necklace felt like it was burning against my skin.

I reached up, finding it, and I held on to it.

"Love you, Dad."

MARIO'S WAS a small restaurant set back from the main road in Pine River. There was some room to sit inside, but their main seating area was a back courtyard. I loved it, everything about it. We were surrounded by a tall fence for privacy and there were vines growing all over the courtyard. A duck came through at one point and went to a small fountain area in the corner. It quacked until one of the employees gave it bread. A second duck had joined it by the time we got our drinks.

While we waited, Theresa went back inside. Soon after, we heard a loud wave of voices.

"Theresa has a lot of friends from Pine Valley," Gem explained. "They're inside."

"I'm from there too," Alred added.

"You don't go to our school?" I asked.

He shook his head. "Nope. I came over today to see what the what was going on tonight. Those girls in there are my friends too, but I'm staying out here because you're amazing."

"Thanks." I grinned at him.

He beamed back. "No problem, sweetie."

Gem started giggling.

"You said this place was a family place?" I asked.

Gem nodded, taking a sip of her water. She motioned inside. "One of my mom's cousins runs it, but we just call him Uncle Hector. The hostess is his daughter. She's also in college."

"You work here sometimes?"

"Yes. Sometimes. When they need extra help or I need money."

"So . . ." Alred laid his arms on the table and leaned forward. "Enough about us. I want to hear all about you. What's your sign? Your horoscope? Do you have a boyfriend, a girl-friend, or both? What are your thoughts on dancing on roller skates? And do you have an online journal? If so, I want to follow you." He motioned to Gem. "I got most of the deets from Gemmie. She told me about your dad and your nasty ex. I'm so sorry about your loss. Also, your mom is a nursing assistant? I met her when I was doing Miss Hettie's nails yesterday." He looked at me. "Your mother is precious, by the way. I wanted to eat her all up."

"I know. She's an amazing mother."

There was another wave of noise, and a moment later, Theresa reappeared, just before four plates of food were brought out.

I frowned. "Wait. We never ordered."

Theresa slid into her seat. "We don't order here. Uncle Hector tells *us* what we eat."

"It's always the best," Gem gushed before thanking the servers.

She was right. After her uncle came over for cheek kisses and hugs, and a few other family members, we dug in. Mario's was the best.

27

RAMSAY

We were leaving when Kira, Ciara, and Leanne were walking in with a few other people. I scanned the guys, but Clint wasn't with them. As we passed, Kira turned around. Her friends had gone inside so she was alone.

"Ramsay."

My whole group stopped with me.

I could feel Theresa's tension, but Kira didn't acknowledge her.

She tipped her chin up, instead saying to me, "You can let Scout know that I won't say anything."

I frowned. "What's that about?" And a follow-up, "Why me?"

She was giving me a smug and knowing look before flicking a glance to Theresa. Then her eyes chilled. "He'll know. We're doing a Homecoming planning meeting next Monday, and we might go to my house afterward. Bring your suit. I've got an indoor pool. Oh, and Gem is cool, but you might want to educate yourself about who else you're hanging with here. Wouldn't want anything to bring down your cousins."

What the fuck?

I frowned.

Theresa growled and started to move forward, but Kira rolled her eyes and headed inside.

Once the doors closed, Theresa exploded. "I hate that bitch! Hate her. God. She's so condescending."

Gem closed in on my side. "What was that about?"

Alred was on my other side. "Do not be fooled by her. She's nasty. Even the girls at my school hate her."

"She wants war again?" Theresa was muttering to herself, under her breath. Her glare trying to burn down the door. "War's on."

"War?" I was reaching for my phone.

Gem hissed, "Theresa, relax. I'm on the Homecoming committee with them."

"Not everything's about you."

Gem tensed. "Come on, Theresa. That's not what I meant."

Theresa suddenly jerked her hands in the air, starting to go for her hair, but Alred hissed, "Not your hair!"

She froze before fisting her hands and letting out another growl. "God. I cannot stand her." Her gaze swung my way. "I don't get along with them. I'm sure that's been established, but there *was* a temporary ceasefire. Looks like that's over."

I frowned. "Do my cousins know about this?"

Gem looked up before sharing a look with Theresa.

Theresa answered, "Cohen does. I have no clue with Scout. I don't think your cousins would know. Girls don't really blast that out, you know?"

My phone buzzed.

Clint: How's it going? Kira just texted, said she saw you.

Me: Yeah. It was something.

Clint: What do you mean?

Me: We can talk later.

Clint: ? Okay . . .

"How bad is it going to get with those girls?" I asked.

Theresa startled, looking as if she'd forgotten I was here. "Oh." She shook her head. "It's nothing new. If you're worried, Kira won't do anything to you. This is my battle."

I had to laugh a little.

"What?"

"I'm not scared of a fight."

She let out a deep breath, her shoulders falling down. "I'm aware. I got front row seats to your takedown against Gabby, remember?"

"Is that going to be a problem?"

Her gaze was sharp. "What do you mean?"

"The overlap. Kira. Homecoming committee. Gabby."

Her mouth tightened and she glanced at her cousins before shrugging. "I guess we'll see."

I guess we would.

I was also starting to get a better feel for the social hierarchy here. I had a hunch more surprises were coming. The other thing I had a feeling about? Was that I *didn't* have a feeling about Theresa.

That'd be a stay-tuned thing as well, but I luh-ved Alred.

28

SCOUT

I was leaving the gym when my phone rang, and since I was
expecting Cohen to call about plans for after the football
game, I answered. "Yo."

"Sweetie!"

Shit. I stilled, just about to open my truck's door. "Mom."

"You don't sound happy to hear from me."

"Well, what do you think?"

She sighed. "Listen—"

I opened my door and tossed my bag to the passenger seat.
"I don't have time, Mom. What do you want? If you're calling to
recite the usual family bullshit, you know how the rest of that
conversation will be."

"I'm not. I'm not calling because of that."

I waited, frowning, wanting to go back inside and pummel
the bag again. "What do you want then?"

"I miss you."

Goddamn it. This was the problem with her. She meant
what she said. "You miss me, then why'd you send me out
here?"

"You know why."

"Yeah," I snapped. "Because you have a dictator father. I have a dictator asshole grandfather, and instead of telling him how it's going to go for your son, you shipped me off to hide."

She sucked in some air. "It's not like that."

"Like fuck it isn't."

"You don't have to yell at me."

I drew in some more control and said through gritted teeth, "I'm here because you're hiding me behind my uncle, the one person who's stood up to Grandfather, and you miss me because I'm your son and you want to be around me, but again, that's on you."

"If you'd just—"

"Just what?" Rage was slowly seeping through me, burning every inch of its path until it was going to cover me completely. "If I'd what?"

She was scared of her father, and while I could say something and had, it wasn't my place. It was hers.

My tone went cold. "You want to see me? You tell Grandfather that not only do I not have any interest in attending his private boarding school or his special Ivy League college *but also* that I won't be joining the family business. And no," I talked over her as she started to intervene, "I'm not going to play along, then do my fighting on the side."

"Scout, you're being unreasonable."

I reached for the handle, and if I could've, I would've ripped the whole door off its handle. "I'm not being unreasonable. You want to see me? You *know* what to do."

"Scout—"

"I'm not talking about his whole plan he's laid out for me."

She got quiet.

She knew what I was referring to.

"Scout." Her voice was so low now.

Fuck. I could hear the pain from her.

I could feel it, and I was back there, hearing—"You don't know what you heard that night."

"Bullshit I didn't."

We'd never talked about it, but she and I both knew, and the next morning she had a plane ticket for me to Oregon. There was the reason she claimed for sending me away and then there was the real reason she'd done it, and I just brought it up for the first time.

"Scout Jamison—"

"Don't full name me. Don't do that. I know what he told you to do, what he demanded you to do, and—"

Her voice rose, "And I did. Me. I did it, and it's nothing I'm proud of, but I did it. You have the wrong idea about what you think happened."

A hard laugh ripped from me. "That's the thing, Mom. I didn't even say anything, and you know what I'm talking about. Lies have to be explained. Truth doesn't."

I wanted to hurt him.

"I was just calling because I miss you. We're doing franchise visits, and I could line one up to come see you and your uncle. I was calling to see if you wanted me to do that."

My blood was rushing through my body. My pulse pounding in my eardrums.

When I didn't respond, couldn't respond, she said, still so quietly, "I can tell you're not ready for that, so I won't come to our franchise site in Pine River. I love you, Scout. I'll call you again later."

There was silence. I had nothing to say to any of that.

I didn't hang up, but she didn't either.

"Don't tell your uncle."

Right. More lies.

She ended the call.

29

RAMSAY

I kept replaying what Kira said, and it wasn't sitting right with me.

On our way to the game, I tried texting Scout, but he wasn't responding. That, combined with whatever Kira was hinting at, I wasn't happy. All of that was churning inside of me, when I heard Alred sigh as we were paying for our tickets. "He's hot, but when he's pissed, he's *hot.*"

I whipped around. "Who?"

He was looking toward the end of the parking lot and nodded in that direction. "Scout Raiden."

Done.

My gut's churning went up a whole notch, and I said, "Don't wait for me. I'll find you in the bleachers."

"What?" Gem asked.

I was already heading his way, and he saw me, stopped, and straightened.

His face locked down.

Good.

He wanted a fight? I was down for it.

I started again.

His head fell back, his nostrils flared, and I caught how his jawline clenched.

Jesus Christ.

All stormy eyes, his pissed off energy, how it was apparent he'd come from the gym, the heat was starting.

His gaze never left mine. He watched me walk the whole way to him, and he didn't move one inch.

I felt an inferno taking me over from the inside out.

"Don't," he said it savagely, just as I got to him.

The roughness in his voice startled me, and my foot stumbled from his ferocity. I jerked to the side before righting my feet.

My heart was in my throat.

I was almost too startled to speak, but as I opened my mouth to do just that, he turned and stalked away. "Hey."

He glanced back once, still going, and he cut past all the vehicles in the lot, dipping into some trees. I followed him to a clearing. Whoa. Talk about weirdness privacy, especially so close to the football stadium. "What is this place?"

His hand was on my chest, just under my throat, and he was in my space.

I stopped talking. I started only feeling, that heat climbing once again. "Scout?"

His nostrils flared again. "You want to talk about an old parking area that they decided not to trim, to try to save the trees?"

My tongue was heavy. "Huh?"

He started moving me back. I went with him, not thinking about anything except his hand just under my throat or the feel of him so close to me that I could feel the heat emanating off him.

"The tree campaign. Cohen told me about it."

My mind was frazzled. "What are you talking about?"

My back hit something, and I couldn't move any farther.

He was right there, an inch from me.

I licked my lip. "What are you doing?"

A whole new demeanor came over him, and he looked between us, at the space there, and he took a deliberate step in, now touching me.

I sucked in some air, my pulse blasting me.

He lowered his head, his mouth so close, too far, not close enough, so close that I could close the distance if I moved a hair toward him. "Scout?"

"I want to fuck you," he whispered, bending so his nose moved down my throat.

Oh God.

I leaned back, moving away, giving him access.

His hand sifted to cup the side of my face, moving to hold the back of my neck. His thumb was right over my carotid. He could feel me feeling him. I licked my lips again because I didn't care. I pressed against him, the whole churning still in me, moving through me at breakneck speed.

"I don't like you."

"I don't care."

"Keep pushing, and I could hate you."

He breathed me in again, this time his mouth grazing against my skin. "You're a fucking liar."

Tendrils of sensation trailed in his path, sending pleasure zinging through me.

He taunted me, "Didn't know you were a liar, Ramsay."

My hand went to his stomach, and I felt zapped by the contact. Further touch. Further need to feel him press all the way against me, to feel him on me, over me. To feel his mouth tasting me. Jesus. Images of us flashed in my head, how it'd feel of him moving inside me. Thrusting.

Holding.

Grinding.

I had to have that, and I didn't care about the consequences.

"You want this now?" He was back to taunting.

"Fuck you."

His smile was so hard, so bitter. So fucking smug. "That's the point, Princess."

I growled again, shoving him so he had to take a step back. "I'm not a princess."

His eyes went flat.

I was on the offense now. "I've never been the princess. You want to know who I was?" I leaned in, and now I was the one taunting. "I was the girl who wouldn't leave her abusive ex. That's who I was. A waste, right? That was me?" I advanced, a hand against his chest, making him go back another step. "Not smart enough to leave. Thinking he'd stop hitting me. Thinking I didn't love him enough. If only I loved him totally unconditionally, it'd heal him. Right?" He stopped, his face looking like cement. "Wrong. I wasn't the princess, Scout. I was the stupid one who couldn't leave the villain. How about that? What's that make me?"

"Ramsay," he gutted out.

"Hmmm?"

Ice cold. Everything froze inside me, but damn him because one look from him, one touch, and a volcano torched it all away. "You want to do this? Fine. Fuck. But rules."

"Rules?"

"I do not like you."

A rough growl left him, ripping out of him, and he advanced again. His forehead went to mine, and I moved back without thinking. He was forcing me to retreat. He was taking the power. "I don't like you either, Williams."

"Good," I spat. "We can't do this if we like each other. If there's feelings."

"Feelings?"

"You know, emotions. Just sex, okay? Anything else, we have to stop this."

"Fine. Sex as long as we don't like each other."

I almost laughed. It was the perfect arrangement.

His hand went to my throat again, holding the side of it. "I'm not going to lie to Alex."

Alex?

Right. My cousin.

"I'll talk to him. I'll explain where my head is."

His hand tightened. "Where *is* your head?"

I shook my head. "We can't do that shit. Sharing. You said it yourself. We're not friends. What we have is attraction. That's it, and denying it is putting us in a situation where I don't want to go."

"Me neither." His eyes flared. "But Alex is not going to understand this."

"Yes, he will." I focused on his chest, knowing what he had pumping just inside there. If I touched him, slid my hand up, over his shirt, under his shirt, I'd feel his heart. If his pulse was frantic or steady.

I swallowed, knowing what was going to happen and knowing I wasn't going to stop it.

We were past our expiration, way past. It was time to catch up.

"You make him understand. You got that?" His voice wasn't quite steady.

I didn't need to feel his heart. I heard how he was affected, and it was my undoing.

I nodded, hunger igniting as he just threw gas on the already blazing fire inside me. Then his hands were on me. Mine were on him. He groaned, backing me up. He hadn't even kissed me. His hands were on my hips. Mine were on his chest, and he moved me until I was against a tree.

Holy shit. A tree. *That* scene was happening, doing it in the woods. He lifted me in the air effortlessly. My legs wound around his waist. I could feel him where I needed him. We both paused at the connection.

I was panting. His forehead rested against mine, and he swore softly. "It's like this and we've barely started."

"Uh-huh." I opened my eyes. We were doomed if we started, but we were doomed if we didn't. "How about no kissing?"

"What?"

"No kissing. Just physical? Kissing can make you feel more. You know?"

His eyes went back to my mouth, and he shook his head slowly. "No way. This time, yeah, because I want to experience that kink, but no way am I saying yes to not tasting you. No fucking way."

Kink. Tasting.

He was speaking porn to me. It flooded my brain. "Fine." I reached for his jeans, my hand closing around the button. We both stilled because if I undid that top button, there was officially no going back.

Did I really want to do this?

Maybe, because no friendship. No feelings. I wanted to stay with that. No emotions. No hurt after.

I growled deep in my throat. "Do you have a condom?"

He cursed, releasing one of my legs as he reached into his pocket. He pulled one out, then cursed again at the buzzing coming from between us. He dug into his pocket and pulled out both of our phones. Clint was calling him, and Gem was calling me.

A different frenzied sensation came over me as I reached for my phone. I declined the call and texted her.

Me: Talking about something. Be back in ten.

Scout read my text and snorted. "Ten minutes? You serious?"

"Shut up."

I dropped the phone on the ground and took his. I held it up to him. "Unlock it."

He adjusted his hold on me, using his free hand to punch in his code.

I texted Clint for him.

Scout: Talking to your cousin about something. About Kira. I dunno.

"Kira?"

I dropped his phone next to mine and shook my head. "Tell you later."

After that, I flicked the button open, undid his zipper, and reached in, finding him rock hard and pointing all the way up at me.

He watched as I began working him, up and down. My hand closed around him, squeezing just slightly. He groaned, pressing me against the tree, and I went back to moving up and down. Slow. Slow. A little faster. I took my time until his forehead hit my shoulder, and I heard him cursing again.

"Put the fucking condom on. We have ten minutes, remember?"

I barked out a laugh and took it from him before opening it. I reached down, rolling it over his dick. He lifted his head, his eyes in pure, carnal agony. "I've not had my time with you."

"Don't worry. I'm ready." I moved up, pressing against him, and he groaned again.

"God, I hope so." He shifted, lifting me so he could pull my leggings down just enough before he moved back in. He touched me, finding me wet, and he panted against my shoulder. "I've never had it like this."

I moved against his fingers. "Ten minutes, buddy."

His eyes shot to mine. "Buddy? That's an upgrade from asshole."

My eyes flashed. "Do you normally talk this much during sex?"

A rakish grin flashed back at me, but then he moved my thong aside, and I felt him line up at my entrance. We both held still for a second before he slid inside.

Oh. God.

It felt good.

So good.

I moaned, already panting.

He began to move, and I stopped thinking altogether. Pleasure whipped through me, sending a sizzle down my spine. Need—all-consuming, primal, earth-moving need—bloomed so deep in me that I almost screamed because I'd had no idea I needed his touch so badly.

I thought I knew.

I'd been wrong. So very *really* wrong.

He kept moving. In, in, in, so deep inside before pulling out. Soon he was pounding into me, and I moved my hips over him, trying to match him. Then finally I stopped and let him have his way. Reaching up, I found a strong branch and tried to pull up so he could go even deeper.

He cursed, doing just that, his hands kneading my ass and under my legs from behind.

"Oh God." My hips rolled against him. "I could do this for hours."

"Jesus Christ." His teeth scraped against my throat. "Shut up or I'm going to come sooner than I thought."

I laughed again, but it ended on a shrill yell because my climax erupted, and I wasn't ready. My whole body felt that. It went all the way to my toes, and I could only gasp and keep breathing. Wave after wave crashed through me.

I held on.

Scout kept thrusting, grunting. "*Fuuck.*"

My last wave finished, and I wrapped my arms and legs around him again, letting go of the tree branch. He pressed me against the tree. I knew I'd have cuts and abrasions from the bark, but it was worth it.

He thrust one last time, a deep guttural groan leaving him. "We're going to do three climaxes next time," he breathed. "I promise."

I wound my arms tighter around his neck, enjoying the feel of him finishing inside me. His forehead pressed against my throat. "That . . . we're so screwed. You know that, right?"

He pulled out, helping me to the ground as I nodded shakily. "I know."

We cleaned up as best we could. He turned me around, sucking in a breath as he saw my back. "We can't go to the game."

"What? Why?" I tried to see, but the burning had already started.

"We were stupid. I was stupid. I should've turned you the other way. Now these need to be cleaned and sterilized."

"Are you serious? I thought my clothes would give me some protection. I didn't feel it during, you know."

"There are a couple of deep ones that shouldn't wait." He smoothed a finger over them, and I arched forward, searing pain coming from his touch.

He was right. I hated that he was right.

"This was supposed to be my first football game here. I missed last week, you know."

He flashed me a hard look. "They have another one in seven days."

"Not the same thing. I was supposed to be making friends too."

His eyes darkened as he stepped back. I pulled my shirt and sweatshirt down, getting my leggings back up and comfortable.

He bent, grabbing our phones, and handed them over. "Text our excuses. We can run to my house—"

"No, my house. It's closer. My mom is a nurse's aide. We

have everything. Plus, Clint's going to go straight there anyway. There'll be less questions."

"Okay with me."

I made up the stupidest excuse, but it was the only thing I could think of. Once we got to his truck, I sent both texts out.

Scout: Your cousin is clumsy AF. She fell down and twisted her ankle. I'm taking her to her house. Sorry ahead of time, but it wasn't my fault. I swear.

I read it to him. He shook his head. "Now you gotta pretend to be limping."

"Just for the night. I can do that."

My phone lit up as Clint called me, so I hit accept and put him on speaker. "Hey."

"What the fuck?"

I could hear whistles and cheering from his end. "Can you even hear us?"

"Yes. Are you okay?"

"I'm fine. More embarrassed than anything."

"What happened? What were you *doing*?"

Scout glanced my way at Clint's tone on that word.

I ignored it, saying, "Nothing. It's all dumb. I just stepped wrong when we were coming back to the game."

"You're lying to me."

My cousins and their freaking lie-detector radar. "I'm not." But *damn it*. Stick to the truth here. "I'm in pain. I got hurt. We're going to my house so I can fix it. All truths."

He was quiet before cursing under his breath. "You want me to leave?"

"No. I mean, not unless you want to, but finish the game. What's the score?"

"We're up ten to three. Alex scored the first touchdown, and Cohen got us close enough for a field goal. Are you sure you don't want me to leave?"

"Finish the game, but could you let Gem know what

happened? I can text her, but it might go better if you let her, Theresa, and Alred know."

"Alred?"

I smiled, envisioning Clint meeting Alred for the first time. "You'll meet him."

"Yeah. I can do that. Okay. I'll text when the game is done."

When the call ended, Scout shook his head. "You're really fucking good at lying."

I grunted, hissing, starting to feel the pain now. "Not with Clint. He knows."

But one problem at a time.

30

RAMSAY

"**W**hy were you bringing up Kira?" Scout asked as he finished cleaning up my back. There'd been some burning, hissing, and curses, but it was mostly done and bandaged. I'd need to watch who saw my back. The lie I had ready was that I fell and scraped my back when I twisted my ankle. It was a stretch, but it'd have to do.

I looked up in the mirror, meeting his gaze. "Because she made a weird comment to me when we were leaving Mario's."

He stilled, and his eyes flashed before his face got hard again.

He clipped out, "She's nothing."

I stilled. "Doesn't feel like nothing. Is there something I need to be worried about?"

He rolled his eyes, putting another bandage on my back before stepping back. "No. You're all done."

I reached for my shirt and pulled it on, not replying, just watching him.

Now he wasn't making eye contact.

What she said definitely had something to do with me. "Scout," I said quietly.

It worked. It got his attention. His eyes came back to mine.

"She said it to me. You don't tell me, I'll go to her. I won't let another person have something over me, not ever again. You get me?"

We continued staring at each other in the mirror until another look flared over his face, so brief, so instant, that it was there and then gone before I could place it. But then we heard a crash downstairs, followed by, "Ramsay!"

It was Clint.

Scout helped the back of my shirt fit better. "Scout."

He started for the door, ignoring me.

Damn it!

I heard him talking to whoever was down there, and it wasn't just Clint. I followed at a more sedate pace, making sure to grab my sweatshirt from my room. I winced just as I stepped out from the stairs.

Clint was there with a couple of guys, along with Kira, Ciara, and Leanne.

Clint's eyes narrowed to slits, taking me in, but before he could say anything, Scout held up his hand to my cousin. "My Good Samaritan part is done. I'm taking off."

Clint ignored him, studying my ankle. "Thought that was twisted?"

Crap. "It was. It still hurts, but I'm of the mindset that I can *will* it back to normal. Must be working if you—"

Clint's eyes flared. He *so* knew I was lying, but he wasn't calling me on it, not in front of our audience. He kept studying me until he finally gave in. "You're better now?"

"Yeah."

Clint glanced back to Scout, who'd paused before leaving and was on his phone. "What are you doing tonight? We were thinking of grabbing drinks and going to hang out at your uncle's gym."

"Uh . . ." He lifted his head and raised his phone. "That was Cohen. He, Alex, and Trenton have it all figured out."

"You cool with that plan? It's your uncle's place."

"Yeah." Scout looked past him to me. "I'm cool with that plan. Want to grab some food?"

"We can all do that together." Kira stepped to Clint's side, leaning into him. "Right, Clint? We were thinking of going to Louie's and getting food to go."

"I'm good with that."

Scout's eyes lingered on her hand on Clint's arm before, "Yeah. I'm good with getting food there too."

Clint looked to me. "Maybe while they get the food, you and I can go get the booze?" He gave me an extra-forceful stare, and it took me a moment to remember his restless energy from school. That was right. He and I were due for doing something stupid.

I mean, I'd already gotten that out of my system, but evidently, he hadn't. "That sounds good to me."

His grin turned wicked. "Awesome."

Oh no.

31

RAMSAY

"I know you and Scout fucked."

Clint dropped the ball as soon as we got in his vehicle.

"Clint!"

He leveled me with a hard look. "What are you *doing*, Rams?"

God. Him and his ability to just know things about me. "It's —look, the attraction is insane. Like crazy insane, and him and me staying away from each other was making it worse. It was messing with us, but it's just sex. There are no emotions. I can't stand the guy. He can't stand me. And we agreed that if either of us starts getting feelings, we're stopping. That'll mess everything up."

"Yeah." His tone was dry. "Because those agreememts always work out."

"Just—"

"You're going to do this. I know you, but I don't like it. And I'm not holding this shit back from Alex."

"Clint."

"No, Rams. No. I'm telling him. If Scout doesn't, I will."

I was quiet, thinking, then I said, "I needed to feel good. I'm sorry, but I did and I do. I don't like him. I'm not going to fall for him. There's absolutely nothing romantic going on, but I felt good for a little bit. He and I know how it is between us. *You* guys are the ones making it complicated. This isn't about you or Alex."

He growled, starting the engine. "Doubt Alex will see it that way."

I pressed my lips together. "If he doesn't, then I'll explain it to him."

He grunted, but he pulled out to the street and I knew my cousin. He said what he needed to say, letting me know where he stood, and now the topic was dropped because that restlessness was still in him. Onto to the next stupid shit we were about to do.

"Where are we going?"

We went through Pine River.

Went over the river.

Went into Pine Valley, which I knew about, but Alred was the first person I knew from there. I'd not been on this side. It was a whole different town, and as we kept driving, I was realizing how much bigger it was. It wasn't a town like Pine River. It was bigger, way bigger, enough whereas Clint hit the blinker and we turned, I saw that it had its own university.

Pine Valley University.

"Clint."

He kept quiet, turning down one road after another before he hit the light and we were down a side alley.

I liked getting into trouble but fun trouble. Clint was different. He liked pushing the boundaries, and I was also now realizing I was troubled-out. I was good. I didn't need this sort of trouble, whatever kind Clint was about to get us into.

"Clint," I dropped my voice. "I can't handle—" We went

across another road and into another alley, but it was the glimpse I got from the road that had me speechless for a moment.

Pine Valley University had its own fraternity row. Every single house looked like they were partying, and the house we drove up to was Rho Mu Epsilon, the fraternity where Max was already a legacy, or would be once he joined. His great, great, great-grandfather was the first member. All the men in Max's family were brothers, his real brother was a current member.

Clint pulled over so his car was hidden behind a dumpster, and I could only whisper, "Clint."

He looked my way. We were completely blanketed by darkness. The side windows on both houses were narrow and closed off with curtains. The front and the back was where the lights were flashing. There'd been people on the front deck, and shadows were moving farther down so there were some people in the backyard, but that was sectioned off by a giant sized fence.

His voice started low and rough. "It's my job to take care of you. It's our job. My and my brothers'. It was your dad's. It was supposed to be your boyfriend's, but he's the one who twisted shit. He broke the vow that all men take when they become men. You got hurt, and you really got hurt."

Pain sliced through me.

"Oh, Clint." They came the very next day after my dad died. They were there, and they stayed forever until Aunt Ailes forced them to go back. Clint made the trip out as often as he was allowed.

His voice turned fierce. "I told my mom that if you stayed there, I was moving and going to your school. Trenton was going to come when football season was done. We had it all worked out. Alex was going to stay, but he'd come every holiday, then he'd stay and I'd come back for baseball."

I couldn't talk. A tennis ball of emotion was smack dab in the middle of my throat.

"We fought so much with Mom and Dad, but I was going. We had that figured out too, how I'd be gone for a while before Mom and Dad would figure it out. Then Mom came to my door, and I had enough time to throw a blanket over my bag on the bed because I was literally in the middle of packing, and she told me you guys were moving here."

I grabbed his arm.

"First time in a year that I'd felt relief. We can protect you here, but he never got his comeuppance." He glanced to the house, the one where Max will join one of its brother houses in another state. "I came here the other time, scouted it out."

My hand squeezed his arm. "That's where you went the other night?"

"They keep their alcohol stock in a room that has two doors. One from the alley, easy unloading, and the other leading into the house. The door to the alley is locked, but the one going to the house is guarded by one guy. Inside the house." His eyes found mine, shining bright. "We break the lock, we can take all of their alcohol and they won't know it until we're gone."

"Stealing alcohol isn't going to hurt them much."

His lip quirked. "You've not seen how much alcohol is in there, and I don't care. It'll hurt the guy who's supposed to be guarding the door. They'll hurt him. One guy. I'd rather go in and steal their drugs, but figured I'd be pushing it enough asking your help for the alcohol."

My hand squeezed again. He was right. Alcohol was one thing. Drugs were a whole other matter. He was also right that they'd hurt the guy guarding the door.

I let go of his arm, the tennis ball of emotion dipping to my chest. "The funny thing is that, even if Max joined this particular house, came to this college, and is a freshman, he still wouldn't be the guy guarding the door. Legacies are treated like royalty in this fraternity."

"I know."

We did this, we'd be signing up for a guy to get hurt.

Maybe a black eye? Would that be it? Hazing?

He'd lose alcohol inventory guarding duty and have to clean bathrooms instead? Would that be his punishment?

My chest was burning up.

It wouldn't be enough, not from who Max took from me.

"Let's do it."

———————————

OUR JOBS WERE SIMPLE.

The fraternity didn't have any special security. It was a lock, so as Clint took out some tools to take off the doorknob—with bolt-cutters to get through if there was a secondary chain on the inside of the door, which Clint said he hadn't gotten a good enough look so we were playing that part by ear—my job was to go inside the fraternity, find the guy guarding the door, and distract him.

My job was easy because it was already getting done for me. The guy had a girl wrapped around him, her legs, arms, and her lips were trying to devour him up. She kept trying to pull him away, but he kept insisting they stay at the door so while he was committed to standing by the door, he was good and distracted.

It was anticlimactic. It was so simply done, but I was still feeling it, my chest still burning because another house like this, the same Greek letters, and it would be where Max would attend. He'd go on, find another girl, and I was sure he already had another one, but he'd hurt her too. I had no doubt about that.

The look was in his eyes when he saw me.

He enjoyed taking away my father.

And he got away with it.

He'd do it again, and he'd get away with it.

And again.

And again.

It would go on and on, never-ending.

Everyone knew what he did to me.

They didn't care.

They cared about Max more, about his family name, about their money.

The police sided with the Prestige family.

The school sided with Max.

My friends blamed me.

"You okay?"

I gasped, rearing back. The hatred burned so hard in me that I hadn't realized I was blinking back tears. "What?"

A guy was there, looking concerned, a beer cup in hand. He was tall, over six feet, and he moved closer, bending over me. "You look upset." His lips moved into a cocky smirk. "We can't have anyone upset at our parties, much less someone as beautiful as you."

God.

This guy even looked like Max. Same almost black hair. Wealth and privilege coming off him in waves. "Do you shop at the same stores?"

He frowned. "What?"

It was the shirt. Jesus Christ. It was the shirt.

Max wore this same shirt, all the time. It was his favorite.

I was now also getting why. It was a Rho Mu Epsilon shirt. The diamond crest on the collar was the same one from the house's sign in front. I never knew that before.

"Never mind." I wiped at my face. No way would those tears

fall for Max. No fucking way. "I'll have something to drink? Would you get me something?"

He took me in again, studying me before nodding slowly. "Sure. We have beer, but I could make you something else?" He took a step closer. "Something special?"

My insides stretched to the point where I thought I'd snap, but I only smiled. "Sure. Be creative."

"No problem." He hesitated and touched his thumb to the indent of my chin. It was a brief flick, but I felt branded by him. I'd not given him permission to touch me.

Asshole.

He lingered, his eyes on my mouth before he pulled away. "Don't go anywhere."

There was a poker around the corner behind me. I could take it and impale it up his ass, hoping it'd go far enough to reach Max himself, and thinking of that, my smile got a little easier. "Not planning on it."

The second he was gone, I grabbed for my phone.

Me: I can't stay in here much longer.

Clint didn't answer right away.

Door guard and his girlfriend kept swapping saliva.

I kept waiting.

Still no answer.

Then, the guy was coming back with a drink in hand. There was no way I was going to drink that, but this guy wasn't going to leave my side. He'd make sure I took at least one sip.

I resent my text again to Clint, then slid my phone into my pocket. I'd feel it buzz if he texted back.

The guy arrived, holding out a purple and pink drink. "The bartender made it, assured me you'll like it. Apparently, the girls go crazy for it, but I have no idea what it's named. Here you go."

My fingers closed around the glass, and I upped my smile. "Thanks."

I swallowed.

The guy frowned. "You're not going to try it? See if you like it?"

My heart picked up, going fast.

"I—"

He moved into my space again. "We didn't exchange names before. I'm Matt." He was giving me a once-over. "What's your name? Do you live in the dorms?"

"I—"

"What the fuck?" a savage growl came out from the side.

Clint was there, looking thunderous. His gaze fixed firmly on me.

The guy stepped back but then shifted to get between Clint and me. "Hey, man. How's it going?"

Clint ignored him, coming closer.

Matt started to put his drink down, his hands going up between us. "Don't know who you are, but the girl is here of her free will. She can stay as long as she'd like, man."

Clint kept glaring at me. "I'd like to let you know that your daughter woke up crying."

"Daughter?" Matt looked my way.

Clint moved to his side. "Thankfully, your other two daughters didn't wake up."

"Two daughters?" Matt edged back a step. "You got three kids?"

"Twins," Clint addressed him for the first time. "Ten month olds."

Matt's eyes bulged out.

Clint's gaze went back to me, dropping to my stomach. "I found the pregnancy test. When were you going to tell me you've got another one coming?"

"Another one?" Matt was in retreat mode by now. He raised a hand, going through his hair, but he turned and ran.

Clint snorted. "See you later, nice to have not met you." He eyed my drink. "Tell me you didn't?"

I snorted. "I would never, and also, you were mom-shaming me. Dick move."

He shrugged. "That kind of guy? I used the one thing that'd get rid of him fast. I could've gone with some sort of disease, but I'd have to make one up and the way he was looking at you, he would've been asking all sorts of questions to make sure he wouldn't get anything from one night with a rubber."

We began heading back out, going a way that Clint must've used getting inside. There were a couple guys watching us, but most were interested in their own conversations. Once we cut through a side door that opened outside, I tossed my drink before leaving the glass behind.

"Wait." Clint grabbed it, using his shirt to wipe it down.

"Are you serious?"

"They're going to be pissed. Trust me."

Once I got to the car, I saw he was right.

The entire back seat was full to the brim, a large blanket covering all of it. In the passenger's seat, he only left enough room for my feet.

"The trunk?"

"All filled."

"Clint, there are cops."

He motioned to the back, already driving away. "Hence the blankets."

"They're going to call the cops."

An ugly laugh left him. "Guys like that, a frat like that, they don't call the police."

My mouth dried up. "How do you know?"

"Because they got worse shit in that house, and cops come, they're not going to risk any of that getting seen no matter how well they think they hide it."

"*How* do you know?"

Clint glanced over. I wasn't looking at my cousin who liked to get into trouble. Not that cousin. This was a whole different one, the one getting in trouble wasn't enough, not in this situation. He wanted to hurt and he was going to do it smart and calculating.

"Because a part of that scouting trip I did? I found their hiding spots."

32

RAMSAY

Sunday night, I was at my desk in my room when my phone buzzed.

Unknown: What are you doing for the night?

I frowned, sitting up and texting back.

Me: Who is this?

Unknown: Theresa. What are you doing tonight?

I glanced at the time.

Me: Studying. What are _you_ doing?

Theresa: We're heading out to watch a fight. Not Scout's. A different guy. Want to come?

Me: Fight?

Theresa: MMA. It's not the official league, but easier to explain it that way. We can swing by, pick you up. You can be back around 2, if you need to know. I'd offer some condolences if that's too late, but you don't strike me as a girl who cares about curfew.

She was right, but only because my mom was working nights. If she wasn't, I'd be staying in and being a good daughter.

Me: I'm in.

Theresa: 20 minutes. Just come out when we pull in.

I didn't answer because I was already up and dressing.

Theresa texting to invite me was a big deal.

After not hanging out with them Friday at the game, I hadn't heard from them all weekend. Gem texted during the game to make sure I was cool. I'd told her a bit of the story with my apologies. She seemed okay, telling me to have fun. Then Clint and I had showed up at Scout's uncle's gym with the booze. The rest of the night had been a lot more chill than I'd thought it was going to be.

Scout was there, but he stayed with Cohen and Alex. Kira, Leanne, and Ciara floated between them. If they were hoping for some action, they were disappointed.

We hung out by the river and drank. The guys built a bonfire.

The girls took off around one in the morning, and after that, I let myself indulge in the booze. It felt good to shut everything off, even if it was just for a night, and I trusted who I was with. I didn't quite remember the drive home, but I woke up the next morning in my aunt's guest bedroom—the one in her she-shed.

Saturday had been hangover recovery day. We went for fast food, and I laid on my couch the rest of the afternoon.

Sunday was studying day for me.

I was all studied out.

My mom had been in and out, but it was her weekend to work, and she was still doing doubles. I cooked and cleaned and tried to help out, but I knew she was going to be dead on her feet tomorrow when she got home. We already had a plan to do movies in her bed. I couldn't wait.

I remembered the crowd from Scout's last fight, so I knew a bit more about how to dress.

I ended up with sneakers, my torn and faded leggings, a white tank top, and then a cropped little hoodie. The ends were ragged, matching my torn leggings, and it hung just under my breasts. My hair went back up in braids, and I wound them around my head. I considered the whole hoop earrings look, but in the end, I went basic—just left my face with natural makeup in earth tones and put two crystal rings on my fingers.

I wadded up some money, a credit card, and my ID and stuck everything into a zipped-up pocket, along with my lipstick and key. I'd keep my phone with me, but if I needed, there was room for that in the pocket too.

I had just gotten downstairs when car lights swept the house.

I headed out, locking the door behind me, and jogged over. It was a black Audi, the sports car version, and I didn't know the guy driving.

Theresa waved from the front seat. She opened her window and called, "Back of me."

I nodded, opening the door and sliding in. Another guy was in the backseat, and at the sight of me, he plastered himself against his door. "Well. *Dayum*, Theresa." He gave me a once-over and a wicked grin. He held out a hand. "Malik. You're Ramsay?"

I shook his hand.

Both guys were dressed in black T-shirts and black jeans. The guy driving had a smoky look on his face, his eyes a little lidded, like he wasn't totally awake. I got the vibe he was very much awake.

Theresa leaned around her seat, popping a thumb in the driver's direction. "This is Kunz, and you just met Malik."

Malik had a very short crew-cut hair style with a fade on the sides. Bright dark eyes and high cheekbones. Kunz scared me. Malik made me want to smile. They were a full dichotomy.

"What up? I'm totally good with meeting you all over again." He positioned himself facing me, leaning forward and resting his chin on his hands and blinking dramatically. "Ramsay, you say?"

"Malik, rest it," Theresa told him. "The Maroney triplets are her cousins, and trust me when I say, they're protective."

He barely seemed to register what she'd said before leaning closer and lowering his voice, "Let's pretend they're not in the car with us. You and me, let's get to know each other. Like a double date."

"Malik!" Theresa leaned back to punch him on the shoulder. "I'm not kidding. I didn't invite her out to get hit on by you the whole night."

He leaned back, acknowledging her with a fake scowl as he smoothed his shirt where she'd hit him. "Excuse me. Why invite a woman, especially one this fine, if you're not going to let me hit on her? That's the whole point."

She fought a grin. "Not tonight." She gave me a rueful look. "Sorry about these two. They'll calm down once we get to the fight. They'll forget we even exist."

Kunz had yet to say a word, but he was driving fast. I remembered Gem had told me Kunz drag raced, and as if feeling my gaze on him in the rearview mirror, he glanced up. He gave a small nod. "What's up?"

Theresa's head whipped to him when he spoke, and when she turned my way again, her smile was a little tight. "Gem was going to come with us, but since the fight is late, she needed to sneak out. Her mom caught her."

"She's in trouble?"

"It'll be fine. She'll be grounded for a night, but that's about all my aunt has in her heart to do." Her smile came back in full force. "I'm glad you came, and don't worry about Malik. He's a softie at heart."

Malik pretended to scowl, cupping a hand over his chest. "You wound me, acting like I'm a good little boy. It's like you don't know me at all, Theresa Garcia."

"A good boy is definitely not how I'd describe you," Kunz drawled.

Malik flashed him a grin, relaxing in his seat and stretching his feet forward. "Thanks, buddy. You do know me."

I caught the look that passed between the guys, and also the way Theresa tightened up.

I was starting to wonder if I should've asked more questions before hopping into the car.

Malik noticed me studying everyone, and his eyes turned knowing. "You're a smart one, huh?" He leaned his head back against the seat.

I moved mine too, mirroring his position, and said softly, "Just not dumb. That's all."

His eyes flickered. "Well, then we're really going to have a fun night."

—

THE FIGHT WAS a little over an hour's drive away, and we were forty minutes in when Kunz asked, "You know anything about fighting, Ramsay?"

We'd stopped at a gas station, and Theresa was still inside, getting snacks.

I shrugged. "Not really, no."

"The Maroney triplets, huh?"

Malik had been focused on his phone, but he lifted his head, putting it away.

"Yeah."

"They're tight with Scout Raiden. You know Raiden?"

My vagina knew Raiden, but I just shrugged. "I know him a little. He's friends with my cousins."

"He's a big name in the fighting world around here."

"That's what I've heard."

I watched Kunz in the rearview mirror, and he watched me back, both ignoring how Malik's gaze skirted between us. For some reason, this conversation was important, as if it mattered how Theresa's whoever-he-was-to-her would categorize me in the aftermath. Someone to . . . what? Walk over? Respect? Pay attention to?

Kunz set the tone. He *would* set the tone moving forward. I wasn't sure what that meant, but I felt it in my bones.

"I lost a lot of money on him in his last fight."

I narrowed my eyes. "You bet against him?"

He didn't reply, but Malik sucked in some air, leaning back as if he could flatten himself against his seat.

"Hey!" Theresa jerked open the door and almost bounced inside. "I got a whole stash. Ramsay, what snacks do you like? I forgot to ask." She divvied them up, tossing bags of Cheetos, chips, peanuts, jerky, and candy at each of the guys before pausing and looking my way. She frowned. "Wha–what's going on?"

"Nothing," Kunz said tightly, starting the engine. "Shut your door. Let's go."

Theresa scrambled, shooting him a dark look. She fastened her seatbelt as he peeled out of the gas station's parking lot and continued to glare at his profile. He ignored her, his jaw tightening.

Malik coughed, clearing the air. "Hey, uh, did you get those gummy bears?"

"Yeah." She handed them back, but she was distracted. "Here you go. Ramsay, you want any of this? I got extra because I wasn't sure what you'd like."

I'd had some pasta for dinner. That was six hours ago so my stomach was growling again, but I wasn't exactly hungry. I gave her a tight smile. "I'm good. Thank you."

There was suspicion in her gaze as she took me in before nodding.

"Oh, score. I didn't know they still made Boston Baked Beans. These are the best." Malik thrust his fist in the air, a bag clenched inside. "Yeah, man. Good call, Theresa, on stopping for snacks."

She gave him a smile. "No problem." She sent Kunz another look before she began to tease Malik about some girl who might be at the fight tonight.

That took up the rest of the drive.

I was glad.

———

THE FIGHT WAS HELD in a warehouse-type building, similar to Scout's. This one was out in the middle of nowhere. We'd been on back roads, winding up and down since we left the gas station. There was dense forest around us, but then we pulled onto a gravel road, behind about twenty other cars, and the drive got a lot slower. As we went up a steep hill, parking attendants directed us to a space in the grass, and after parking, I saw a bunch of other steel buildings set up. In the main one, the large doors were pulled open, showcasing the ring. Some chairs had been set up right by the ring, but after that, people were standing everywhere.

Malik and Kunz headed off in front of us, and Theresa caught my arm, slowing me down. "Did he say something to you at the gas station?"

I watched Kunz. He and Malik looked back our way. "No. Why?"

"It was weird when I came back with snacks. Why was it weird?"

"He asked about my cousins and brought up Scout."

She pulled me to a stop, her fingers pressing into my arm. "What did he say about him?"

"About Scout?"

"Yeah."

"That he lost some money on his last fight."

Her eyes narrowed. "What else?"

"That was it. I asked him if he bet against Scout, and then you got into the car."

"That was it?"

"Yeah." I looked down at her hand still holding my arm.

She released me, stepping back. "Sorry. I—that's weird. It was tense when I got in. I thought something else had happened."

"Like what?"

She shook her head. "It's nothing." She started forward.

"Hey." I grabbed her this time, holding her still. "You don't actually know me. Going to something like this is something I'd do, but I'm not reckless. If something's going on—something with your boyfriend and me or something with him and Scout —I need to know."

She pressed her mouth into a tight line. "It's fine. It's nothing."

She stepped forward again, but this time, I got in her way. "I mean it. Kunz might have tender moments with you, but he's dangerous. I felt it as soon as I got in the car. I need to know what I'm stepping into here."

"It's nothing. I mean it."

"Is there bad blood between him and Scout?"

She frowned, shaking her head. "What's your fascination with Raiden? He was just a fighter he bet against. That's it. You're making this a bigger deal than it is."

"Then why'd the car get so tense that you're asking me about it twenty minutes later?"

"It's nothing. For real. Yes, Kunz has a dangerous side to him, but he's not as bad as you're making him sound. He doesn't know you, and you're connected to the Maroney triplets. That makes you connected to Raiden. He's probably just unsure how to proceed with you at the fight because Kunz has some enemies here. That's all. Nothing really to do with you or Scout. Just Kunz getting the lay of the land."

"Is this a fight Scout would come to?"

She shrugged, looking behind me to where the ring was set up. "I don't know. Sometimes he comes, sometimes he doesn't. If Scout's here, he's got a whole other group he hangs with. We don't mix with them."

"Why not?"

She bit down on her lip. "I can't get into that. It's not my business, but I didn't invite you out for any of this. I swear. Kunz mentioned checking out this new fighter. Malik came without his brother, so that means it's just meant to be an easygoing match to watch—nothing serious, or trust me, Malik's twin would be here. Then I wouldn't have come myself, let alone invite you."

"Good to know about the twin."

She shook her head. "You'll never meet him, so don't worry. If you do, it'll be at one of Kunz's parties, and if that's the case, Gem and Alred will be with us. Totally different vibe."

Right.

She went around me and caught up with the guys who were waiting just ahead. I heaved a big breath.

Had I made a mistake coming tonight?

33

RAMSAY

Maybe it was against my better judgment or maybe it was just me being stupidly stubborn, but I didn't text my cousins or Scout to say where I was. I didn't want them driving here and worrying, only to find me just fine and ream me out, and I didn't want to push the thing with Scout. If he was here tonight, it was easy to miss him. The place was packed with probably three hundred people.

There didn't seem to be any lingering tension coming from Kunz once I joined them. We went in and found some breathing room on some bleachers that were pulled out. Kunz jumped up, and there was room enough for one more, so Theresa went too. She stood, offering me the seat and indicated she could sit on Kunz's lap. I shook my head, feeling the need to stay in the back. She frowned but sat beside Kunz. Malik leaned against the wall by me, but fortunately, he loosened up on the flirting.

Once the fight started, Theresa was in Kunz's lap by the second round, and Malik was straining to see better.

I nudged him and gestured with my chin. "Sit up there."

He shook his head. "I'm good."

I shook mine back. "Climb up. You can see better."

He gave me a lingering look.

"I'm not that invested, and I'm restless. There's room up there to see. Jump up. Watch. I'm good. Really."

"You sure?" He didn't seem to believe me.

"I am. I mean it." I nudged him with my hip. "Go."

There was another cheer from the crowd, followed by boos right after, and he finally nodded. "Okay. Stand close, though. Okay?"

I nodded, moving in as he jumped up.

Kunz gave him a small grin before focusing back on the fight. Then he was standing. Everyone was standing. Theresa stood on the seat in front of them, and Kunz held her by the waist.

I had no clue what was going on. Three tall guys were in front of me, so I couldn't see much. Slinking back against the wall, I did what I always did when I was in a situation where I didn't feel totally safe and secure.

I weighed my options and read the crowd.

It was similar to Scout's fight.

The guys were entranced, most holding a beer. Some were just regular dudes, but a large majority looked as if they could be fighters themselves. As for the women, there were quite a few like myself, dressed in leggings and sweatshirts, but there was a good amount in tight dresses and some in barely there bikini tops and shorts. People were fully into the fight, cheering, cursing, and drinking.

I wasn't expecting to recognize anyone unless Scout or Cohen were here, but Theresa knew Cohen, and she'd said nothing about him, so I figured he wasn't in attendance.

After another scan and not seeing anyone I recognized, I settled back to watch what I could of the match.

MY NERVES WERE SHOT by the time one guy got knocked out, and the other guy didn't look like winning had been worth it. He had blood pouring from every orifice in his face. Only one of his eyes looked like he could see out of it, but the referee held up his hand, and the crowd went wild.

"Hey!" Theresa jumped down. Her eyes were jazzed. "Do you need to go to the bathroom? I gotta go. Oh—I know her!" She tore off, skipping around a bunch of guys, and was gone the next second.

"She's a social butterfly at these fights. Her cousin fights, so she knows a lot of people," Kunz said. He had jumped down, but Malik was still on the bleachers, talking to a group of people. Kunz smiled. "We usually wait out in the front for her, but if you want, I could show you where the bathroom is?"

"Uh . . ." I turned, trying to guess where the bathrooms might be. "If you just point me in the right direction, I could probably find them myself."

He pointed ahead. "They're just out those doors."

Outside. The far left doors. Okey-dokey. "Thanks." I gave a polite smile before starting off.

Getting to the other side of the ring was the hardest part. Most everyone wanted to stay, stand exactly where they were, and talk with everyone around them. Some people were pissed. Most were drunk or high. There were a lot of giggles, and some guys bumped into me.

When I got outside, the air opened up dramatically. It wasn't as congested with people.

Spotting the porta potties, I went over and got in line behind a few girls. They were on their phones when suddenly one exclaimed, "OMG! He came!"

"What?" The second one whipped around, grabbing her phone. "He did?"

The first one started hyperventilating. "Ohmygodohmygodohmygod! We have to find out where he is."

"The picture was taken out front. He's with Selina and that whole group."

"He's just so hot. I can't wait for his next fight."

"I know! I wish he'd fought tonight. Did you go to his last one?"

We kept inching forward to the porta potties, and the first girl squealed in agreement before the door opened again. Her friend pushed her forward. "Hurry! Your turn."

"Hey!" Theresa zoomed up to my right side, sounding out of breath. She grabbed my sleeve and lifted up her foot, fixing something on her shoe. "Sorry about that. Kunz said you went to the bathroom. I saw some of my friends from Pine Valley. Did you enjoy the fight?"

The whole time she spoke to me, she wasn't looking at me. She was scanning the crowd, holding on to me for balance.

"Did you take something?" I asked.

Her eyes snapped to mine. "Like . . . Tums? Or something?"

"Like Ecstasy. You seem high as a kite."

"Oh." She started laughing, tipping her head back. "No. I'm sorry. I get like this when I'm at these events. I don't know what it is, like something in the air. I just, I feel high, but I'm not. I swear. I'm not into drugs, like, at all." Her tone went flat, and some of my tension eased. She did seem a little more sober now.

"Right."

"But did you enjoy the fight? Isn't it crazy? It gets in your blood, and you feel like you need to fuck." She twisted around, biting her lip and looking back the direction she'd come from. "Where are the guys?"

"Your man said they would wait in front for you. That's where I was going to go after using the bathroom."

"That sounds good. Some people mentioned a party closer to Pine River. Would you be interested?"

No. "What kind of party?"

"A house party. Nothing huge. We wouldn't stay too long. Can't. School."

The girl in front of me came out of the bathroom, so I held up a hand before slipping inside.

I went as fast as possible. Who enjoys being in these things? But when I got back outside, Theresa wasn't there. I assumed she'd gone into one of the other bathrooms, so I stood to the side and considered my options.

Nothing bad had happened. I mean, there were sketchy vibes from Kunz. And Malik seemed nicer, more stable, but he still gave me dangerous vibes. Then there was Theresa, who everyone said was solid. She hadn't seemed that way here, but she'd admitted it was the pheromones in the crowd and the energy of the fight affecting her.

That made sense. It would've affected me the same way if I'd been someone else—or been with people I knew and felt safe with. In all honesty, Kunz hadn't done anything to make me question being safe. We drove to a fight, watched a fight, and now I was waiting outside of a bathroom.

We came. We watched. We were going to leave.

All good. Right?

Yes. I sucked in my breath, counted to ten, and released. I was just out of my comfort zone, and that was a trigger by itself.

Everything would be fine. All fine.

Theresa came out and flashed me a smile. She was glowing, her cheeks flushed. "Ready? The guys are at the car."

I nodded, my neck tense.

She looped her arm with mine, and as we started forward, she asked, "So, party?"

"Um . . ."

We headed around the front. Theresa called out to a bunch of people, but she didn't leave my side again. As we passed, a rather large crowd had congregated around a wagon. I couldn't see who was sitting on it, but it almost seemed like celebrities.

I recognized the two girls who'd been gushing over whoever *he* was in front of me in the bathroom line. They were standing with some guys and a couple of other girls, but they looked transfixed by whoever was on that wagon.

"Who was that all about?" I asked after we'd gotten down the path a bit.

"That?" Theresa glanced back.

"Yeah. Some girls in front of me were going nuts over some guy being at the fight."

Kunz and Malik were sitting on the back of the car, and they got up as we approached.

Theresa answered absentmindedly as she went to the front passenger side. "Oh. That was Scout and his fighting posse. Told you. He has celebrity status here." She breezed inside, shutting the door, and I was left standing, the only one not in the car.

"You ready?" She opened her door again, grinning up at me.

Right. Yeah. Right. I jerked forward, getting inside.

Scout and I weren't friends. That was obvious. Though he would've stepped in and helped me get home—because of his friendship with my cousins.

But I was fine. This was all fine.

34

RAMSAY

The party wasn't super huge so much as a house that looked filled with people who had spread out into an unattached garage. There were ping pong and pool tables in the front yard. As we walked in, Kunz and Malik kept stopping to say hi to people.

Theresa tugged my hand. "Come on. This is their realm so they'll be out here a while. Let's go get some drinks."

Okay. I was wrong. Inside, the house was packed. We could barely get through the door, but someone yelled Theresa's name, and she waved, tugging me through a group of girls to where a guy was standing behind a bar. He was tall and lean, wearing a Hawaiian shirt unbuttoned with a white tank beneath. His hair was messily rumpled, but it worked on him. He leaned over. "Hey. Surprised to see you here."

Theresa lifted a shoulder. "Kunz wanted to check out the fight."

His eyes moved to me. "Who's your friend?"

"This is Ramsay. She's new."

"Hi, Ramsay." He held a hand over the bar. "My name's Ben."

"Ben knows Gem." She gave him a questioning look. "He used to work at Mario's. You're still going to the university?"

He nodded. "Yeah. I haven't seen Gem in a while. How's she doing?"

"She's good."

Ben nodded his head. "Awesome. Tell her hi for me, and any friend of Gem's is a friend of mine." He slapped his hands on the counter. "What would you like, ladies?"

"I'll have a beer, whatever's on tap," I told him.

"Whatever's on tap. Got it." He grabbed a glass and began pouring, then raised an eyebrow, waiting for Theresa's order.

Her head wafted back and forth. "Uh . . . make me something you've been wanting to make all night and haven't yet."

He handed me my beer, saying to Theresa, "You sure about that? Some might say you're being awfully brave, letting a bartender pick your poison."

She rolled her shoulders back and smiled widely. "Let me have it, Ben. I believe in you."

He chuckled. "All right. Sit tight and watch some magic then."

As he worked, he asked, "So you're here with Kunz, huh?" He looked up at Theresa when he could. "I thought that was over?"

Some of her smile faded, but she shrugged, watching what he mixed together. "He—I . . . I don't know. He wanted to check out a new fighter, so here we are."

Ben nodded. "I heard about that fight. A lot of those guys are heading over here afterward. We were warned to double our inventory, triple it with some bottles." He finished up, and I had no idea what was in the drink. He'd poured blue stuff, pink stuff, some purple stuff, and it came out looking yellow. Topping it off with an orange, he handed it over. "Voila. My own little cocktail."

"Thanks, Ben." She sipped it, and her eyes rolled back. "Ohhhhmygawd. This is amazing. What do you call it?"

He smiled. "Right now it's Ben's Bender, but don't let the name fool you. It'll just cause you to *want* to go on a bender. But not you ladies because you're underage and you shouldn't be drinking, am I right? I'm right. Now get out of here before my conscience gets the best of me. All these people, I don't know. I don't know how old they are, but you and her, I do know. Get out of here and be the normal rebel high schoolers I know you are."

Theresa laughed, taking another sip. "See you, Ben. Give Gem a call sometime."

He held a hand up, already filling another order.

"Gem?" I inclined my head. "And him?"

Theresa laughed, ducking out through a side door to the side of the house. "It's not like that. I mean, it would be for Gem. She had a huge crush on him, but Ben's not like that. He looks like a stoner, but he's the hardest working kid I know. Ask her about him and enjoy the blushing fireworks. It's a whole Fourth of July show."

We walked around the house, and she spotted the guys, who hadn't moved from the pool table in the front yard.

She sighed. "They're going to be talking the whole time. We might as well go have fun somewhere else until we want to go." She looked my way. "What are you thinking?"

"What do you mean?"

"What do you typically do at parties? You know, hide in the kitchen? Hide in the basement? Flutter around like a butterfly? Party tricks? Karaoke? Or do you find a Playstation and join the gamer room?"

"Honestly? I used to find my people, sit, and laugh with them the whole time."

"You're one of *those* people."

"What people?"

"The ones who make others come to them. *Those* kind of people."

I thought about it. "I guess. Maybe? But I know I'm not the fluttering around type. That shit makes me nervous."

"Okay." She looped our arms again, and we turned around. She pointed at a bonfire where some people were sitting around. One guy was strumming a guitar. "I know those guys a tiny bit. They're cool. If we're going to sit somewhere, that's where we should go."

I nodded. "Sounds good to me."

THERESA WAS RIGHT. The bonfire people were cool.

I *was* one of those people, I guess.

It was an hour later when Theresa decided to find Kunz because, though we were having fun, it was time to head back. She went to the front while I went inside to use the bathroom.

I was just coming out when a girl pushed past me, almost flattening me against the wall. She tore down the hallway to join her other friends, who were all waving for her to hurry her ass up. As they shoved through the screen door, I expected it to bang shut, but it didn't because other people were pushing out too.

I went with the herd, wondering what the hell was going on, and then saw a crowd starting to form outside. I checked my phone to see if Theresa had texted me, but she hadn't, so I pushed through to see. When I got there, a few feet back from the edge of the crowd, I paused, because a guy was in Malik's face.

I had déjà vu from the cafeteria because Scout was standing behind the guy in Malik's face. And just next to Malik was Kunz, who was glaring at Scout. But this time, Scout looked indifferent.

I looked through the crowd for Theresa, but couldn't find her.

Me: Where are you?

I took a pic of my location and sent it to her in a second text.

"This has nothing to do with you, Winslet," Malik yelled. "Why are you in my face about it?"

The guy stepped back, and he was big—like Hulk big, bodybuilder big. He drew back a hand and pointed at Kunz. "I'm in your face because it was your buddy making noise about Raiden."

Malik eyed him warily before casting a look in Kunz's direction and then Scout's. He rubbed a hand over his jaw, taking a step back. "I can't answer on that matter." He spoke to the guy, though it was obvious he was asking Kunz to step in.

He just leaned back against the pool table and dug into his pocket, pulling out his phone.

Malik cursed under his breath, shaking his head before seeing me and giving me a little chin-lift.

I didn't respond, just put my mouth in a flat line.

He looked back to Kunz.

The big guy was also looking at Kunz, and he threw a hand out toward him. "You want to join in this conversation? Since you're the one with his balls all twisted up because my guy wouldn't take a dive in his last fight for you?"

A girl gasped next to me.

A couple of guys shouted.

"Shit!"

"No way he just said that."

I heard one guy near me mutter, "That's just wrong."

Kunz lifted his head from his phone and began looking around. His eyes got hard. "What do you want me to say? I never asked him to take a dive. I just asked if he thought he was going to lose. There's a difference."

"Yeah, man." The guy near me muttered again. "There's a *real* big difference with those two."

"You asked me to lose, you dipshit." Scout stepped forward.

The crowd quieted.

This was a whole different world, with different rules and different dynamics. A whole different culture.

Kunz turned his way. "That was your interpretation."

Scout went still, eerily still. "We both know how that conversation went down." *Danger.*

He didn't seem mad, but Scout was getting there.

Someone bumped into me, and I looked over, annoyed, but it was Theresa.

"Hey—" I started to say, but she stepped out of the crowd.

I went with her by accident, falling forward.

"You asked him to take a dive?" She shook her head, a gurgling sound coming out of her.

"Theresa—" I'd reached for her when I was plucked up before I could register what was happening.

A strong arm wrapped around my waist and carried me away. "Hey!" I twisted around enough to see Scout scowling at me. He was not happy.

"Put me down."

"Hey! Ramsay!"

I yelled back at Theresa, "Um, okay—"

"You came with her?" he clipped out. He walked into the crowd. They parted, all eyes following us as he strode toward the street where he was parked.

"Put me down. It's fine."

"Garcia is fine." He scoured me with another look. "You are not." He set me down once we reached the truck, only to unlock his door. Then he opened it and put me inside.

"Hey!" I reached for him, but he shut the door and locked it. "Hey!" I tried to open it, but whoa—did he have child locks on his front passenger door? That was . . . then I cursed myself. Of course he didn't. I just wasn't pulling the handle the right way. Figuring it out, I opened the door and started out, but Scout wasn't far. He'd just turned to talk to a bunch of people who'd followed us.

He whipped around, slamming his arm against the door, trapping me in.

I ducked, trying to go under his arm, but he used his legs to cage me.

"Scout."

"Get back inside."

Some of his friends edged back a step. The girls gave me nasty looks. One was blinking back tears. Another guy had moved forward to stand just behind Scout.

"Get back inside!" he barked. "I'm not fucking around."

I eased back, eyeing him and brushing a hand over my forehead. "Theresa," I croaked.

He gritted his teeth. "Get inside while I figure shit out."

I nodded because really, what could I do? I only knew Theresa and he seemed to know everyone else here. Plus, what was the point of making a scene? Once I realized this, the fight left me, and my entire body felt ready to drop.

I got back into his truck.

He stood there, watching me until I sighed and just sat there.

He left the door open and turned his back to me, blocking me in.

"Kunz took off with their girl with them," said the guy who'd stepped forward. "Now we just need to know what you want done with her?" His gaze switched to me.

Scout glanced back at me, folding his arms over his chest. "You came with Garcia?"

I nodded. "To the fight."

His eyebrows twitched.

"Then here," I added.

"You guys here with anyone else? Gem?"

I shook my head. "Kunz and Malik were in the car with Theresa and me. That was it. We were going to leave when I came out and saw your confrontation with him."

His mouth tightened, and he raked a hand over his hair before looking at his friend again. "Nice of them to leave you behind." He turned back to me. "You ready to go?"

Theresa took off? Just like that?

I sank even lower in the seat. "Yeah."

35

RAMSAY

"Don't start," I warned Scout.

We shot forward in the truck, and Scout drove just as fast as Kunz had. His knuckles were white as he held the steering wheel. I settled back, just waiting for him to light into me. It was inevitable.

"What the fuck were you thinking going *anywhere* with Kunz? Do you know anything about him?"

I unfolded my arms from my chest, tilting my head to the side. "I didn't know we were going with Kunz when Theresa invited me."

"Who'd you think she would be with?"

"Gem." My voice got quiet. "Alred?"

Scout started laughing, a bitter sound. "Not likely. Garcia, I get her. She's going to make stupid decisions, especially with that piece of shit, but she has other friends around here. She's not alone. You? You're all fucking alone. If Kunz tried something with you? I was at the fight. I'm not dumb. I know word gets out when I'm at these events."

Gah. He was right. I lifted a shoulder.

Another biting laugh came from him, but he relaxed his

hands. Not all the knuckles were so white now. "Fucking stupid, Ramsay—"

"Don't call me fucking stupid."

He shot right back. "I'm not calling *you* stupid. What you *did* was stupid, and you know it. That guy is dangerous."

I couldn't argue. I'd felt it the moment I got in that car. And dammit, I'd been trying to tell myself that I was fine, all fine, but my instincts were telling me otherwise.

"Why didn't you text me?"

I shook my head, feeling the full force of being a dumbass. "I was just trying to tell myself I could get through the night. Nothing would happen, and then I'd know never to go with them again."

"Why didn't you text me?" he asked again, gentling his voice.

"Pride."

He snorted, and I caught him rolling his eyes. "At least you're honest about it."

"Fuck you, dude."

He glared at me. "Fuck you."

"Fuck you!"

"Jesus. We're children."

"Look," I burst out. "It was dumb, okay? I get it. But Theresa invited me out, and I was tired of being at the house alone because my mom works double shifts every night, so I went. My mistake was assuming she was with Gem and Alred because that was who she was with the last time I hung out with her. That was my mistake, but everything was fine until your confrontation."

"You should've texted me," he clipped out.

"We're not friends!"

"Jesus Christ. We fucked. I'm friends with your cousins. You knew I'd help, and you still decided not to text me."

My whole body was tense. "I let myself lean on my cousins, but I learned a year ago not to rely on another male."

He bit out a harsh laugh. "Glad we're keeping it real here."

"We are. Because that's how you and I are, remember?" I gave him a dark look.

He met it with his own.

We drove the rest of the way in silence until we pulled up to my house. He parked, cutting the lights and taking the keys out. He leaned back, sighing. "Your mom's not here?"

"We are *not friends*. You don't get to ask that."

"Stuff it. I'm asking for other reasons."

Oh.

Oh.

I was getting where he was going, and as soon as it clicked, my body felt like it was strummed tight. I was down for feeling *nice* tonight.

I opened my door. "Park on the street, just in case."

He nodded.

I went to the house, unlocked the back door, and stepped inside.

He came inside not long after. I'd already gone upstairs to the bathroom, but I came back down as he was shutting the door and locking it. I motioned to the counter where I'd set a glass of water for him. He grunted a thanks before taking it and following me upstairs.

I didn't know what his plans were, but he went into my bedroom, and I went back to the bathroom. If I could fall asleep after, I didn't want to be screwed for school in the morning. So I got ready for bed like normal.

When I went into my room, we switched. He went to the bathroom.

I was waiting for him when he came back in. He had his phone in hand and looked around. "Can I plug this in somewhere?"

I motioned to my desk. "There."

He plugged it in, setting it on the desk, and turned to me.

His eyes darkened.

My body was already heated up.

"Not that I'm aiming to do this, but if I fall asleep, will you freak out?"

It was almost three in the morning. "That would be dumb of me considering we gotta be at school in five hours. Will your uncle get pissed?"

He shook his head, pulling his sweatshirt off.

My mouth watered as his shirt came off next, and his muscles contracted with the motion. *Goddamn.* He was a gorgeous specimen, all ripped and corded muscles. He was perfect.

He dropped his jeans, then his boxer briefs, and began stroking his cock. He worked it quick. It was already half hard, but he finished it up, then looked at me. "Did we talk about condoms?"

"Do you have some?"

"I do." He nodded, reaching for his wallet. He grabbed one and put a couple more in my desk drawer before coming over to me. He knelt down, tugging the sheet off my body, and his cock got a whole lot harder. He groaned. "*Fuck*, but you're hot."

"You didn't answer about your uncle."

"What? Oh, no. He knows I went to a fight tonight, and so long as I show up for training tomorrow after school, he'll just assume I crashed somewhere." He crawled over me, his head bending, and this time, his mouth caught mine.

Oooh! Pleasure swirled through me, electrifying me, making my tummy tingle. I gasped, my mouth opening, and his tongue slid inside. Oh boy. I was really, really happy we'd decided not to go with the no-kissing rule I offered.

Scout could kiss.

I reached up, wound my arms around him, and pulled him down to me.

I wanted to feel good.

I FELL ASLEEP AFTER, and when I woke hours later, Scout had a leg pushed between mine and one arm wrapped tight around my waist. The second time I woke, I looked over. He was still in the bed but turned away, his back curled and one of his legs half off the bed.

I looked up at the clock—just after six. My mom would be coming home around the time I needed to be getting up.

But if he'd parked on the street . . . I stopped caring and fell back asleep.

The third time I woke, I felt something rubbing my clit and gasped, realizing it was his mouth between my legs.

Scout lifted his head. His eyes were dark, stormy, but drowsy too. "Is that okay?"

In answer, I took his head and pushed it back down. I was groaning and falling apart not long after, and then he was back over me, sliding inside. He went all the way to the hilt, pausing as I wound my legs and arms around him.

He began to move.

The fourth time I woke to my alarm.

I was alone in bed. Scout's keys, clothes, phone, and wallet were gone.

I reached over and snoozed my alarm for another ten minutes.

I was going to need it.

36

SCOUT

Alex: We need to talk.

I had one guess what that was about.

Me: Just parked at school. Where do you want to do this?

I grabbed my keys and my bag, and my phone buzzed again as I was getting out of my truck.

Alex: The old weight room.

Of all the ironies. That building was only used by a few of the athletes and it was right next to the tree square where I fucked Ramsay.

Me: omw

I started for the football field because both were in that direction.

Cohen: Staring at you going the wrong way, dude.

Me: Alex needs to talk.

Cohen: Everything okay?

Me: Stay tuned

Cohen: Shit.

Amalia: HE LEAKED THE PICTURE OMG OMG OMG HE LEAKED THE PICTURE

Shit.

Double shit. That was not good.

Me: I need to handle something, but we'll figure this out. Don't worry, okay?

She buzzed through, but I was already texting Cohen.

Me: That thing we were worried about with Amalia and Rice just happened.

Cohen: WHAT? She's blowing up my phone.

Me: I'm pretty sure that's illegal, but I don't know. I need to talk to Alex. Can you grab Amalia and take off to the police station? Call my uncle.

Cohen: Dude. I'm calling MY uncle.

Me: He's good too.

Which he was because he was a detective.

Me: I'll call Miles and let him know what's going on.

Cohen: Sounds good, and I'm not responding anymore. Amalia's freaking out. Taking care of her first.

Me: I'll hook up with you in a bit.

I stopped just short of walking into the old weight building because, fuck. Fuuuck. If anything could go wrong today, I had a feeling it was going to happen. Today was a 'brace day.' You braced for what was going to happen, and I needed to prioritize.

Alex first because I was here and he was here. We were going to have some real honest best friend bullshit going on, but after that, Amalia.

This shit was not good.

The door opened. Alex said from the doorway, "You coming in or what?"

Right.

"I'm coming in."

37

RAMSAY

Theresa was at my locker, waiting for me as I approached. She was alone.

"Hey."

She straightened, glancing around. "Hey."

I looked too. "No Gem?"

She shook her head, glancing down, and some of her hair fell forward over her shoulder. "I asked her to do something in the library for me."

I opened my locker, stowing my bag inside. "You did that on purpose?"

Her head lifted. Regret flashed over her face. Her mouth tightened, but then her face cleared. She raised her chin up and shrugged. "I wanted to talk to you first."

I waited, grabbing my phone, my book, my notebook, and my pen.

I was still waiting by the time I grabbed all that, going slow too.

"Okay." She rolled her eyes. "I took off last night and I didn't check on you. I'm sorry for doing that." She looked away before focusing on me again. "I shouldn't have done that. I should've texted you or called you, or something. Honestly, I should've thrown a huge fit to make sure you were okay going with Scout, but I didn't. And I didn't do that because in that moment last night, I chose Kunz." The regret was there again. She grimaced. "I'm really ashamed. Shit's going down between my guy and Raiden, and Raiden scoops you because I get it. You're part of his side because of his friendship with your cousins, and I figured you might be better off with Raiden, but still. You came with me and Kunz, and I should've gone ballistic in trying to get to you."

This whole apology looked like it was costing her.

I frowned, sensing there was deeper stuff going on. I asked, "Why didn't you?"

Her eyes jerked to mine. She was struggling.

Her lips parted. "Because if I had, he would've left me."

Boom.

Truth explosion.

She swallowed, her head folding down again. "I didn't want to admit that to myself in that moment, but still—"

I held up a hand. "Apology accepted. You knew I was safe with Scout, so stop tormenting yourself." I shut my locker and leaned back against it, my arms folding everything in my arms. "Are *you* okay?"

"No," she admitted, her body shuddering. "I—just—last night when I knew I needed to check on you, when he should've been cool with letting me check on the new friend who came because I invited her—I knew it then. Knew in my gut. He would have no problem leaving without me, and I'd go a week without hearing from him because he'd be too busy fucking other girls. Then he'd come back and the worst part of it is that when he'd come to me, he wouldn't apologize. That's . . . a really hard pill to swallow."

I was gathering. "I'm sorry."

She shook her head, her eyes closing and holding before

opening. "I wanted to make things right with you before Gem shows up. Could I ask a favor? I'm aware that I totally don't have that right considering the circumstances."

I frowned, straightening up. "Sure."

Her gaze lifted and she pinned it down the hallway, but at the same time her jaw clenched. "Could you not mention any of this to Gem? She really likes you and wants us to be friends. I had fun with you last night, and I'd like that too, but I know I probably messed everything up. Give me another two weeks to try to make it up to you before dropping the hammer about what happened last night to Gem?"

My mouth twitched. "Your whole shame and blame yourself thing is a little overboard. You're having guy revelations, meaning you're more into your guy than he is with you and you're making yourself face that head on, and you knew I'd be safe with Scout last night. The main crisis happening here is more with yourself. I'm good. I won't hold a grudge against you, and you coming up and really putting it all out there makes up for you not checking on me last night. I'm way more into being your friend now than I was yesterday."

Her shoulders dropped dramatically. "You serious?"

I nodded, thinking we needed to start heading for class.

That was until someone screamed.

38

SCOUT

"**Y**ou're fucking my cousin?"

I paused.

He took my pause the wrong way, fury twisting up his face. "Clint told me, and it's messed up if you think my triplet isn't going to share that shit with me."

Okay. First—I shook my head. Too many fires happening right now.

I held my hand up, closing the weight room door behind me. No one else was inside. "I told her I wasn't going to lie to you."

"When did it happen?"

This morning flashed in my head.

The time before that.

The time before *that*.

"It is a recent development."

He exploded, "Fuck you, Scout! She's my cousin. You know the shit she's gone through, and now this? You? What are you —" He was tense, and his hands were in fists.

I had two seconds to start explaining or my best friend was going to swing on me.

I got to talking. "Ramsay and I aren't like that."

"BULLSHI—"

"Not, not like that." I raised my voice because, fuck this. He needed to hear me. "And I told her that I wasn't going to lie to you. She also said she can't lie to you guys, and I'm figuring out now she meant that literally. But, fuck, okay. Yes. I fucked your cousin."

Maybe the wrong thing to say because he started for me.

I backed up. "*But* it was making it worse not to do it."

He stopped, but his head flew back. "That is the most messed up shi—"

"You gotta let me talk. Jesus fucking Christ, Alex!" Now my shit was going to explode because fuck this. Amalia's life was crumbling, and I was here handling this, for him, for my friendship. "Look. Your cousin isn't some chick who's looking at me with wide eyes. This thing between us has been there from the beginning."

He started shaking his head.

"I mean it. Ask her, but goddamn, the first fucking time we saw each other, it was there. And neither of us wanted it. Believe that. I love you. I love you and Cohen and Amalia and, right now, shit's going down with Amalia. They need me, but I'm here with you because you're my brother too. I mean that shit. I really do." He frowned, his eyebrows dipping down. I kept on, "Ramsay and I? I don't know what's going to happen with that, but I can tell you that I don't feel like I'm going to combust from my organs because her and I finally gave in."

"Jesu—" He started to turn away.

"I don't have pretty words to explain it, but Ramsay and I can barely stand each other."

"You fucked her."

I was at a crossroads. I could take the road he'd like me to take, but I remembered sliding into Ramsay this morning, needing to taste her, and I needed to be brutally honest.

"I am fucking her."

He froze, his head twisted.

Right. He didn't like hearing that.

I was on the ready, knowing he could swing on me.

I still said it. "We're fucking. We're going to do it again."

He was eerily still. His head cocked to the other side. "I didn't hear that right because I swear you just said—"

"Gonna fuck her again."

His face turned thunderous. He started for me.

I didn't back up, saying as he came, "I cannot leave her alone."

Something in my tone got through to him. He stopped, but his chest was rising at a fast pace.

His nostrils were flaring.

I started to shut down, but fuck this. I had no other option here. "I don't know the reason, but I know that I'm going to keep fucking her. And she's the same."

He was listening.

Thank God.

My chest rose, just a little, and I felt some space clearing in there. I could talk a little more free. "I said it, but I'm saying it again. Your cousin and I can't stand each other, but it's the same with needing to touch each other. I don't get it. I don't like it, but it's there. There are no emotions between us. She and I know exactly where the other is with this thing."

His eyes were narrowed. "You got other stuff to get out? Like how this isn't going to end in catastrophe and Clint scraping Ramsay off the floor, *again*, because we've all done that with her. That was in another city, but no way am I going to be okay letting my *best friend* be the next guy who does that to her."

Hot anger scorched me because fuck him. Fuck that. Fuck what he just said.

My tone went cold, *"The fuck you just say?"*

His eyes were just as cold as his tone. "The fuck I just said."

I started for him this time.

39

RAMSAY

A girl shrieked right after that scream, "Shut up! Put that away."

I started for them, not thinking, just feeling. My gut was telling me to get over there.

It was a group of three girls, all glued to their phones.

The one who screamed was gaping at her screen.

The one who shrieked was reaching for the screamer's phone, and there was another girl who looked like a deer in headlights, complete with a tear falling down her face.

Theresa was moving with me, and said under her breath, "They're Amalia's friends."

Amalia. It took a second for that name to register. Right. Cohen's sister. Like Scout's sister. The same one where something was going to come out about and my cousins and I let the school gossip instead focus on me. Whatever they'd been worried would come out, hadn't, and I was not going to take a wild guess that it came out now.

"Got it."

"She's been keeping a super low profile, so I wouldn't be surprised if she's not here at school."

Also good to know.

We got to them, and none of them realized we were there. They were still transfixed to their phones.

The one who had shrieked was now fighting the screamer for her phone, saying, "That's not cool, Tal. Erase that. I mean it."

The screamer yanked her phone clear and stuck her face into her friend's. "Like this hasn't already been sent out. That loser released it. That's not on us."

"It is on you if you don't delete it, and it's even more on you if you sent it to someone else."

The other one who hadn't said a word saw us, but she only blinked. Her eyes flooded with more tears. She rushed off, her bag thumping against her arm.

"Hey!" Theresa snapped at the two.

They froze, saw us, and gulped. Both of them.

"What's on your phone?"

Their eyes darted, as one, to me, and both paled.

I was getting an even worse feeling and frowned, stepping forward. "Show it or I'll sic my cousins on you."

The screamer was getting hot in the cheeks and rolled her eyes, but she cursed at the same time she shoved her phone our way.

Theresa took it, showing us both.

It was a topless image of a girl. She was wearing jeans, but they were opened and pushed down.

This was what Scout had been worried about.

The good thing was that it didn't show the face, but we knew. These girls knew. That meant everyone would know because the one was right, this hadn't just been sent to her. It was sent to her email. He'd used the school email system.

"Holy—" Theresa started shaking. Her hand first. Her arm. Her chin. Her head.

Her torso.

Her legs.

She was vibrating. "Holy fuck. Fuck. Fuck! Fuck that piece of shi—"

That was the precursor.

"FUCK! FUCK! FUCK HIM. FUCK HIM TO HELL AND BACK! FUUUUUUUUUUUUUU—" She rounded, knowing that everyone was watching us. Anyone who had their own phones out had stopped what they were doing to now watch this new entertainment happening live and in person. She thrust the phone in the air and began walking. "IF ANYONE, AND I MEAN *ANYONE*, SHARES THIS IMAGE, YOU WILL HAVE ME TO ANSWER TO!"

"AND ME!" That came from Gem, who was farther down, Her face was beat red, her eyes blazing, and her chest moving so fast I wasn't sure she was breathing at the same time.

Theresa froze, looking at her cousin.

Everyone was focused on Gem, who was visibly panting, her arms full of papers, and after a second, she threw them all down. "AGHHHHHHHHHHH!"

I jumped back from the ferocity of that scream. It was bloodcurdling, and I only needed to count down the seconds before teachers would be rushing out into the hallway.

One.

As soon as Gem quieted, Theresa picked up the gavel, "YOU WILL DELETE THIS SHIT! NOWWWWWW! And if you have a thought of saving it, I will find people who can hack shit and they will expose you for keeping *UNDERAGE PORNOGRAPHIC IMAGES* ON YOUR PHONES, COMPUTERS, TABLETS, IN YOUR INBOX, I DO NOT CARE! THEY WILL FIND IT, AND I WILL TAKE YOU DOWN!" She gasped at the end, drawing in a breath.

Two teachers had come out. I forgot to keep counting.

No one was moving.

"NOW! DELETE IT *NOWWWWWW!*"

I scrambled for my own phone, going to my email and deleting it.

That was when I saw a text that had come through, a different text, one that had nothing to do with Amalia, one that I hadn't noticed.

My heart stopped.

40

SCOUT

I stopped after taking two steps because *fuck him*. I didn't know if I could stop myself from hurting my best friend. Not right now. Not after what he just said.

"You think I'm like that piece of shit? That I'd do what he did to her?"

Alex was still so still as he studied me, but I was too caught up in my anger to really care. I was already breathing red, my blood rushing through me. "That guy? That murdering piece of anal shit who should never have been born? That guy? You think I'm like that guy?"

Alex eased back, but his head was lifting.

"She told me what he did. She said I'm the first one she told besides her mom and the cops, that she didn't even get to tell you guys because you were told by someone else. She said it was the first time she brought it up, and I'm guessing she meant outside of a law enforcement setting, but fuck you, Alex. Fuck you if you think I'd do that to her." If Max Prestige were here, right now, in this situation, I would killed him.

I wouldn't blink.

I wouldn't have second thoughts.

I'd do it, so it'd be done, and then I'd do the one thing I made a vow early in my life to never do—I'd call my grandfather. And no one knew the *weight* of that promise.

"I'd fucking kill him, right here, if he was here. I'd do it in a heartbeat, and it wouldn't be for you. It wouldn't even be for her. It'd be because that piece of shit shouldn't have been born. Or hell, maybe we should go another step and take out the dad because it was semen that produced that piece of shit and raised him. They created him. It's their fault he's such a fuck-up that he killed her father and sent her pictures of it. You think I'm like that guy?"

Alex was all the way calm now.

That was starting to penetrate, just slightly. I was still envisioning killing her ex how he killed her father.

"That guy is going down. If you think I'm like that guy, then you and I aren't friends. We never were if that's the case. But I'll tell you this, that guy comes here, you don't need to worry about protecting her because I'm *going to end him*." He could take that however the fuck he wanted.

My phone was blowing up, and I realized I was almost breathing Alex's air.

I roared, ripping myself back, and that was when some clarity began to sink in.

"What the fuck?" Alex whispered, his phone out in his hand.

I knew. I fucking knew.

He lifted his head, his eyes stricken. "This is the shit you were talking about?"

I winced, seeing the image of someone who was like a sister to me on his screen. "Delete that."

His thumb moved in a flash. "Done." He was back to watching me, and I was seeing how we'd switched roles. Now he was wary around me. "Scout..."

"Fucking hell, Alex. I'm not going to hurt Ramsay, but I'm being honest. I can't stop fucking her. I just know that too."

He narrowed his eyes and held for a moment, as if thinking something through. Then he nodded and heaved a deep sigh. "I don't like it." He held up a hand, holding off anything I was about to say. "But I'm getting that you won't actively hurt her. I swear to God, though, the second feelings come into play, you end it. The very second. We cannot handle watching Ramsay get hurt again. I don't think you understand how on edge we all are. Me. Trenton. Clint's the worst. I don't even know what shit he's been doing lately, but I know he's doing something. I'm terrified. I almost lost my cousin. I can't lose my brother."

I frowned, but my phone was ringing.

That was Cohen's ring.

I couldn't wait any longer.

I was turning and answering at the same time, "I'm coming."

41

RAMSAY

Traitor 1: Thought you should know about this. (link)
I had clicked on the link, feeling my heart trying to beat itself out of my chest, no longer paying attention to the storm still happening in the hallway.

I Was Manipulated, announced the headline of the article.

A male presence had come to stand by us. His low baritone voice drowned over my head, speaking to the others.

I took a step away, my chest hurting, unable to believe I was reading what I was reading.

Oh, I couldn't. I *just* couldn't.

My ex.

My ex had written an article about how I'd manipulated him into beating me up and killing my father.

He was the victim. He was. *Him.*

I wanted to kill him. I wanted to *eviscerate* him.

I—no, no, no. I was sick to my stomach. My whole body began shaking.

No one was around me. I looked up, panicked, but people were going to their first periods.

I didn't know where Theresa or anyone else went.

The hallways were emptying.

Doors were closing.

It was just me.

I read the article, not able to stop myself.

My hand was jerking so hard. I almost dropped my phone.

I'd been stupid, so very, very stupid.

I thought this would go away. I thought *he'd* go away. Eventually.

It wasn't. He wasn't.

He was always going to do this.

None of this was ever going to go away. Ever.

I shot to my feet and sprinted for the bathroom.

Tore through the door.

To the first stall.

I fell to my knees.

I emptied everything and anything that was in me.

And once that was done, I was throwing up bile.

I couldn't stop dry-heaving.

42

RAMSAY

Shit went down today. When I left the bathroom, it was only because the last bell wrang and I had to force myself to stand. So I stood. I was washing my hands, had just wiped some vomit from the corner of my mouth when the bathroom door opened. In came whoever.

I didn't see faces.

I didn't think about names.

I wasn't checking my phone.

I was in zombie mode, going through the hallways.

To my locker.

Getting what I needed.

To class.

My cousins were there.

They were talking.

I said whatever I said, I didn't know. It was enough to appease them. I might've got some frowns. I might not have got some frowns.

I had no idea.

I'd think later that I didn't remember seeing Gem or Theresa later.

Kira stopped at my locker one time. She was saying something about Homecoming.

I nodded, said whatever to her, and she went away.

Then on I went to the next class . . . and the next . . . and the next.

Books dropped down on the table next to me in the cafeteria, and Scout dropped down right after. "Yo."

I exhaled a ragged breath, looking away. "Not today."

Wait.

I hadn't seen him all day, and this morning. Amalia.

"Are you okay?"

He raised an eyebrow. "What?"

"Amalia. The image. Are you okay? Is she okay?"

He snorted, eyeing me. "Surprised you care. According to Alex, you've been incommunicado all day."

I frowned. "Have you been gone all day?"

His eyes narrowed, his eyebrows pulling down. "I've been at the police station with Amalia and Cohen. I got brought back here because my uncle realized I actually *didn't* need to be there. Heard crazy shit happened here too."

Yes.

Also, I had no idea what the aftermath had been.

I frowned, more to myself. "Theresa and Gem went crazy about the picture, and then . . ." I didn't know.

Scout was waiting for me to finish, but at my silence, his head lowered. "Rice fucked up. He used the school email system to send that pic. Kira told me that he's been expelled. Pretty sure there's something illegal about what he did, which the school will bring charges against him for so their ass won't get held responsible. Bottom line, we don't need to worry about that dick being back. That's what." He leaned closer. "Have you *not* talked to your girls?"

God.

My girls. Gem and Theresa.

I was still in a haze.

We were in study hall now.

I spent lunch in the bathroom, asking for mouthwash from the nurse afterward. She'd been convinced I was trying to get drunk and stood guard while I used it.

After that—just class.

Zombie mode.

I needed to stay in that mode.

One more hour.

One more, and I could fall apart.

I was trying to stay in that mode. It was helping me get through the day.

"Hey. Williams."

Full zombie mode. I had to get back into it or I was going to lose it. Scout had a way of either pissing me off or making me come alive. I couldn't come alive—not right now, not here.

"Shut up."

But it was working.

I was waking up.

I couldn't wake up.

The detention teacher wasn't here.

I grabbed my books and left.

I concentrated so hard on not tripping over my own feet, that I didn't notice Scout on my tail at first. I opened my locker and stashed my books inside. He closed it and grabbed me by the waistband of my jeans. He dragged me behind him until we hit the parking lot. He let go after that, but he kept an eye on me.

I didn't fight him. I had nothing in me. I just went, grateful to be going *away*. Just away.

I didn't care where.

I just had to go.

We got to his truck.

I got in. He got in.

He was glancing my way, not saying anything.

That didn't last long until he growled, "You going to tell me what the fuck is wrong?"

"Where are we going?" I considered reminding him we weren't friends, but who was I kidding? At this moment, I needed someone.

"What's going on with you?"

My stomach rumbled. That was my answer.

He sighed, hitting the turn signal and taking a right. "Guess we're going to get food."

"I'm not hungry."

"I don't care."

"I am."

Okay. We were going to get food.

We went to Carby's, which I liked on a normal day. They had healthy stuff, but they also had the best greasy food too. We did the drive-thru, and the girl got really excited when she found out it was Scout ordering. When we pulled to the window, three more employees were there, all smiling at us.

A couple of businessmen were in the background, and I only knew they were businessmen because they were wearing suits. Also, they looked all authoritative. One looked way higher up on the wealth chain than the others.

Scout cursed, but ripped the bag from the employee, threw a twenty dollar bill at her, and drove off.

I made a note later to ask why that'd been so weird, but I didn't have the bandwidth in that moment.

Scout bought me a burger, which I didn't eat.

"Where are we going?"

"My place."

"Your place?"

He started on his burger. "You're weirder than normal, and I'm not sure what to do with you. Figured I could watch you better at my place. Are you going to eat your burger?"

"No." My stomach twisted, and I felt like I could hurl again. God.

I couldn't think about Max. I couldn't . . .

"We can chill at my house until I have to go to training."

Training. That made sense.

"Are you tired?" I asked.

Scout nodded, fighting a yawn as we reached his house. After parking in front of the garage, he motioned for me to follow him. We went inside, and he dropped his things on the counter, going into the kitchen. "You sure you don't want to eat anything?" He gave me a once-over, opening the fridge door. "I'm going to make a smoothie. You want one?"

"You just ate."

He shrugged.

I shook my head. "No, but do you have an extra toothbrush I could use? And toothpaste."

He pulled out a carton of almond milk, set it on the counter, and stared at me. "Why do you need to brush your teeth?"

"I threw up my lunch."

His eyebrows lowered. "Are you sick?"

"No."

"Why'd you throw up?"

I ignored that question and answered one he didn't ask, "I went to the nurse's office and used some mouthwash, but actual toothpaste would go a long way."

He studied me for a beat before giving in. "Okay. Yeah." He headed up the stairs to a bathroom on the second floor. I followed. He opened a closet, and there was a whole tote of toothbrushes there, all new and still in the wrapper. He pulled one out and grabbed a travel-size toothpaste. He gave me that too.

"Why do you have all of those?"

He smirked. "My uncle has a lot of one-night stands." He stepped back. "You need to shower?"

"What? I didn't get vomit all over me. I was more just dry-heaving into the toilet." I closed my eyes. Agh.

He shrugged, backing out of the bathroom. "Do whatever you need to do." He motioned to the right. "My room's in there if you need a change of clothes or something. Second drawer. I'm downstairs. You sure you don't want a smoothie?"

I frowned, my stomach rumbling, and I felt a little light-headed. Maybe something in my stomach would be okay? "Could you make me a coffee-flavored smoothie?"

"You serious?"

I shrugged. "You can put healthy stuff in there, but if it tastes like coffee, I'm more likely to drink it."

He rolled his eyes. "That's what's wrong with women these days. They'll eat or drink anything as long as it tastes like coffee. No respect for proper nutrition."

"Uh. Okay, *Dad*."

He made an exasperated sound before going back downstairs.

I shut the door, eyeing the shower because that had some appeal. Not because I needed one—I'd showered this morning.

I finished brushing my teeth, and when that was done, I didn't move.

Scout woke me up. I was back to feeling. I was back to remembering.

I didn't go downstairs. I didn't leave the bathroom.

I stared at myself in the mirror, my visions tunneling in and out.

I was back in Cedra Valley.

There was a layer of dirt and revulsion and *gross*. It settled over my body like another layer of skin. I felt it again. It seeped into my body, and I felt it taking my skin's place as if it were pushing out all the new freedom and good things I'd started to feel being here.

Cedra Valley and Max Prestige were back inside me, and I couldn't get them out.

That article. I had to fight back. I had to, and I hated that he was making me do that. If he'd just stopped . . .

If he'd just go away . . .

I felt the tears coming, but no. I would not cry over that piece of shit. Would not and could not.

The door swung open. Scout stood there, his phone in hand. "Is this why you threw up today?"

I could see the headline for the article that Max wrote.

"If I asked you to, would you go over there and beat the shit out of him?"

I was joking, wasn't I? I tore my gaze away and turned for the shower because I really, really needed to clean myself off for some reason.

"Yes."

I swung back to him. He was serious. His eyes were darkening. Anger.

He was angry *for* me. My mouth opened. My throat was dry. "Are you serious?"

"What he did to you, to *any* girl? Fuck yes, but now that he did *this*? He's legit asking for a beating. I will be shocked if I'm the first one to get to him."

I stared at him. Just stared and breathed, and that bathroom suddenly felt so small and sweltering. I wanted him to do it.

I wanted Max to hurt, just an iota of what he'd done to me. He took my father away from me.

He *deserved* to hurt.

I couldn't respond to Scout. If I did, I'd say something I couldn't take back, even though everything in me wanted one person to take up for me against him, to make Max hurt for me, one person to stand up because it was so hard, so tiring, to always be the only one.

But I had my mom, my cousins. They were all behind me.

That was right. I wasn't alone. I had family. I had new friends.

I was here. Max couldn't get to me here.

"Do my cousins know about that?" I nodded at his phone as I reached to turn on the shower.

His eyes darkened all over again, and he put his phone on the counter. "Kira sent it to me, so I'm guessing yes. She asked if you're missing some Homecoming thing because of this. She would've sent it to your cousins."

As if on cue, my phone lit up.

Scout was closest to it, and he looked down. "Clint calling."

"Turn it off."

He frowned at me, but he reached down and powered off my phone. "You didn't answer me. You want me to beat the shit out of your ex?"

My heart beat so hard in my chest, trying to tunnel its way out of me. "Of course I want you to do that."

His eyebrows lifted. "Yeah?"

"But that's what he wants. He wants me to send a guy after him. He wants a reaction from me. He wants anything to do with me."

"I could do it and not get in trouble."

I reached back, testing the water. It was almost scalding hot. Perfect.

I reached for my shirt, taking that off first. I did the rest, not looking at Scout as I stripped naked. It wasn't until I'd backed into the shower that I looked at him again.

He'd moved farther into the bathroom and was leaned against the counter, his arms folded over his chest. He watched me.

I tipped my head back, feeling the burn soak me from head to toe. "Can't do anything to him, and we both know it."

"Speak for yourself."

"You go after him, I guarantee he'll somehow use it to

further ruin my life and yours. I can't have you as collateral damage."

Not you too.

"Offer's there. I'd do it in a way that I wouldn't get caught."

If I were a cat, that'd be catnip to me. As it was, I tipped my head back and closed my eyes, let the scalding water boil down over me. I welcomed the heat. Hotter the better. I needed to feel pain, to feel something other than him. I needed him *out of* me. His family. Their power. Their reach.

I welcomed the burning.

I needed it.

After a moment, the water cooled, and I opened my eyes to find Scout in front of me.

He'd stripped and shut the door. When the water was a more normal temperature, he looked down at me, his eyes flaring.

Fine. I'd let myself get burned another way.

43

RAMSAY

I reached for him, but he was already bending down to me.

Our mouths met, and I felt the heat again, this time it was inside me. It was pushing out what had seeped into me, and I wrapped my arms around Scout as he picked me up. My legs wound around his waist.

"Condom?"

"Fuck." He groaned.

"I'm on the pill."

"I'm clean."

I knew I was too, and as I lifted my head, his eyes searched mine for permission. I reached down, touching his stomach enough to move back, adjust myself.

He moved his cock, putting it at my entrance, and I slid down. That was my response.

Jesus. That felt so good.

We both groaned from the contact. His forehead went to my shoulder, and then he began to move—or we began to move because I was going with him, moving my hips with his as he thrust up into me. Sex this good shouldn't be right, but it was—and thank God it was.

Sensations raced through me, deep carnal pleasure exploding, tickling the base of my spine until I climaxed.

I gasped, almost feeling tears at how *fucking* good that felt.

Scout kept going. He'd been holding back, but now, he wrapped his arms around me, curled his fingers over my shoulders, and he pulled me down as he pounded up into me.

I bent down, my teeth grazing his shoulder, and he roared, but he kept going.

He hadn't released yet, so I moved my mouth over his shoulder to his neck and nuzzled for his mouth. He groaned, cursing as his mouth found mine.

I opened up, wanting him to explore me that way.

The kiss was hot, almost desperate and crushing at the same time. I loved the feel of his tongue against mine, the soft rub there, so different from what he was doing to my body, and I felt the tingle at my spine again. I was going to come again, and I slipped a hand down to rub my clit. He moved my hand aside, using his hand instead, and I came a second time.

My whole body was limp, but I clung to him, riding out the waves, gasping because this was so *good*.

"Shit." He lifted his head, turning to the door.

We stopped just as the doorknob twisted.

Locked.

Thank goodness. Relief flowed through me, but someone was knocking.

"Scout?"

I didn't recognize the voice, a deep baritone.

Scout cursed before raising his voice, "Showering!"

"What are you doing home? Is this about Amalia?"

"No." He frowned at me, but called out, "Needed to get a start on training."

"So you're showering?"

"Uh . . ." Scout grunted, the sound strained. "I'm not alone, Uncle."

I tightened my legs around his waist, scowling at him.

He laughed under his breath. "What? He's going to know anyway."

There was silence for a moment on the other side of the door. "Jesus Christ, Scout. Hurry and finish, then take the girl home."

Scout snorted, burying his head back in my neck. Goose bumps broke out over my body.

We heard footsteps moving away. Then a faint rumble of . . . I was guessing the garage.

"He's going back to the gym."

I hit Scout's shoulder. "That was embarrassing."

"Got him to leave." He smirked, starting to move inside me again. "He wouldn't have left otherwise. My uncle has an enormous bullshit radar."

I groaned but held on to him, closing my eyes because, God, he was making me feel good all over again.

"Now, shut up and let me come, woman."

He did, and I did again.

He'd finally achieved the three-release promise.

***

HE MADE ME A COFFEE-FLAVORED SMOOTHIE.

As I came down from changing clothes—well, somewhat changing. I wore my jeans, underwear, and bra, but I'd put on one of his muscle tanks. It was gray and faded, and I liked how the black lettering was chipped. It was also a little baggy on me.

My hair was wet, and I'd put it up in a French braid. My face was scrubbed clean too. I felt very clean, or as clean as I could. Max had entered my life again today, and I didn't think I'd ever scrub that feeling out of me, so I was choosing to ignore it. At least for the day.

"Here." Scout motioned to the smoothie. "There's healthy shit in there, but ignore it. Only focus on the coffee flavor."

He was being sarcastic, but I smiled at him. "Thanks."

He snorted, bending to grab a bag. He put it on the counter and began rifling through it.

He'd changed too, now wearing gray gym shorts. The kind that were old, faded, and had holes in them. He looked delicious. He wore a muscle tank, but it was barely there. He was basically shirtless. I had a feeling that shirt would get ripped off at the gym because, what was the point?

"You wear those shirts?"

He shook his head, not looking at me. "I give two fucks about what I'm wearing when I work out. This was the first thing I grabbed." He looked up. "Why? Wrong fashion choice?"

I frowned, sipping my smoothie. "Why are you pissed at me?"

"Because I'm late for training, and I have to take you back to school, don't I?"

"I could go to the gym with you."

"You want to work out?"

"No. I'd tan."

He snorted, rolling his eyes. "You're not coming to the gym with me." He began heading for the garage, his bag in hand.

I took another sip of the smoothie and followed him.

He hit the button, and the garage door started to raise.

"Why not?"

He walked to his truck. "Because I don't want my uncle to know you're the girl I'm fucking." He got in.

I got in on my side. I took another sip. "Why not? The two of you seem very casual about your sex life."

He started the engine. "Because I know my uncle. I don't fuck girls at the house, so he'd want to know who you are, and knowing him, he'd probably reach out to your mom. And your mom is hot. My uncle would try to sleep with her."

I waved my hands. "I don't want to hear any more. Please, stop. No, no, no to your uncle and my mom." I had a flash of that tote filled with toothbrushes. "Especially if he has that many one-night stands."

Scout chuckled, backing out of the driveway.

"Just take me home," I told him. "I don't need anything from school."

44

RAMSAY

"**Y**ou're a dick."

I was in the kitchen, making spaghetti because, for once, my mom wasn't working, and I was happy. And I was leaning into that happiness because everything else, I'd deal with later. Mom and daughter night tonight, hell yes.

Clint had declared that, coming in from the back door. Trenton and Alex followed. All had scowls, but when my mom came out from the bathroom, the scowls disappeared.

"Hey, you guys. Are you coming over for dinner?" She greeted each with a kiss to their cheeks, one by one. They rotated around for her.

"Uh . . ." Clint gave me a meaningful look. "We are now."

I didn't respond, but reached out and grabbed another huge handful of noodles for the pot. We'd also need a second sauce jar. "I'll grab the sauce."

"No, no." My mom came over, patting me on the arm. "I'll grab it."

I noticed how she grabbed her phone on the way. She was probably calling my aunt to see what was up. The guys had come in with attitude.

Alex watched her go down the hallway. "She's in her room," he announced after a moment.

"She's calling Mom," Trenton added.

"Who cares." Clint hadn't stopped scowling at me. "Thanks to *Kira*, we know what's going on with our own cousin. What the fuck, Rams?"

"You're mad at me about the article he wrote?"

"We're mad we didn't hear it from you. Why didn't you tell us?"

I was aware of a peculiar look Alex was giving me, but one thing at a time here. Ducking my head, stirring the still-hard noodles, I shrugged. "It's—wait a minute." I remembered why I hadn't told them and whirled around, the spoon in hand. "A lot happened today." I shot Alex a peculiar look right back because Scout informed me of their come-to-Jesus moment. "I fully intended to air everything out with you, but then I came home and forgot my mom had tonight off. It's a mom/daughter night."

"Yeah. Well." Alex leaned forward, grabbing my spoon and nudging me out of the way. "We're not leaving."

I measured him with a look. "Do we need to talk?"

He growled but ignored me, still holding my spoon. "No. Scout and I had it out. I do not like it—"

"None of us fucking like it," Clint corrected.

Alex kept going as if his brother hadn't spoken, "But also aware you do your own shit. Trust and believe, though, that I made him promise that the second any emotions start acting up, he cuts it off." His face got all serious. "I mean that, Rams. We've each picked you up, and I will not let my best friend be another reason we're picking you up from the floor."

My throat swelled up, but I blinked, pushing past that and jerked my head up and down. "Got it."

"No emotions. And that's such a weird thing I've even—let's never talk about this again? How about that?"

I started to smile, then thought better about it. That might be pushing it. "Okay. No emotions. No more talking about me and him."

Alex shot me a warning look.

Now, it was my turn to get serious—or, more serious. "My mom doesn't know about the article. Don't tell her. Okay?" I pointed at each of my cousins. "Got it?"

Clint was still scowling. "She needs to know."

"I know, but not tonight. I want a night of normalcy. I need it. I'll talk, but not tonight. This is a safe zone here."

Alex was still stirring.

"Guys!"

Each one gave me a grudging nod.

I was relieved, then frowned at Alex. The water wasn't even close to boiling. "You don't have to actually stir—"

"Yes, he does!" Trenton and Clint said, giving me a look.

I closed my mouth.

"What?" Alex frowned at me, at his brothers.

Clint and Trenton were looking away, fighting laughter.

Alex pointed at them with the spoon. "You have to stir the whole time or you get limp noodles." His eyebrows lowered. "Right?"

I closed my mouth.

New understanding dawned over Alex, and his mouth fell open. "Those douchebags told me I had to constantly stir. Are you saying you don't?"

I wasn't touching that. "I mean, yeah—who wants to eat those noodles?"

Clint and Trenton started laughing.

"You guys are dickheads." Alex took the whole pot and was about to launch it.

"Hey! No!" I yelled. "I want spaghetti tonight."

He put it back. "How long do you actually need to stir? I was trying to be nice."

His brothers were still laughing.

I gave them a nasty look before putting the lid back on the pot. "To each their own, but generally, you wait for the water to boil and then put the noodles in. I maybe stir it once or twice, and I take the lid off once it's boiling."

He growled, "You guys are such dicks."

———

IT WAS AFTER FAMILY DINNER, which had been fun and awesome, and *light*, which was what I needed tonight. My mom stopped at the door to my room, sticking her head through the doorway. "I'm going to take the boys back. Will you be okay while I'm gone?"

I had come up to grab my laptop while the guys watched TV downstairs. "Uh. Yeah. Are you going to be long?"

"Hopefully not too long, but you know how it can be. Adult conversation."

I nodded. "Wine."

She grinned a little. "Maybe I'll indulge in one glass."

I sat at my desk. "I'll be good, Mom. Take your time."

"I'll try not to be too late. You want to do a midnight movie if I'm back?"

That was code for watching a movie in her bed and falling asleep. I loved those nights. I smiled. "I'd love that."

"Okay." She crossed the room, catching my face with her hands. She pressed a soft kiss to my forehead. "I love you, honey. Be back."

She headed down, and the guys yelled out their goodbyes a second later.

"Turn on your phone!" Clint added.

I groaned, but he was right. It started blowing up a few seconds later, and I waded through the texts and voice messages.

Gem had left one. Theresa too.

From Alred.

I skimmed through what my cousins had sent, seeing mostly what they'd said to me in person.

There was one from Kira.

Unknown number: This is Kira! I saw the article. Are you okay? Asking genuinely. Also, we're doing another Homecoming meeting at my house Friday before the game. Come with Gem. We'll all go to the game together and come back for a party. You are invited for the party. Obvy!

I didn't reply, knowing that invitation was riddled with problems and deciding to tackle it all tomorrow.

I was crawling into my mom's bed, determined to start watching the movie whether she was here or not, when my phone buzzed again.

Traitor 1: Just so you know, he's getting pushback on the article. You have people in your corner here.

I didn't want to think.

I didn't even know *what* to think.

So, I turned on the movie and snuggled in.

I was somewhere that I felt safe.

That was all that mattered to me.

45

SCOUT

M y phone rang as I turned down the road to my uncle's gym. Considering it was past midnight, and considering that had my uncle's ringtone, I was guessing he just got to the house. I answered, swinging in and seeing Alex standing at the back of Cohen's truck. Cohen was just getting out of the driver's side, and both jerked their chins up at me, but I pulled to the side and answered the call.

"Yeah?"

"I know you're not home so before I get into asking where you are, I got a call today. There's a guy out of Cedra Valley, asking to fight you. You wan—"

"Yes."

He got quiet. "You don't know when it is."

"I don't care. I need a fight."

"You just had two fights."

"You only tell me about fights if you think I should take them. I want to take this one. What are *you* doing? Do you think I shouldn't take it?"

"No. I—I just talked you into a fight so soon after another one and you pushed back on that. Now, nothing. You're suddenly all eager when you don't know who the guy is or when the fight is going to happen."

"I trust you."

He was silent again. "Why am I getting the feeling I don't fully know what's going on here?"

Right. He needed convincing. "Remember what went down today. I need something to focus on or I'm going to rip someone's head off that probably wouldn't help my career. You got me?"

"Okay." He didn't sound like he was accepting it. "Well, I can give you the details tomorrow. Where are you?"

I checked his own phone's tracker and smirked. "How do you know I'm not home again?"

"Because I have my ways. Where are you?"

I turned off the engine, but didn't move. "Doing the same thing you're doing." I was watching Cohen in the rearview mirror. He wasn't saying anything. Neither was Alex.

My uncle was quiet. "How's Cohen doing?"

"I don't know since I just arrived, and I'm talking to you. I've not gotten out to assess him. How's *your* best friend doing?" His best friend was the reason Cohen and I even knew each other. He was Cohen's uncle.

"How do you think? Been spending all afternoon talking with his sister about his niece's nude picture being spread on the internet."

I frowned. "It got that far?"

"Yeah. One kid, but he was tracked and we think we got it contained. Lucky break, though."

I heard how Garcia and Gem went crazy. That helped. "Yeah."

"Cohen told him that some of the girls went nuts in school? The principal called, wondering if they should be punished or praised. They had to ask the police about those legalities."

I grunted. "There were a few different parties that threw

down, made it known their lives would be not fun if they didn't delete that picture asap." I wasn't lying. Kira had thrown her hat into the ring too. Garcia had the fear factor, and after today, people were a little scared of Gem, since she came off unhinged, but most were scared about Garcia's threat of hackers. I was thinking the details hadn't been told to either the principal or Cohen and Amalia's uncle or that would've gotten to my uncle and then he'd be asking me about these said hackers. But again, Kira's power at the top helped too.

"I've got a feeling some of the weight that happened in your school might not have happened if you weren't there."

I frowned, knowing what he was trying to say. It was his way of thanking me for being me, a total dick and at the top. "Save your breath. I wasn't even there."

"You know what I'm saying."

Yeah. I sighed. I did. "It wasn't me this time, Miles. The girls saved the day this time."

He got quiet before sighing from his end. "I got the report. Amalia finally tapped out fifteen minutes ago. Angel called, asked if I'd head over. I swung by to grab a few things, saw you weren't there, and now I know where you are. You're at the gym?"

"Cohen likes the river."

"I remembered. If you use the gym, make sure everything is turned off and lock up before you leave. You got me?"

I took my keys out and opened the door. "Got you."

"Hey. I got a call today from your mother."

I closed the door again. "Yeah?"

"She said some execs were in town, said they saw you."

Shit. "I swung by for food."

"You shouldn't go there anymore."

"It's the popular place to eat. I don't go there, I'll look weird for not going."

"Just say you're cutting weight."

"They got salads there. Or I could do what I normally do when I'm cutting weight, I eat water." He didn't get it. "It's weird if I don't go."

"Look, all I'm saying is that if word got to your mom, then you know word got to your grandfather. He knows you're here."

"I wasn't hiding."

"We weren't broadcasting you were here either."

I shook my head. "If he wants to know where I am, you know he just needs to make a call. They have an entire division of private detectives. He knew I was here the second *your sister* booked my flight."

"Yeah. Well, I'm just bringing it up because there might be more drama coming from him. I want you to know."

I was done with this conversation, at least this portion of it. "Then get ready, Uncle, because all the bullshit he pulled trying to make you live the life *he* chose is what he's going to do for me. This will be just round two."

He grunted. "I know, but enough about that. Go take care of your best friend."

"You do the same."

I headed to where Cohen and Alex were still waiting.

"Hey."

Cohen met me, hand up, and we did our half-hand shake. Alex gave me a nod, both of us sharing a look because it hadn't been that long ago when we were having a whole different type of exchange.

"You got it?"

I motioned to the gym. "I'll get it." I glanced Alex's way. "You brought your shit?"

He rolled his eyes, but reached into the back of Cohen's truck and hauled out a whole box. The clank of bottles inside told me he followed through. "I don't know where the fuck Clint and Ramsay got this, but yes. A whole shit ton of booze."

Cohen was eyeing it, hungrily, angrily, but he was holding off.

I held up my keys. "One second. I'll get the bag."

After jogging to the building, I let myself in, turned off the security system, and opened one of the giant garage doors. Then I started rolling out one of the mobile punching bags. I nabbed some tape, though knowing they both probably had their own gloves.

Which was the case as I rolled it all the way over to them.

Cohen was gloved up, warming up his arms.

Alex was standing back, a beer in hand, and watching Cohen warily.

This was what we did if one of us needed the other.

I'd done this more with Cohen than Alex, but we'd been there for Alex a couple times last year. Course, now those nights took on a different feel because at the time he said he needed a night to get drunk and hurt something, said it had something to do with his cousin. We hadn't asked details because we weren't those guys. If the other one wanted to talk about it, he'd talk about it, and we'd listen. But this, we showed up.

We drank together and we hurt something.

My uncle found out about our tradition. How, I had no idea, but the next morning after the first night, he told me I needed to clean off the bag and lock up. I had locked up, but I hadn't cleaned the bag off.

I'd make sure to do that this time.

I set it up and stood back.

Cohen was on the bag in the next instant, and Alex was holding out a beer for me.

I took it, moving farther back.

I didn't say anything.

We watched Cohen swing on the bag through one beer.

Another beer.

I took a break.

Alex kept drinking.

He broke the silence as he was reaching for a fourth. "It's messed up."

I braced myself, knowing he needed this night too.

Alex started his fourth. "I want to hurt him."

Cohen stopped, breathing hard. "Rice?"

"Huh?" Alex tipped his head back, taking a long drag.

"You want to hurt Rice?"

"Fuck no. I want to hurt Prestige."

Cohen frowned. "Who the fuck is Prestige?"

Alex stepped forward. "How the fuck do you not know?"

I stepped between them, hands in the air. "You both got your heads in your own situations. He's talking about the guy who hurt his cousin."

Cohen kept frowning. "I want to beat the shit out of Rice."

Alex burped. "Me too."

"What? You just said—"

"He's on his fourth beer," I said to Cohen.

"Oh." He wiped one of his gloved hands over his face, rolling his shoulders back. "Sorry. I got my own shit going on. My little sister."

"I know. I'm just saying."

I nodded at the bag behind him. "Want to let Alex have a go? Thinking he needs it now."

Cohen considered it and shrugged, stepping back, taking off his gloves.

"Hell yeah!" Alex handed off his beer, rushing the bag, and he was going at it without his gloves.

Cohen watched him before shaking his head and handing me Alex's beer. "I need to cool off. One minute."

He rushed past me, hitting the dock, and a second later, we heard the splash as he jumped into the river. Or I heard because Alex had jumped up on the bag, trying to pummel it from the top.

Cohen joined me a little later, taking Alex's beer back and sniffing it. "Did he drink this?"

"He started to."

"Oh." He set it down, grabbed a new one, and eyed Alex. "What the fuck is he doing?"

I shrugged. "I think he's trying a spidermonkey version of fighting."

Cohen narrowed his eyes. "Looks like the bag is winning."

It was. Alex was barely hanging on to the bag, but he was still swinging with one hand. His ass was going to touch the ground soon. When it did, and Alex let go of the bag, laid back, and began kicking at it from below.

"He's not even touching the bag."

"Nope." The bag began swinging from Alex's first kick, and he was kicking up with both of his legs in an upward bicycling motion, the bag was swinging over him and he was missing every time. He wasn't making any contact. "Pretty sure he's drunk."

"Ahhhhh!" Alex jumped up and launched himself once more, crawling to the top, where he began hitting the top with one hand. We both settled back, knowing we were about to see a repeat.

Cohen grunted. "Clint and Trenton are way better fighters."

"They're also better drinkers."

"I can hear you, you fuckfaces."

Cohen and I both grinned.

This was what we did for the next two hours.

When Cohen needed to fight, he took the bag.

When Alex needed it, it was his turn.

They offered it to me, but I shook my head. It was my night off, except to chaperone these two, which was what they needed because between the two, they drank almost every bottle that'd been in that box.

There was drunk talk. Drunk cursing. Drunk promises were made, but this night was just about being around each other. We showed up for each other.

After I drove both home, I pulled my phone out.

Scout: Your mom working?

Ramsay: No. It's a mom night.

Ramsay: How's Amalia?

Scout: She'll be okay.

Ramsay: Good.

46

RAMSAY

T hings settled over the next few days.

And the rumor mill had stopped talking about me, the article, and Amalia. I had a feeling that everyone was too terrified to gossip about anything because of Theresa's threat of hackers.

Clint was back on a tear for his own form of vengeance, and he declared it at my locker a few days later.

"I want to go back."

I shut my locker, saying, "No."

He glared at me. "You owe me."

I snorted. "I don't because I'm saving your life right now."

"I want to go back."

He was talking about going to the fraternity house and stealing more alcohol because, in Clint's mind, of course they wouldn't be thinking someone would try to steal their stash again. Oh no. They'd have the same setup. They wouldn't remember us, and we'd be able to waltz right in, crack open the door, lay a conveyor belt and happily and peacefully ship off every piece of alcohol once again.

I was saving his life. "You're not going."

He opened his mouth.

I said over him, "And if you do, I will tell your brothers what you're going to do."

His mouth closed. "You're not being cool. It's about revenge. Vengeance. Come on. He has to pay."

"Max is not going to pay by you stealing booze from his future brother frat house. Trust me." I leaned in. "You're the one who's going to pay, and it'll be worse because you'll be another person he's taken away from me. Do you want to live with that blood on your hands?"

He was glowering now. "Totally not cool, and you're over-dramatizing."

"Hmmm. Nope. Not even a little bit. We're not going back."

Gem arrived, literally running in and taking a leap to land in between us. "Where are we not going?"

I shot Clint a look. "You're not going back. I'm aware that in your head you heard Gem said 'we' and somehow you're playing on her words. You're thinking that since I'm not going, so Gem's 'we' doesn't count so you're now thinking 'I'm going' as in you are going without me, *and you're not going.*"

He frowned.

I flushed. "I do not care if that makes no sense. I just know how you think, and I also know that made total sense to you. You cannot word play your way out of this one."

Gem was skirting between us, her eyebrows up.

Clint growled before taking off.

"You're not going to tell me what that's about, are you?" Gem motioned where Clint went. "Right? It's like a family thing?"

I was shaking my head as Kira and Ciara came over to us.

"Hey, peeps." Kira was all smiles.

Ciara was beaming next to her.

Both had color-coordinated their outfits. Kira was in pastel pink, top and skirt. Ciara was in pastel blue. I had a feeling Leanne would be in pastel green? Yellow? One of those.

Gem was gaping at them. "You guys look like Easter."

Kira fought back a smile. "It's on purpose because ta-da! We picked our Homecoming theme. Candyland!"

Ciara added, "But sexy."

"Yes, so you guys know first so you have first dibs at getting your dresses. We're announcing next week so go this weekend."

Homecoming.

I was on the planning committee. That meant I had to go.

I hadn't planned that far ahead, of me going or not going, but crap. My cousins would be expected to be there. They'd have dates. They'd be doing their own thing. I was overthinking all of this.

Gem would want to go.

"That"—Gem was barely breathing—"is awesome! I know we voted last year, but I didn't know what we picked."

Both girls' smiles faded. They shared a look.

"Well, the winner was a write-in where people didn't want a theme, but we have to do a theme so this was the one we picked." Kira got all serious. "Don't tell anyone that, but the theme's been picked and"—she focused on me—"totally understandable why you skipped our last meeting, but don't skip this Friday. To keep it secret until next week, we're meeting at my house before the football game—"

"I have to work," Gem blurted out. Her eyes were huge. Her mouth turned down. She looked horrified. "Omg. I have to work. I have to miss it. I'm so sorry. My uncle specifically asked for me to help with Mario's, but I'll be done by nine. Can we do the planning then?"

Kira's eye twitched. "You want us to postpone our planning until nine o'clock on a Friday night, after the football game, for you?"

Even I winced at her tone. It was almost scathing.

"Theresa can fill in for her."

Both snapped their gazes my way. I refused to flinch, saying, "I know you don't get along, but it'll be one meeting. She'll be taking her cousin's place. Get along for one time? I think you can both do that. Right?"

Ciara sucked in her breath.

Kira's eyes narrowed. "Keep her in line, and we'll be fine." She cast those eyes on Gem next. "You can only miss a few times before you're kicked off the Homecoming committee."

Gem visibly swallowed. "Yes. Okay. I won't miss again. I promise."

Kira and Ciara took off, and Gem whirled to me. "It's family! I can't let down my family, and they'll be disappointed in me if I can't help out because I told them I would. What am I going to do? I can't not be on the Homecoming committee. And we totally have to go dress shopping this weekend. Alred will go with us. He lives for this sort of thing."

I wasn't sure what she meant, but I took her shoulders in my hands and leaned down. "It'll be okay. It's not cool that Kira's picking the planning times based on her schedule. Friday? Really? But just mention it to your uncle and aunt and see if they can work with you over the next month or so. It's only until Homecoming."

She was blinking, her eyes going back to normal size and her cheeks looked less haggard. "Right. You're right. It's only until Homecoming, and you're also right. My uncle and tía will totally work with me. They'll be understanding." A different thought came to her, and she began shaking her head, walking away.

I frowned. "What?"

She kept shaking her head and went faster. "No way am I going to be there when you tell Theresa she's my fill-in. You're on your own with that one."

"Wha—"

But she was gone as the first bell rang, and . . . crap.
I hadn't thought that out either.

47

RAMSAY

heresa only *said* she wanted to murder me, but she agreed to being Gem's replacement. She had a weird look in her eyes when she said that, so I wasn't sure what to prepare myself for, but it was happening.

The plan was to go to Kira's for the meeting, then head to my place before the game. Which is what we did, and the whole meeting had been more of an excuse to hang out.

Kira and her group stayed on one end of her living room. Theresa and I were on the other side. In between were a bunch of other people, and they were all excited now that the theme had been picked. They brainstormed about different decorations, and where each decoration should be for the dance, the parade, and the procession. People were picked to handle voting for Homecoming King and Queen and all the rest.

After a couple hours, we headed out.

"You can stay and get ready here? Go with us." Kira's offer was being extended to me, not Theresa. That was obvious from the nasty look she was giving Theresa, who rolled her eyes and harrumphed. "I'll wait for you outside."

"We're good. I need to get something from my house."

She nodded, her gaze lingering on the door. "My parents are gone this weekend, and I'm taking advantage. We're pre-partying until the game. You're welcome to come back and join, or join us after the game? We're all coming back here. Your cousins usually come over." Before I could ask, she made an exasperated sound. "And yes, Gem is obviously invited. She's on the planning committee, and I'm aware where she goes, her cousin goes. As long as you're around, Garcia can come, but you're responsible for her. Anything bad that happens, you have to handle it."

I opened my mouth, not sure how to respond, but then I figured it was a win. I'd take them when I got them. "Thanks."

She gave me a grudging nod, still giving her door a hard look before I left.

Some of the other girls not in Kira's main group were also leaving. They gave us a ride to get food and then to my place. We'd just gotten dropped off when my phone buzzed.

Scout: What are you doing this afternoon?

Then, right after, it buzzed again.

Clint: PARTY! WHERE ARE YOU?

Me: Theresa and I are pre-partying at my house. We just got here.

Clint: Where were you?

Me: Kira's for Homecoming stuff.

Clint: Your mom's working?

Me: When is she not?

Clint: True, true. We're at Marky's house. Want us to swing by and pick you up?

Me: Sure.

I must've made a sound because Theresa asked, "What?"

I typed as I replied, "Clint has already started drinking. He's with some of his baseball friends."

Theresa grinned. "Clint is funny when he's drunk. Also, he's funny to watch with you. You have your own language."

I paused mid-type. "We do?"

She nodded. "Oh yeah. It drives Kira nuts."

"How would she know?"

"Everyone knows. The first day you showed up, you were *big* news. You have no idea how big."

My phone buzzed again, but I let us inside before putting my quesadilla on the counter and reading it.

Clint: We'll pick you up in an hour. PJ is driving.

Me: DON'T FORGET

Clint: NEVER!

"We've got an hour. They're going to pick us up."

"So..."

I looked up.

Theresa looked concerned as she set her food next to mine. "We're, like, actually going to the game with your cousin and then the party afterward?" I'd filled her in on the way over.

"Yeah. Is that okay? We'll get home. I promise. Clint or Alex or Trenton will make sure we're good."

She reached for her phone and began typing. "Could we crash here tonight then? Me and Gem?"

"That'd be fun actually. I'll let my mom know, but she won't care."

"Speaking of your mom, wine?"

I laughed and went to find it. I gave both of us a full glass. Then, I sat down and began unwrapping my quesadilla.

"God. I love you." Theresa took a sip of the wine first.

My phone buzzed again.

Scout: Answer?

Oh, shit.

We'd not talked since our shower, which was fine with me. Even in study hall, we'd stayed away from each other. It felt right. I mean, there was always the pull for him, but that mixed with the push away when he began talking and I'd been emotionally exhausted from everything. It'd been easier to stay

away, but now, he was texting and seeking me out, and I was
remembering how nice it felt with him.

I'd started texting him back when there was a knock at the
door.

"Yo . . ." Scout just walked in, but he trailed off, seeing
Theresa at my counter.

I grimaced, holding up my phone. "I was just texting you
back."

He hit the door closed behind him. "Garcia."

"Hi." She looked between us.

He walked past us to the fridge and opened it.

She looked my way, her eyebrows going up.

I ignored her. "*Sure*. Make yourself at home."

He ignored me, pulling out a water. He stood on the other
side of the counter, pulled my food over to him, and took a bite
of my quesadilla.

"Hey!"

He watched me while he ate the food. He reached for
more.

I batted away his hand. "Stop. That's my food."

He shrugged me away, pulling my food more firmly in front
of him, getting comfortable. "Garcia. What's up with you and
Kunz?"

I was distracted now and wanted to know, too, but, gah. My
stomach was growling. Slipping off my stool, I got another plate
and put half of my food on it. I slid that in front of Scout before
taking the rest away .

He transitioned to eating that instead.

"I . . ." Theresa shook her head. "Right. Uh, nothing. We're
on a break right now. Had a fight. The usual."

I didn't know what the usual meant, and was just going
to ask.

"Until he wants to fuck and gives you a call?" Scout
narrowed his eyes.

Theresa choked on a sip of wine. Pressing a hand to her mouth, she wiped it clean. "I . . . how's that your business?"

His eyes slid my way. "You chose him over her. She's my best friend's cousin. I'm making it my business."

She choked out a sound, her head folding in. "I—we're off, and with all due respect, fuck off about it. I've apologized to Ramsay about that. And again, Kunz and I are *done*. He's an asshole."

"But you like screwing him."

Her mouth flattened. "Fuck. Off."

He kept eating, kept watching her with the same impartial expression. Then his eyes slid my way. "Your cousins are only half badass since you came to school."

"What?" I reared back. "You're starting on me now?"

He stopped eating, now fully focused on me. "Rice is gone. We don't need to worry about him anymore, but what about your ex? What if he comes here? How are your cousins going to handle that?"

"We'll be lucky if they don't kill him," I said back frostily. "They're not half badass since I've come to school. You're trying to piss me off."

His eyes narrowed.

What was he doing?

He said, "You interfered once. That messed them up."

I glared at him. "No. What messed them up was you threatening me. You did that. Not me. Don't put that shit on me."

His eyes twinkled, but the rest of his face was a blank wall. "Your cousins have gone soft since you showed up." He was doubling down.

"Jesus Christ, Scout." I was fully aware of Theresa watching this exchange with avid interest.

"You know they haven't. Why are you saying this?"

He kept watching me, his face still blank. "I took a fight against a guy from Cedra Valley."

All the oxygen left my body.

I couldn't respond, not right away. I felt punched sideways. I was seeing stars, feeling stars. "Why would you do that?" I asked quietly.

"You know why."

I felt the room swimming around me.

"Apparently, he's a big deal there. Has a lot of friends." He waited another beat, watching me. "I made sure that the fight was here. Make him come to me."

Him. I knew Max wasn't the fighter he was talking about, but we were both referring to Max. "I don't want him here. This is my place," I said, forgetting Theresa was in the room. If there was a fight happening anywhere near me, Max would be there. He loved the local fights. He loved pretending he had a say in who won.

He would salivate over coming to a fight here.

Scout leaned down. "So, we'll do the fight not here, but close. I want home advantage. We can do it at the place you were at last week."

That would be fine. I nodded. "Just not here. Not in Pine River."

He studied me again. "Okay. If something else goes down, are you going to interfere again?"

That was why he was asking all of that?

I started to shake my head, but then more understanding dawned.

In his way, his fucked-up way, he was asking if I wanted my cousins involved.

"No. They can't be a part of that."

His eyes flared. He knew I was telling him to do whatever he was going to do away from my cousins.

I had friends who never said a word back in Cedra Valley. I came here for my family, but here was Scout. He was willing to do this for me? I knew he said it before, but it didn't make sense to me. Why would he get involved?

"Why?"

"He doesn't deserve to walk around. I'm going to do something about it."

"Scout."

He kept watching me, and his eyes were blazing. I knew he wanted to touch me. He wanted to lift me up on the counter and sink deep inside. I recognized the look, felt it inside me. My body was heating, and if I'd been on the other side of the counter with him, I would've stepped toward him.

"His family is powerful."

"Even better," he said, shaking his head. "This is the shit I know how to do."

He remembered we had an audience before I did, his eyes sliding to Theresa. He straightened up from the counter. "Where's your booze? I can drink tonight. I got one more night. I want to booze it up." He picked up his plate, taking it with him as he went searching for my mom's liquor cabinet.

I reached for my wine and drank half of it in one gulp as I rounded the counter. I was going to need something stronger.

Max was coming here. He'd hear about the fight, and he'd come.

I felt sick to my stomach.

"Don't let that piece of shit make you feel like that." Scout returned, a bottle of vodka in hand. He put it on the counter.

I blinked back tears because fuck Max. "Stop, Scout."

"*You* stop. Get mad, Ramsay. What that piece of shit—"

"*I know what he did!*" I had to take a breath. God. My chest heaved. "I know what he did. I loved my dad, and I'm the reason—"

He leaned down, getting in my face. "No, you're not. You're not the reason for any of this. Did you give him the gun he used? He beat the shit out of *you*. Your cousins showed me the pictures."

"Stop." I shook my head.

"He broke you. You—"

"*Stop!*" I shoved him back, and I kept shoving him because that felt good. To shove him. To shove someone. "Stop it! You don't know anything."

"I know there's a time to heal, and there's a time to fight back. You're at the point where you have to fight so that you can get *back* to healing. You shut down. That article—"

"Stop, Scout!"

He didn't understand.

I grabbed the vodka and took it upstairs.

I WAS IN A MOOD, so I opted for faux-leather pants, black, and a simple gray T-shirt. Normally it wouldn't work, but I made this one work. The shirt was torn down the front, almost halfway. I was going for sexy messy. It was a little over the top for a football game, but I didn't care. People could wonder where we were going afterwards.

"Hey." Theresa pushed open the door, coming in to sit on my bed. "I gotta say, my head is spinning from whatever is going on between you and Scout Raiden." She looked up at me. "*And holy shit*, you look *hot*."

I groaned, finishing my makeup at my desk. I liked to do it here instead of the bathroom. I had a better setup, but I'd go in there to finish my hair.

I shook my head. "He's such an ass."

"Yeah, but he's an ass that cares, and girl, I'm telling you I have *never* seen Scout talk like that to anyone. I didn't know he had that in him. He's always shut down. That was eye-opening. He's let you in. That's not something to dismiss. Kira would be eating her underwear in a fit of jealousy if she'd glimpsed even ten seconds of that conversation down there."

"He makes me so mad."

"Well, he shouldn't. That was hot. Him. *Hot*. You should fuck him."

I pressed my lips together.

She groaned, lying on my bed. "Man! You don't understand. That guy—he's not let anyone see into him. How he was down there? Just now? That was worth *all* the crushes the girls in school have on him. So totally worth it."

"I'm kinda more interested in you and Kunz." I eyed her over the makeup mirror.

She paused and then cursed. "Kunz and I are done. For the last time. If I get lonely, I'll find someone to scratch that itch."

"I'm sorry."

She sat up, shrugging, but she couldn't mask the sadness in her face. "I kinda want to drink a shit ton of wine, go to a football game, and then party it out of me tonight. You game?"

I smiled. "Totally game."

Scout was gone when we went downstairs, so I quickly finished eating and filled two thermoses. One with wine for Theresa and something stronger for mine. After that, a car swung in, and I met PJ for the first time.

We were off to the football game.

48

RAMSAY

Clint's eyes almost bulged out of his head when he saw me. "You're wearing that? That?" He looked down at his outfit, which was a Pine River sweatshirt and jeans.

But he was a guy. He could wear almost anything, and it had no bearing on his social status.

"I think you look great." PJ's tongue was almost out of his mouth.

Clint rounded on him. "My cousin, dude. Like my sister. Like my best friend."

PJ didn't care. His smile only widened. "How do you do, cousin/sister/best friend of Clint?"

I snorted, laughing.

"Not cool, PJ. Not cool."

"She's cool enough for me." He kept looking me over.

"Uh. Hey, guys." Theresa waved. "Since we're in the football parking lot, maybe we should go to the game?"

Clint shook his head.

PJ nodded, his smile still stretching wide.

Marky was with him, a big hulking guy, but he'd taken off as soon as we arrived.

Clint groaned. "This is going to suck. What's with your mood? Someone or something has you all worked up."

Theresa glanced my way, but she didn't say anything.

I started forward. "Nothing's with my mood. Maybe I just got tired of trying to blend in for once." Maybe that *was* it? No. I knew who'd gotten to me. Scout and every freaking word he said to me.

I took our thermoses and gave them to PJ. "Here. We're going to go in first. Meet us behind the concessions, and pass those to us." I motioned to the line of trees, where security wouldn't catch us.

He looked at them, frowning. "Why can't I go in with you?"

"Because that's alcohol."

Clint just groaned. "You're going to ruin my night. No booze. Nothing fun. I'm going to be on Ramsay-babysitting duty all night. I can just see it."

"You owe me for last week."

He snorted, but he trudged behind us as PJ took off, veering through the cars to around the back section. And he wasn't being inconspicuous at all, walking with a super-straight back, and moving his feet like he was wearing a jetpack. The whole looking around every three seconds didn't help things either. I could see why Clint took me last week and not PJ.

"He should never consider a career as a criminal."

Clint laughed, moving up to walk next to me. He gave me a grin, and I grinned back. Our cousin fight was already over.

Theresa just laughed. "PJ is hilarious." He was now crouched behind a neon blue car, though no one was looking at him. Then he scurried to the next car and repeated the same action. He continued this way on down the row.

"Clint!" Kira waved from closer to the ticket counter. Ciara and Leanne were with her. The other hulking friend was there, Marky, along with some other guys. More baseball friends.

Kira's eyebrows were up. "See you changed."

"Yep." Clint nodded. "They're party bound too tonight."

Kira just gave me a confused look.

I shrugged, not sure what to say.

Theresa noted, "PJ's probably been arrested by now."

Kira's mouth curved down. "What?"

"Nothing." I hurried off, and yes, I was aware of the looks.

I'd been in a mood when I dressed, but the mood was waning, and I was on the verge of regretting what I'd chosen to wear tonight. But, ugh. Oh well. *Own it.* I wore it. I'd own it.

Theresa bumped me. "You look amazing, and everyone knows it," she whispered. "Don't you dare start feeling self-conscious about it, Queen Ramsay. Wear the crown."

A knot had started forming in my stomach, but at her words, it eased. "Thank you."

She grinned. "For what it's worth, I'm glad Gem wouldn't shut up about you."

"Same."

"Oh God. PJ."

"PJ!"

We paid for our tickets, and I gestured to Clint where we were going. He gave me a thumbs-up. PJ was lounging against the fence when we got there. He straightened. "Finally. I gotta take a piss now."

"Nice," Theresa said.

It was a chain-link fence. The holes were big enough to pass the thermoses. I reached over and made sure the tops were on tight before pulling them through. "Thank you."

He'd gone back to looking at my legs. "Thank your pants. Damn, I wish you weren't Clint's cousin."

Theresa gave me a knowing smirk. "Scout hasn't seen you in them yet."

My stomach tightened. "Girl."

She burst out laughing. "I'm kidding. You ready to tackle the bleachers?"

I nodded, sipping some of my vodka.

We moved back to where everyone was sitting. I felt the attention as soon as we started up the stairs of the student section. Kira and her friends were smack dab in the front row, but Clint was farther up. He waved, indicating there was space by him. I nudged Theresa and jerked my chin up. "Clint's up there."

Theresa headed on up, but I lingered, and *then* I felt him.

Scout was coming in from the far end of the bleachers. His eyes were right on me, darkening as he drew closer.

I couldn't move, not at first. I swallowed over a lump in my throat before heading where Theresa had gone.

He followed me.

"What's up, man?" PJ had his hand out for Scout, who was behind me.

PJ moved around me to greet Scout.

Theresa shifted so I was between Clint and her, and we clinked thermoses, taking another drink.

"I want some." Clint reached for my thermos.

I let him have it.

"Yo, man. Up here," someone called. A couple of the guys moved over so Scout ended up right behind me.

Oh boy. I was going to feel him the entire game. His attention. His presence. His heat. Him, him, all him, and yeah, the throbbing had full speed ahead.

"Hey, man." Clint turned, greeting Scout.

"That what I think it is?"

"Yeah." Clint grinned. "It's hers."

"Can I have some?"

Clint handed it over. "You're drinking tonight?"

"Taking a night. Then back to training tomorrow. I took a fight—"

"Stop!" I twisted around, locking eyes with Scout.

Clint frowned.

"I mean, nothing." I turned back around. Then cursed because Scout had my vodka. I twisted back and took it from him. "This is mine. No sharing."

I felt a hand on the back of my shirt, pulling me backward. A tattooed arm came around me and took the thermos back out of my hand. Scout took a long drink before putting it back into my hands and letting my shirt go.

My body felt like an inferno.

I caught Theresa shaking her head, and when I looked over, she mouthed, *So hot.*

This was going to be a long-ass football game.

49

RAMSAY

I was not getting drunk. I didn't even have a good buzz. Scout and Clint had consumed most of my alcohol. I tried sipping from Theresa's, but she caught on and drank most of it before I could force her to share with me.

So, she was buzzing at least.

However, I *was* buzzing from having Scout continuously grab my shirt and pull me back so he could get to my vodka. It took me halfway through the game to realize he was also looking down my shirt, and then during the second half of the game, he managed to rub his finger on the inside of my shirt.

I looked around, but somehow, only a couple of people were watching us. The guys on both sides of him were standing forward, blocking his movements. It took me only a little longer to realize they were doing that on purpose. And by that time, I didn't want to slap his hand away.

Clint just kept shaking his head. At one point, he leaned over to me. "The second *any* feelings start, you're done. Remember that shit."

Shit. I gulped. "I will."

He looked back and gave Scout the middle finger.

Scout just tugged my shirt, working his entire hand under to press against my back.

I shuddered.

Theresa kept trying to sip more of her drink, the drink she'd finished before halftime.

The buzzer finally sounded, signaling the end of the game.

"I have to piss." Clint jumped around me, rushing off.

Theresa turned my way, biting her lip. "You gotta go too?" I asked.

She nodded.

I waved. "Go. I'll catch up."

She thrust her empty thermos at me, so I was now carrying two. I stayed in the stands because most everyone around me was talking to each other. Kira and her friends had moved down to the sidelines and were standing front and center.

Scout moved down to stand next to me. "You're going to Kira's?"

I glanced up. "Don't touch me right now."

He gave me a dark, wolfish grin, his eyes smoldering. "Because you want me to or you don't want me to?"

"Both." I made a point of looking straight ahead.

"Let me give you a ride to Kira's. Theresa can go with your cousin."

"Like that wouldn't be obvious."

"Your cousins know."

"Theresa doesn't."

"She suspects, and who cares?"

"I do."

"You lie well. So lie." He smiled. "Well."

"You're such an ass."

"That's why what we're doing works. You don't want to like me as a friend. I can be an ass to you. You like it."

I was burning, just having him solely focused on me. And

damn him because he was making sense. "You're still an asshole."

"And you can be a bitch."

I shrugged. "Truth."

"Let me give you a ride. You don't even have to make something up. Garcia *knows*. She won't say anything."

"I'm not going to do that to her. I'm not that kind of friend. Stop asking. You know what kind of guy that's making you." I shot him a look because he'd just been on Theresa about doing the same thing to me that he wanted me to do to her. Ditch her for a guy.

He eased back. "I had to ask because, if I hadn't, you'd be thinking, *Why didn't he ask?*"

I rolled my eyes, though, there was some truth in that too.

The crowd started to thin, so we began moving down toward the restrooms. I moved ahead, and Scout lingered, responding to people who said hello to him. When we got to the area where the restrooms and concessions were, Kira and her friends were standing in a group.

"Ramsay!" she called. Her smile got bigger when she saw Scout. "Hey, Scout. You and Cohen doing anything tonight?"

Scout glanced at me. "Heard something about a party?"

She blinked a few times before straightening. "Yeah. I mean, yeah! At my house." Her eyes slid my way. "Who do I thank for your presence? It'll be twice this year. It's a record."

He stared at her, an impenetrable wall. He didn't comment.

She blinked a few more times. "Okay then. Tell Cohen I said hey."

He moved out, and his hand grazed the back of mine as he went past.

A couple of guys fell in step with him, but Scout wasn't like them. It was obvious. They were talking around him, and at him, and he barely gave them the time of day.

It wasn't just in the way he had built his body or that he was taller than them. It wasn't even in his tattoos. Though, he wore a T-shirt tonight and I fully appreciated all the tats on him now. He had a full sleeve on one arm in full display for everyone.

But it was more.

It was in the way he walked. It was in the way he just was, the air around him, how he said nothing but that spoke volumes, how he barely did a thing and everyone was aware of him. It was in how he held himself, as if he had decades of experience on the guys around him.

The guys around were a little jumpy, cocky, and excited.

They were normal. Scout was different.

And though he and I were surrounded by so many others as we began heading to the parking lot, Scout glanced back at me and I was zapped. It was like we were the only ones walking in that moment.

I was in such trouble.

50

RAMSAY

Everyone knew the instant the football players arrived at Kira's party. A whole wave of greetings rose up in the house. I was in the kitchen, waiting with Clint. Theresa ended up knowing a group of people so she was with them outside, and Gem had disappeared into the basement. Turns out, she's a gamer. And really good at it.

Scout had headed out after the game. I was assuming he was doing the same thing as us somewhere, waiting on Cohen.

But since the team lost, we'd been waiting for Trenton and Alex.

Alex came in first, holding his fist up and bumping it with a bunch of guys on his way to where we were in the kitchen. "Hey, hey." He nodded to a few more people, then came around and gave me a hug. "Hey."

He lifted his chin up toward Clint. "Hey."

"Yo."

I stepped back, frowning. "How are you?"

He grimaced. "I want to drink. Who's driving tonight?"

"Uh . . ."

He took my drink and downed half of it in one gulp.

"Not you, apparently."

He frowned, taking another drag from my drink. "What?"

"Nothing." I started making myself a second drink.

"Hi, Alex." Kira came over.

"Kira. Nice party."

"Only the best for the best." She posed, lifting her head and fluttering her eyelashes.

He grinned at her. "Cool."

"Kira! Kira!"

"I'm being called away. I'll talk to you guys later?" She gave a wave before heading off, passing Trenton. She touched his shoulder, giving him a smile.

He gave her a smile back but then focused on me, on my drink. "Nice."

"If you touch my drink, I will scream bloody murder." I'd just finished pouring it.

He pulled back his hands. "Uh, is there beer?"

"Try the fridge." Alex nodded behind him.

"Oh." Trenton opened it and found two entire drawers of beer. He snagged two, opening both and closing the door. "Score."

"Double-fisting?" I asked.

He shrugged. "It was a rough game."

Alex let out a deep sigh. "I want to get fucked up tonight."

I held up my drink. "I propose a game."

They held their drinks up to mine, all ears.

"Every time a girl comes up to you and flutters their eyes at you, we drink."

They both laughed. "We'll be drunk in five minutes," Alex noted.

"They don't flutter them that much . . ." Their looks said otherwise. "Do they?"

They shared another laugh.

Oh, boy.

Alex turned serious, frowning at me. "I need to say something to you."

My heart sank. "What?"

"I'm out of here," Trenton said under his breath.

I grabbed his shirt, holding him in place. "You're staying."

"You're fucking my best friend," Alex said.

I started to pull Trenton so he was blocking me from Alex.

Trenton shook his head. "No way. I'm not getting in the middle of this talk. Also, here's my say. I don't like it, but if I don't see it, I'm going to pretend it's not happening. With that, I'm out of here. Love you, Rams, but I need a female touch tonight that's not related to me by blood." He pointed at my hand, still holding his shirt.

I let go.

He left.

I focused on Alex, who watched me with a not-happy look on his face. His mouth was in a flat line.

"You're pissed?"

"I'm not happy, so go from there."

"Did Scout explain how it was messing with our heads?"

He nodded stiffly. "He did. I'm like Trenton. I don't like it. Scout and I had words, and I mean where we almost came to blows. My best friend. After you, my two brothers, I love that guy. But I got eyes. I saw how he's tormented by shit too, and I saw his reaction to something that says more than even he knows."

I straightened. "Like what?"

"That's not for me to say. I'm just repeating what we already said earlier. The second, the very instant feelings start, you two are dunzo. You hear me? Otherwise, it'll get messy, and I don't want to lose my best friend." His eyes flared. "Because you know it's family. It's always family. You, my brothers, I'll always choose you guys over anyone else. But having said all that, I've watched you two. You don't seem like you're falling for him, and

I get that he can say things to you we can't. Maybe that's something you need?"

That was kinda the truth. "He got in my face today about not talking about the article."

"He did?"

I nodded. "He yelled at me, said I let Max break me this week."

Alex got quiet.

"He might've been a little right."

Alex nodded. "He has that tendency sometimes—that, and wanting to rip someone's head off."

"I've seen that side."

He got a whole new weird look over his face before he shuddered, and wiped his expression clean. "I'm not going to ask about that." He gave me back my own emptied glass. "Make me another drink."

"I—"

"You're banging my best friend."

I closed my mouth. "Another drink coming right up."

Once I was done with the bartending, he pulled me to his chest, giving me a hug. "Love you, cousin. Nice having you here."

I squeezed him tight. "Love you too."

"Now." He turned me around, his arm around my shoulders. "Forget the eye fluttering game. Clint's probably making out with someone already, let's cockblock him. He'll explode on one of us, and when he does, we both empty our drinks."

"Who wins in that situation?"

"The one he doesn't explode on."

I considered it. "Let's do it."

THE PARTY WAS WINDING DOWN. It was past one in the morning.

Most had gone by now. Gem and Theresa took off an hour ago, catching a ride with some of Theresa's friends. It'd been fun to go around, playing pool with my cousins, hearing Gem laugh with the gamers, seeing Theresa happy in her corner with her friends, and being able to enjoy this old feeling again. Socializing. Hanging out. Not being scared when someone was going to say something to target you, ridicule you, and when you'd have to 'fight' albeit that be emotional, mental, verbal, or the worst of the worst, physically.

I was heading inside when I saw Gabby, Amalia's friend who spread my business from back in Cedra Valley here. She was in the kitchen, grabbing food, when I'd just come in from the patio outside.

Our gazes met.

She froze, and I felt a kick in my gut, remembering a promise I made her that I was the kind of enemy that would wait, watch for the perfect timing, and *then* pounce for my revenge.

She was alone. I caught the look in her eyes.

I wasn't.

I had friends all around me. Kira was actively trying to befriend me.

My cousins were here.

She was on the bottom of the social ladder, and I wasn't. We were both aware of how our positions had changed, and I knew that I could hurt her, right then and there.

I was walking through the patio door. She was unprotected in that very instance. She knew that much, and in the time it took me to close the door, I considered it.

I wouldn't let it get out of hand. I was salivating over it, let her feel a tenth of what I felt when she put it on her social media about me, about Max, about my ex who took my father away, about how I felt feeling him violating me here, in Pine

River, where it was supposed to be my sanctuary, but the truth was that I could never outrun my past.

Would *never* be able to.

He'd always catch up to me.

What he did to me, who he took from me, and I'd have to live with that. I'd have to deal with it, but in that split second, I wanted to put some of that pain on her.

But what I did instead was close the door, let her meet my gaze, hold it, and I raised my chin up. I asked, "How does it feel?"

She swallowed, turning to me, her hands holding a plate of food in front of her. Her chin wobbled and her hands shook as she held onto that plate. "How does what feel?"

"To be vulnerable?" I moved forward a step, knowing it was perfect timing.

How a predator feels when they had their prey cornered.

I was feeling that way now. It was liberating. Addictive.

It also wasn't right, and I knew that, but I was holding off from dropping this moment.

Just a little.

I wanted her to get a window into what she gave me.

She swallowed again, dropping the plate to the counter because she couldn't hold it steady anymore.

Yes. She was feeling it.

Good.

"I don't know what you're talking about." She was lying. Her voice was unsteady too.

One more step. I wanted to draw this out, just one more second.

I raised my chin higher. "This. Right now. What you're feeling. You're scared."

She reached behind her, holding onto the counter.

We were both feeling the undercurrents. The vibe you get

when you turn down an alley and your gut tells you no, it's not safe. She was feeling it. So was I.

I was the one bringing it to the surface. "You know that I could humiliate you. I could say something in just the right tone, in just the right way, and others would come in. They wouldn't even know why they're coming, but they'd join me. They'd taunt you in a way that they'd laugh later, saying you couldn't take a joke. But they would know, deep down, just like you would, like I would, that this would be done to hurt you, to cut you deep inside, and they'd do that with me." I had to end this.

But I liked feeling this way . . .

I wanted to keep going. I wanted to do what I was saying.

I just wanted to hurt her.

Then I felt the prick on the back of my neck.

Him. Scout. It was the same feeling I always got when he was near, and I looked up, seeing him just coming in from the front entryway. Cohen was with him and almost walked right into Scout when he stopped short.

His nostrils flared, as if he could sense what was going on between Gabby and me. He asked, his voice low, cautious, "What are you doing?"

My gut came alive. Anger filled it, and I switched targets. "What do you care?" I shot at him.

His eyes narrowed.

"Whoa." Cohen took a step to the side, toward Gabby.

Now the undercurrents were there, between Scout and me, flowing back and forth. And these grew charged, a dangerous vibe adding to them.

Gabby drew in a breath.

I said to Scout, "This is none of your business."

His gaze went to Gabby for a split second before coming back to me and staying on me. He was dismissing her. She wasn't important. I was, and he raised his head up a fraction of an inch. "She's friends with Amalia. Watch whatever you're doing."

My gut was really flaring alive.

The charge that was going between us was sparking something else inside me, something I wasn't sure what it was, what I was feeling, but I'd never felt this before. I felt alive, in a way that was foreign to me. Something dark. Something powerful.

Exhilarating.

Like now that he was here, I'd found my *real* challenge.

Gabby wasn't a worthy adversary.

Scout was.

Scout was stepping up to the plate, one that I was hungering for that I hadn't realized until now, until I unlocked some of my darkness. Because I was so goddamn sick of being the one that got hurt. I wanted to hurt someone else, if only one time.

"She's not a friend."

I heard Gabby mutter, "Excuse me?"

And Cohen hissed, "Don't. You really want to tangle with her right now?"

"I'm just saying."

"She looks ready to murder you. He's gifting this for you, taking her on." Cohen made some disgruntled sound before saying, "Let's go."

He hurried her out, going back out of the kitchen through the front door.

There were others in the living room.

They'd been in there the whole time, at first chattering in the background when I came in and was talking to Gabby, but the second Scout showed, they went silent.

They were all watching, listening.

The patio door opened behind me, and I could feel more people coming in.

"What's going on in here?" That was Kira, coming to stand to the side, somewhat between us.

"Shit. Fight. Hell yeah." A guy said that, hopping up on the kitchen counter. He was sat back, feet swinging. The crunch of a chip bag was crinkled next. Someone was eating them.

People were getting snacks.

"Why are you protecting her?" I ignored them, my stomach still churning.

I needed to get back to whatever I was feeling before.

"Because, what the fuck were you going to do? Punch down, *metaphorically* speaking?"

I came alive again. "Metaphorically? That's a big word."

"You want to fight?" He took a step closer. Now looking down at me. "Is that what you want?" His eyes grew mocking, still so cold. "Take me on, Ramsay. I can handle your shit. You tired of hurting? Want to spread some of that pain around so you don't hurt so much?"

He got closer.

His head bent, almost breathing on me.

His eyes were so cold, like a snake waiting to strike. "Like you're the only person hurting around here? Like no one else has baggage? Trauma? Is that what you think? You get a free card to hurt someone 'less' than you because you got more than your fair share of something shitty that happened to you?"

I was loving this.

I wanted more.

I taunted right back, my eyes almost in slits, "Less than? That's how you think of her?"

"She is, and you know it. She can't handle you."

"That shows how wrong you are because that girl can end someone's world just by typing some words on her phone screen and clicking share. You think she has less power than me? You're wrong if you don't see how powerful she can be, all because she can hide behind her phone, her computer, using others to do her bidding, sharing the bullshit gossip she wants to spread because she knows it's going to hurt someone. And what's worse? She didn't know me when she clicked post. You want to come at me because I was having one conversation, *one*, in person, face to face, where I was pointing out how it felt with the situation reversed. That's all you interrupted. I hadn't said shit to her."

"That wasn't the vibe I was getting. I was getting the vibe you were about to tear into her carotid."

I wished I had. He took that away from me. "You were getting how I wanted to, but I hadn't said shit." I took a step back from him. "You jumped to conclusions and came to her defense, not waiting to see what I was actually saying. It's nice to know that's how you think of me. As someone who'd so easily bully someone else."

"Like you weren't going to," he shot back at me.

Fuck this.

I surged back at him, my head back, my teeth showing. "Because I wanted to! I *wanted* to. That was it! She was vulnerable. She felt it. I felt it. I was pointing it out. That was it." I reached up, intending to shove at him, but he moved.

He caught my hands.

An electrical charge seared through us.

My eyes latched to his.

He felt it too. He was affected too.

Then Trenton growled behind me, "What *the fuck* is going on here?"

51

SCOUT

S hit.

    Trenton's eyes were feral, trained on my hands on Ramsay.

"Trent—"

He launched himself, ripping through two guys in front of him and shoving me back. "Get your hands off her!"

"Trenton." Ramsay tried to get between us.

It was useless. He was too gone.

He was either just that drunk or on something. Either way, he wasn't rational, and I needed to handle this before it got out of hand.

"Trenton!" Ramsay was yelling.

He had shoved me against the kitchen island, his hands on my shirt. I was holding him in place. So far.

I looked over his head at Ramsay, and she was scared. I saw the agony she'd been enduring when I first came into the kitchen, but it was swimming under the surface. She'd let something out, something ugly, something that my gut told me was going to end with her hurting someone.

Trenton reared back.

He was going to punch me.

I twisted, an arm locking around his, keeping him immobile and I slammed him to the side, my foot wedging in between his. I was using my body to hold him in place. The fucker could bite me, but I didn't think Trenton was that kind of fighter.

I snarled over my shoulder at Ramsay, "He's not thinking clearly."

Her eyes flashed. "Obviously."

Jesus. I'm in the middle of a physical fight, and she's sparking back at me, and I was liking it.

I had some sick obsession with her. It's the only thing that made sense to me.

Trenton was struggling, and it was working. He was getting an arm free. When he did, well, the fight would be on.

"I need Alex or Cohen."

Her eyes flared again. She raked a hand through her hair. "Trust me, you do not want Alex right now."

Trenton growled, and another surge of energy reared through him. He got his arm free.

I shoved back, yelling at the same time, "Get Cohen then!"

A stampede of feet was coming.

People were shoving. Shouting.

Trenton took me in, those eyes clouded over with rage. His head was down, looking like a bull about to charge.

"Trent!"

That was Clint.

I shifted gears, preparing to take on two of the triplets.

"You got it wrong, Trent—"

He growled, "It's Trenton! You don't get my nickname. You had hands on her."

"What?" came low, primal, and furious from Clint, now stepping into the cleared space.

Moving as one person, both triplets stepped toward me. Circling me.

I backed up, moves flashing through my head how to dismantle one so I could take on the other.

"He had hands on Ramsay," Trenton said to Clint.

Wrong thing to say. Clint joined him in not thinking clearly. The need to hurt was genetic.

I hit up against a counter and tried reasoning. "I'm not that guy." They wanted to hurt someone who had hurt Ramsay. I got it. I did, but this was dangerous. "It wasn't like that."

"Yeah?" Clint taunted. "How was it then? I can't think of any scenario where you should have hands on my cousin when she doesn't want them." He frowned suddenly, his head slightly turning to his brother. "They were fighting, right?"

"Oh yeah."

Clint focused back on me, and there was the trouble maker. He thrived on it. I saw it then, had heard about it, but it was clear as day to me now. Ramsay had that same look on her face when I came into the kitchen.

She needed it like it was a release for her.

"Guys—"

A shout was heard from behind me, the door was shoved open, and I recognized Cohen rushing in. "What the fuck, guys?" He stopped right next to me, and I pushed off from the cupboard. I'd been planning on using the cupboard if it was two against one, but with Cohen wading in, different moves needed to be handled. I'd taught him how to use takedown moves so he could twist, get one of the triplets in a move, hold them until I got the other handled.

I didn't want to hit them, but they were putting me in a situation where I'd have to. "Guys, it's really not what you think it was."

"I tried to shove him." Ramsay was back, and she waded in, standing between her cousins and Cohen and me. Her chest was rising up and down rapidly. The back of her shirt was wet, down her spine. The darkness was gone from her, whatever that'd been, and she was scared. "Don't do this. You got it wrong."

Clint's head reared back, his chin tipping up, and he took in a breath as if he were a wolf lifting his nose about to howl. When he lowered his head, his eyes were more clear. He was listening to her. Adjusting.

Some of her tension softened, just a little.

I moved to the side so I could see better.

She was waiting, eyes on Clint, who gave her a slight nod, and more tension left her.

She held up a hand, palm out toward Trenton, and she approached, her voice coming out softly. "He and I were having a verbal exchange. He said something that made me mad, and I moved to put hands on him. It was wrong. He caught me to defend himself. That's what you saw. I swear."

His eyes were still feral, and he wanted to swing on me. So bad.

He was thinking about it.

I readied myself. Clint wouldn't jump in. I could handle Trenton in one move. He'd take a little nap, and then we'd deal with the fallout when he woke up.

"Trenton!" Ramsay snapped, standing at her fullest height. "I was in the wrong. Not him."

He growled, "Those words don't hold much weight, not after your last guy."

Clint's face snapped to his brother.

Ramsay's entire body flinched.

I saw red. "You fuck—"

52

RAMSAY

S cout moved so fast.
He was by the cupboard one second, and he had an arm wrapped around Trenton and was lowering him to the floor the next. I screamed. Then screamed again because there was sudden movement behind me.

Thud.

"Fuck," Clint rasped, grunting.

I turned. He and Cohen were locked in a battle.

Clint was trying to get to Trenton. Cohen was trying to hold him back.

They adjusted, but Cohen went down to the floor, his legs wrapped around Clint's waist.

Then another *thud*.

Trenton was unconscious and Scout was stepping back from him, keeping a wary eye on me and Clint.

"You—" Clint let loose a savage roar, reaching down, punching Cohen so his legs let loose. It worked. Cohen fell to the ground, and Clint started for Scout, who jumped up on the counter and used his feet to block him.

Clint threw a right punch. Scout blocked it with his feet.

His left.

Scout caught it with his left foot, using his right to push back on Clint's hip. "Stop, Clint. I put him to sleep. That's all I did. A normal body lock takedown. He would've kept pushing it, and you know that." Clint knocked one of Scout's feet aside, punching at his thigh, and he made contact.

Scout winced, but then he was off the counter, and he had a hold on Clint in the next instant.

Déjà vu from a moment again. Different cousin, same hold.

I couldn't handle it. "Stop! Stop it!" In the background, I was aware of a door being ripped open, then slammed shut, and more feet running our way.

"What the—" Alex.

Alex was coming.

My chest broke free from the chunk of ice that'd frozen it in place.

"MOVE!"

Someone moved.

"What is going on?" Another beat and, "Let go of my brother!"

Cohen jumped up and got in front of Alex, who was yanking his shirt up and over his head. "It didn't need to get to this."

Alex shoved him away, going to my side, but stopped abruptly. "Trenton?"

Scout and Clint were still in a standing wrestling battle. Scout was trying to contain Clint, and Clint was trying to get free so he could hurt him. It was consisting of a lot of fast arm movements, too fast for me to see all of it. They were moving in a blur, and at one point, Scout had his legs wrapped around Clint again, but Alex started for him.

"Shit!" Scout ripped himself away, hitting Clint back with one sudden kick to his chest as he flipped his body over the kitchen island, landing on the other side. "Stop! Fuck."

"You put hands on my brother?" Alex was saying, advancing from the left.

Clint was going to the right. "He had hands on Ramsay."

Alex froze. "*What?*"

It was the wrong thing to say.

No one else was wading in.

Cohen was standing on the side. "Scout?"

He was waiting for him to tell him what to do, but Scout was focused on two of my cousins again. And Trenton? I looked and found that he was waking up, blinking rapidly.

This was going to get out of hand, already was out of hand.

"STOP!" I had to end this.

My head was swimming. The violence. The anger. The thirst for blood.

The fear.

Chilled sweat was trickling down my spine.

None of this was right. None of this was good.

I choked out, "Stop it."

Clint started for me. "Ramsay."

I shot up a hand. "Stop. Just stop. It's all a misunderstanding." They were listening *now*. "I was in the wrong. I was going to say something that I shouldn't have. Scout came in and jumped to the wrong conclusion. Or maybe the right one, I don't know, but he and I were exchanging words. That was it. That was all. I swear. I tried to put hands on him. I was wrong. Me! This is all my fault. Trenton came in, saw the wrong thing and—"

"I didn't care." Trenton was now standing, rubbing at his neck, wincing. He was rational again. His eyes were clear, though clouded in pain. "I knew I shouldn't swing on him, but I did. I *wanted* to." He raised his chin toward Scout. "Sorry, man. Misplaced anger. It's that real fuck I want to—" He stopped himself right as Clint hissed at him, and both swung their gazes to me.

"I'm sorry. I'm so sorry."

How did I fix this? It felt like it was beyond repair.

They'd swung on each other.

Cohen cleared his throat. "We can handle this—but not here and not with an audience."

"Not tonight." Alex was looking around too.

Clint was nodding. "Ramsay, we'll take you home."

I glanced in Scout's direction, words I'd like to say were on the tip of my tongue, but seeing the frostiness in his gaze, they died in my throat.

I was hoping to believe Cohen, but not with Scout and me.

What we had was well and truly done.

53

SCOUT

I heard the beep just after I dropped Cohen off, and knowing nothing good was sent this late at night, I checked my phone.

Ramsay: I know it's not much right now, but I'm sorry for everything that happened tonight.

I frowned.

Me: It's not your fault.

Ramsay: Feels like it.

Me: It was a mix of misunderstandings and pissed off guys who care about you and not being able to do what we're supposed to do. The real guy they want to hurt wasn't here. I was. Not on you.

She didn't reply, but I didn't think she would. I just laid down some deep shit, so I checked my inbox while I was waiting.

Rothchelton University: We are looking forward to—I cursed, clicking on the email.

Congratulations! We are excited to meet you for your admissions interview. We'll be arriving at Portland and will conduct the meeting at the Chelton Hotel at . . .

I stopped reading, checking the date and time.

They were coming to meet me on Monday.

My grandfather did this. This was his Ivy League school.

Shit.

He was doing it, actually doing it. My uncle was right. My showing up at Carby's, his execs seeing me, knowing me, recognizing me had all gotten back to him. I'd been hiding, but now, in the twisted and morphed way he thought, he'd think this was me being disrespectful. I let others know where I was, and he'd been informed about me. It happened without him declaring it should be because he wanted to control everything. I only should've been seen if he had given me permission and that hadn't happened.

He did this as retribution. I'd be expected to show, and if I didn't, he'd use it as a further excuse to do more, trying to rein me in.

I hated him. *Hated* him.

My phone beeped. Ramsay had texted, but I didn't read it.

I swung around, heading for her place.

54

RAMSAY

My phone buzzed when I was in bed, trying to sleep.

Scout: I'm outside. Can I come up?

I rolled over, going to my window. I lifted up my curtain and saw his truck parked on the road.

What in the world?

Me: Back door.

I went to meet him, unlocking the door. He came in, and immediately, I could tell something was off with him. He was usually guarded, but this was different. He had snarly energy, a restlessness to him. Edgy.

He looked to where my mom's room was, but I touched his arm, shaking my head.

The door was locked, and we headed up to my room. He waited until we were inside before asking, "Is your mom here?"

"She just texted. A girl is coming in early for her so she might be rolling in soon. What are you doing here?"

His eyes were on my mouth, darkening.

I didn't need to ask that question again.

"Scout," I started.

"I don't want to talk." His voice was as rough as his energy.

Gruff. "I came here because I need *not* to talk, not to do anything except feel good. We've done that in the past." He started for me. "Can we do it again?"

My eyes held his the whole time, until he was right in front of me. Barely an inch separating us.

His energy was blanketing me. Taking me over.

I felt on edge.

I felt restless.

I needed to touch him.

I was taking on his needs, but they were mine now, and I nodded, reaching for him. "Yeah."

His mouth was on mine. Hot. Hungry.

He tasted good.

I wrapped my arms around him, feeling him picking me up.

We went to my door, and I felt him reaching behind me. I heard the click of the lock, the lights went out, and he walked us to my bed.

He lowered me, his mouth never leaving mine.

I could kiss him forever. I realized that as I stretched out under him, savoring this connection.

His tongue slid inside, tasting me back, and he took his time, which was a dichotomy from his earlier almost frenzied air about him.

"Scout." I groaned as his mouth left mine, sliding down my throat.

His hands slid around my back, lifting me up so I was tipped more fully against him. We paused, holding in that position, relishing the almost hug before he let me back down. His hand moved to my stomach, resting there before sliding inside my shorts and going under my thong.

He feathered kisses down my throat at the same time he circled me.

I held still, my eyes closed, loving how that felt. So good. So nice.

He slid inside, his thumb moving to my clit at the same time, and he began working me. Sliding in and out. Rubbing. Circling. Pressing. At the same time he was tasting me, moving down to my chest, nuzzling aside my shirt until he could taste one of my breasts.

I reached up, grasping the back of his head as I was buckling under his hand below.

Sensations were building, rising in me. Pleasure was coating my insides.

I didn't know why this guy. Why he had the ability to make me feel like this, but he did. I could become addicted to this, just this, how he could make me soar inside.

I was going to come. I wasn't ready. I gasped, trying to push him back. "Scout, no—"

His finger slid back inside, going deep, and holding. He lifted his head up. "You okay?"

I was panting, my chest lifting up and down. "It's too soon. I want to—"

His finger twitched. I went over the edge, gasping, my back lifting so my chest pressed against him.

I exploded and cursed, riding out the waves.

When I came down, he was grinning at me, but his eyes had darkened again and were back to being focused on my mouth. "That's one."

My eyes widened, not getting his meaning, until he was gone.

My shirt was off.

His shirt was next.

My shorts were yanked away, tossed to the floor, and he had his jeans off before he came back down. This time, he nudged aside my legs and his mouth found me.

Oh.

Oh.

That was what he meant. He was working on number two already.

Oh, dear God.

I reached down and held on to the back of his head.

I was coming apart not long after that, and then he was up and sliding into me.

The third time wasn't the last one.

He slowed, taking his time with the first two climaxes, as if he needed to give that to me, but when he was inside me. Whatever had been bothering him, whatever had brought him to me, took over. His thrusts grew frenzied, almost desperate, as if he were chasing something away and he needed to get lost in me to do that.

His hands gripped my hips, and he angled me higher for him. He slipped out, sitting up until he was somewhat kneeling between my legs, and then he was at my entrance again. He slid in, rearing back and going again.

And again.

He was pounding into me.

I groaned as I pressed my palms to my headboard.

He lifted me up, going hard and fast and rough, but still going.

Sensation after sensation was hitting me, making me almost blind from what he was doing to me, how he was bringing me to the edge, right there, and I was just about to climax, when he'd pull back, hold off. He'd wait, over and over again, sliding in, bringing me to the same point, and holding.

I was ready to scream for release, but I watched him. He wasn't looking at me.

This was all him. It was as if he were punishing himself, not letting himself release, until finally, a savage roar erupted from the back of his throat, and gripping my hips again, he slammed into me.

I jolted upright, sitting from the explosion that tore through me, but it was good.

Too good.

He caught me before I began to slump back down, and held on to me, half-hugging me. He was riding out his own climax, his body shaking before he pulled out, letting both of us fall back down to the bed. He curled in behind me. "Shit. Sorry about that."

I laughed, my body weak in the most glorious way from what we'd just done. "For what? That was . . . that was another level."

He laughed shortly, brushing a kiss to the back of my shoulder before he started to sit up.

"Hey." I covered his hand on my arm with his. "Stay."

A shadow crossed over his face. "I don't know."

I settled more into my covers, reaching for a blanket and hauled it over us both.

He wasn't getting up, but he wasn't relaxing either.

I yawned, knowing even my toes were relaxed after what we just did. "Do you want to talk now?"

He tensed, his arms tightening before his hand dropped to my stomach. My other one stayed on his so it moved with him. "About what?"

"I thought this was over. You and me." I flipped around so I could see him better. We were face to face until he shifted so he was a little on his back, but his hand stayed on my stomach, his thumb beginning to rub back and forth in a small circle. "After earlier."

"Oh." He frowned, that shadow still in place. "No. I mean, I meant what I texted. That's not on you."

"Will you be okay with my cousins?"

"Yeah. We're guys. The only thing that could get between us is you, and well, they already know about this. Think some wrestling moves and punches will be nothing."

I frowned. He really meant that, saying it so casually. "I was worried."

He shrugged into the bed. "Don't be, not about that."

"Okay." I wanted to ask what brought him here, what made him look like that, as if he had the weight of the world on his shoulders. This was unlike him, where he was showing me he was a human. Not a machine. Not just cold and locked down, only coming alive when he was inside me. This was a whole different Scout, and I didn't want him to go. When he'd go, the coldness would come back.

He'd return to locking me out unless he was in my space, getting in my business.

I liked getting this glimpse.

I laughed at that realization.

"What?"

I shook my head. "It's nothing. Just . . . sometimes it's like you're a robot, always guarded. Showing no emotion." He didn't reply so I moved my head to see him. He wasn't looking at me, looking off into the room. So screw it. I asked, "Why'd you come tonight?"

His face tightened. The old mask was going to fall in place.

I said before it could, "To me. Why'd you come to me? Why'd you need to feel good tonight?"

He stilled before his eyes found mine.

He hadn't totally locked down. I was still getting a little window to him, a small one.

I said quietly, "You know all of my bad shit. You put yourself in all of my bad shit."

He tensed before some of his rigidness softened. "My family's wealthy."

Now I stilled. "What?"

"Really wealthy. Carby's, we own that."

Wait. What? "The local one—"

He shook his head, not looking at me. "Not the local one. The whole thing."

Oh.

He was talking about . . . I pushed myself up, staring down at him. "The global franchise? The whole thing?"

His eyes had gone back to being stark as they met mine. "The whole thing. My grandfather started it."

My mouth was hanging open. I was trying to close it. Trying, but failing. "Whoa."

He snorted. "When I say that my grandfather is a narcissist dictator asshole, that's being kind."

I lowered back down, still stunned. "Your grandfather owns Carby's." The way the staff acted with him the other day, the executives in the back, how he reacted, getting us out of there as fast as possible. It was making sense.

Some of it.

"Wait. Who knows this about you?"

"No one. Well, one of those suits works for my family. The local staff never knew, but how they looked at me, I'm sure Richard said something about me being here. I can't go there anymore."

I twisted to face him, laying on my side. His hand moved to my hip and began tracing circles there. I asked, "No one else knows?"

He shook his head. "My uncle, but that's a whole other story."

"Cohen?"

He shook his head again. "I know Cohen and Amalia because my uncle and their uncle were in the military together. They're best friends—or, more like brothers. I'd come out to visit my uncle every summer when he left and settled here. I feel like I've known them all my life, but no. They don't know this about me."

"But how? Your last name—"

"I have my dad's last name, who I don't have a relationship with, and I don't want to get into that either. You're lucky with the family you have. Your cousins. Your aunt and uncle. Your mom. You guys love each other and you don't make plays to try to ruin the other person's life in order to make them heed and do what you want. That's the shit that happens with my family. Saying they're powerful, privileged, and cutthroat wolves is an insult to wolves." He went back to looking at the room, which felt smaller suddenly. "I got a notice that my grandfather wants me to do something, and I'm not going to do it."

"What will happen?"

He let out a long sigh. "Nothing good."

I could see the weight crushing him, and I wanted to push it away. I wanted to help keep it away. "Hey."

He looked my way.

I took his hand, rolled to my back, and pulled him with me.

He settled over me, his eyes falling to my mouth.

I reached up for him, sliding my hand up his chest, opening my legs so he could fit better between them, and as he did, as we both felt his cock come in contact with me, we both groaned.

I tipped my mouth up, whispering, "Let's feel good again."

He groaned, answering me and he was thrusting inside of me soon after.

As he was moving in me, I knew this night had changed things.

55

RAMSAY

I woke the next morning entangled in Scout's limbs—me in my tank and underwear and him in his boxers. His chest was pressed against my back, and one of his arms hugged my waist.

I registered that first.

Then I registered that it was fully sunny outside.

Then I registered the clock. Nine twenty-three AM.

I bolted upright. "Oh shit!"

Scout yawned, sitting up at a much more leisurely pace.

It wasn't fast enough for me.

I jumped up and ran around him, my finger to my mouth because ohmygodohmygod, I didn't want to get into this sort of trouble with her. A boy in my bed? Sleeping over? When she did so many doubles? I was an ungrateful daughter, sneaking a guy in when my mom was literally breaking her back for me.

I had the belated thought that I needed to get a job. I needed to help her out.

"My mom," I hissed to Scout.

He nodded as he reached for his pants. He was pulling them on as I slipped out of the room and tiptoed downstairs. I heard a fan buzzing from Mom's room as I passed, but I needed to make sure.

Her purse was on the counter. She'd come home. There was a note.

Hey, honey. I have the weekend off. Let's go to a movie tonight. You pick! Love you so much - Mom

P.S. How was the game? The other girl was a no-show. I got in a little late, so do me a favor and keep quiet until three or so. If I can sleep that long, that'll be great. I'll probably be up around one-ish, but I'm hoping for three.

I exhaled a breath. Thank God. Going back to her room, I slowly cracked open her door, and there she was, burrowed under the sheets. Her blinds were pulled, and I could hear her soft snoring. I grinned. Her snores sounded like a rabbit sneezing.

We were okay. I shut her door and headed back upstairs, stopping in the bathroom to clean up. Scout was looking at his phone when I came back to my room. "My mom's sleeping."

He rubbed his hand over his jaw, nodding. There were bags under his eyes. "Sorry I fell asleep."

"It was late and an intense night." I fell back into my bed with a yawn. "I'm going to sleep a little longer."

He stood by my bed, looking down at me.

"What?"

"Nothing." He turned to leave.

"Hey." I sat back up. "What is it?"

"I'm going to ask my uncle for the weekend. I'll start training on Monday."

"That's what you were just thinking? Not about . . ." His grandfather?

"No. I was thinking about what I was going to do today."

I frowned. "What do you usually do on Saturdays?"

"I go to the gym and stay there all day. Then shower and head out with Cohen and probably your cousins."

"The guys will want to hang out today."

His lips curved up. "We'll see. Sometimes they need a day. I'll reach out later."

His eyes held mine.

I remembered the frenzied energy he had when he showed up last night.

"Hey."

He'd started to leave but looked back.

I settled deeper into my pillows. "Thanks for making me feel good last night too."

He gave a slight nod before leaving.

I didn't sleep. Instead, I reached for my phone because we'd talked a little about his stuff, but my stuff had been in the back of my mind since yesterday.

I needed to know what was going on in Cedra Valley.

I texted Traitor 1.

Me: What do you mean he's getting backlash?

She texted immediately.

Traitor 1: People are starting to talk. More are believing you. There's a whole group that's formed for justice for you and your dad.

Traitor 1: I'm sorry I didn't stand by you. There's no excuse. I'm sorry.

I blocked her.

My heart pounded. I couldn't go there. I needed a wall, but . . . something stirred inside me.

People were starting to believe me.

56

RAMSAY

D*ad.*
     It's been so long. Too long. I'm sorry that I've not let myself think of you or talk to you or feel you. No matter how bad it still hurts, it's not a good enough reason. I'm sorry.

I'd be pissed if I was on the other side, watching me, and you weren't talking to me. I'm hoping you're with mom today because I'm dress shopping for the Homecoming dance. It's not my idea. I'm being forced.

I have these new friends. Gem. Theresa. Alred.

I'm really liking Gem. Theresa is . . . I think we'll be good friends. We'll see. Jury is still out. And Alred. I'm sure you already know that I luh-ve Alred. He has flair, is hilarious, and very kind. You used to tell me to trust my gut, which . . . I didn't, Dad. I'm sorry.

I didn't listen to that voice when I should've, and it's my fault. Everything's my fault.

Logically, I know it's not. It's his, but logic doesn't seem to matter when it feels like my fault. And I have to pretend around others that I don't feel this way, but I do.

Is that okay?

I'm scared to ask about what you think about how I'm doing? Am I doing okay?

Me and Scout . . . okay, I don't think I want to know what you think about him. He drives me crazy, but sometimes he's not so bad. He makes me feel, though. I've not felt anything for so long. I get mad at him. I want to yell at him, curse at him, shove him. I want to deck him sometimes. He has that effect. He's an asshole a lot of the times.

But he makes me feel alive.

And Mom. Are you checking on her for me? She's working herself to death.

I don't know what's going on with Aunt Ailes and Uncle Nick. With his affair. I forgot about it for a while, and I've not told Clint and the guys. What do you think? Should I tell them? They have a right to know, right?

Aunt Ailes said she was going to tell them, but I don't think she has, but I also don't think it's my place, you know?

Can you help? Is that even fair for me to ask? After what you gave for me?

You were trying to protect me. You were being the dad, and you were the best dad ever.

I'm so sorry.

I'm just so very sorry.

I really miss you.

Pinkie promise me you're living it up on the other side? Dancing with Grandma, annoying Grandpa? Also, if you're able, can you please help me prank Clint? Are you able to get birds to shit on him? That'd be awesome.

Totally not sure if it's cool that I ask that, but if it happens, YOU'RE AWESOME, DAD!

Okay. Signing off because Alred is bringing a red dress, which isn't at all my color, my way and he has a look in his eyes. I'm sensing a battle coming.

Love you, Dad. Always. Forever.

Ramsay

57

RAMSAY

Clint: What are you up to?

Me: Dress shopping with Gem, Theresa, and Alred. You?

Clint: At Scout's. Cohen's here too.

Me: You guys are okay then?

Clint: Yeah. All good. Just being stupid. We're thinking of going to the movies tonight. Want to join?

Me: Yes! I asked the rest. Theresa and Alred are in. Gem has to work at Mario's for a bit.

Clint: Cool. See you there or pick you up?

Me: My mom will drive us. They're going to sleep over and we're going to have a dance party tonight. Want to join in that too?

Clint: Um . . .

Me: It's cool. You're too cool for a dance party, unlike two summers ago when—

Clint: Keep talking, and I'll unleash Cousin Prank War again.

I stopped texting. *No one* wanted Cousin Prank War to happen. Trenton ended up in handcuffs the last time.

PINE RIVER'S movie theater was The Fritz Movie Cinema, one of a national chain that were known for their large movie screens, lounge chairs, and also a giant slide that each one had extending from the side. Pine River's was no different, except it was on the river where one side had a screen for those in the river and the rest of the screens were inside. The outside was made of brick with a large marquee in flashing red lights that displayed the theater's name. A person could go up to the third floor, go down the slide that took you outside of the building, and then come back in through the side door. It was important to note that the third floor was only built for the slide. It was a small loft area, while sometimes it seemed stupid to have a third floor because of a slide, it was a genius marketing plan. While we stood in line, I counted thirty people going up for the slide. That was people, little kids, teenagers, and even adults.

All in all, Pine River's movie theater was kinda awesome.

My phone buzzed, and I pulled it out to check the text.

Gem: I like having a job. I like working with family. I like having $$! BUT I really hate having a job this weekend. The game and now the movies without me?

Me: Dance party after.

Gem: Gah. Agh. Gah. Agh! That's what's getting me through. Theresa's picking me up when you're done with the movie.

Theresa nudged my elbow. "That Gem?"

I nodded, putting my phone away.

"She still pissed that she's missing the movie?"

I nodded as Alred shoved in too. "She's more pissed she's not going to the movies with those five gorgeous specimens." He pointed to my cousins, who were at the concession stand with Scout, Cohen, and my mom. She'd insisted on paying since she was the adult who'd been honored with an invitation to the movie night. Honored. Invited. Of course she'd think like that, and she was glowing.

Alred groaned, biting his lip. "I can't decide whose butt is the cutest. I think it's Scout's or Trenton's. Both have top-notch asses. And Scout is tied for best biceps with Cohen. Clint has the best face. And Alex has the best chest."

Theresa and I looked at him.

He held up his hand, still looking at the guys. "I took Scout out of the running for that. He's a fighter. It's not even fair. Your mom, though." He tipped his head, his grin softening. "She has the best smile of them all."

I smiled. "Thank you. I'm going to tell her."

"I hope it goes to her head because your mom is a hot mama."

I shifted to watch them. My mom was at the counter, pointing to the popcorn prices with Alex. Scout and Cohen had stepped back. Scout's face was locked down. He looked as if he was bored but I could tell he was uncomfortable with my mom paying for him.

I texted.

Me: Let her pay. She gets a high from it.

He pulled his phone out and glanced my way. His gaze was hooded.

Scout: Doesn't feel right. Your mom does double shifts at the nursing home.

Scout: And I've been banging her daughter while she's working those shifts.

I sighed.

Me: Let her pay. It's how she shows love. She's in her element right now.

I didn't tell him that we used to have money. That my mom used to love taking my friends and me to the movies and paying for the snacks. She also used to put together snack boxes and gift boxes for when Traitor 1, Traitor 2, and Traitor 3 would sleepover. And the traitors loved getting those boxes because my mom put thought into each gift for them. It was her love language, and she hadn't been able to express it for a long time.

Scout looked my way one more time and put his phone back into his pocket.

My mom motioned for him and Cohen, and he stepped toward her.

Thank you, I mouthed.

He just shrugged and told her what he wanted. And dear Lord, my mom was checking him out. It wasn't obvious, but she stared at him a little longer than she needed to and then swallowed. I caught a blush on her face before she shifted to Cohen's order.

"Did I . . . ?" Theresa asked.

"You did," Alred confirmed. "Your mom's not dead. That's all that means." He whistled as we reached the front of the ticket line. My mom had given me money, and Clint had shoved some money from his mom into my hand before they veered to the concession stand.

I counted out the money he'd given me and realized why. Aunt Aileen had given me more than enough for the tickets and half the concessions. I used her money for the tickets.

"Theresa, Alred." Warmth oozed from Kira as she stopped next to us.

Ciara, Leanne, and Gabby were with her, and there was another girl who seemed to be trying to hide behind Gabby.

"You guys are going to the movies too?" Kira asked. "Which one?"

Alred's eyes went flat. "Girl."

Theresa nudged him, shooting him a look. "The new Marvel one."

Kira smiled. "Us too! We all need to sit together." She looked beyond us. "And your cousins. And Scout—"

The girl hiding gasped, her head jerking up. "Who? What? Where?"

Gabby started laughing. "Why?"

The girl's eyes got big. "Oh no . . ."

Theresa said, "Hi, Amalia."

Amalia. Oh. Oh! Cohen's sister Amalia.

"Oh. Hi, guys," she said. "I didn't know you'd be here–"

Cohen came storming around the group, his head cocked to the side. "What are you doing here?" He glared at his sister, who shrank back behind Gabby again. "You said you were hanging out with Gabby and friends tonight."

"I am," she squeaked, motioning to the ticket counter. "At the movies."

"You didn't say at the movies. You said at a friend's house."

"We were at Kira's house and decided to come here."

Gabby shot me a nervous look, which was warranted, but I wasn't about to start anything. Especially not after the fiasco that happened last night.

I felt a presence behind me, and both Gabby and Amalia's eyes lifted up, up, up. I knew who it was

"Heya, Scout," Amalia squeaked.

He nodded. "Right." He turned, touching my arm and pulling me away with him. Theresa and Alred followed.

Scout took me to the hallway over by the concessions, where my mom and cousins were waiting. He let go of my arm. "Got her."

I handed out the tickets. My cousins went in first. Theresa and Alred were next.

Scout held back, watching for Cohen.

My mom tugged on my arm, motioning for me to go down the hallway a little.

"So . . ." She held on to my arm with both hands and looked at Scout. "Your aunt Aileen just texted me, and she said she'd be up for a drink."

Oh, no, no. I knew what she was going to do. "Mom. No—"

She pointed just out the door. "There's a cute little bar right next to this place. Apparently they have great appetizers, a happy hour right about now, and a few cute bartenders." She wiggled her eyebrows.

I swallowed the disappointment and nodded. "I'll come get you when we're done?"

She squeezed my hand, pressing a kiss to my forehead. "Amazing. You're the best daughter ever. I love you, sweetie."

"Mom."

She turned back. "Hmm?"

"You're going to join in with the dance party, right?"

"Of course. It's like old times with your other friends." She dropped her hand to mine and squeezed before leaving. She waved to Cohen, who was going into the theater with Kira and her friends.

Scout was still in the hallway waiting for me. I walked over, slowly because suddenly the movie didn't seem so fun.

"She ditched?" Scout asked.

"Drinks next door with my aunt."

"That's cool. Maybe she'll meet someone."

I scowled. "I'd be fine with a flirtation, but meeting someone? It's too soon."

"Right." He nodded. "Only the daughter can get some."

I rolled my eyes. "Why are you an asshole and then sweet at other times?"

He shrugged. "When have I been sweet?"

I shot him a look, but grinned.

When we got in, there were two seats open behind Theresa and Alred. Kira and her group had filled the rest of the row with my cousins.

I'm sorry, Theresa mouthed as we went past her.

I shrugged. A movie was a movie to me. I knew Scout wouldn't be talking. I took the seat by the stairs.

AN HOUR IN, I had no idea what was happening in the movie, so I didn't feel a bit bad about hauling butt out of there. The lobby was quiet despite the steady flow of people coming in for other movies. I grabbed a water and went to sit at a corner table. They had a few set up on the far side of the theater. It was a great people-watching perch which is why I saw Scout heading out not long after me.

He dipped into the bathroom before coming to stand at the end of my table instead of heading back into the theater.

I cupped my water protectively. "If you dare try to drink this, I will bite your hand. I have rabies."

He smirked and went to the concessions, returning with a black coffee. He slid into the seat across from me, moving so he had his back against the wall and he could people-watch with me.

"Coffee?"

He shrugged, glancing down the hallway before answering. "There's nothing healthy over there. I'm tired. Figured caffeine's not the worst choice." He lifted his eyes my way. "You're out here because of your mom?"

I shrugged, looking away. "I like watching movies with my mom."

"Even though all of us are here too?"

My throat tightened. "She'd go with my friends and me back in Cedra Valley. It was fun. I've never been the daughter embarrassed of her parents. I love my parents." The tightening got worse. "And you know I don't get a lot of time with her."

I could feel him watching me steadily.

I didn't used to like it. I was accepting it now.

He turned to face me, his back going to the hallway leading to our theater. "Something's going on with your aunt."

"What do you mean?"

He shrugged. "Been around their house lately, picked up on some tension."

The affair.

Which I'd forgotten about.

Which I'd known about for how long and hadn't told my cousins?

Which ... Aunt Ailes asked me not to so she could, but she hadn't.

Shit.

"I'm seeing I'm right." He'd been studying my face.

My gaze snapped to his. "Don't say—" Crap. Alex was his best friend. "I—Aunt Aileen told me she was going to tell them."

"Guessing whatever it is or was, she hasn't." His eyes were narrowed, intent on me. "What is it? Your uncle cheated?"

My eyes bulged out. "How did you—" I sucked in my breath and pushed back in my chair. "Don't say anything."

He laughed. "You and me? My being inside you? That's business a best friend has to say, but the uncle being inside someone not your aunt, *not* my business to share. Now if that shit was still going on, I'd have to say something. It ended?"

"That's what I was told. Also, can you be more crude?"

"Yeah. Do you want me to be?" He was serious.

"No! Jesus."

Another shrug before he scooted back so he could see the hallway again. "So that's why you're out here?"

"No. Yes. I don't know."

His eyes slid sideways so he could see me. "What is it then?"

I moved in my seat, adjusting. "It's none of your business."

His eyes went flat. "Right. Back to that."

Guilt flared in my gut. "I haven't—ugh. Okay. I've not been letting myself think about my dad. When I have, it's just in facts. Max killed him. He's gone. Those are facts. That's how I've been processing his death, but today ..." A burning started in my chest. "Today, I thought about him. I thought *to* him, if that makes sense? We were shopping for dresses, and I had a fleeting thought about what he would think of this dress Alred picked out for me. It was so skimpy and very red, which is *not* the pastel theme we're doing, but I laughed and thought my dad would have some joke to say about it. Then I remembered, and . . ." My throat was back to tightening. "It went from there. I had a whole conversation in my head, to him."

"That's cool."

Was he being serious or making fun of me?

"What?" he asked with a shrug. "That's normal. Your dad's gone. Your piece-of-shit, abuser ex took him away from you. Think it's normal to be doing that."

"Doing what?" I was cautious in asking.

"Doing whatever. That's grief. Don't think there's a manual on how to grieve. Do it in the way that works for you."

I was a little surprised. "That's kinda mature of you."

He smirked. "That must be why you like my dick. I'm *mature*."

"Well, you're being a dick right now."

"See. It goes back to my cock."

I rolled my eyes and grinned a little. In his weird way, Scout helped.

"Think we should go back?" I asked.

"Fuck no. Cohen and Kira were making out, and Alex was sticking his tongue down Ciara's throat when I left."

"Oh." Also, "Gross."

He laughed. "Some other chicks were in there eyeballing Trenton, so Clint had moved to sit by Leanne. You're safer out here."

I considered asking how he was so okay with my cousins after last night, but he'd already told me they would be. The explanation made sense to him so I was letting it go.

"Can I ask about your dad?" I asked instead.

"*I have my dad's last name, who I don't have a relationship with, and I don't want to get into that either . . .*"

His smirk vanished, and his lips thinned. "No. Actually trying not to be a dick here, but that's a story I never plan to tell anyone. He's a piece of shit and I'm better off without him."

My heart squeezed.

His dad was alive and not in his life. My dad was gone, and I'd give anything to have him back. "I'm sorry."

His eyes held mine.

I added softly, "Everyone should know a good dad."

"I do."

I waited.

He flashed me a hard grin. "Nick's not a great husband, but he seems like a good dad." He finished his coffee and tossed it into the garbage by us. "And maybe you can tell me about yours? I can know a second one."

Pain sliced through me, but something else was mixed with it. It was bittersweet. "I'd actually love to do that. He was so great, it's part of the reason he's not here anymore."

"Then you definitely need to tell me about him." He snagged my water and stood. "Come on, Williams. We might as well watch the end of the movie." I went with him, snatching my water back. "You just said you didn't want to go in?"

"Changed my mind."

"Why would you want to watch the end without watching the whole movie?"

He shrugged. "If I like the ending, I'll rewatch and enjoy the whole thing. If I don't, I'm not going to waste my time."

"That also makes no sense." We got to the door and paused.

"Good." He pushed it open, his hand at the small of my back, and he gently shoved me ahead of him. "Because I'm totally fucking with you."

58

SCOUT

There were a lot of situations happening after the movies.

One, Ramsay's two friends were all over her, sneaking looks my way. I was sure she was being interrogated about our mid-movie disappearance, but Ramsay looked as if she were holding her own, waving them off. The guy was steamed, sent me a withering glance before frowning to himself.

I almost laughed.

Second, the guys wanted to go drinking at the river. We had a bonfire ring with seating around it for a reason. Miles liked knowing where I was if my friends were drinking. I knew this because he'd told me many times.

The other ordeal was Amalia.

Cohen didn't want her drinking with them.

Kira declared that if Amalia left, Gabby should go with her.

That was a whole other situation because when she said that with Gabby looking hurt before she sent a nasty look in Ramsay's direction. I had no clue what was going on. I just knew that I was staring at Ramsay and thinking that we could've had a quickie in the time it was taking for everyone to figure out what the fuck they wanted to do for the night.

In the end, Ramsay's guy friend huffed, "We're doing a dance party."

Theresa added, "Just us. No one else is invited." She turned to Ramsay. "We need to pick up Gem and grab our stuff."

Clint drawled, "Damn. No cousin tonight." He was being sarcastic, hanging all over Leanne. "Love you, Rams."

"Shut it, Clint. Love you too."

He smirked at her.

Trenton clapped his hands together. "That all seems settled so can we"—he swept the group in an exaggerated motion—"can get going?" His arm fell down around his girl's shoulders. Her friends giggled, thinking that was hilarious.

I was tempted to opt out of everything and see if I could hide in Ramsay's bed until her friends passed out, but then we were on the move and heading to the parking lot.

Cohen veered my way. "Can you take Amalia home?" He nodded toward Kira, whose face was flushed. "Because, you know."

I gave him a look. "It's my uncle's gym."

"We can wait until you show up before the girls need to use the bathroom. We'll be good. You know that." He flashed me a grin, heading off to catch a ride with Kira.

Ramsay was staring intently at her mom and aunt before they broke off to their different vehicles. The only cousin who caught the exchange was Clint, who shared a look with Ramsay before she slid into the car with her mom. Theresa and their dude friend, who waved at me, got in with them.

I focused on the two left. Amalia and the chick who my chick hated, or the chick I was banging hated.

"So."

Gabby started crying.

Amalia hauled her in for a hug.

I had no clue what any of this was about.

I sighed. "Shit."

59

RAMSAY

We made it to my house an hour later with backpacks, sleeping bags, and pillows in hand. Gem was also with us.

I sprinted upstairs to change into some pants and a tank, keeping a bra on. They were getting the sleeping bags situated when I came back downstairs.

We heated up leftover food, turned on the music, and turned off the lights. My mom brought out a disco ball and placed some LED lights around the room. After that, it was dance party all night long.

She stayed with us until two in the morning. Once she went to bed, a movie was turned on but they wanted to know what happened at the party after they left. I'd already told them when we were dress shopping, but I told them again.

They wanted to know about Scout.

Alred had been to a drag show last night so I wanted to know how that went.

Theresa teased Gem about all her new gamer guy friends.

Alred wanted to know about those guys.

We ended the night gossiping about Kira and her friends

After that, I checked out. I mean, I'd been checked out most of the night, to be honest, but I still loved it. I loved the dancing. I loved the friends. I loved how many times Alred made my mom laugh.

Once they'd all fallen asleep in the living room, I waited until they were all been snoring before I snuck back to my room. It was close to four in the morning.

After using the bathroom, I crawled into my bed.

That was when I reached for my phone.

"Everyone should know a good dad."

"Maybe you can tell me about yours? I can know a second one."

That'd been in the back of my mind all night, in replay. So maybe because of that, I texted him.

Me: You awake?

He texted five minutes later.

Scout: Leaving Cohen's, going home. What's up?

Me: Want to pick me up?

Two minutes later . . .

Scout: Heading over. I'll be parked on the street.

That was all I needed. I was up, changing into dark sweats and a black hoodie. With my phone and keys, I tiptoed out the back door.

He wanted to know about my dad.

I wanted to tell him.

That was making me feel so many different things, all things I didn't want to feel right now.

I went to the street and sat on the curb to wait.

His lights turned onto the street a few minutes later, and he pulled to a stop right in front of me. I got in, and after giving me one hooded look, he headed off.

60

RAMSAY

I lay on my stomach, and Scout was moving inside me from behind. He sank down, his back arched and his forehead pressing to my shoulder blades as he thrust in all the way, grinding in and going slow.

That was not what I wanted.

I needed to feel only him, only what he could make me feel. Needing to forget, I wanted to explode and then explode again and again and again until my body was so tired that I could only focus on keeping my eyelids open.

Pushing up from the bed, I reached out, shoving him off me. He went willingly, his cock sticking up.

I flipped around and pushed him to his back, then climbed on, my legs going to either side of him. He touched my hips, helping me align myself, and I sank down. This time, a hand to his chest, my eyes closed, I rode him.

It was all me. My pace. My rhythm. The way I wanted to feel him inside.

Feeling the beginning of my release at the base of my spine, a whisper of a touch, a little tingle, I opened my eyes. His hips moved with me, but his eyes weren't into it. I could tell.

"What's wrong?"

He reached up, palming my breast, his thumb rubbing over my nipple. "Nothing." He lifted his hips. "Keep going."

I went slow. Moving both my hands to his chest, I held myself upright as I rode him. He continued to watch me. This time, he was into it, but I still frowned. "Something's wrong. I can tell."

His hand clamped down harder on my hip, and he shook his head. "Nothing. I'm into this, but what's your issue? I can tell."

My nostrils flared as I rode him a little harder. "That's the basis of this, whatever we're doing. We make each other feel good."

He sat up, and I gasped as he wrapped a hand around me, holding me in place. "Like I said . . ." His mouth was inches from mine. I sank deeper onto him as he said, "I'm into this, but you're forcing it. You've never forced it."

As if in defiance, I ground over him. His eyes closed from the sensations. This was a new experience for me—bickering while fucking. Somehow it made it hotter.

He reached up, palming one of my breasts again.

I opened my eyes and bit my lip.

His eyes flared, and he grabbed my leg. He began pulling me against him. I gasped, my release teasing me again.

I was so close.

I wanted another explosion. Please. One more. Another one—and Scout took over again. He flipped me, put me back on my stomach, and sank in from behind. But he held himself over me as his mouth went to my ear, and as he thrust into me, he asked, "Is this what you wanted? Rough?" He pounded into me, reaching over to grab the headboard.

He started slamming into me.

I gasped, my head sinking into his pillow. *Yes.* That was

exactly what I wanted. I wanted to forget. I wanted to feel *only* him, not to think. He was delivering.

He gripped my hip so hard I knew there'd probably be bruises tomorrow.

I loved it.

He thrust so hard my head almost hit the headboard. He caught me, holding me upright so that didn't happen. I plastered myself against him as his hips pistoned into me.

And then I erupted.

A strangled cry ripped from my throat, and fuck, I saw stars. I almost blacked out as the climax tore through me at a breakneck speed, and the waves had me crying out all over again. My whole body trembled. I fell to the bed, on the side of him, and when I looked over, he had a hand around his dick.

I knocked it aside and put my mouth around him.

"Jesus!" he hissed, but as I deep-throated him, he threaded his fingers into the back of my hair.

I began sucking, and soon, he groaned and began guiding my movements. His free hand snaked down my body and between my legs so he could rub my clit.

I moaned over his cock because that felt so good, and as I writhed around, he exploded in my mouth. I exploded all over again, and *then* I lifted my head and swallowed, wiping my mouth before I collapsed onto his bed.

"You got people at your house," he said after a moment.

I yawned, the exhaustion finally hitting me. "I do." My eyelids were heavy.

He was quiet for a beat before he got up and tugged me with him. "Come on." He patted my ass. "I gotta drive you home so you can sneak back in."

I grumbled, but he was right. I dressed, smelling like sex and not caring, and watched as he pulled on his own clothes. As we headed back out, I almost had a heart attack when I heard movement inside another bedroom.

He flashed me a grin and tugged on my hand. He led me back out to his truck, and when we got in, I hissed, "We woke your uncle up?"

He laughed a little, backing up before turning around in the driveway. "He's getting up for the day. He's gotta meet some fighters for early-morning training."

I groaned, slumping down in the seat. "Oh God." I didn't know what was worse, that his uncle might've heard us again or that we woke him up. Either way, I was mortified.

"We didn't wake him up. I promise. He sleeps with this huge fan on because he knows when I'm not training, I get up and do shit. It used to drive him crazy."

When he wasn't training. I side-eyed him. "You have one more day before you start training again?"

He nodded, yawning and rubbing a hand over his face. "Yeah. I can't do this starting Monday. I'm going to need ten hours of sleep every night. You want a booty call? You need to start planning ahead."

"Sure. I'll tell that to my PTSD."

He glanced over to me. "That's what tonight was?"

"No. I don't know."

I didn't want to talk about my dad, and maybe he sensed that because he didn't push me. We didn't talk until he pulled up at my place. He paused on the street, and I sat up, taking a breath because I'd have to sneak in.

"Hey." He touched my hand. "Thanks for calling."

I frowned. "I called more for me."

He shrugged, his hand moving to cup the back of my head. "I don't care." His mouth opened over mine, and I let myself get lost in the kiss. It was thorough, almost claiming. My heart was beating hard by the time he pulled away, and I frowned at him. "What was that for?"

He got serious. "Just being clear. I want to keep doing this."

"This?"

"This. You and me. Calling when one of us wants the other. Whatever we're doing, I want to keep doing it."

I stared at him, weighing his words, trying to decipher if there were other messages in there that I wasn't hearing. Then I shrugged. "Okay." I scowled. "Don't fuck someone else."

"Back at you. Also, I need to teach you how to hit because you suck at it. I noticed that when you were hitting my bag before."

I rolled my eyes as I got out. But as I walked up to the house, I couldn't lie to myself.

I was smiling.

61

RAMSAY

They crept into my room the next morning. Theresa was carrying a cup of coffee and when they saw I was awake, they started grinning.

Theresa put the coffee on my desk as Gem and Alred climbed onto my bed.

"That's from your mom," Theresa said.

"Your mom is awesome. She's making pancakes that look like they have Skittles inside. I don't think they do, but I'm loving the rainbow theme." Alred sighed happily from where he lay at the foot of my bed with his head resting against the wall. Gem was on her back next to me, and she yawned. "We need to decide what we're doing for the day."

"Yeah."

Theresa sat on my loveseat, pulling a pillow onto her lap. "Wanna do lunch at Louie's?"

Gem held up a hand. "I was thinking more along the lines of studying. I worked this weekend, so I got almost no homework done."

Alred groaned, rolling to face us. "You guys are boring. Homework. Studying. But I'm down for Louie's."

"You don't have work to do for your school?" I asked.

"I get that done during my classes."

I was still curious about Louie's.

"What are you thinking? You down for Louie's?" Theresa asked.

I grabbed my phone and sent a text to Clint.

Me: What are you doing today?

A few seconds later, a new text sounded.

Clint: Waiting for you to come over.

"I think I'm needed at my cousin's today," I told them.

Theresa nodded before half jumping on Alred, who shrieked a little as he pushed her off.

I was waiting for one of them to mention my sneaking out last night, but no one brought it up. I was relieved. Not that I wanted to keep Scout a secret, but it was just easier not to answer questions. When my mom called up that breakfast was ready, I slipped into the bathroom and cleaned up for the day. I headed downstairs in leggings and an oversized hoodie, my coffee in hand.

Everyone was seated at the island.

Gem waved her fork in the air. "Yourmom'spancake-sareawesome."

Theresa laughed. "Do I need to translate that?"

I took a stool as my mom put a plate in front of me. Alred was right. The pancakes had Skittles.

My mom had set up the whole island for breakfast. There were bowls of fruit, chocolate chips, sprinkles, whipped cream, candy, Nutella, and bacon bits. Each one had a little tag to label it. She'd gone to the store and gotten balloons as well. They were in one corner of the island, along with four brown goody bags for me and my friends.

"Ramsay." Alred almost dropped his fork. "What's wrong?"

I couldn't look away from the goody bags.

My mom came over, wrapping me in her arms. "It's always

good to keep moving forward," she whispered. "New friends. New memories. Good things in life."

I reached up and held on to her hands.

"I love you, sweetie."

"If I haven't said it, you are the *best mom* I could ask for."

She untangled herself. I turned so I could hug her better.

I motioned to the bags and the island. "My mom used to do this for me back before . . . everything. With my other friends."

Gem squeezed my hand. "Are you still in touch with them?"

I thought of Traitor 1's recent texts and shrugged. "They sided with him at the time. It doesn't matter what they think now."

"Then they're assholes," Theresa declared. "They're kicking themselves for their stupidity. You're amazing, and they know it."

"If they don't accept you for you, they weren't knowing in the first place." Alred's eyes were distant before he blinked, clearing a flash of emotion away and dug back into his pancakes.

I paused, studying Alred for a second.

I'd heard these things before, but it never took away the truth that when I needed my friends, they weren't there for me. The other truth? That feeling never left a person.

My mom stayed close until they left, giving each a hug and their goody bag.

Maybe it was the nostalgia, or maybe it was the glimpse I got of my old mom coming back, or maybe it was something deeper inside me, but whatever it was, I turned to her once they left.

"I need to tell you something."

She only grinned. "You're going to tell me about the boy I found in your bed the other morning. The one who only wanted mints from the concession stand."

I—what?

She laughed, patting my hand. "If you think I didn't know, you're going to have to do better." She pretended to drop the mic. "Bomb dropped."

I didn't blink.

My throat was burning. "Max wrote an article about how he's the victim."

She froze.

My whole chest was burning now. "He blames me for everything, and it's online. I couldn't bring myself to tell you." I started to look away.

How could I explain that, sometimes, I didn't want to bring something up because that meant I'd have to deal with it *again*? I'd have to feel it *again*. I'd have to experience it *again*. How was I supposed to move forward when I was yanked back?

Again.

Again.

So many *agains*.

When would it end?

My bomb won.

62

SCOUT

"What's going on with you? You're distracted," my uncle asked, wrapping his hands around the bag I'd been punching for the last thirty minutes. He held it in place, and I began whaling on it even harder.

We were not supposed to tire ourselves out, but I was at the end of my training for the night, so I let everything out on this bag. "I'm good," I told him.

He knew about the email from Grandfather.

We'd talked about what I should do, which was not show up.

He knew it. I knew it. We both knew there was a shitstorm coming afterward.

I was hoping he wasn't going to bring it up.

He stared at me, pushing the bag back my way.

I dodged it, stepping aside, and soon that was the new training exercise: me jabbing, then seeing if I could retreat fast enough for him.

He grunted. "Leg kick."

I did a roundhouse and punched with my opposite arm.

He shook the bag, shoving it back at me.

I kept jabbing. Jab, retreat. Jab, retreat. Jab, retreat.

"You're slow on your feet today."

This was my first day back to a hardcore training regime, but he was right. I knew better, and I began bouncing on my toes, focusing on that as I continued jabbing. I was good with grappling, but I excelled at jabbing. I leaned on my strengths when I was tired, and my mind wasn't thinking as fast as I needed it to in a fight.

"This anything to do with that girl I saw you driving back Sunday morning?"

I scowled at him. "No."

"You didn't get a lot of sleep that night."

I frowned. "I'm fine." I delivered a good kick, hard enough to knock him back, and I retreated before he could throw the bag at me.

He stared at me, hard.

I ignored him.

"Your shoulder's dropping."

I gritted my teeth. "My shoulder's not dropping."

"Who's the girl?"

I jabbed again. "No one."

"She's not no one."

I stopped, resting my hands on my hips. "Why do you care? You've never cared about anyone I fucked so long as I didn't get anyone pregnant."

"Because you've never brought a girl to the house before. She's been there twice. I don't want you distracted. You have a fight coming up."

"I'm not distracted. And it's just sex between us."

He frowned. "That sounds logical. You're in high school."

"Meaning?" I hit again, throwing a kick right after. Then I changed it up and did the same with the opposite arm and leg.

"You're in high school. Emotions are involved. Your brain's not fully developed."

"Jesus Christ. It's just sex."

"You've slept at her place a couple of times too," he added. "Don't think I didn't notice."

"You've never given me grief about where I sleep, as long as I don't fuck up training or school. Are you giving me a curfew now?"

I was too far gone for that. He and I were both too far gone for that.

He sighed. "You're not far from getting signed. I don't want you losing your focus. And . . ." He hesitated.

That made me stop altogether. My grandfather—or, no, he had a different look on his face. "You talked to my mom?"

"She called."

I suppressed a curse. "About?"

"She doesn't know about the email. She was calling to hear how you're doing. I told her you're doing well."

Relief hit.

"What's he going to do when I don't show up?"

He settled back on his feet, a hand leaning on the punching bag. "He's going to call and tell me how you not showing up is an insult to him. He's then going to talk about what a great guy he is because he'll get that school to agree to another interview, but he'll say you have to fly there to them. We both know he'll show up either before or after the interview, but we also know you won't show up for that one either. You're not doing what he wants you to do will enrage him. After that, he'll either target your mother, me, or I don't know. Eventually, he will try to find your weakness and exploit it until you agree to do what he wants."

I wanted to end him—straight up, right then and there—because he wouldn't stop. He'd never stop.

Unwrapping my hands, I let the tape drop to the ground. "Good to know."

I started to head for the stretching area when my uncle's hand came to my shoulder. "Hey."

I stopped.

"You do not worry about him. Got that? I will deal with him, and if push comes to shove, so will your mother. I know my sister. She loves you more than she's scared of him. It might be taking her a while to get there, but I have no doubt she'll get there."

"Yeah." I grunted, turning away again.

"Stretch, wash up, go home. Wrap ice packs on your shoulder tonight. You got homework to do, and get ten hours of sleep. I mean it, okay?" He reached out, grasping my shoulder. "Ten hours. I want a two-mile run before school tomorrow."

"Two?"

"Five. Do five instead. And grab a smoothie on the way out."

Putting on my headphones, I spent thirty minutes unwinding my muscles enough to where it was safe to shower and drive home. Miles was watching me as I left, my bag over my shoulders. I gave him a quick nod before grabbing a smoothie from the counter and ducking out the door.

My phone buzzed on the way, and it was like they'd planned it together.

Mom: I've not heard much from you lately. How are you?

I got into my truck before I texted back.

Me: I'm fine. Training. School. Staying out of trouble.

Mom: I talked to your uncle. He said you might have a girlfriend?

Me: No girlfriend.

Mom: You sure?

Me: Yes. What about you? Do you have a girlfriend?

Mom: I'm dating someone.

Me: Did she move in yet?

Mom: It's not like that.

Me: You get attached right away.

Mom: I didn't text so we could start fighting.

Me: Then why'd you text? All we do is fight.

Mom: I'll give you a call later in the week. Love you.

I sighed. She'd call, hoping we wouldn't fight then, but we would because we always did. That was just how it was between us right now.

Me: I'm doing fine, if that's why you were texting. No girl-friend. It's just sex. You don't have to worry.

Mom: Okay. Love you.

Tossing my phone aside, I decided to get some food before going to the house. I texted Ramsay when I got to the grocery store.

Me: Hey.

Williams: Hey. You want to come over?

Me: What time?

Williams: uh, 8:30 maybe?

Me: See you then.

63

RAMSAY

A week later, I felt like I was treading water.
I couldn't shake it. I didn't know where this feeling was coming from, but it wouldn't go away.

The bed shook as Scout got up, reaching for his boxer briefs and pulling them up as he stood, looking around the room. We were at his place, and I was lounging.

It was already ten at night, and I needed to sneak out—not that sneaking was necessary at his house. His uncle knew I existed. Scout had said as much, but we never crossed paths. The guy came home late. Scout said he trained guys at all hours.

This night, though, I just couldn't make myself move, and I watched as he glanced back. He frowned slightly before going to his desk and booting up his computer. "You okay? You came, I thought?"

I gave him a little grin. "I did. Twice."

He smirked before turning to his screen again. I watched as he booted up his emails and clicked over to his social media. He read through everything, not responding to anything, and pulled up a Word doc.

Okay. He was going to do homework.

I still lay there, yawning, and my eyelids started getting heavy.

———

"HEY." Someone was shaking me.

I jerked awake, but it was dark, and my heart leaped into my throat. Panic seized me. *Max.* It was Max! I flailed to fight back, not fully able to see.

He cursed, twisting away. "Christ. Stop. It's me—Scout."

I shot forward, planning on jumping and going for the door, but his voice got through the terror. He twisted and caught me before I fell off his bed. My legs were still tangled in his blankets. I gulped for air, curling a fist into his shirt.

Scout. I breathed him in. That was him. Not Max.

Scout. Not Max.

But the panic was real. The terror.

I'd been back there.

I curled away from him, still in his arms, and a guttural cry came out of me.

That sound was from an animal in a trap.

"Hey." His tone was gentler this time, and he moved closer, sitting with me on the bed. "Hey."

His door shoved open.

I flinched, pressing my forehead into Scout's chest. He began rubbing his hand up and down my back.

"What's wrong with her?"

I tensed, not recognizing that voice. But I was in Scout's house. That was probably his uncle.

Scout spoke over my head. "She fell asleep. I woke her—"

"What's *wrong* with her?"

I drew in a breath, shoving aside the last of the fog on my brain. It was time to be strong.

"My guess? PTSD shit," Scout said. "And before you start, I was doing my homework. She fell asleep. I was waking her up to take her home."

He was still so tense. I rubbed my hand over his side. I felt bad that he was having to deal with my stuff, deal with his uncle on my behalf. I should've been gone by now.

"Does she need anything?"

"Space, probably."

"Okay. Just, let me know. I'm heading to bed, but I'll still be up for ten minutes or so."

The door closed. Scout cursed before he moved. He kept a hand on me as he moved to switch on a fan, providing some noise in the background. As he turned to me, I could make him out in the soft glow of the lamp on his desk.

"Your mom?" he asked.

I frowned, moving back to sit against the wall. I had to remember what night it was. *Wednesday.* "She's doing a double tonight."

"She does *a lot* of them."

I curled in on myself. That felt safe, making myself as small as possible. If only that worked . . . I frowned. "We need the money, and they're short-staffed. I was going to get a job, but Kira's been having us do Homecoming planning every day after school. My mom gets time and a half. She's paying rent on that house. She didn't want to move me into an apartment, thought I'd have trouble being in a small space with strangers around me—like in the hallways or the elevators."

He cursed softly under his breath. "I didn't even think about stuff like that."

I closed my eyes. My hands were trembling.

"You want to sleep here tonight?" he asked. "I get up early to run, could drive you home then."

I tipped my head back so I could really see him. His face was guarded, his eyes shadowed.

I'd be lying if I said I wasn't becoming addicted to him, to his body.

Or to the feel of being in his arms.

I couldn't tell anymore. I was all jumbled up inside.

But I was so tired, and I didn't want to go home and be there alone.

Leaning forward, my forehead went to his shoulder. It felt like surrendering as I said, "I'd like to sleep here tonight."

He smoothed a hand down my back. "You want the bathroom first?"

"You go first." My heart was still stampeding through my chest. I needed some time.

The bed dipped as he got up, moving around the room before going into the bathroom. I stayed, curling the blanket tighter around myself. I heard Scout in the bathroom. The bathroom fan switched on. The toilet. He showered. A few minutes later, the sink was running. The bathroom fan turned off.

There was a murmur of male voices.

He was talking to his uncle, and I sat up, knowing my turn was coming if his uncle didn't insist I go home for the night. I checked my phone and saw a bunch of texts from Gem and Theresa. A few from Clint. A couple from my mom.

Mom: I'm on my break. About to switch shifts so I have to give a report to myself. Haha! Love you, honey. Let me know when you head to bed. Did you get all your homework done? Ailes said you're so vigilant with going home to study this week. I'm so proud of you. I don't think I've told you that enough.

She'd not pushed the talk about Scout. She'd not pushed to know if I was still having sex with him, but I knew my mom. She thought she knew where I was every hour of the day, so she thought it had stopped.

If she actually asked, I'd tell her.

I needed to tell her. And that made me feel even worse.

The door opened. Scout came in, freshly showered and only wearing boxer briefs. He was holding a whistle and a green thing.

I frowned. "What are those?"

"They're from my uncle." He held the whistle up, handing it over. "For you to blow if you're ever in a situation where you need to blow it."

My stomach turned to lead, but I took it. "A rape whistle?"

"Yeah." He held up the other thing, showing me how to use it. "This is pepper spray, and he also offered to give you some self-defense lessons if you want."

A rape whistle. Pepper spray. Self-defense lessons.

I took both items. "Will you thank him for me?"

Scout nodded. "Yeah, but he's not expecting it."

I didn't know what to think of that, but I stood to move past him.

"Hey."

I looked back. He was holding up a new T-shirt. "If you shower."

I took it and slipped into the bathroom, hitting the lock. I took a second to gather my bearings. This house was so male. There was nothing soft about anything. There was a barbell on the ground by the toilet as if it were normal to lift weights while they were taking a shit.

I shook my head and looked down, staring at the whistle and spray in my hand.

Maybe I should do the self-defense classes?

Even the thought sent panic through me, and I shut that down. I'd think about it later.

After showering and brushing my teeth, I hit the lights and opened the door.

And stifled a scream because a guy was standing in the doorway of a room across the hallway from where I stood.

He held up a hand. "Sorry. I didn't mean to scare you. Just . . ." He trailed off, staring at me, probably processing that I was wearing his nephew's shirt.

I got my first good look at Scout's uncle.

He was older but still looked young. Maybe late thirties? Early forties. It was obvious he worked out. Golden brown skin. Dark eyes. Dark hair that was long enough to comb back. He had a rugged look to him. A square jaw. I could see why Scout said his uncle had a lot of one-night stands—if that was true. In all the time I'd spent here, his uncle was barely around, and if he was, he never brought a woman. Then again, it'd only been three weeks.

He coughed. "Scout said you're staying the night. I just wanted to introduce myself so you'll know who else is in the house, in case you get up during the night or something. I'm Miles. I'm, uh, Scout's uncle."

He seemed nervous, which eased my fear a little. I didn't know why. "I'm Ramsay."

"Ramsay." He nodded. "It's nice to finally meet you. I'm serious about the self-defense lessons. I do a course every Tuesday and Thursday night at six. There are a bunch of other women who take it, a few bring their daughters with them. You're welcome to join. I just started a new class. You'd only be behind by a week, and that's nothing."

Scout's door opened, and he stood there, still shirtless, frowning at us. He didn't say anything.

"Right." His uncle held up a hand. "I'm off to bed. Uh—"

"'Night," Scout ground out.

His uncle barely gave him a glance, only giving me a tight smile before stepping back into his room and shutting his door.

I swung my eyes to Scout, who shook his head before stepping back inside.

I moved around him, putting my things on his desk and getting ready for the morning.

Scout tossed a charger on the mattress by me. I plugged it in on the other side of his bed and attached my phone. Then I moved to the far side of the bed. I'd been over here enough times to know he liked being on the outside. I got the wall. Normally, that would freak me out, but not with Scout.

I lay down and scrolled through my phone. He moved to lay next to me, doing the same. The lamp was still on, so I knew he'd get up at least one more time before going to sleep.

After a few minutes, Scout put his phone away. "What'd my uncle say?"

I lowered my phone to my chest. "He wanted to meet me, and I think to offer the self-defense classes. What'd you tell him about me?"

"He asked about your PTSD. It's obvious you were, you know, attacked. He didn't want the details, but I think it was mostly for him to know if you felt safe here or not. He has a soft spot for women and wants them to feel safe."

I looked at him. He didn't add anything, so I pointed out, "You do too."

He looked my way, but he didn't react. "That was basically it."

"I liked it," I told him.

"Liked what?"

"That he offered the classes. And the whistle and pepper spray. I liked that he gave them to you to give to me."

He frowned. "He wants to meet your mom."

"What?" I sat up.

"He said that's a stipulation of your staying here tonight. He wants to make sure she knows you're safe here."

I swore, slumping. "She and I haven't really talked about you and me."

"You told me she knew earlier this week."

"I did. She does. She did. But it's been a week. I think she thinks this stopped."

"She might like knowing you're safe."

I gave him a look. "You're a fighter. The last guy I slept with . . ."

He grimaced slightly. "Why don't we just let my uncle talk to her then?"

"That would be worse."

"Look, she knows about us. My uncle also knows, but he doesn't know the extent. You aren't usually here when he gets in, so let's . . ." He shrugged. "Let's just have him talk to her. They can figure it out. He can reassure her you're safe when you're here. Maybe it'll help?"

I gave him another look. "It'll make it worse."

He sighed. "He's going to meet her whether you want him to or not. But that's all he'll do. He sticks his nose in to make sure everything is okay. I'm still training, still going to school, and if that doesn't get messed with, he won't care." He made a face, his mouth flattening. "He thinks you're my girlfriend now."

"Are you going to—"

He gave me a look. "What? Tell him the truth, that we're still just fucking?"

"I could hit you with a pillow right now," I deadpanned.

"It's better if he thinks that. Easier to explain."

I growled, but who was I kidding? I understood. "My mom is going to want you to come over for dinner."

"We can tell her we broke up."

I laughed, and once I started, I didn't want to stop. The knot inside me was still there. It might always be there, but the laughter softened it.

A bit later, Scout got up for the last time, turning the light off before he slid back into bed.

I pushed my phone to the floor. I knew Scout's alarm would wake us up. "Thank you for letting me stay."

He didn't reply, but a second later, his hand found mine.

"I'm going to Portland tomorrow night for a fight. Do you want to go with me?"

"Is your uncle going? You're fighting?"

"No to both. He has a class tomorrow night, but he knows I'm going. A friend of mine is fighting. I'm going to support him, but I also want to scope out the guy he's fighting. He's been asking me for a match. It'll be a late night coming back, but do you want to go with? You don't have to—"

"Yes." I didn't know why, but I really, really wanted to go.

He was quiet for a beat. "Okay. I was planning on leaving around four. Time to get there and eat something."

I turned on my side, facing him. "Thank you for inviting me."

He turned to face me. He was always just watching me. Always with a wall up, not letting anything shine through, but I knew what this invitation meant. I knew what me staying here meant. I knew what him holding my hand meant.

"Can I ask you something else?"

"What?"

"What happened with your grandfather?"

He tensed up all over again, and I let out a soft sigh.

"I shouldn't have asked."

"No. It's—I didn't do what he wanted me to do, and now we're waiting for his second assau—" His eyes flicked to me. "His second attempt."

I said softly, "You were going to say assault."

"Bad word choice."

"Is it, though?" I was studying him as I asked, "Is that how it feels when he does things or tries to get you to do the things he wants you to do?"

He slowly let himself relax. "It's like war with him. He launches an assault, and he delivers a direct blow. I didn't do what he wanted so he'll launch a second assault. Just waiting to see what it is."

"Then what?"

"Then I'll figure out how to react to whatever he does. The problem is that he uses money to control everyone else in our family except my uncle and me. My dad has money, which I got from him even though he and I are estranged, and my grandmother set up a trust fund for me. My grandfather doesn't even know about that money. He and my grandmother are divorced. They hate each other's guts. He can't hurt my dad. He can't hurt my uncle because my uncle walked away from the family. The only person he can hurt is my mom . . ." He hesitated, rolling to his back and letting go of my hand so he could rest his palm on his stomach. "I can't do anything to stop that. He's been hurting her since before I was alive."

A sick feeling took root in me. "Hurting her?"

"Not like, well, I don't know what you mean, but he's emotionally abusive to her. And other things, but she's an adult. She won't leave."

My heart was thudding hard against my sternum. "Scout—"

"You can't say anything to me that I haven't heard or thought about before. I won't live my life with him in it, and the only move I had was to leave." A hard laugh left him. "Sad thing is, my mom's the one who told me to go. Bought my ticket. She opened the door, and I walked through it. She's regretted it ever since, but I won't go back."

I frowned. "What do you mean she regrets it?"

His eyes found mine. "She goes back and forth, wanting me back. Then her mom side kicks in and she knows it's best for me if I'm here."

"I'm sorry."

He shrugged, his eyes closing off. His whole face shuttering closed. "It is what it is."

I studied him, seeing all the thoughts I had about him, that he stood apart, was true because he did. He was different from the rest. He was aged in ways the rest of us weren't, myself included. A family that waged war on each other? I couldn't imagine.

A different thought occurred to me. "You told me you weren't scared of Max or his family. You really aren't, are you?"

He rolled back to his side, the granite effect softening. His hand found mine. "Not even a little bit."

That almost made me smile.

"My turn. Can I ask you something now too?"

"What?"

He looked so serious. "Did you tell your mom about the article?"

My chest tightened, but I nodded.

"Do you want to talk about the article?" she asked.

"I will never want to talk about the article."

"Okay, then I'm going to tell you what I'm going to do." She waited for me to look at her. "I understand how you're feeling, that you've been pushed down by him so hard that it's pointless to even stand up. That he keeps hurting you and getting away with it. That you're so far down, it's easier to close your eyes and turn away." Her face and tone grew fierce. "I'm not having this, not after all he's taken away from you. I'm going to call our lawyer. We're going to get that article taken down, and then we're going to file a suit against the Prestige family."

My heart ached and tightened because, if we did that, what else could they take from us? "Mom, no—"

"It's not up for discussion. It wasn't just you he hurt. He hurt my daughter. He took my husband. He may not face criminal charges, but he's going to face some other repercussions. This article was the last straw." She caught my face in her hands. "You are my world, and to see you hurting, that hurts me. It's going to stop now, but you do not worry about it. You do not give him one thought. We're going to keep on and we're going to find reasons to laugh every day. There's always good happening. It's our job to find it. I want you to do that. Can you do that for me? Find a reason to smile, honey?"

I told him what she said.

He didn't say anything, but his hand was so tight over mine the whole time.

That made me admit something.

"Scout," I whispered.

"What?"

"I think we're friends."

He didn't reply, but he also didn't pull his hand away.

Yeah. We were friends.

I didn't know how I felt about the friendship, but I went to sleep with someone holding my hand. *That* meant something to me.

64

RAMSAY

"**Y**o." Kira caught me at my locker. I shut it and turned my back to it. "Yo."

She gave me a slight grin. "You need a date for the Homecoming dance."

I couldn't disguise my wince.

Her eyes narrowed. "Come on. I've seen you at our meetings. A part of you likes doing this."

"I do, but a date?"

She flicked her eyes up. "Like you're not going with Scout."

"What are you talking about?" I knew what she was talking about, my cousins knew what she was talking about, Scout knew, but *Kira* should not have known. It was then that I also remembered the comment she'd made when I'd been leaving Mario's.

I never did find out what that was all about.

Her smile turned knowing and smug. She lifted a shoulder as the bell rang and then turned to turn to leave with the crowd. "Just saying."

Just saying?

Just saying what?

WTF? But she brought that up to me before study hall, which I shared with Scout, which he wasn't in the cafeteria with us.

I got in there, saw Kira and her buds at a table, and huffed because I didn't like the little grin she was giving me.

I pulled my phone out.

Me: Where are you?

Scout: Getting some training in before we go.

Now I was steaming because did Kira know about us and Scout knew she knew, but he didn't tell me that she knew? Was that the deal? If that was, I wasn't happy, but here I was, at study hall and I couldn't get any answers because he wasn't here. But he was working out, which made sense, and logically, I could chill. I could and should and would wait to bring it up in the vehicle on the way to Portland, but we were going to Portland and, what if this led to a fight? That was a long time to spend with someone you weren't happy with, but ugh. What was I doing?

I was overthinking.

I was being that girl, though I knew plenty of guys who were overthinkers too, but still. Chill. Relax. Bring it up later.

That was what I was going to do.

I DIDN'T BRING it up, mostly because I got distracted.

And I got distracted because everyone and their cousin—in my case, literally—were hanging out at my locker after school. I didn't know if Scout and I were telling people where we were going together, so while Clint was peppering me with questions about hanging out, I was lying.

I couldn't hang out because . . . fill in the blank.

Anything I said, Clint knew was bullshit.

He knew I was lying.

That made me lie even more, and that was making me feel an excessive amount of guilt because I didn't want to lie to my cousin. He just would not be happy that I was driving to Portland and back with Scout. Call it cousin intuition because Alex and Trenton were also feeling it. They were all standing there, all staring at me, all knowing I was lying, and each of them was giving me this side-eye look, but they couldn't blast me because, who else was there? The theme was cousins today, so yeah, we had Gem and her cousin, Theresa, also there, who were listening in, holding their books to their chests, their heads downs, and their eyes skirting left to right, following the interrogation happening.

In the end, I somehow concocted a story about how I'd decided to look for a job and I had to go alone and I wasn't really sure where all I was going to apply because who knew? Maybe I'd end up seeing if some craft store in Pine River or a stamp store in Pine Valley were hiring? But I had to go alone because who'd want to hang out with me while I'm running in and out of stores, filling out applications? At that part, my cousins started to back off because that rang true for them. They didn't want to do that with me. Clint was starting to sweat that I was going to try to talk him into applying with me. Which, if it'd been true, I would've.

Alex and Trenton backed off when they realized going with me would cause them to miss football practice.

They left after thirty minutes. I had Gem and Theresa to dodge next.

They turned out to be easier to talk around because I mentioned that Kira brought up Homecoming dates. Theresa was out at that point. She didn't want to talk about that.

Gem was the last hold-out.

She wanted to talk about how we're doing our hair for the dance.

That was when my phone buzzed.

Scout: Outside. You ready?

"I have to go," I blurted.

She stopped mid-sentence, her face perplexed.

"I'm sorry. I-I have to go." I grabbed what I needed from my locker and headed out.

Gem was walking with me. "You okay?"

I picked up speed.

So did she.

I went faster.

She matched me.

We were both almost sprinting for the door.

"Ramsay—hey. Wait."

The door was right there. Within reach, and I looked out, seeing Scout waiting by the curb in his truck.

What was I doing? For real. What was I doing?

She was on the same wavelength because she asked, "What is going on with you? And don't give me the same story about job applications. You know I'd go with you." She rethought that. "You know I'd try to talk you into working at Mario's. You said that to get your cousins off your back."

"You think?"

She nodded, her eyes so somber. "I'm starting to get to know you, you know. Really know you. What's going on? You can tell me."

I didn't trust friends. Family, yes. Everyone else? No. But, Gem picked me. She saw me and she chose me and she had no idea who I was. I . . . I didn't know what Scout and I were doing. I didn't know what it meant that he invited me to go to this fight with him, or that I was going, or that I was excited to go. It could mean I wanted to get away, get distracted even more from life, or it could mean other things, other things that frightened me as well.

But I had a sleepover with Gem, and I was closed off to letting her in.

I was realizing it now.

She was watching me, waiting for me, and I had a decision to make. Let her in or keep her out.

"I'm going to Portland with Scout."

She gasped.

I wasn't done. "We're going to watch a fight."

Another gasp.

I was going for broke here. "And we've been sleeping together."

She careened backward and dropped. Literally. It was a hard *thud* as she hit the ground. "Wait. I'm good. Sorry. I'm up." She shot a hand up before scrambling to her feet. "Sorry." Her face was beet red. "I—Holy, holy, holy, holy, holy! I can't believe what you just said!"

Steam was starting to rise from the top of her head.

Her eyes were bulging out. "You're slee—"

I clamped a hand over her mouth, and she finished but her words were muffled against my palm. I still got, "Howyuck-howyuckhowyuck!"

I was guessing she was saying holy fuck.

I was holding my breath, waiting out her reaction as the door opened behind us. We'd turned around at some point, I'd not noticed, so I turned to see Scout coming in, a frown on his face. He spotted us and stopped half in, half out of the door, and Gem began shrieking. She clamped her own hand over her mouth, still making the same sound as she began jumping in place.

Scout's eyes slid my way.

Her gaze kept bouncing from him to me, him to me, him to me, as she kept jumping, her hand clamped over her mouth.

He sighed. "Fucking hell." He turned and left, the door swinging shut behind him.

Gem didn't look like she was going to stop, so I reached out and caught her arm. "Please don't tell anyone."

She stopped jumping and began vigorously nodding, her hand still over her mouth.

I gave her a tentative grin before following because, what else was there for me to do? Had that been a good move or not?

So yeah.

All that happened, and that was why I forgot to ask him about Kira's comment because when I got in his truck, I wasn't thinking about Kira. I was thinking about Gem.

She was the first friend outside of family that I'd let in. I glanced at Scout.

She was the second outside of family.

65

RAMSAY

I 'd gone to Scout's fight with my cousins.

I'd gone to a fight with Theresa.

Neither of them prepared me for what it was like to go to a fight with Scout.

The drive had been long, but I'd spent most of it flustered over everything that happened after school and before he picked me up, so after we stopped for food, gas, did a bathroom break, I was relieved for some quiet. I needed it to regroup.

I would have no idea how much I needed that before we arrived to this fight because when we arrived, I learned the level of Scout's celebrity status. Legit.

The fight was held in an old gymnasium. There was security, but we got waved through and sent to a special parking area. All the security guys wanted to say hello to Scout. All of them. There was one selling tickets across the lot, and he had to rush over to give Scout a manly handshake and shoulder pounding before he headed back to continue his job. And the people who were waiting for him, they saw Scout, and the phones came out.

Women came over. Smiling. Flirting. Not giving one fuck I was there.

Most had to hug him. Some gave him lingering touches on the arm.

Scout was unfazed. This was normal for him, which stunned me.

And the guys. There were so many who wanted to talk to him. Not just a hello. A real conversation. It took us thirty minutes to cover five feet once we got through the first set of doors. Once we got into the main arena area, the more professional people approached him, and they had a different vibe to them. Smarter. More business-like. Brisk. Intelligent. They were all in hella good shape. Most looked like they'd been fighters themselves, but all came over to talk with Scout or shake his hand.

Once the first set of pictures started being taken, I held back.

Scout came over, breaking away. "We can watch down by the cage or up there. It'll be more comfortable up there."

"Whatever works best for you to see."

His eyes narrowed, studying me.

Up there meant a section above the normal seating area. We had a slight balcony to stand behind, and we stood even though there were seats to the side. A few other people had congregated with us. Scout introduced me to them, and I wasn't surprised to find out that most were also fighters. They were nice enough, but I was thankful when they left before the fight started.

66

SCOUT

Bad move bringing Ramsay with me.

I didn't know what I was thinking, and I'd thought about telling her something came up, I had to go alone. I should've done that.

But I wanted her with me. It was stupid.

It was distracting. She was distracting.

Instead of watching for how Pieter dropped his shoulder before he swung and didn't protect his left side, or cocked his head a slight centimeter before making a move, I was watching Ramsay.

I loved fighting.

Loved everything about it. The feel of walking into the gym. Of hearing the sounds of someone pounding away on a bag. I liked the smarts that it took to be a great fighter, the challenge, the need to outmaneuver your opponent. There was something about going from being pinned and about to tap out to finding that opening and reversing so you were on the offensive.

I loved all of that.

And I was really loving being here, at a fight, with her, knowing I could touch her if I wanted.

Fuck's sakes. It'd been so hard at my fight, feeling the pain and the exhilaration coursing through my body, then looking up, seeing her, and knowing I couldn't take her like I wanted.

Now was different.

Now I could do all the taking I wanted.

I moved over, lined up behind her, and leaned in.

RAMSAY

He was against my back.

We were at the balcony, and he'd settled in literally behind me.

I was going to combust.

The whole thing was a lot. The testosterone.

The reek of sweat, sex, and need compounding through the room.

I turned around, looking up, seeing Scout's eyes all dark, all focused right on me, and that look in his eyes, the same one that told me he wanted to be pounding into me. We were barely touching, but I felt him in every sense.

Every cell.

My heart was thumping so hard, almost deafening.

I wet my lips, and his gaze locked on that movement.

The fight had just started.

Scout was supposed to be watching it. He was watching me, and I couldn't look away. There was an invisible pressure on both of us. If I looked away, I felt like I'd die.

A whimper left me as I bit down on my lip.

His eyes went feral, and he yanked me from the balcony.

He half-carried me, half-dragged me through the door,

down a hallway, through another door, and everything else went silent. It was just him and me.

The door slammed shut. The light was left off, and my back was shoved against the wall.

His mouth hit mine—hot, persistent, demanding.

Oh, damn. *Damn.*

I was drugged. I was drunk. I wasn't thinking clearly. Pure, blind, unbridled hunger took over as he lifted me.

My legs wound around his waist.

His hands were under my shirt, pushing it up.

Our mouths were battling, devouring each other.

I went to his pants, reaching in, and closed around him.

He stilled, his forehead leaning against mine. He said under his breath, "Fuck. *Fuck.*"

Right. I was there with him.

"Fuck. Rams—" He squirmed as I smoothed up and down, my thumb running over his tip. His forehead went to the wall beside me, his shoulders began to shake, and he breathed out heavily. A deep pant.

I kept going, squeezing, pumping. He growled as he batted my hand away. "Scou—"

He pulled me from the wall, turned me around, and was on my back in the next second. His heat against mine. We both paused at the contact, right before a second growl erupted from him.

He kicked my feet wide, making room, then ran his hands up the outsides of my legs.

I was squirming now.

He breathed in, right in my ear, "How does that feel?"

I moaned, starting to turn around.

"No," he clipped out before nipping at my ear.

A shiver went down my neck and spine, but he pulled my pants down and was cupping me from behind.

His thumb moved to my clit as two fingers sank in.

He went hard and fast, not giving me time to adjust. He began pumping like I'd been pumping him. This was tit for tat.

A savage sound came from me as I tried to shove away from the wall.

I didn't want it this way. I wanted to sink down on him. I wanted both of us to come together, but this felt different.

Scout was different. More alpha. More primal.

He wanted to dominate.

I couldn't handle it.

I'd be stripped down, needing, feeling raw and he'd indulge how he seemed fit. He'd have all the power. The control.

He wasn't giving me a choice, his fingers kept thrusting in until I gaped, plastered completely against the wall because my knees were knocking. I was going to fall down.

"Scout," I choked out, just as my knees gave away and a climax ripped through me.

He moved in, catching me, his fingers helping to lift me off my feet. He held me in place, letting me rest completely against him as my entire body was shaking, trembling.

He waited until the waves faded, then pressed a kiss to my neck and growled, "My turn."

I was turned around, my legs whipped up. He barked, "Wrap."

I wrapped them around his waist.

"Lock."

I locked my ankles.

He slid inside, pushing all the way to the hilt. He paused for one second before he gripped my waist, tipping my hips a bit, and then he was fucking me.

So deep. In and out. He was rough. Almost frenzied.

I was going to climax again. I felt the release starting, waiting, holding, building.

I could only hold on to his shoulders.

I exploded, a strangled scream poured out of me right

before his mouth slammed back on mine. He drank me up, and he released right after, his whole body sagging against mine. He continued to hold me up, waiting until both of our pulses slowed.

"*Fuck*," he breathed against me, his fingers sinking into my skin before he pushed back, letting my feet drop.

He sighed. "Fight's almost done, I bet."

I frowned as we began fixing our clothing. "Sorry?"

He laughed, flashing me a short grin.

God. He was hot when he was pissed off, but that smile transformed his whole face. He was stunning, reminding me of the first time I saw him smile. I liked it. I wanted to see it more.

He got suddenly serious, straightening up. His hand fell from his hair back to his side.

"What?" I asked, straightening too.

"You think we should talk about this?" He motioned between us.

My mouth dried up. "No."

He frowned. "No? We're fucking almost every other day."

I reached past him, my hand closing over the door handle. "I like fucking you. Why would you want that to stop?"

"Rams—"

I wasn't listening as I opened the door and breezed past him.

I liked what we were doing.

I liked not thinking.

I liked that he could make me feel good, chase away the demons.

I didn't want to lose that.

Still, I couldn't ignore the little spark of doubt and fear that took root in me because, if he brought it up once, he'd bring it up again. That was how Scout was. He didn't hide from something, instead he was like a bull, literally charging at it head on.

While normally that'd make me respect someone, I didn't like it in this instance. Not one bit.

So distracted by wanting to get away from Scout before he insisted we had that kind of talk, I hadn't paid attention to where I was going. I turned down one hallway and then another, eventually finding myself in front of the concession area.

"The Maroney triplets' cousin." A body stepped in front of me.

I almost collided with them, and they reached up, hands closing around my arms to steady me as I braked suddenly.

I looked up. Kunz was staring at me, a hard, cocky glint in his eyes. He didn't let go of me as his eyes trailed past me, and a mocking smirk twisted the corner of his mouth when someone else stepped up to his side.

Macon Rice was with him. He was sneering at me. "I remember you."

I frowned, almost paralyzed because that ugliness in him was bringing up old memories. He wasn't like Max, but he was on the same path. He would become another Max, without the same privilege that protected him, and because of that, Macon would only live a life in and out of prison.

Pity washed over me, and seeing it, some of his sneer disappeared, then it was back and reinforced. "Word on the street is that you're fucking Raiden."

Kunz's fingers tightened on me, just slightly. "Is that so?"

The paralysis lifted. I began to try to rip myself out of Kunz's hold, which I thought was going to be a waste of energy before I was suddenly free. It took me a second to realize it was Scout's doing, and he currently had Kunz pushed all the way back to the concession counter. People scattered, some squawking.

Some guys were shouting.

Some girls screamed.

Funny. I had a thought in the back of my mind that these

people were here for violence, but when it happened uncontained, their view suddenly changed. It got a lot more scary to them.

"You're not going to put hands on her. You hear me?" Scout had a hand to Kunz's throat, holding him pinned in place. He wasn't doing anything else, he wasn't touching him anywhere else, just that one hand against his throat. The very real promise he could and would hurt Kunz was keeping him in place.

Kunz's eyes hardened, first focusing on Scout before looking at me.

Scout growled, moving to block him. "You don't look at her."

Security guards were running in. They got Scout off of him, and I was about to move forward when a slimy hand touched my arm, and I was being pulled backward.

No!

"Hey." I tried to twist around, but Macon's grip on me was constricting. He was already leaving bruises. "Stop!"

He kept dragging me backward, through the crowd that had gathered to watch Scout and Kunz, and through a door.

We were in a locker room, and suddenly, another guy was there. This time, he was big, an older adult. Maybe in his forties. He ripped Macon's grip off me and slammed him back against the door. "What the fuck were you going to do to her?"

Before Macon could answer, the guy looked at me. "Get the fuck out of here."

I swallowed. He looked vaguely familiar. Dark hair. His eyes . . .

Why'd he look so familiar?

He snarled, "Now!"

I took off, glancing back once and seeing he was gone with Macon.

I ran around the corner and right into a hard chest, but

relief hit me because I knew this chest. Arms wrapped around me on reflex. Scout tensed and then swept me up and against him. "You okay? Where'd you go?"

"I—" I looked back, but the guy was coming back out of the locker room. He had a hold of Macon, and as Scout cursed, his entire body becoming like cement, two security guards were approaching the guy and Macon.

"Fuck—" Scout growled. "Winslet."

"Yo." One of the guys that Scout had introduced me to earlier materialized by his side. "Keep watch of Ramsay for me."

"Got it." He was a big dude, and he gave me a wink. "Which fight did you enjoy the most?"

My eyebrows pinched together as I watched Scout head over to talk to the guy. Macon was being led out by the two guards, and as Scout tried to go after him, the guy blocked him. They exchanged words, and judging by how rigid both were as well as their clenched jaws and fists, I was guessing it wasn't a good exchange of words.

The whole thing only lasted a few seconds before Scout turned and stalked my way.

"Your boy's not happy." Winslet was eating a carrot, not sounding bothered. He gave me another wink. "Word of advice? Start a fight in the beginning of the ride back. He'll settle down by the time you arrive in Pine River. Happy trails."

He sauntered off, still eating that carrot.

Scout was back and glaring over my shoulder. "Let's go."

"Wait. What?"

He took my hand, and we began winding our way through the crowd. The few who looked back, glimpsed him in time to recognize him, stepped back, started to say his name, but he ignored them all as he pushed outside and headed straight toward his truck.

I waited until we got into the truck. "What happened back there? Who was that guy—"

"Don't," Scout barked, not looking at me once as he clipped on his seatbelt, started the truck, and peeled out of the parking lot. "Don't bring up that guy."

"Wh—"

"Ever, Ramsay." He seared me with a look before blinking, and his usual mask was back in place over his face. "And Rice is going back to jail."

"Wha—just like that?"

"Just like that."

"Wait. What? You need to explain that to me. I was the one he was trying to drag into the locker room." My voice rose.

He cursed and then swung into a parking lot. It was after-hours so it was empty. A lone light was in the middle. Scout pulled over, putting the vehicle in park. "What do you want to know?"

"I—" I snapped, sick of being hauled around and all the angry tones. "I don't know! Maybe what was Rice going to do to me? Why's he going to jail? Don't I need to give a statement? What happened with you and Kunz?" And since I was on a roll. "And I don't want to talk about you and me or what we're doing. I like what we're doing. I don't want it to end. Okay?"

He didn't answer right away.

"Okay?"

He was scowling at me as he quietly said, "If they need your statement, they'll contact you. If you want to give one, I know the number, but they don't need it. Rice isn't supposed to be anywhere in the same vicinity as this league's fights. He was banned a while back. Him catching trespassing charges will violate whatever bond he's out on, and he's going to go back to jail."

"It happens like that?"

"Sometimes. With him, I think so. Cohen's uncle is a detective. He's told me things about what could happen with Rice."

Oh. "And Kunz?"

"Kunz and I had words. That was it."

His phone lit up.

Scout muttered a curse, accepting the call. "You psychic now?"

There was silence before a smooth laugh came through. "You were talking about me? Hope it was all good." It was Kunz.

"It'll never be good about you. What do you want?"

"I just heard what Rice did—or tried to do, and wanted to reach out. He wasn't there with me. He knew I'd be there, found me, and asked if I wanted to employ him." He waited a beat. "I turned him down. Latest rumor spreading is that he saw Williams, thought he could threaten her to get her to get you off his back about Amalia." Another beat of silence. "He's not the brightest. But, again, he had nothing to do with me. I'm not endorsing what he tried to do. I'm calling to let Williams know that she didn't need to be scared of me tonight, and if anything is said to Theresa, you know, put the right slant on it."

Scout cursed. "You're calling so we'll put in a good word for you with Garcia?"

"Not a good word. Just not a wrong word. That's all."

I stopped listening to them.

Macon was going to threaten me. That was sinking in. Threaten.

New relief hit my sternum. I could handle threats. Other stuff—ice lined my organs.

Scout had been studying me, seeing my reaction. "Thanks for the info."

"Now, about you—"

Scout ended the call, still focusing on me. "You okay?"

I swallowed, the pit moving up in my throat. "Not really."

"I didn't think—I'm sorry. It was a bad idea to bring you here."

I swung back to him. "Why?"

He paused.

"Why do you say that? Before Kunz and Rice, I liked it. I liked being here." With him.

A shadow flickered in his gaze. "The violence. The undertones—"

"Violence doesn't scare me. It's a part of life. What scares me is how it's used, and you've never used it the wrong way for me. Kunz wasn't hurting me when he was holding my arms. I almost walked into him, and he caught me so I didn't fall back. I was about to step away, and Scout, he would've let me go. I knew that in my gut. Rice, though. He was different."

His eyebrows lowered. "Kunz isn't a good guy."

"Maybe not, but tonight, he wasn't the one who scared me. All I'm saying. That's it."

He continued to hold my gaze before slowing nodding. Some pressure in the truck lifted, easing up. "Okay."

I bit my lip, unsure. "Can I ask who that older guy was?"

His mouth flattened before he sat back, his hands going to the gears. "No. It's not personal. Just, he doesn't matter."

I had a feeling he did, but I didn't ask again.

We drove in silence for a while, stopping for gas before leaving the city. Once we were back on the interstate, he broke it first. "Before that shit happened, I had fun." He glanced my way. "With you. I had fun with you."

I would've responded, but my stomach fluttered.

Then it sank.

This wasn't good.

BY THE TIME we got to Pine River, I had convinced myself that the stomach flutters weren't flutters. They didn't mean anything. I'd also made up my mind that I was going to focus on the first part of the night.

Not the parts that involved Kunz, Rice, or anyone else Scout didn't want to talk about. So barring all of that, it was a good trip.

I was glad we'd gone.

Then I realized my phone had been silent all night. I'd accidentally muted it. I didn't know when that happened or how, but the notifications stopped me from wondering anything else.

Missed calls (23)

Text alerts (64)

I clicked on the first one.

Alex: You knew our dad was having an affair? NOT COOL, RAMS

Trenton: Wtf?

My mom had left messages. My aunt. My cousins.

My heart sank.

Our night went from good to bad, and it was about to get worse.

67

SCOUT

"**W**hat's wrong?"

Once Ramsay opened her phone, she made a guttural whimper and hadn't moved a muscle since. She was frozen in her seat, holding that phone in her lap, her chin resting on her chest.

"Ramsay."

She still didn't move.

"If you don't say a word in the next five seconds, I'm pulling over. What is going on?"

She whispered, "I messed up." She raised stricken eyes to me, and damn. Damn. I never wanted to see that look in her eyes again. Ever. Felt like a hole just punctured my chest. She kept whispering, "I knew about something, but I never told them, and I should've told. They found out, and they know that I knew before them."

"You're talking about the affair?"

"I forgot I told you."

We were pulling up to her house, and after seeing every light on and three vehicles parked in front, I said, "Looks like everyone knows now." I knew those cars. One was her aunt's. Another was Alex's. The third was Trenton's.

Clint's was missing.

Ramsay had paled, but she jerked forward, seeing what I was seeing.

As soon as I pulled over to the curb, she was scrambling for the door at the same time the front door of her house opened. Out ran her mom. Trenton and Alex were next. Her aunt was last, staying on the front step, holding her phone clutched to her chest.

This was not good, so very not good.

"Oh God! You're okay! You're okay." Ramsay's mom had her in her arms, her hands smoothing down Ramsay's hair and back. "Oh thank goodness. We couldn't find you or get in touch, and I had no idea."

Another two vehicles were coming up the street. My uncle's and Cohen's uncle. Angel Reyes.

Trenton and Alex stayed on the other side of my truck by Ramsay, and both were scorching me with looks. I got out and closed my door as my uncle's truck pulled over to the other side of the street. Angel pulled up behind, but as I crossed to my uncle, Angel got out of his and was meeting me.

My uncle got out, shutting his door and leaning back against it, his arms crossed over his chest. He was looking past me. "You know what's going on?"

I shook my head. "We just got back."

"You took her to the fight with you?"

"Yeah."

His eyes were knowing. "Learn a lot about your opponent, huh?"

"Come on."

Angel moved in. "Glad to see you're okay."

"What are you doing here?" I asked him.

He nodded toward everyone on the other side of the road.

"Cohen got a call from Alex, who couldn't find his cousin, who also couldn't get ahold of you. So, my nephew called me to see what I could do."

My uncle added, "Ten minutes ago, that call changed to them now not being able to find one of the triplets."

"Clint's not here." I indicated the vehicles. "That's Alex's, Trenton's, and their aunt's."

"Why weren't you in communication?" my uncle asked me.

"I had my phone on, but I didn't check it. Ramsay pulled out her phone when we were coming into town. That was when she saw all her notifications. Clint is missing?"

"She say anything to you?" That was from Angel, who was studying me intently.

My gut twisted, remembering the look on her face. "Nothing about Clint missing."

"Okay." My uncle sighed. "Let's go over and see what we can do to help."

Ramsay was off to the side, her head bent close to Alex and Trenton's.

My uncle approached her mom, and now Mama Maroney was coming down the walkway. Her face was just as tear-stained as Ramsay's mom's.

"Ma'am."

"God, no. I'm Christina, Ramsay's mother. Call me Chris."

Ramsay's head jerked up, a plea in her gaze as she looked at me.

I moved over, letting the adults do their introductions.

"What's going on?" I asked.

Trenton cursed, jumping back on his feet.

I wasn't liking the restlessness coming from him.

Ramsay filled in the blanks. "My uncle is leaving my aunt."

Alex was glaring at me, his jaw clenching.

"Alex," I started.

He shook his head. "Don't even, man. You were off with my cousin? You couldn't answer a fucking phone call?"

I hadn't looked at my phone all night. How could I explain that he rarely called me, and the only other person I wanted to hear from was with me? That Cohen was aware I was at a fight and knew I tended not to answer because I was usually in work mode, studying, networking, that sort of stuff. I hadn't noticed any of the notifications.

Ramsay said, "Clint's missing."

Trenton shifted back to the group, but he was still edgy, like a firework that'd been lit and just hadn't been tossed yet. "He's getting himself into deep shit. That's what he's doing. We gotta find him before he either puts someone in the hospital or he gets put into the hospital."

"Yeah." Alex was eying his brother. "We just gotta figure out where he'd go."

Both shared a look. Then, as one, they turned to Ramsay.

Her eyes got big. "What?"

I was on the outskirts, not understanding these cousin dynamics.

Trenton smirked.

Alex rolled his eyes. "We know he was doing shit, and he pulled you in. Where'd you go? What'd you do?"

"The booze," Trenton added. "Where'd you get it?"

"Oh God." Horror flared over Ramsay's face as she took a step back. "Oh no. He wouldn't—"

"He's not thinking clearly, and he wants to hurt something or someone. Where'd you go that night?"

Ramsay actually wavered on her feet. My hand shot out, catching her.

At the touch, she centered and drew in a deep breath.

Both her cousins noticed, noticed my hand too.

"There's a fraternity on the other side of Pine Valley," she whispered.

"We're going." Alex started for his car.

"No." I held up my keys. "I'm driving."

Trenton's eyes narrowed.

Alex didn't look happy.

Ramsay moved so she was between them and me. Her hand went to my chest. I didn't think she even knew it, but her cousins did. They were very aware of every move between the two of us. She was saying, "If we run into trouble, we're going to need him."

"This is a family thing." Trenton's head lowered, still glowering.

Alex didn't say anything. Neither did Ramsay. As if knowing it was his decision, we all waited. Finally, he sighed. "Ramsay, you're in the back seat. I'll text mom, let her know we're going to get Clint."

The adults had moved inside the house.

I got in the front. Trenton jumped to the back.

Ramsay climbed into the back seat, and Alex got into the passenger seat. He had his phone out.

"Who are you calling?"

He didn't look my way. "Cohen. If we really do need all hands on deck, we'll need him too. We can pick him up." He had pulled up Cohen's number and hit the call button as he looked at me. "If something happens to Ramsay, we're going to need someone who can talk you down because, sure as shit, none of us will be in the mindframe to deal with you."

I wasn't sure if that was an insult, a dig, or just solid fore-thought.

I was going with the latter.

68

RAMSAY

My uncle hadn't stopped the affair. That was what my cousins told me, which was also what all of them were told tonight when Uncle Nick sat everyone down in the living room. The affair never ended, and he'd made a decision.

He was leaving Aunt Aileen.

The aftermath was Clint and Trenton going apeshit on him, making him pack his bags because they'd kicked him out of the house. After that, they showed up with their mom at my house as my mom was getting home from her shift.

They piled into the house, and it was pandemonium as they filled her in on what happened. When they were trying to find me because I wasn't in my room like everyone assumed I would be, it got even worse.

That'd been my bad.

I hadn't thought about letting my mom know I'd be gone as long as I had been.

I thought we'd be back before her shift ended.

But that happened, and when they were calling me and panicking, and also looking for Scout and further panicking because he wasn't picking up his phone either, that was when Clint took off.

Then we rolled up and now we were heading over to Pine Valley University.

I gave them directions on where to go, and we parked on a street away from the Rho Mu Epsilon house. "That's him." Trenton took off first, running up a back alley.

I moved to go after him, but someone stopped me. I looked. Scout was holding onto the back of my jeans, his eyes locked on Trenton, who was now wrestling with Clint.

Alex muttered a curse, heading over to them, and a moment later, both brothers were dragging Clint back with them. They shoved him forward before creating a wall. Cohen joined.

"What?" Clint yelled at them, getting in their faces. "I'm not doing shit."

Alex got back in his. "You were going to."

Trenton's mouth was clamped shut, but with Trenton, who knew what that meant? Right now, he wasn't backing down from Clint.

Swinging around, seeing me, Clint did a double take. Then he saw Scout's hold on me, and an ugly snarl came out. "Right. No fucking feelings, huh?"

Ignoring that, I jerked forward. "What are you doing here?"

"You brought them here."

"Of course I did! I told you last week to leave it alone. They're going to be looking for us."

"For you guys?" Alex prompted.

Scout began pulling me back to him.

I resisted, but I wasn't trying to break free.

"*What'd* you do?" Again from Alex.

Clint was skewering me with a look that clearly said if I talked, I'd regret it. I was getting the message, but Trenton was still being quiet. That was making me more uncomfortable than anything else.

I raised an eyebrow. "They already know."

"What'd you do? You need to say it." Alex shoved Clint backward, who almost hit me, would've if Scout hadn't yanked me out of the way. He stepped in, taking the hit and holding Clint steady.

"Get off me!" Clint shoved away before focusing on Alex. "Nothing. I did nothing—"

"Tonight."

All eyes went to me. I added, "Tonight, you did nothing." And because this was stupid, I filled in the rest. "Max's family belongs to that fraternity. He'll be a legacy. He's going to join that fraternity at UConn next year."

Both Alex and Trenton sputtered out curses.

Alex was biting out with sarcasm. "You stole all that liquor from them, didn't you?"

"That was thousands of dollars' worth of liquor," Cohen spoke. "Whoa."

Clint quieted before jerking a hand in my direction. "I just scouted the first trip and took pics of some other things. She helped me."

Scout lined up right behind me, his body a hard wall. He growled, and I felt the vibrations from his chest. "Helped how?"

Clint gave him a nasty glance. "You were supposed to stop fucking when you got feelings."

There was one second when everyone froze.

Then everyone sprang into action.

I threw my arms up, trying to stop Scout.

Scout began to lunge for Clint, who turned, ready to face off against him.

Alex and Cohen jumped in the middle.

Trenton was the only one who didn't move a muscle, except to slide his eyes down the alley.

"Stop!" Me.

"Don't!" Alex.

"Hey, man." Cohen.

"Let him fucking come at me. If he's going to hurt my cousin, I want to hurt him back. Rather do it now than later."

"No, you don't!" Alex turned his back to Scout and shoved once at Clint's chest, making him fall back a step. "You're hurting because of our parents. You want a target, and we're here, stopping you from doing whatever the fuck you were going to do. So, now you want a different target. Scout's my best friend."

"Your best friend is fucking our cousin."

I felt like I should say something.

Alex yelled, "And she's letting him! Ever fucking think about that? Huh?"

Everyone got silent again.

Alex kept on, his face getting red, "I went at Scout. Him and me. We almost brawled about it, but I saw what even he couldn't see. Think, dude. Think." He stabbed a finger at his head. "The attraction was there from the beginning. Neither wanted it. They didn't like each other, but that didn't seem to matter. What does that tell you? I'm his best friend. He has two friends here. Scout's not the type who fucks over friends, and still, he—"

Clint's sarcasm was just as biting, "And still, he decided to shove his prick into her."

Now I was seeing red. "You—" I lunged, but a cement arm wrapped around my waist, and I was being carried away. I struggled to get free. "Come on. Let me go! I know how to fight him."

"I'm sure you do." Scout walked me away before setting me on my feet, and when I tried darting around him, he stopped me, getting in my way. "Stop. Listen, okay? Listen." He lifted a hand, hesitated, and then placing it against the side of my face.

I froze before looking up at him. His eyes were clouded. His face was shadowed, but he was fighting for his own control.

His hand trembled against my face. Holding it steady, he brushed a thumb over my cheek. "Just listen."

A pent-up growl erupted, and I tried shoving away, but Scout held me against him.

Then I listened, and my heart began to break.

"He's going to hurt her." Clint.

"Maybe." Alex. "Maybe not."

"What are you on? You have to be on something. Yeah. It's Ramsay. She does what she wants, but she came to us broken. He broke her. You're going to let another guy—"

I tried to twist away from Scout, but he wouldn't let go, keeping himself frozen in place at the same time.

"That's fucking bullshit, and you know it."

"Cohen," Clint warned.

"No, fuck you. You're saying shit about my best friend. He's like a brother to me, and he's never screwed over a friend. He doesn't have them for a reason. You wake up, dude. He could have a million friends, but does he? No. He has Alex and me. That's it. I mean, there are guys he hangs out with at fights, but we're it. We're the only ones he lets in, and her—she's in! I'm pretty sure he tells her things that even I don't know, and I've known him almost all my life. Think on that. Just fucking think on that, Clint. You'll realize how far up your own ass that you stuck your own pole. Yank it the fuck out, and see!" Cohen was almost yelling.

"Guys." A hiss. Trenton. "Shut the fuck up. NOW!"

Everyone quieted.

Scout stepped around me, and we could hear footsteps coming down the alley toward us.

I started around him, but Scout yanked me back, herding me against the wall behind the corner. The other guys had all hidden.

A flash of headlights pulled down the alley, going slow.

It stopped.

A slight buzzing sound.

"Yo, man."

"What's up? You got my stuff?"

"Yeah, yeah. This what you wanted?"

"My man. You are awesome."

A slapping sound. The slight buzzing sound again.

The headlights flashed and went down the rest of the alley, racing past us. Too fast to spot us.

"Shut up!"

The footsteps had started down the alley, but they paused at hearing one of my cousins. Then they started again. Going slow. Getting louder. Getting closer.

He appeared, and he was staring right at me. One of the fraternity brothers from Rho Mu Epsilon. I barely recognized him. He might've been the one making out with the girl, guarding the alcohol door, but his eyes bulged out. "What the fuck?"

Scout cursed.

The guy tore out of there, yelling, "We got company?"

"Scout, stop!" Cohen raced to get in front of him so he couldn't go down the alley. "Think, man. He's going for backup. You want to fight them here or in the street?"

Alex said, "Or how about we don't fight them at all?"

No.

No.

I felt in a trance, stepping to the side, now clearly visible in the alley. They could see me, and they were looking. A group trickled out from the house at hearing their brother yelling. That guy stopped on the street, turning to point at me.

It was the guy who'd been hitting on me.

He wasn't alone.

I felt a presence next to me, heard the slight scrape of a shoe on the gravel, and knew it was Clint. "Holy fuck." His voice was low, disbelieving. "Is that?"

"Yes," my voice scraped out. Because it happened, when a brother fraternity road-tripped to see another brother fraternity. I didn't know why they were there, but they were.

"Guys," Clint said. "They've got company."

"Who?"

He stepped out from his own brothers, other guys that I recognized because I'd partied at their house, partied with the guy who I thought I'd loved at that time.

"Max's brother. His *real* brother."

69

SCOUT

Christ. The guy's brother looked like all the typical douchebags I hated. Salmon-colored fucking shorts. A blue polo. The dickwad was an Easter egg. He had the thick square jaw that I loved breaking when guys like him used to step up to me, thinking they could best Kincaid Raiden's kid. Jock. Muscle.

They were the ones who fell the fastest.

Maybe it was knowing who he was related to or the way he was staring at Ramsay. He looked ready to eat her up after fucking her in every hole and wanting her to resist it. Or, maybe it was because I just hated assholes like him.

I was going to break this kid's jaw.

I stepped around them, knowing Cohen glanced my way.

Alex too, but he was distracted, keeping an eye on Ramsay and Clint because the Trouble Twins were out in effect. Ramsay wasn't hiding. She wasn't scared. I recognized the look in her eyes too. She wanted blood. Vengeance. She'd joined Clint in his need to cause mayhem.

"Ramsay Williams?" The brother came forward, sneering at her. "It *is* you."

"Spencer." Ramsay's tone was so cold.

Spencer Prestige. Max Prestige.

I *loathed* their names. Fancy-ass, wealthy, privileged weasel dicks. These were the assholes my grandfather would've wanted me to befriend. Hell with that. They would've been beneath me. I didn't even want to know how much worse the pricks would've been, the ones my grandfather would've chosen to be my friends.

"That's her." One of the frat guys was pointing at Ramsay. "And him. He came into the house to get her."

Another guy stepped forward, bigger, older. Probably the one in charge of the house. "You're the ones who ripped us off?"

"Ripped—" Prestige's brother laughed, tipping his head back. "Absolutely priceless. Ramsay Williams. I cannot wait to let father know about this. He's just waiting to pull the trigger on a lawsuit. Just you wai—"

"Shut up!" she yelled, stepping forward. Her whole body was riddled with tension. "Just shut the fuck up, you three-inch dick. They even know the history? Do they know?"

He quieted.

"Yeah." Her laugh was hollow. "I'm guessing not."

The leader frowned. "What's she talking about, Prestige?"

He was glowering at Ramsay. "Nothing. She ain't talking about shit."

"Or she is." Alex raised his hand, rolling his eyes. "You might want to know the history going on here, like the fact that this guy?" He was pointing at Prestige's brother. "His little brother used to date my cousin." His finger swung toward Ramsay before dropping. "And the whole reason she's here is because that prick's brother not only beat her up but also killed her dad. My uncle." All three Maroney triplets stepped forward, their very violent promise clear on their faces.

The fraternity leader was taking everyone in before swinging my way and holding. He cursed. "You kidding me?"

He stepped back.

"What?" the Spencer fuck asked.

A few other fraternity brothers were looking from him to me, and then another one cursed, raking a hand over his face. "Well, fuckers."

"What?" Prestige's voice rose sharply. "Who is that? Who are you?"

"We're not going to fight you guys, not when you have Scout Raiden here."

Yeah. He knew me.

"Who's Scout Raiden?" The brother was still looking back and forth before focusing on me. Judging me. Deciphering me. "Who are you?"

One of their guys moved forward, a hand to Prestige's arm. "Dude. Maybe step back."

Prestige shook his hand off, still only focused on me. "You want a piece of me?"

I went feral.

Yes. I wanted a piece of him. I wanted a whole head piece of him, and I started to answer, letting him know this when Cohen spoke up.

"You should rethink your odds." His voice was calm. Rational.

It wasn't welcome.

He motioned toward us. "You have no idea who you're taking on here. I'll get to my best friend later, but take in the triplets first. They want blood. Literally. Your guy's brother put her in the hospital and killed her father. Think on that." His hand swung wide. "These guys love her and have picked her up from the floor, and your brother's real brother is the reason she was on the floor. Trust me. They've got a bone to pick, and they are *looking* for an excuse to pick that bone. Don't underestimate the power that adrenaline can do to a human body. You got the numbers, but we want the fight *more.* And now let's get to my best friend, who most of you have heard of—except the one he really wants to pound, of course." His voice got quiet, and he stepped forward, like a showman between two rivaling teams. He paused before he said clearly so everyone could hear, "There's a reason these guys don't want to take him on. Though, *please*, I think I speak for everyone on my side that we would love for you to find out firsthand." He raised his chin, holding a second before moving on. His words were for the fraternity's leader. "Then again, you might want to know that we witnessed your guy over there"—he pointed out the one who first found us—"doing a drug deal. So, yeah, we can wade into a fight, but when the cops come, we'll be telling that story too."

The frat leader started to respond, his big mouth opening.

Clint said, "I got pics."

The group descended into silence again.

"The first time I came, I went around your house. I found your stashes. You weren't real good at hiding them."

"Bullshi—"

"The drugs behind the library door."

The frat leader snapped to attention.

Clint said, "The drugs in the upstairs bathroom behind the medicine cabinet." He was now wary, eyeing the rest of the fraternity guys who were all pointedly looking anywhere but at him. "Do you want me to keep going? The cocaine in the freezer, which is a sucky hiding spot. The needles in the base-ment, tucked next to the pool table. That one confused me. I still can't figure out how you get them out if there's people around, but to each their own idiotic hiding spots." He stopped, still eyeing them. "I have pictures. I have video of another drug deal you did. I have it all. Take me down, I don't care, but trust me, I'll take your entire chapter with me."

"You're lying—" Prestige started.

The fraternity leader got ahead of him, slapping a hand to his chest. "Do us a favor and shut the fuck up, Prestige."

His chest bolstered up. "Now, listen, Grant—"

"You're done. I don't care about your last name or that you're a legacy. I want you gone and on a flight by the end of tonight." He motioned to his other fraternity members. "Pack their shit up. Escort them out of here."

A sound of frustration ripped from Ramsay. "No!"

The leader looked her way. "Listen, I'm sorry for what—"

"That's it?" Clint exclaimed. "I just threatened you with some evidence and you're tucking tail and running."

"We ain't running from shit, but I've got sisters. I'm not down with what you say happened to your cous—"

A car alarm blasted through the air.

Everyone stopped and then twisted.

The car was back by the fraternity house. A black Pagani, tinted windows, black rims. The type of car that screamed wealth.

Trenton was standing next to it. Its lights were flashing, and he waved. "Hey. Hi. So. Hope this is one of yours . . ." He lifted the bat that was in his other hand. He smiled. "You guys are talking a lot, and I'm kinda tired of it."

His waving hand fell down.

His smile dropped.

He stepped back, swung the bat up, and brought it down on top of the Pagani's windshield.

70

RAMSAY

We were going back.

I was squished between my cousins in the back seat. Cohen and Scout were in the front. No one was talking. I didn't know what was going on in my cousins' heads, but I was thinking back to what just happened.

When Trenton smashed the windshield, everyone sprang into action. They were starting to fight when a loud horn sounded and everyone froze. The head guy from the fraternity was the one who'd sounded the alarm, and he lowered it, pointing at Scout. "We're not going to fight."

His fraternity brothers started arguing, but he only raised his voice and added, "I know who you are." He was saying that directly to Scout. "I know who your *family* is. We're not going to fight you." His guys had quieted, and he turned toward them. "Everyone inside *now!*"

When they began trickling inside, the leader looked back and at me. "I'm sorry for what Prestige's little brother did to you. I'm saying it to you straight. I would not have been okay with that. I have little sisters, and I would murder anyone who did to them what was done to you." His eyes cut to Clint. "But having said all of that, if I see your face at one of our parties again, we're going to beat the shit out of you."

More than a few confused looks went Scout's way, but he was moving first. He plucked me up, carrying me back to the truck, and within a minute, we were leaving.

We were lucky. They had an entire house against our six.

No matter Scout's skills, no matter our adrenaline, it wouldn't have been a good ending for us.

We were crossing the river, leaving Pine Valley behind. Turning onto the main road, then we'd go by the river until we needed to turn off on my road. It might've been cold out. It probably was. We were in the back and I wasn't feeling a thing.

Except the adrenaline was starting to leave and exhaustion was creeping in.

I had no idea the time. I had no idea about a lot of things, but by the time we pulled up to my house, I was fighting back tears. I had no idea why. Alex saw me first and pulled me against him, his arm going around my shoulders. "A lot of shit went down tonight. Cry it out. We'll be fine."

I forced myself to sit up and patted his chest. "Thank you."

He frowned, seeing my face.

"Shit," Clint muttered, peering at the house.

Scout and Cohen's uncles were gone, but my aunt's was still there.

"Your car, man." Trenton was looking at Clint.

Who grimaced. "We'll get it tomorrow. I parked back a road. I don't think they'll spot it. It should be fine." He looked my way. "What was that guy saying about Scout's family?"

The truck turned off, and Scout's door opened. The passenger door too. Cohen was getting out.

Clint vaulted from the back of the truck. Trenton was right behind him. Alex and I followed, but at a more sedate pace. Clint had asked the question, but I knew he wasn't the only one wondering about Scout's family.

"What'd that guy mean about your family?"

Scout looked over Clint's head to me. I pressed my lips together.

He shrugged. "My dad's known in the fighting world. That's all, and I'm estranged from him." His tone cooled.

Clint was studying him, nodding slowly.

Cohen frowned his way.

The house was still lit up, and I didn't want to even look at my phone. I had silenced it earlier so I was sure there were so many messages from my mom.

"I knew." Clint's voice broke the slight quiet that had descended over the group. He was facing the house, his hands in his pockets, and he had a whole broody look over his face. "I knew about the affair. I walked in on Dad on the phone with her and overheard. They were talking about their next meet-up. He told Mom that they had stopped, but they hadn't." His jaw clenched. "I hate him. I've not said a word because I didn't want you to feel what I did when I found out our dad is a cheating bastard."

Alex and Trenton moved in closer to him.

"I knew," I said, my voice hoarse. "You guys knew I knew, but I didn't know that he was still cheating. Your mom asked me to wait. I didn't say anything because she said she wanted to do it, but she never did, and I . . . I should've said something. I'm sorry."

Were they mad at me? They could've been.

As if reading my mind, Clint sent me a sad smile. "Not mad at you. Don't go there, okay?"

Right.

My throat was thick with emotion, but right. I jerked my head in a nod. "Thanks." My voice was still hoarse.

"I don't think I want to go to college." That was Trenton.

"*What?*" Clint asked.

"You what?" From Alex.

Trenton held up his hands. "I thought we were sharing. I'm not saying I'm not going. Just saying I don't want to go. Sharing circle here. Clint said his thing. Then Rams. I thought it was the right time to do mine. Don't be so harsh, you know, considering the other truths revealed tonight." He motioned toward the house and Scout before dropping his hands back down by his side.

Alex shot him a glare before shaking his head. His shoulders hunched forward. "I told Ciara and Leanne that I'd take both of them to Homecoming."

Everyone's eyebrows went up.

He let out a deep sigh, his head falling down even more. "I said it when I was having sex with them at the same time."

"Holy shit." Clint's hands went in the air. "I gotta walk away on that one."

Trenton was eyeing his brother. "Both of them?"

Alex nodded.

"At the same time?"

Another nod from Alex.

Trenton's eyes rolled. "That's not really something pivotal to share here."

Alex huffed. "It is for me! I don't want to take them both to Homecoming. Do you know how expensive that'll be?"

Trenton's lips twitched.

Cohen let out a laugh.

Even Scout grinned. "They won't do that to you."

Alex sent him a look. "You think?"

"It was a heat-of-the-moment thing. No way will they think you're taking both of them to the dance."

Cohen added, "But you'll have to choose, and I gotta say, your ass will be in a sling from the one you don't choose."

"Thanks," Alex muttered, shooting him a dark look.

Cohen shrugged, grinning. "I'm taking Kira to Homecoming."

"That's the truth you're sharing?" Trenton griped. "You need to do better than that."

Cohen thought on it. "I really, *really* want to do something to Macon Rice for what he did to Amalia. It's not enough that I already beat the shit out of him, and it's not enough that he's in jail. I drive by his house all the time. Sometimes, I park and watch his place, wondering who he loves that I could hurt so he'd know what it feels like?" He asked Trenton, "That good enough?"

"Plenty, and holy shit, dude."

Scout glanced Cohen's way. "Don't do anything that'll put you in jail. That'll hurt Amalia even more."

"I know."

Clint grunted. "But also, *ditto*." He gave me a pointed glance before looking back at Cohen.

I felt that look, felt it all the way to my toes. It knocked me back.

I said, almost to myself, "I can't believe I saw Max's brother tonight."

"He wasn't backed by his frat. It's not much, but it's something." Scout moved over so he was closer to me.

"It's not enough." Clint cursed. "It'll never fucking be enough. I'd take any of the Prestiges without a pulse and buried six feet down, and it wouldn't ever be enough. How's that for another share from me? I daydream about taking a shovel and beating the fuck out of that kid, and then when he's dead, I'm still wailing on him. I can't stop. I fucking breathe that fantasy at times."

"Clint," I whispered, half horrified, and half heartbroken.

His angry and blazing eyes flicked my way before looking away. The emotion in there zapped me all over again. "Can't help it, Rams. That's how I'm built."

There were no words because I couldn't take back what happened.

I couldn't make it unhappen.

I couldn't bring my dad back.

I couldn't stop myself from falling for a guy like Max in the first place.

I could only hope and wish and heal and do something so others wouldn't do what I did.

That was what I'd do.

I'd make amends that way. Or try.

Alex had come back and said quietly, "You gotta share something Scout."

"That true about your dad?" Trenton asked him.

Scout moved so he was right by me and I could feel the tension coming off him. "We're estranged. I don't want to talk about my dad."

I looked up, tipping my head back.

He tipped his head down, his eyes finding mine.

I said it softly, "You should tell them."

I meant about his family because I didn't think it was his dad that the fraternity guy was referencing, but it wasn't for me to say. It was my place to prompt him, to give him a nudge because he was allowed support. That much I knew.

His eyes flashed.

"Tell us what?" Alex asked.

Still holding my gaze, where I was feeling he was looking inside of me, he shared, "That Clint's right. I'm starting to like your cousin, and no, I have no intention to stop fucking you. How's that for a share?"

That hadn't been what I thought he was going to share.

71

RAMSAY

Over the next week, a few things changed. One was Gem, who wanted all the details about Scout and me. I shared what I could.

"We're sleeping together so no feelings would start."

"No feelings?"

"Except sexual ones. That's changed now, though."

"You don't have sexual feelings now?"

"No, we do. That was there before we even started."

"But other feelings changed?"

"Right."

"Now you have feelings? But you're not sleeping together?"

"No, we are. We're not stopping."

"So . . . you're sleeping together, there are feelings, but you're still not friends?"

"I think we're friends now."

"But, wait. What?" She had her hands twisted in her hair. "Are you a couple then?"

"God, no."

"Wha . . ."

Theresa had come over to us, so we'd stopped talking. Gem tried asking later, but it was the same conversation.

"Okay. I get it now."

"What do you get?"

She gave me a long and inscrutable look. "That you have no idea what you're doing."

"Well." Duh. "Yeah."

After that, we were on the same page. It felt good.

A second thing that changed was Homecoming. The planning ramped up.

Also, that Alex was going to be Homecoming King. That wasn't really a change, but it was news to me. The other guys elected for Homecoming court were Clint, Trenton, Cohen, and four guys I didn't know.

The big surprise was that Scout's name wasn't on the voting sheet. He wasn't even an option.

I asked him the night after we voted.

We'd been at my place, in my room, on my bed, with the door open. My mom was home.

It'd been a week since Family Explosion. That was what I was calling the night Nick dropped the bomb he was leaving my aunt, all the other bombs we dropped after the run in with Rho Mu Epsilon, the bomb my mom dropped after everyone else had gone home.

If I was going to keep doing whatever I was doing with Scout—those weren't her exact words—we needed rules.

Rule one: Scout and his uncle came over for dinner.

That hadn't been awkward. (Sarcasm inserted.)

Rule two: Scout and I needed to be *defined.*

"It's not for you. You can think whatever you kids think nowadays, but I need to know. What do I call him? Are you having sex?" she said after dinner the next day, but then she shot a hand out. "No. I don't want to know. I should know. I need to be a proactive mom here, but I'm not blind. It's obvious whatever you're doing, that

you've been doing a while. I'm playing catchup and I'm worried about my daughter. Just tell me you're being smart? Are you being smart?"

We were folding clothes when she started. I lifted the fitted bed sheet, took in the three knots she had tied it into, and nodded. "I'm being smart."

Her chest lifted and held as she bit her lip. "What is he to you? So it makes sense to me."

What were we? "He's my Homecoming date."

Her eyes lit up. A big smile started, and she burst into tears.

Turned out, Homecoming was a sensitive topic around the house, which was what I was currently trying to explain to Scout. That she cried because she was happy I was being "normal" again.

He seemed stuck on one point.

"I'm your what?"

"Homecoming date, and also, why weren't you on the voting ballot again? You're one of the top guys here."

He sat up. "Is this your way of asking me to Homecoming?"

Okay. Now I was sitting up. "Were you planning on going stag?"

"I wasn't planning on *going*. That was why I got my name off the ballot."

"What?" Also, "How did you do that?"

His eyes narrowed. "I have my ways, and the whole point was so I wouldn't have to go. I don't go to dances."

My eyes narrowed right back. "You're going to this one."

"I don't like dances."

I sighed, sitting back on my butt and crossing my legs in front of me. "You're saying that like you have a choice in this matter."

"I do."

"You don't." I leaned forward, leveling him with a look. "My mom was asking me to define us. After you told my cousins you were starting to like me and not adhering to the original rule of stopping what we're doing, which we haven't." I raised my eyebrows.

So did he. He was following me.

I kept on, "Your uncle came over and met my mom. My mom met your uncle. There's now a whole 'thing' going on."

"Thing?"

I ignored that. "And since I have to go to Homecoming, and my mom is asking for a title for us—"

"Title?"

I ignored that too. "I went with the least responsibilities choice. Homecoming date. You. Me. You're going." For added clarification, I said, "*With* me."

His eyes went back to being narrowed at me. "Homecoming is expensive."

"Right, Heir to the Carby's Empire and whatever other businesses your grandfather dictates."

"I'm not getting any of that money."

"You don't need it, your words exactly. If you wanted to play the poor card, you shouldn't have told me about your grandmother's trust fund."

His mouth went flat. "I'll do this if you do something for me."

Now my mouth went flat. "That's not how this works."

"It's how it's going to be. I'm not doing shit then. I don't care what you say."

I growled. "Fine. What is it you want me to do?"

"I want you to come to my uncle's gym for a self-defense lesson."

My stomach flipped over. It didn't drop or tighten. It just did a somersault. "What?"

He nodded. "Just you, or you can bring your friends, but one class. I want you to come. Try it out."

"One class?"

Another nod, slower this time. "One. But you gotta stay the whole time."

"One. Fine."

His eyes narrowed. "Good."

I held up my hand, my pinkie finger out toward him.

"I'm not doing that. I'm not Clint."

No. He certainly wasn't. "You know, you messed up with me. You never should have told my cousins that you're starting to like me. Secrets and sex. That should've been the foundation for us. Alas, that ship's sailed. You're stuck with being my Homecoming date." I grinned. "And you have to ask me in a very cool and elaborate way, but you can modify it to still meet your 'cool' standards."

"Two self-defense classes."

"What? No way. That's not our deal."

"It is if you want cool and elaborate.'"

I growled, but my mom chose that moment to sail into the room, pushing my door open all the way. "How's it going in here? Scout, are you staying for dinner? The boys are coming over." Her eyes lit up. "Wait. We can talk about Homecoming. This will be fun!"

Oh boy.

72

RAMSAY

Theresa parked at Mile High Gym the next Thursday.

I was already there and waited for them to get out, but as they did, I turned to stare up at the sign. For some reason, knowing the reason I was here today, that sign was bigger and more ominous than it had been the other times I'd seen it.

Theresa, Gem, and Alred came to stand next to me, all staring up with me.

"What are we doing here?" Theresa asked.

Gem poked her. "Are we here to stalk Scout?"

"Not me," Alred piped up. "Theresa told me where you said to meet, and I was in. I'm so in."

I looked at them for the first time, and my mouth fell open. "What are you guys *wearing*?"

"What?" Theresa frowned, tugging at her sports bra strap. "You said to dress for the gym."

"I meant like workout clothes. Not . . . ." I didn't even know how to process what I was seeing.

They were wearing tutus. Ballerina tutus. And leggings.

And Gem had tie-dyed hair ties holding back her hair. She could've been in an '80s workout video.

Alred was in all black. Black tutu. Black leggings. But he was also wearing black gym shorts and a black T-shirt. Theresa was in a white tutu, white leggings, and booty shorts. She had a sports bra and a tie-dyed tank top on top.

I blinked a few times, but I still couldn't process this. "I . . . agh, what?"

Alred held up a hand.

"Yes?"

He smiled. "It's always been my dream to do a music video here. We're wearing tutus so if we get the chance? We're ready to go."

A truck pulled in, gravel moving under the tires. A door opened and shut.

Footsteps crossed to us.

Scout's uncle clear his throat. "Ramsay?"

I whirled, knowing my neck was flushed even though I was *not* wearing a tutu. I'd changed into a sports bra, one of Scout's workout tanks (he'd left it at the house one time), and normal workout shorts. My hair was up in a braid. "Hi. Yeah. Mr.—uh, Miles. Hi. These are . . ." I motioned to them. "These are my friends."

All of them waved.

"Hi."

"Heya."

"Have you ever been asked if someone could do a music video here?"

I groaned, closing my eyes for a moment.

"Uh, you're here for the class?"

"Yes." I lifted my head.

"We're here for a class?" Theresa asked.

Gem elbowed her. "Shhh . . ."

Alred had turned toward the gym, a giant barn-like structure with the front two doors pulled open. A fighting ring was visible inside with a ton of shirtless guys exercising. A few guys were hitting the bags outside.

Alred breathed out, "Whatever we're doing here, I'm *in*."

Miles chuckled, raking a hand over his face. "Okay."

Just then, Scout drove past and parked next to his uncle's truck. He got out, a bag over his shoulder. Instead of coming over, he headed to the building but paused just outside the large doors.

Alred waved. "Hi, Scout!"

Gem started laughing.

Scout frowned.

His uncle shouted, "Warm up, then hit the bag. You're doing grappling tonight."

He held up a hand, turning for inside, but watched me for a moment, without saying a word.

I felt his uncle watching me too, but he didn't comment. "Class starts in five minutes," he said instead. "You can see if you like it before paying. I'm not going to take your money if you don't like the class. Bathrooms and water are inside, but we'll be having class over there." He indicated a section in the grass. A couple guys were carrying over a large mat, and as we watched, they dropped it on the ground. A few women, some girls I recognized from school, and a couple other guys were lingering around. Some were chatting. Some were stretching. A few looked nervous. Some of the girls were looking our way, a couple laughing.

"I'm going to self-defense their asses if they keep laughing," Theresa said loudly, pointing right at them.

The girls turned around. They shut up.

Theresa harrumphed. "That's what I thought."

I gave her a look. "I think, of all of us, you might be the one who shouldn't take self-defense."

"Fuck that. I'm totally in." She pointed toward the gym. "I

saw a couple of girl fighters in there. I might join. I feel like my soul is clicking into place, and fighting is what I'm supposed to be doing for a living. I *love* that you invited us here."

"I'll be your trainer."

She gave Alred a look. "I'm going to need a professional trainer."

"Then I'll be your warm-up hyper, or the trainer's assistant, or whatever you need. Water boy. I'm it."

Gem looked around, biting her lip. "This is all aggressive and making me nervous."

Theresa's eye twitched. "Get used to it because this is about to become my second home."

Gem didn't say anything, but continued to bite her lip.

Theresa and Alred went inside for the bathroom as Gem and I headed toward the mat outside. I nudged her. "It's just self-defense. I'm sorry I wasn't more forthright, but I—"

She stopped and grabbed my hand. "No." She was fierce. "Whatever helps you, we're doing it. Okay?"

She grabbed both my arms. "For what it's worth, I'm really glad you asked us to come today. You just made all our days, but you really made Theresa's. She came alive when she saw a girl crossing the parking lot to go into the gym."

"Thank you."

She nodded, smiling.

Theresa and Alred joined us at the mat, bouncing from excitement.

One of the trainers led us through some warm-up stretches before a woman instructor and Miles came out of the gym. The lady held up a hand. "Hello, everyone. I'm Rachel. I'm one of the instructors at the gym. I know Miles usually teaches you, but I'm going to work with you all today while Miles brings the new students up to speed. We all know the first-day lessons are so key. Everyone, line up with a partner. We're going to practice the heel-palm strike, the knee strike, and the eye strike. Ready?"

Miles motioned us to the side. "I figured it's important to go over the basics, and we have a couple other new students joining as well." He looked beyond us, and Theresa shrieked.

"Oh my God!" She ran over to hug Cohen and Amalia.

Gem hugged Amalia too. "What are you guys doing here?"

Cohen was looking my way as he responded, "Scout mentioned the class. Thought it might be a good idea."

I felt Scout's uncle watching us. He gave us a little nod, clapping his hands together. "Okay, everyone. Come over here."

There was a general introduction made. He told us about him, about the gym, about the intention of the class, and after that we lined up. He began laying out the basics for us.

He said to trust our instincts.

He explained how to avoid being an easy target—make them work for it, if they were going to target you.

He said we should use our body to let an attacker know we weren't weak or vulnerable. We should verbally let the attacker know we were not the ones to mess with. He explained how to keep a relaxed but confident stance, and how to use that for the element of surprise if someone did attack. He told us how to maintain a safe distance.

Then, after all of that, Miles began running us through some techniques.

After that, we rejoined the other group, practicing how to break your attacker's nose, how to go for their eyes, and how to go for their groin.

We were nearing the end of the hour when we moved on to how to break out of body holds—the headlock, the chokehold, and the rear bear hug.

I was paired with Cohen, and we watched everyone else go through the techniques, learn how to get out of them, but I didn't want to do it. Nope. No, thank you. I was sick to my stomach.

They were wrapping their arms around their partners and choking them.

"You okay, Ramsay?" Cohen asked.

I shook my head, but I couldn't talk.

"Ramsay?"

Sweat ran down my back.

We were up next. Everyone else had done it. They'd all done it so well, made it look simple and easy, and I wanted to throw up because they didn't know. I bet none of them knew what it was like to feel like you couldn't breathe, to fight someone because you were so fucking scared for your life. Terrified that, at any moment, any second, you might black out, and they could kill you if they wanted. Or worse.

I bet none of them knew that.

But I did.

"Cohen? Ramsay?" Miles stepped toward us.

Everyone was watching.

I couldn't do it.

"She's shaking."

"Ramsay?"

I was frozen in place. I couldn't move.

Miles frowned, a flicker of emotion flashing over his face. "Get Scout."

I wasn't here anymore. I was back there with Max the night he'd gotten through the door, when he'd grabbed me and squeezed—when I couldn't knock his hands off my throat. And the aftermath ...

My dad.

I shook my head. "I can't. I'm sorry. I can't."

Then Scout was there. "Hey. Hey." He moved into my personal space.

I stepped back, feeling Max. Feeling *him*. "No." I whimpered, and God, it sounded like it came from the depths of my soul. "No. I can't."

"Ramsay." He touched my elbow and stood right in front of me. "It's me. *Me.* You know I won't do anything—"

I shook my head. "I don't know shit. He said that too. He did."

"Babe. It's *me.*"

Babe. I shook my head. "He said that too," I whispered.

Tears. God. Tears.

I could taste them. I hated them.

All this shit. He had no idea. No one did. One day to break us down. How much work it took to build back up. Maybe years to stand back up. Maybe never.

No one saw that. No one stuck around for the progress report. All good? That was what they asked. They wanted to hear, "Yep" so they could move on and live their lives while we were still fighting just to *try* to live ours.

"Hey. Hey." Scout was still in front of me.

I shook my head, trying to get away. I was in full fight-or-flight mode.

"Hey." He gentled his tone, touching my face. "Hey. Look at me." His thumb swept over my cheek. I felt his forehead touching mine. "I need you to look at me."

God. *Look at him.* I blinked, coming back to where I was standing.

I was at Scout's uncle's gym, and we were standing on a mat. Scout was in front of me, and I needed to do a chokehold technique.

I was remembering. I was back.

"I'm okay."

"You're not."

I wanted to shove him away, but he was right. "He tried to choke me before," I whispered. "I thought he was joking, but then I knew he wasn't. He would've, if he could've. Then he did.

He just kept—I couldn't shake free." I gasped. "I couldn't get away from him."

"We're going to teach you to do that. Today. So you'll never be in that position again. Okay? Never again." Scout was fierce, staring at me. "*Never* fucking again, Ramsay. You can control it. You can say no, and you'll not only mean it, know it, believe it, but you'll say it as a *warning* to *them*."

Yeah. I was down for that. That sounded good.

"To do that, I have to wrap my arm around your throat. I have to apply pressure." He looked tortured. "But you think, and you listen, and you do what my uncle tells you to do. You *think*." He touched my forehead. "That's Fighting 101. You always have to be thinking. Okay? You think and listen and then do."

Think.

Listen.

Do.

I nodded, my body still shaking as Scout slowly moved to stand behind me and wrapped his arm around my throat. He was barely pressing, but it didn't matter.

I knew he could.

Miles was speaking. "You have two options, Ramsay. One, you can reach behind him and go for his nuts. That's the easiest route, and ninety-eight percent of the time, you should choose that route. You can do that. *Or* you can grab his arm, twist out of his hold, use your leg to trip him, and then you can punch down."

The nuts seemed the most logical option, but I forced myself to breathe and think and do what Scout would do. He'd go for the second option. He'd want to hit back.

I did that option, and Miles said it again. He gave me instructions, step by step.

"Grab his elbow."

I grabbed his elbow.

"Twist down."

I twisted down.

"Turn your head."

I turned my head.

"Slip his hold."

I pulled my head out of his hold.

"Yank his wrist up."

I pulled it up behind him, forcing him down.

"Hit your knee behind his."

I did.

"Punch down."

I raised my hand and held.

"Then you run."

I let go of Scout's arm and stepped back, still trembling but not as badly as moments ago. I'd done it.

I'd gotten out.

He watched me. His uncle watched me. I knew the entire class was watching, and as I felt tears streaming down my face, I gulped for a breath and said, "Can we do it again? But faster."

"Yeah," Miles said. "We'll do it as much as you want."

Good. I nodded. *Good.*

73

SCOUT

The kitchen light was on when I got home, but it was empty. I didn't think much of it as I headed for the stairs.

I was passing the front door when my uncle called my name.

I paused. "Yeah?"

He came to the kitchen, standing in the doorway, a drink in hand. "You were with Ramsay?"

I gave him a nod. "I'm later than I intended. Kinda a big night tonight . . ." Then I got a good look at his face. "What's going on?"

He motioned behind him. "We're in the front office. Can you come in with us?"

"Us?" I asked as I walked in and trailed off as I saw her.

She rose from her seat, smoothed her hands down her pants, and gave me a nervous smile. "Heya, buddy. How are you?"

I didn't answer because, if she was here, giving me her scared look, that meant nothing good. That meant disaster was coming.

I sighed. "Hi, Mom."

74

RAMSAY

The intercom was staticky when the vice principal was announcing next week's themes for each day. Monday was Out of This World Day. We were supposed to dress up as our favorite galactic being because our future was "So out of this world." It was a little cheesy, but I had to admit that a part of me was excited to see everyone's costumes on Monday. Except, as I walked into school, I had a feeling no one was talking about any of those topics. All eyes went to me. Conversations muted as I approached, then picked up on whispers as I passed. I had a sinking feeling that I was the newest topic. Or, to be more specific, Scout and I were because, after last night at his uncle's lesson, we were out and out in a *big* way.

Someone had been recording us. That video was on social media.

Alred had been the first one to see it, almost immediately after the lesson ended. We were still at the gym. He jumped up and thrust his phone in my face. "Look at him being all there for you as you're breaking down? I'm swooning. You're *out*, out!"

Though, Theresa's reaction had been the loudest. She stared at me with her mouth on the floor. "You and Scout

Raiden?! Are you kidding me? I knew it. I mean I suspected, but then you and him. And him with his forehead to yours. And the whispering, but I heard him call you babe. You're babe to him. Yeah. I so knew it."

Gem was quietly smiling until Alred yelled, pointing at her. "You knew!"

Theresa started to launch for her, but Cohen and Amalia joined us and everything got forgotten because Cohen broke the news he was taking Kira to Homecoming to them.

Turning down the hallway to my locker now, I saw Gem waiting at my locker, her back to it, her head down, and she was studying her nails. I made my way to her. "Hey."

She smiled back, saying, "Hey back—"

"About time the two of you came out," Kira's voice cut in as she swung around to stand in front of Gem with the Homecoming planning committee in tow. She put her arm around my shoulders and leaned half into me. "And since he's taking you to Homecoming, the sex has got to be great. I'm impressed, Williams. Impressed. Good job."

Gem's mouth had twisted up, then fell by the end of Kira's statement.

Kira didn't notice, leaving just as quick as she showed up, giving me a two-finger salute with a smirk.

Gem frowned. "Kira knew?"

"No. I knew she knew *something*, but I kept forgetting to push Scout when we were alone, and then things got crazy the night I did tell you."

"Crazy how?"

I'd just stepped wrong. I'd not said anything because my cousins didn't want anyone to know. Their family business was their family business. I was respecting it, but I didn't know how to separate our run-in with the fraternity from what was going on with my cousins so I'd kept quiet.

"I can't say. I'm so sorry."

"Say to me?"

"Say to anyone."

"But *Kira* knew?"

"I—" I didn't know what to say to make it better because she was looking hurt, really hurt, by that fact. "I don't know what Kira knows."

"She obviously knows something or knew something."

"Gem, I . . ."

"You know, don't. I get that you went through something seriously messed up, but I was so excited when you told me about you and Scout. You were dropping some of the walls. Finally letting me in, but I'm right back to where I was before. Have I done anything to you for you not to trust me?"

"It's not like that."

"Then what's it like?"

"It's . . . nothing. I did let you in."

"But Kira knew before me?"

"I'm telling you that I don't know *what* she knows."

Gem had gone from smiling, to being confused, then to hurt, and now her whole face went blank. "I think I know what it is. I thought you weren't like the others. Not about being popular. About cutting people out, but I'm starting to see I was wrong. So wrong. Have fun at Homecoming with *Kira*." She bit out the name before she darted ahead.

She was gone.

I wanted to scream. I hadn't foreseen any of this happening like it was. Spying Scout at the end of the hallway, I started for him, then paused because he saw me, stopped, and turned the other way.

What?

"You gotten any grief?"

Alex joined me, studying his phone. His backpack was still on him.

"What?"

He looked up, putting his phone away. "The vid of you and Scout is all over social media. You've not gotten any grief from anyone back in Cedra? I'm hoping you haven't."

"No." I frowned. "Or I don't think so. I haven't checked."

"Do yourself a favor. Don't." Those were his parting words as he veered off to his locker.

Trenton was at the end of the hallway, talking to a girl, but when he saw me, he jerked up his chin in a greeting and headed down the opposite hallway.

Seriously. Was it me today?

What was going on with my people today?

Clint came out of the bathroom, whistling, swinging his hands in front of him.

He saw me, flashed a smile, and headed right for me.

Finally. My body relaxed. It wasn't me, whatever was going on.

"I need your help," he announced.

I perked up. "I'm in."

"Good. I wanna blow up my dad."

"What?"

He flashed me a grin as the first warning bell sounded. We both started for class at the same time. "Not literally. He's my dad, but I wanna blow up his spot. You know, he and that lady he cheated with. He's staying with her."

"No."

He pulled open the door, letting me go first and then following me to our table. As we slid onto our seats, Clint hunched forward so no one else could hear. "Her husband didn't move out. He's staying in the house with their kids, so she moved out. I was in a mood last night and staked it out. They're both there. I want to hurt my dad, do what I can to help Mom for the divorce because—not sorry to say this—but my dad's an asshole. He's selfish. He's going to fight Mom on everything."

I'd missed the cold look in his eyes, but I didn't miss the smile he gave me now. It was chilled and calculating.

He added, "You in? Do whatever we gotta do to help my mom?"

"We have Homecoming next week."

He shrugged. "We can do both."

Right. Both.

He held up his pinkie. "Trouble twin?"

I melted, circling his pinkie with mine. "Trouble twin."

Hopefully this wasn't going to end in disaster, for us.

Then he asked, "What's going on with you? You look horrible."

KIRA TO HOMECOMING PLANNING COMMITTEE:

URGENT! URGENT! Emergency meeting ASAP! We were just approached by a CHELTON HOTEL THAT'S BEING BUILT THIRTY MINUTES FROM HERE! They've offered to host our Homecoming dance in their grand banquet in addition to one of their penthouse suites as part of their soft opening. I talked with Mrs. Charlotte and Mr. Karpoti, and they've approved the move. Come to the gym after school today for an emergency meeting. We'll go over everything.

This is SO EXCITING! The announcement will be made next Monday, so it's hush hush until then!

75

RAMSAY

Clint was calling when I got to the gym. I'd forgotten to tell him about the emergency meeting, but Kira was waving everyone over to the corner, and she had her boss look on her face.

I declined the call, texting instead.

Me: Emergency meeting for Homecoming right now. Wait for me and I'll go with you to do whatever we need to do.

Clint: Are you serious?

I frowned, starting to respond when Kira called out my name.

She motioned with quick, almost frantic hand motions. "Come over here. Quick."

Uh . . . I put my phone away, feeling it buzz, and hoping Clint wouldn't be upset.

"Okay, guys." Kira climbed up on one of the bleacher seats so she was looking out over everyone. I glanced around for Gem, but couldn't find her. "Listen up!" Kira's face was flushed, her eyes were blazing. "Okay, this is an amazing and exciting change for us. You all know the Chelton Hotels? How they're amazing, and upscale, and the definition of luxury. Well, they've built one on the coast, on the other side of Pine Valley."

"Wait. Over Dragon Abyss? By Wembley Creek? I thought they were building a Walmart there. A Chelton Hotel makes so much more sense. That's so cool. That place rocks."

"I thought they were building a Gaylord."

"I thought it was a prison."

"Okay," Kira clipped to the last guy who interrupted. "What are you doing here, PJ? You're not on Homecoming Committee."

He shrugged as he adjusted the basketball under his arm. "I was playing hoops and you guys ran in so I joined. Seemed the thing to do. Go with the flow. This is exciting. I'm in."

She continued to half frown, half glare at him before rolling her eyes. "Whatever. Fine. If you breathe a word of this to anyone, I'll murder you in your sleep. I know where you live."

He'd been pulling out his phone, then froze at her threat.

"Anywho!" She clapped her hands. "Here's the plan. We need a leader from each subcommittee, and you're going to come over with me today. We're going to walk through the hotel—" She paused, her mouth flattening as a hand shot up. "What, Brittany?"

The hand went down. "So, are we not going to talk about how they were building a Chelton Hotel so close to us and we didn't know? I mean, how lit is that?"

A few others jumped in, all excited as well.

"I mean, it *is* thirty minutes away." Kira rolled her eyes. "But yes, yes. It's very cool. That hotel franchise is the beyond of beyond of hotels, but that was the whole point. They built it, and now they want to announce their presence at our Homecoming. That's the beyondest of beyond. Oh, and they're going to have a photographer there too."

"Whoa," Brittany breathed. "That's out of this galaxy beyond."

"So lit." PJ was nodding.

"Shut it, PJ. You're not even supposed to be here."

He wasn't fazed, a lazy grin spreading over his face. "But how lucky am I, huh?" The sarcasm was noted, making the others laugh.

"Okay," Kira was back to snapping. "Listen up. Everything is switching over there. Coronation is going to happen during the game, but we'll do another royalty introduction at the hotel. The dance will be there. We'll open up a penthouse suite for the after-party."

PJ asked, "Are we in the presidential suite? I heard they have those too."

"No. Just one of the penthouse suites."

"Why not the presidential one?"

"Are you serious with this?"

He smirked. "Kinda. It's fun to get you riled up."

A few girls snickered, and he shot them a cool and cocky look.

"Okay. So, are we good on the plan?"

"Wait." Another girl shot her hand up. "Dragon Abyss is thirty minutes to the coast. Do we have organized rides there or—"

Kira's mouth was flat again. "It's the same thing you were already planning. Do your own rides."

"But some people have rides for here, not for there. What about those people?"

"Yeah." PJ joined in. "We should plan something for everyone. Maybe like a bus service? That's a great idea."

Kira clipped out, "You want to offer a bus service to students when you know we're all going to be drinking?"

PJ gave her a sly grin. "This is a student activity. No alcohol should be provided."

She rolled her eyes again.

"Don't worry, Kirakins. My uncle has a party bus. I'll talk to him, see if he can help us out."

"Don't call me that, and you need to get that approved by Mrs. Charlotte and Mr. Karpoti."

"They both love me. It'll be fine."

"Whatever. Fine. Okay, other business is permission slips. When the announcement comes out on Monday, each of you are going to give out permission slips to everyone going to the dance. They can't attend if they haven't gotten their slip signed."

"You know there are some students who won't get their slips signed. Their parents only let them attend activities on campus. That's not cool for them."

Kira's response was to lift a shoulder. "I'm sure they'll figure it out."

I frowned. That wasn't right. "Wait. Are you serious?" All eyes went to me, including Kira's who was giving me a meaningful glare, which I was ignoring. "You can't do that. You're separating the kids with privilege and the ones without. That's total bullshit."

Someone gasped. I didn't look to see who it was.

"Are you serious, Miss I'm Dating—"

I didn't know what she was going to say or what she actually knew, but I raised my voice, "You won't go there."

Another couple of girls gasped.

"Are we going to get a cat fight? 'Cause I'm down." PJ shifted in the crowd, coming to stand by me. He draped an arm over my shoulders, ignoring my tension. "Also, Kirakins, if a mutiny is happening, I'm with the Maroney triplets' cousin." There was more shifting in the group, more lining up on my side and it was evident Kira would lose some standing if she kept pushing back.

She opened her mouth, but held it until she seemed to surrender. "We'll get it sanctioned. Somehow."

That only meant she wasn't giving up the Chelton Hotel and already knew a way around it so all students could attend. She would've been fine letting those students not attend because of their homelife.

What an elitist snob.

"RAMSAY!" Kira called my name after the meeting.

I was heading out, intent to find Gem, Scout, and Clint. I just hadn't decided who I needed to find first. "I can't talk," I said over my shoulder as I turned the corner for my locker.

"Make the time." She got to me as I was opening my locker.

"Make it quick then. I have people to find."

"I don't want to be enemies with you. I keep saying that to you."

I frowned, pulling out my bag and checking my phone. There were no texts or calls from either of them. "What are you talking about?"

"Inside. You pushed back on me. That wasn't cool."

I gave her all my focus. "Are you kidding me? What you were going to do wasn't cool. You know some of these students don't come from great homes. A dance is the only thing they're looking forward to, and their parents won't sign off on letting them go to a hotel. That's not okay what you were going to do."

A flicker of regret flashed over her face before she masked it and squared her shoulders. "I'll make it okay. We just have to get more chaperones. It'll be fine, but don't do that again. Okay?"

"Do what?"

"Speak against me in front of the group. Come to me in person next time. It's humiliating. You threatened my authority—"

"Are you kidding me, *again*?" I snapped. If my locker had been opened, I would've slammed it shut for effect.

Kira's eyes widened.

"You can't call an emergency meeting and not expect opinions to be shared. That's the entire definition of a meeting. You just want blind loyalty. There's a different word for that, and I've got no problem using it for you."

Her mouth went slack, but I saw the steam building.

"You don't want to fight with me, but clue in, Kira. I'm not going to fall in line. You better make right with that because I'm not changing. I took on an entire school last year. Warring with you, I don't want it, but I'll take it on if I have to."

"Is that a threat?"

I rolled my eyes this time. "Of course you'd take it that way. To me, I'm only telling you that I'm going to be me. I'm not a follower. You choose if you're okay with that or not. Ball's in your court. I have to go."

I shrugged past her and had made up my mind who to find first.

76

RAMSAY

S cout wasn't answering his phone, and I needed a vehicle.

It was time to make an executive decision, and that was that I needed a car. I didn't want to be on the bike all day, not for all the miles I was guessing I'd need to cover. I headed home, grabbed my mom's extra set, and went to the nursing home. From there, I locked my bike up and took off in her car. My mom never left on her break so I needed to gamble. I hoped I could get it back before the end of her shift. She'd never know.

I went to the gym, but Scout's vehicle wasn't in that parking lot. He'd been incommunicado all day. It was starting to bug me. I mean, this was the whole reason we were supposed to stop doing what we were doing because of this. Because I didn't like this weird pit in my stomach. It shouldn't be there. Not about him, but it was, and I wasn't liking how it was a bigger pit than I wanted to admit.

I headed to his house, and his vehicle *was* there. Success.

The garage door was open. It looked like he was in the middle of training with his equipment pulled out into the middle. A few bottles of water were on the floor along with a roll of tape. His shirt was lying next to them, but no Scout.

I went to the door, a brief knock before I opened it. "Scout?" I moved inside. "Are you here . . ." I trailed off as a woman stepped out from the kitchen. Tall. Narrow shoulders. Thin and short red hair. A strong jawline. A slightly pointed nose that worked for her. And Scout's eyes.

"You're Scout's mom?"

He had her eyes, but that was all. It made me wonder what his dad looked like.

"Hi!" She'd been holding a towel, but after putting it on the island behind her, she came my way. She started to hold her hand out, but then hesitated and ended up crossing her arms as if she was hugging herself. "You must be Ramsay. I heard about you."

"You did?"

Footsteps stampeded down the stairs. Scout rounded the corner, saying, "Mom—" His eyes latched onto me, and they flashed before they hardened. "What are you doing here?"

"I—"

His mom cut in, her voice warm, "This is Alex's cousin. It's so good to meet you finally." She patted his arm fondly. "This one has said everything got turned upside down the minute you arrived to town. I've not met the triplets, but I'm dying to do so."

"The triplets. Yeah."

That was all he'd said about me?

Scout wasn't looking at me. He was staring at his mom, his expression unreadable.

I didn't like that. Not one bit.

"Can I—" I indicated Scout. "Can we talk?"

He gave me the slightest nod.

I led the way, going up to his room. He shut the door behind us.

"Your mom is here?"

"Hold on." He passed me and turned on the fan before his hands went into his pockets. "What are you doing here?"

"Why's your mom here?"

"My mom's none of your business."

I took a step back. "Scout."

"You know—no. Don't do this shit. We fuck, and that's it. Right? I'm tired of all this shit I'm getting about you and me. If I wanted people up in my business, I'd tell them my business, but I *don't* because I don't want this."

This. He didn't want this.

My chest started tightening. "This?"

"Yes," he snapped, a hand thrusting through his hair. "You and me. This shit. Alex is up in my face. Trenton and Clint threatening to beat the shit out of me, then trying how many fucking times? I'm done with this bullshit. You're in my face. We had some moments—"

"Don't!" My tone was cold right back. I didn't know where *this* came from, but he'd been avoiding me at school. I was seeing why. This—him—fuck him. Just fuck him.

His words struck and they struck deep.

God.

They pierced me harder than I wanted, cutting me.

I refused to let him see that my hands were shaking. I tucked them behind me. "Don't do this. Why are you doing this? I don't understand."

What had changed? What was different?

He was tense, not looking at me.

His mom. "Your mom is here—"

"My mom is none of your business."

I held firm, not stumbling back from that shout.

He wanted to be done with this? With me?

I was burning up on the inside.

My chest was all the way tight now. "Fine."

"Fine."

We both glared at each other.

"I'm up in your face because you said something to Kira, who said it in front of Gem, and I need to know what it was because my real friend is pissed at me. So, what did *you* say? Not *me*. You."

He was still scowling before he blinked. He raked another hand through his hair, turning away. "Jesus Christ. This bullshit."

"What'd you say?" My voice rose.

"Nothing."

"You're lying, like you've been lying all this time."

"What? I never—"

"What'd you say, Scout? That's all I need to know."

God. His face was so hard. His eyes blazing so fierce.

Did he care? Even a little? Was this ripping his insides out like it was mine?

But no. Shut it down. He didn't care. He said it himself.

Shut. It. Down.

I was shutting it down. I forced a breath around a giant boulder squishing my lungs.

"Ramsay—" He'd gentled his tone.

He didn't get to gentle his tone. Not now.

"*What'd you say*?" I screamed.

"Nothing!" he yelled back. "She could tell at your cousins' barbeque that I wanted you. That's it."

"That's it?"

"That's it. I told her to shut her face."

I winced, imagining those words being said to another girl, but not now. I couldn't think about that now. I nodded, the numbness starting to slip in. The boulder edged to the back. The answer was gotten. It was time to retreat.

I couldn't look at him anymore. It was searing me, so I jerked my gaze to the side and rasped out, "We're done."

I rushed past him for the door, but he blocked me.

"Ramsay."

I wasn't looking at him. I wasn't paying attention to how his tone sounded regretful.

"Listen," he started.

I clipped my head from side to side. I was done, so done. "No."

"I—" He cut himself off.

I would not cry over this one. I was done crying because of guys. "Move."

"Listen—"

"Move!"

He waited until I yanked my gaze up to his, and I fought past my own emotions to see he was battling something as well. His jaw was clenched, and his eyes were focused on something beyond me before he stepped away, gutting out, "Fine. We're done."

I yanked open the door, then heard his parting words. "It's better this way."

I didn't ask what he meant. I was gone.

77

SCOUT

I knew she'd come in because there was no way she hadn't overheard that. My door creaked open a minute later. "Honey?"

I was throwing my shit into a bag. "I don't want to talk about it."

The floorboards protested as she came in. "She's not just Alex's cousin, is she?"

"Mom." God, I was fucking tired. Of everything. "Don't—"

She rushed forward. "Listen to me, Scout. Listen."

More floorboards sounded and then her hand was on my arm. She pulled me to look at her. She'd been crying. "Listen to me. You can't do this."

"Mom—"

She'd never understand how tired I was of this. From my whole life.

Her fingers tightened, a determined expression hardened her face. "This isn't your fight. You've been saying this all along. This is mine. I'll handle it."

She'd said this before.

She'd made all the promises.

That she'd protect me. That she wouldn't let my grandfather dictate my life, how I lived, where I went to school, who I hung out with, what I did after, or what I did for the rest of my life because, no matter the luxury trappings, I wouldn't be living my life. I'd be living his.

I'd never be free.

With me, how I am, I couldn't live like that. And until she showed up here, I'd vowed that I never would.

Things changed.

"Mom, you told me what he was going to do to you. It's my turn to protect you. I have to do this. I'm going."

"No." She stepped back, letting me go. "I didn't know you had a girl here."

Pain sliced me. I waved that off. "She's nothing."

"She's *not* nothing. I know you. I gave birth to you. I know when you're hurting and when you care, when you don't want to show it, and that girl meant something to you. You've never let anyone in except Cohen, his sister, and Alex. Those are the only three Miles have mentioned. He didn't mention her. That says everything."

"Stop. Okay?"

"No." She was vehement. There was a new look in her gaze. A look that I'd never seen before, not once in my whole life. She shook her head, a tear falling all the way to the floor. I doubted she knew it was there. "You've been saying it for a long time, and I've not been listening. I was too scared, but knowing you have a chance at happiness—it's my time to do something. I'm so sorry, Scout. I'm so sorry." More tears fell. She still didn't know they were there, and she began to turn for the door. "I'm going to fix this. I'm going to fix everything."

"Mom—"

She rushed out, her door slamming shut a moment later.

I could go to her. Yeah. I could be that son. Going in. Telling her to stop whatever she was thinking because it was fleeting. That was how she was.

My grandfather had always been controlling. He'd always been an asshole. He'd always been abusive in his way, and she folded every time. I grew up with that, watching that, watching how he treated her, how it paralyzed her, and she had moments like this.

She never followed through.

She wouldn't follow through this time, so when she showed up here with a bruise on her arm, and knowing there were more on her body that she was hiding, it'd been enough.

He'd gotten physical. He'd do it again, and I couldn't let that happen.

Ramsay . . . It hurt. It did. It really did, but this was best for us. For me. She said it, but I'd known the second my mom had shown up.

I was letting go of us, what 'us' there had been because it was my turn. I was tagging my mom out. I'd go in, live the life my grandfather wanted for me, and he'd leave her alone. That was the deal I was going to make with him.

I went back to doing what I'd been doing.

I finished packing.

78

RAMSAY

I refused to cry. Refused to, but my God, I couldn't stop my hands from shaking as I sent out the text to Theresa.

Me: Where's Gem? 911

Theresa: At Mario's. She's filling in for a cousin.

I tossed my phone aside and drove, still fighting back the tears but knowing my chin was trembling and that was because of Scout. Him.

I was over guys hurting me. Completely over them.

He'd—tears streaked down, and I tasted one. Gah.

My phone was buzzing on the passenger seat, but I was only focused on getting there. I had to make it right with Gem. It'd all been an accident. A miscommunication. Surely, she'd see that? She wouldn't hold it against me?

I needed a friend. A non-cousin friend, who'd listen and agree that Scout should go to hell. Tequila might help too.

I got there, pulled in to the back door, and Gem was stepping out, frowning down at her phone before she lifted her head. I must've looked a sight because her eyes widened. Her mouth dropped open. I could almost hear her gasp through my closed windows before she stuffed her phone in her pocket and came running to me.

I'd just turned the engine off as she opened my door, and she was right there. Kneeling down. Her hands on my face, wiping my tears away. "*Dios mío*. Are you okay? What's happened?"

I couldn't undo the seatbelt. It was imperative I get out of the car, but the seatbelt wouldn't move an inch. I cursed, almost punching it.

"Ramsay. Stop." She was so gentle, moving my hand aside and unhooking my belt. Then I was in her arms. I didn't know if I launched myself at her or if she yanked me out, but either way, my arms were tight around her and she was hugging me back just as hard.

I cried out, hiccupping at the same time, "I'm"—*hiccup*— "so"—*hiccup*—"sorry. I didn't know"—*hiccup*—"what Kira knew. I really didn't. I mean it, and I went to ask Scout"—*hiccup, hiccup, hiccup*—"what he told her." I managed out the rest as we sat in the gravel parking lot, arms still half-hugging but leaving enough space for me to tell her everything.

"What the ever-loving fuck! That rat bastard," she seethed through gritted teeth.

Tires driving over gravel sounded behind us.

A car was coming up. Theresa behind the wheel. Alred with her. They parked and both ran over, dropping down around us. I moved back a bit more so all four of us were in a circle, our knees touching.

Arms were lifted around our shoulders, so we were literally hugging each other. Heads bent forward, and I filled them in.

"He did what?" Theresa growled.

"I can't believe it!" Alred was aghast.

"I'm just sad, and I also want to slip some razors in his toothbrush." That was from Gem.

"Oh my god." Alred was aghast again.

Theresa eyed her cousin warily. "Gem."

Even I winced at that one.

"I will never do anything or say anything to end up as your nemesis," Alred loudly whispered to Gem, who shrugged.

Okay then.

We sat there for another twenty minutes before the back door opened.

"Gem?" An older woman's head poked out. When she saw us, her eyes flashed with concern. She came toward us, speaking Spanish, then switched to English. "Is everything okay?"

"Tía Lupe, what would you do?" Gem filled her in on everything.

The door opened a second later. One of the busboys came out.

Then two of the dishwashers.

One of the servers.

Uncle Hector was the last one.

All listened to Gem, Theresa, and Alred fill them in, and we were given their opinions after.

Uncle Hector gave his first before heading back inside. "I'd leave that boy alone. He's not worth the tears or your time. A better boy will come, especially for someone so beautiful and kind-hearted."

Theresa laughed a little, shooting me a look. I was on the same wavelength. I wasn't sure if I'd call myself kind-hearted . . .

The server's opinion was that I should slash his tires, then give him a bag of spikes as a gift so when he'd open it up, it'd be so full that the spikes would fly out.

I was thinking the server was also related to Gem.

The busboy told me to brush it off, he'd take me to Homecoming.

And he was kinda cute, but everyone else said, "No!" at the same time, so I was taking my cue from them. Tía Lupe pretended to swat him up the backside of his head, her Spanish coming out fast, but I caught enough to know she was saying how he was too much of a lothario. He was ordered back inside. "The tables aren't going to clean themselves."

The dishwashers had the best advice, in my opinion. The first one was tall and lanky, a crooked grin on his face suggested I stop dating boys altogether, wait for men. He gave me a wink.

It wasn't his advice that I thought was the best.

The second dishwasher, who was shorter with a bit of a tummy on him and some frizz on his chin thought I should let it all go because the universe obviously gave me a red flag. I should kick back, chill, enjoy some gummies because they came in all colors of the rainbow, and wait for a leprechaun to bring me my pot of gold. He also said he'd be up for sharing. (The gold and gummies.) And he mentioned listening to Pink Floyd's *Dark Side of the Moon* album at the same time we enjoyed the gummies.

He was shooed inside right after.

The aunt gave me a hug, telling me it was early love and everything would get better. She gave me a kiss on the forehead before she headed inside.

It was the four of us.

We looked at each other.

After a pause, Theresa said, "Let's get ice cream, then some alcohol, and go and get wasted at the river by his uncle's gym. When he shows up to train, we'll go to his house and put bleach in his laundry basket."

"If we're drinking at the river by his gym, won't his uncle catch us?" Alred asked.

"There's a sitting area to the side, kinda hidden. Scout and the triplets party there sometimes."

We had a plan, and all of us stood. We turned almost as one entity, and stopped again.

"Wait." Theresa pointed to my car. "When did you get a car?"

I winced. "I didn't. I kinda stole my mom's."

"Okay. Let's revise the plan."

The plan was revised. We returned my mom's car and took my bike back to my place.

Gem asked once we were really on the way for the original plan, "If we're drinking, how are we going to get to his house?"

No one said a thing. No one had an answer.

I said, "Let's revise that too as we go."

"Right. We'll figure it out later." Gem nodded.

"What about the mom? You said she was there?" from Alred.

Theresa, Gem, and I looked at each other. As one we said, "We'll figure that out as we go too."

WE GOT THE BOOZE, candy, and ice cream.

We found the bonfire area, and we did drink.

We had lots of candy.

Most of the ice cream melted or got dirt in it.

We laughed so much because, well . . . booze, that we forgot to watch for Scout's truck to show up. We also never went to his house, too worried about running into his mom catching us dumping bleach into his laundry basket. It was more the concept of revenge that was the most helpful.

By the time I got to bed that night, I was sore from laughing and from smiling because, turns out, I had some really great solid friends.

In my mind, that was the best revenge ever, and I wasn't meaning against Scout.

For that revenge, I was just going to tell Clint. Clint would handle my vengeance all by himself.

Then I remembered and gasped, jerking upright in bed.

Clint! I'd forgotten all about him.

I rolled over and grabbed my phone.

Me: Hey! I'm so sorry. Some stuff went down today between Scout and me. I'll tell you later, but are you okay? What did you end up doing? Can we do it together tomorrow?

HIS RESPONSE CAME through in the morning.

Clint: All good. I handled it.

Me: Handled what? What'd you do?

Clint: Best if you don't know.

79

SCOUT

C ohen met me at my locker first on Monday. "Dude. What the fuck?" He dropped his bag on the floor, his arms thrown up from frustration.

I ignored him, turning and opening my locker. I was ignoring everything, everyone. There seemed to be extra chaos going on in the hallway, but I didn't care. None of it fucking mattered anymore.

"Let it go, man." I stowed my bags.

"I called you Thursday night and nothing. Goddamn nothing. I know shit went down. Alex told me, and nothing. You stonewalled me Friday. Went to the gym, and you weren't there all fucking weekend. My uncle told me to steer clear. Your uncle told me to steer clear. I'll repeat, what the fuck, Scout?" His voice rose, and people were starting to look.

"I told you. Let it go." The bell would ring soon. I didn't want to come today. I didn't want to come at all this week, but my uncle argued, said I needed to. My last week of freedom, so what was the point? I'd be sent off, going to the Privileged School of Assholes by next week. At this point, it was—I saw her. Ramsay.

Fuck. She looked good.

And haunted.

She was coming down the hallway, her friends completely circling her. Even Alred was there with books hugged against his chest. I wouldn't put it past him to have transferred just for Ramsay. It was her. She inspired friendships like that. Loyalty.

People knew she was good people. They wanted to keep her —and I was torturing myself.

"Scout—" Cohen tried to get in front of me, but I wheeled around him.

"I told you. Let it go—" *Slam!*

I was hit hard from the side, shoved into the lockers. People scrambled. I might've ran into someone else, and I started to look, but the fist was in my peripheral vision. It was coming fast. I ducked, moving clear of whoever was coming at me.

It was Clint. His face was full of fury, eyes wild. "You little fuck. You piece of shit." He shoved at me again, hitting my chest.

I didn't move this time, and despite the threat of him, despite the madness happening all around us, I looked up.

She was right there.

Everything melted away.

The pain was there, so close to the surface. She couldn't hide it, not right away, until she did, masking it. Cold hatred glared back at me before she blinked again. Another mask, cool indifference this time.

I would've taken anything, the hatred even, over the indifference.

Her friends were chattering, trying to pull her away, and then Clint was in my face again. "You're next in line after a murderer. How's that feel, you fucker—"

Sheer agony flared in her gaze, and she gasped, unable to put that away. "Oh God—" She'd been hurt by me. That was obvious, but she was haunted by what else had been taken from her.

I knew Clint was going to do something, say something. I'd been ready for it, willing to stand, let him get his hits in, but that? Bringing up her father? I snapped.

He came at me again, and I twisted. My shoulder and head dropped. I went down, then came back up with a punch, getting just under his chin, and his head flared back.

He flew backward, his body following suit. He was airborne for a second before he came back down, tripping and falling into the opposite lockers.

I moved in, following his movements.

As he landed, his head hit again, and he began to slide down to the ground.

I grabbed his shirt, yanked him up, and held him. I shouldn't have done that move, but he wasn't going to go anywhere. I'd stunned him enough, and my fist was back. I had perfect line right next to his eye. Real damage could've been done, but then a guttural scream sounded and a body yanked down on my arm, hanging on me.

It was Ramsay.

I knew it before she was there, knew she was coming. Of course, she'd come in, save her cousin, save another one she loved.

Of course, I just handed her own nightmare to her, live and in person, and knowing that, feeling the instant regret, I caught her as her hold slipped. She was going to fall. I slipped an arm around her waist and yanked her against me.

She stiffened, but I put both arms around her and moved her backward until we were beyond the crowd that'd gathered, moving us into an empty room, and I held her. I needed it more for me because I didn't know if I'd ever hold her again.

"N-no! No!" She wrenched herself out of my arms. "No!"

She hit at my arm. "You don't get to do this. Not after you ended things."

"Ramsay—"

"No! I said no!" She was pawing at her hair, trying to clear it from her face, but the strands were sticking for some reason. Giving up just as someone tried opening the door, she reached for the handle and opened it herself.

Clint, Alex, and Trenton were all there. One or all of them grabbed for her, pulling her through, putting her behind them.

I started for her, not meaning to, knowing I shouldn't, but I did it anyway.

I had to. I just had to go to her. She was like gravity for me.

"No." Alex moved to the front, his hands braced against the doorframe, barring my way. His brothers were next to him, all wearing murderous expressions.

This was my best friend.

This *had been* my best friend.

His gaze was dark, ominous. "Stay away from us. Stay away from her. Got it?"

Everything was ricocheting inside me. Who I wanted. What I couldn't have. Why I couldn't have her. What I couldn't do. Knowing I'd be leaving—none of it mattered. None of this mattered.

It was over. My life here was over. This week was just . . . the universe's joke on me. I was getting a live and in-person tease of what I was leaving behind and would never get back again.

I didn't move, but I withdrew. Alex sensed it, a slight frown showing before I clipped out, "Not a fucking problem. Get out of my way, Maroney."

80

RAMSAY
FIVE DAYS LATER

"Oh." My mom sighed behind me. "Honey."

I met her gaze in my mirror. She was taking me in, her eyes starting to shine as she leaned against my doorframe. "That's your Homecoming dress?"

It was a dark mauve-colored dress that felt like silk, with lacy sleeves. It changed colors depending on the light and the angle. From the side, it looked completely black. The front crisscrossed across me, wrapping to the side with a braided pattern weaved throughout the dress.

It almost looked Grecian.

My hair was swept back with long loose curls. I'd been nervous to do it, but I skipped the football game to give myself enough time. Theresa and Alred dropped by to help and had just left to pick up Gem on the way to the dance.

I nodded, smoothing out the front before turning to her, dropping my shoulders. "What do you think?"

Her eyes were now watering. "You look beautiful."

She said it so softly, wistfully.

My throat swelled, seeing her emotion. "Mom," I whispered before looking away.

"You've decided to go then? To the dance?"

She knew about the end with Scout. I came home that night and she'd been here, on one of her nights off. I hadn't wanted to lie. She took one look at me, opened her arms, and I walked into them.

"Yeah." I met her gaze again, giving her a somewhat sheepish grin. "It's at that new hotel, and all the planning I did . . ." I raised a shoulder. "Gem, Theresa, and Alred will be there. A lot of Theresa's other friends too. I've just started to hang out with them. They're fun."

"I think that's good. Your cousins too."

I gave her a nod.

"Your father would be swooning over you and crapping his pants at the same time. You are so beautiful, and there is going to be *so many* guys. He'd be so worried he would either need to go to the gun range or go to the store to get medication. But he'd be so proud of you." A tear streaked down her cheek. She only took a deep breath, her smile turning sad. "I know he's here, and I know he's swooning over you, saying how proud he is of you, but we can't see him."

Totally choked up here. I rasped out, "He can see us."

"Yes, he can. He can see us." She came over, hugging me.

"How about you and me go back sometime? Go visit his grave?"

I pulled back, searching her face.

I blinked. "You're serious."

A somber but serious expression was there. Her hands dropped to the sides of my waist. "Yeah. I mean, the Prestige family is starting not to have the pull they used to, from what I've heard."

"That's what the lawyers are saying?" I asked, knowing she promised me that I wouldn't be pulled in unless it was absolutely necessary. I'd gotten other texts from my previous friends saying the same thing.

"That's what they're saying. I believe them. Quite a few people have reached out."

Oh. *Oh.*

That had me all choked up, all over again.

So many of her friends turned their backs on us. Some turned against us. If you have an injustice done to you, no matter the kind, and you find the courage to speak up, say the truth, and find that those who professed to love you didn't believe you? That was a betrayal felt in the soul. To have them turn against you, siding with lies that were being said, that was a whole *different* kind of betrayal. That was the kind where you asked yourself how you could've been so wrong in choosing to love someone because, for them to do that to you, you *must've* been wrong in realizing what kind of people they were. That was the kind of betrayal that made you not believe in yourself, and in some ways, I felt that was the very *worst* type of betrayal.

My mom never deserved that.

She saw the tears, and another sad smile graced her face. She framed mine with her hands, moving in and resting her forehead to mine. "I am so proud of you. You are strong. You are beautiful. You are kind. You are fierce when you need to be. You are a warrior, and I am *beyond* blessed to have you as my daughter."

She enfolded me into her arms, and we stayed there again.

It felt right. It felt healing.

My phone beeped, and I glanced at the text.

Gem: Where are you?? We're heading to the dance. Are you sure you don't want us to pick you up? Also, BEN IS BEING OUR DRIVER!! CAN YOU BELIEVE THAT?! He's in town this weekend and came into Mario's to pick up some shifts and overheard us talking about Homecoming. He agreed to be sober-cab in case, you know.

Gem: Also, he's no longer cute. He's HOT.

81

SCOUT

I was pummeling the bag when a vehicle pulled into my driveway. Glancing over my shoulder, seeing it was Cohen's truck, I went back to the bag. After going for another two minutes straight, I took a break.

Cohen was there, a water in hand waiting for me.

"Hey." I took the water.

As I took a long drink, he asked, "You seriously not heading to Homecoming?"

"Why would I?"

"Uh, because it's Homecoming and Ramsay is going to look damn good."

I scowled, tossing my water to the side before squaring off against the bag again. "She ain't mine to look at. Never was."

He stepped around, holding the bag for me. "You know that's bullshit."

"I'm leaving." He was the only one I told.

He flicked his eyes up. "Look. You say shit sometimes. You say shit you don't mean and right now, you don't mean what you're saying. Pull your head out of your ass. You leaving or not leaving, you need to be at that dance."

I swung, my fist making contact. It wasn't satisfying. I needed to hit it again, harder. Faster.

I swung again, but it wasn't feeling right.

I glared at Cohen. "Can you leave? Let me train in peace."

"No, because I know you. I didn't know about your rich granddaddy or about all the bullshit you think you're signing on, but I know you. I know that, no matter what you said to yourself, to Ramsay, to anyone who'd listen, you liked her. I knew that because I know you. You kept going back. You'd never do that if you didn't have feelings. You'd never face off against Alex. You know I'm right on that."

"Shut up, Cohen." My teeth ground against each other.

"You go and you don't make it right with her, that'll scar you. Go to the dance, Scout. See your girl. Make it right. Do it or you'll regret it."

I started to shake my head.

"That girl's been through enough. Don't add to her list."

I cursed softly. "I hate you sometimes."

He flashed me a grin. "No, you don't. Ramsay's tough, but if there's any night she's going to want to see you, it'll be tonight. Get your ass to that fancy hotel, and—"

"Wait." I straightened to my fullest height, rolling my shoulders back. My hands dropped down. "What hotel?"

He frowned. "That fancy new one. I thought it was supposed to be a new Amazon warehouse. The dance is there now. They made the announcement on Monday. Didn't you . . ." He trailed off before grimacing. "That's when everything went to shit."

I cut the rest of the day, not wanting to be around. I'd only talked to Cohen during the week, tuning everything and everyone out.

"What fancy new hotel?"

"The Chelton Hotel. It's on Dragon Abyss—"

The Chelton?
No, no, no.
My gloves dropped to the ground.
I sprinted for the door.

82

RAMSAY

I'd been to one Chelton Hotel during a field trip to Washington D.C.

A part of me was curious about what one looked like so close to Pine River and Pine Valley. Clint's friend mentioned Dragon Abyss, and once I got there, I understood. I pulled into the parking lot, the hotel looked like a modern day castle, set on the edge of the highest point over a cliff. Literal fog was floating up from where the ocean waves were crashing in against the rocks, into a small clearing below.

With the forest, mountains, ocean, and cliff, it had a magical, but poignant and mysterious feel.

The inside had a lush red carpet with a gold crest pattern accent set in the carpet. There was gold all over as well—on the elevator, on the counters, on some of the tables set around by a bunch of couches.

A man approached me, wearing a Chelton Hotel uniform and white gloves folded in front of him. "Ma'am, how may I help you?"

I was figuring my dress was a dead giveaway, but I said, "I'm here for the Pine River Homecoming Dance."

"Ah. Yes. May I enquire as to your name?"

"Ramsay Williams."

He barely blinked, folding his head slightly. "I'll escort you. If I may?" He indicated the elevator.

I led the way. He followed at a discrete distance, hitting the elevator button, and once inside, he pressed another button. We went up, and up, and we kept going until we ended on one of the top floors. The door slid open.

He went first, waiting for me to follow, taking me to a double door. He knocked briefly, standing to the side, his hands folded again in front of him as he waited for it to open. Once it did, he stepped forward, his head slightly bent forward.

I couldn't see who was inside, but all of this for a dance? Kira mentioned we were using one of the suites so was this me getting into that room early? He conversed with whoever was inside before he stepped back, turned to me. "Have a pleasant evening, Miss Williams."

The elevator doors slid open behind me, and he stepped onto them before the door swept farther open so I could see whoever was inside. A woman was there, maybe in her thirties. Reddish hair swept up in a bun with soft tendrils loose, framing her face. She wore glasses, a pencil skirt, and a soft silk shirt. All lilac colored, the glasses included. She gave me a bare smile, indicating for me to step inside. "Miss Williams, please come in."

I didn't move. "What is this?"

She frowned slightly. "Miss Williams?"

"I came here for a Homecoming dance, and I'm doubting Kira is inside waiting to jump out and yell 'surprise.' What is this?"

"I don't know who Kira is." Her mouth moved slightly, pressing more inwards before she cleared her throat. "Mr. Rothchelton wishes to speak with you."

Mr. Rothchelton? *Chelton?*

She was gone before I could regroup enough to ask her. As soon as the door closed behind her, another door on the opposite side of the room opened. An older man strode forward, stopping just inside the door to study me. It was a brief perusal before he dismissed me and went to take a seat on one of the couches. He threw a leg over his other, and placed a hand on the back of the couch, now tipping his head back to give me another study, this time longer.

The brief look had been nothing, as if I were a bug under his feet. The second one he was looking at me with amusement. I was entertaining to him.

"Who are you?"

A different, almost thoughtful, expression flared in his eyes before it was gone. "You don't know me?"

"The lady said you're Mr. Rothchelton?" I gazed around, the dots connecting. I hadn't gone to a penthouse suite. I'd been taken to the presidential suite. "You own this place?"

"I own everything."

He said it so simply, expecting his words to have power. Knowing they would.

Authority clung to this guy. He was the boss of all bosses, used to everything he said, or even thought, happening before he needed to do anything more than simply stating what he wanted. Mid-sixties. He kept himself trim. Dark hair, long enough where he had a whole curl swirled on the top of his head, probably sprayed to stay in place. He had a goatee, a slight beard. Darkly tanned skin. He could've been a villain in a cartoon. I almost expected him to produce a gold cane that he used for decoration or to have handy so he could use it as a weapon.

His suit was three-piece, obvious wealth. Much like his shoes. I didn't know much about shoes, but even I knew those were probably custom-made and made from some personal shoemaker over in Switzerland.

"Like this hotel?"

"I own the hotels. I own the universities—" He kept on, giving an impressive list, but the university caught me.

"Chelton University?"

He stopped, his mouth turning down before he heaved a deep sigh and sat forward. His arm dropped from the back of the couch, reaching for a coffee that was already placed on the coffee table as if whomever placed it there knew he'd expect it. It was there for him, no one else. There wasn't a second cup either.

"The *Rothchelton* University." His mouth went flat. "It was named after my great-grandfather."

The Rothchelton University. That name—I'd heard of that before.

Scout.

He said that was the university his grandfather wanted him to go to.

All the dots connected because I didn't believe in coincidences. I was reeling. "You're Scout's grandfather."

Also, Scout was a *Rothchelton*?

"*I have my dad's last name . . .*" He talked about his family, that they were wealthy and like cutthroat wolves. He'd not been lying. Owning the global franchise of Carby's was only one of his grandfather's empire, and he was here, in front of me, after having me escorted to seeing him. Alone. On his territory.

The floor seemed to dropped out from under my feet. This was all a setup.

"What are you doing? Why am I here?"

"My grandson has talked about me?" He sounded pleased.

"Yeah, as in he hates you."

His eyes sharpened on me.

I couldn't be here. Panic was starting to claw at me. My being here wasn't good. This was all too familiar, too reminiscent of being around Max, around his family. Scout's grandfather was like *them*, with their money and power and prestige they wielded like weapons, but his grandfather was more. He put Max's family to shame. He was leagues above them.

I started for the door, the need to get out of there, escape, retreat, was so overwhelming.

"I wouldn't do that," he said as I reached for the door handle. "I would listen to what I have to say because I came here to be of service to you, Miss Williams."

No, no, no.

Every instinct was screaming for me to go, but those words. *Of service.* I was frozen.

The same power Max had was washing over me again. The same abusive power. Did all abusers have it? The same power? Was it me? It was as if Max had carved out a hole for his power to slip in and control me, and because Scout's grandfather was also an abuser, I was just as vulnerable?

I needed to fill that hole so no other power could slip in there and control me. It was me. I needed to push it out of me.

"What do you want?" I didn't recognize my voice.

Fear was pulsing through me. My vision was blurring on the ends.

"You have a problem. I have a problem. I'm here because I believe we can help each other out. Would you stay? Hear me out?" He had stood. I didn't know when, but he held a hand out to a chair not far from me.

It was farther away from him than I had been, which was the only reason I sat. I almost scurried there, wanting to get away from him and wishing I could just leave.

Despite his lack of reaction, I could tell it pleased him.

"From what my sources tell me, you and my grandson are in a relationship. Is that correct?"

My lips thinned. "Were."

"Right." He was still studying me. Weighing me. Judging how he could use me in the best way for him. He never sat.

"You already had a previous relationship with a Max Prestige."

God. I sucked in air. Him saying Max's name was too much. Too threatening.

He knew too much.

"I've taken the time to familiarize myself with your situation and the incident that occurred between your previous boyfriend and your father."

No, no . . .

He couldn't talk on that. It wasn't his to talk about.

"You've been given a bad hand, and you have my sympathies, but—"

But he didn't care.

But he would use it, weaponize it.

He had no right to say any of this to me.

My pulse was so rapid, heart thumping so hard in my chest, that I swore I felt it though my whole body.

"I've also been told of a recent incident that occurred at a nearby university, where another Prestige's vehicle was vandalized. Did you know they had that car shipped here specially for the trip?"

Oh God. Oh no.

Trenton. He smashed Spencer's windshield.

"Are you also aware that Mr. Prestige was planning to bring charges against your cousin? I believe he's the one who did the vandalism. Or that the Prestige family has been financially supporting your father's family who are challenging his will?"

I couldn't talk.

All this information, all coming at once were like blows against me.

"I've stepped in on your behalf."

My gaze jerked to his. He liked that. He was loving the manipulation that was washing over me. He was thinking it was working, that I was too impressed, too scared to stand up, to speak against him, to do what I wanted. To leave this hotel room.

"Once Mr. Prestige was aware of the connection you and I have, he changed his mind. He changed his mind about other things as well."

My stomach took a nosedive. Connection. What other things? What other ways had he been thinking of trying to hurt me? Hurt my mother?

I couldn't stay here. I was going to be sick.

I tried to stand.

"You should remain sitting, Miss Williams."

"No," I choked out. I couldn't. I had to get out. I started for the door, looking at it like a lifejacket on a sinking ship. I needed to hold on to something to keep from drowning.

"Ramsay!" he barked disapprovingly, but the door shoved open.

Scout was there, and he was *seething*.

83

SCOUT

R amsay was pale as a ghost. All the blood was drained from her face, and I'd never seen such panic in her eyes before. She took one look at me and stuttered to a stop. "Scout."

She even sounded weak.

He did that.

I moved past her, locked on my grandfather, who was behind her.

"What the *fuck*? You don't get to talk to her. You don't get to look at her. You don't get to breathe the same air as her." I was still going at him, but Ramsay got in front of me.

"Scout."

"His real name isn't Scout." He laughed. He fucking laughed, all condescending. "It's an insult to your family, insisting on using the name that man gave you."

"Shut up before I come over and break your face." I was two seconds from doing it, fuck the consequences.

God. If he'd hurt her—

Cold rage filled my veins. If he had hurt her. . .

"Did he hurt you?" Her hands were on my chest, and she began walking me back. I resisted. The thought of him in a

room alone with Ramsay was maddening. He didn't get to
know anything about her, talk to her. Nothing. He didn't
deserve to even know about her. "I swear to God, Ramsay. If he
hurt you—"

"He didn't." She held her hands up. "All he did was talk
to me."

Talk?

Fuck.

I was going to lose control. The rope was stretched tight,
and it was going to snap. "You didn't expect me, did you?" I
taunted him, going on the offense first. That was what he
taught me.

He tipped his chin up, his shoulders set back as if he were
resigned to dealing with me.

Well, he was going to deal with a whole ton more than just
me right now. I moved in front of Ramsay, saying under my
breath, "Go. He won't bother you again."

"Scout." Her hand reached out, touching my arm. Her
fingers curled around me.

I pulled it free, not roughly, but gently. "Go, Ramsay. I'm
okay. I won't do—I won't do what I wanted to do seconds ago. I
promise." I moved forward, feeling her leave. This was the only
time I could say what I wanted to say. After today, there'd be no
freedom for me. "You messed up, old man."

His eyes were trained behind me, watching Ramsay leave,
before they switched back to me. "Messed up?"

"I was coming to you anyway. You didn't need to do this. Set
whatever this was up for Ramsay. All of it was wasted. Your
time. Your money. All of it." I spat. "I was coming anyway."

His eyes flared, a peculiar look there. "You were coming
to me?"

I couldn't give him that last bit of victory. I'd already said it
twice. Another time? I couldn't. I just couldn't. "When did you
start building here?"

His answer was swift. "The day your mother bought your plane ticket. We started planning this hotel the next day. Locals were told it was something else. I'm surprised you didn't hear about it."

"This place is thirty minutes from Pine River. I don't give a fuck what locals talk about." He was a toxin, invading everywhere. "You did this so you'd have a hold here? Own the area? Run it? Have a say over the local politics because your ego couldn't handle losing another one of us. You lost your mark. We're thirty minutes away."

"Close enough. And I've not lost you. I've not lost any of my children."

"Except your son."

"I only have one son. He's in his rightful place."

He'd disowned his other son. I wasn't going to let him forget him. I tipped my chin up. "Your son, Miles. My uncle, remember him? He's taken me in."

His mouth went flat.

"He's given me a home."

His mouth turned down.

"He built a gym to help train me."

His mouth parted. I saw his teeth then.

Good. Satisfaction surged through me because it was only this one shot. "I was coming in, you fucking Viagra limp dick. I was coming in. You didn't need to hurt my mom. She's your daughter."

His eyes narrowed.

God. I wanted to hit him. I wanted to keep hitting him. Knock him down, but he stood there, listening to me.

My voice went low. "I know your plans for me. I'm fully aware that, once I come in, you'll ship me off to that school. You'll pick my friends. You'll pick my hobbies. You'll pick everything you want me to do for you for the rest of my life, and I know you'll ensure it by making me do things, *bad* things, that'll hurt people. And you'll have that on me, whatever evidence there'll be. You'll send people after me, probably pay for my friends to narc on me. My professors. You'll handpick the girls you want me to fuck. Pick my wife. Name my future children. And if I don't fall in line? You'll either threaten to release whatever dirt you have on me or you'll hurt my mom. *Again*. And you'll do it over and over again until I'm so fucking numb, that I'll need to be a cokehead in order to live the life you've chosen for me. And, for what? *Why*? What goddamn reason? For your ego? Because I'm blood? You think blood means anything—"

"It means *everything!*" he snapped, roaring back at me.

He'd lost some of his control. Good. I zapped it up, using it.

"What you made my mom do for you? All those men you had her fuck? All the videos you had them record of your own daughter?"

"I wasn't recording her. I was recording them." He was trying to regain his control. I saw it, how his eyes were bouncing back and forth. Some wildness showed in there.

"And that makes it any better?" I scoffed. "You're getting old. How long do you think you can last living this life of blackmail and threats? It corrupts from the inside out. You know that. You've taught your other son to do that with your rival companies, sending him off to find the poison in your enemy so you can exploit it. You ruin lives when you do it."

"I believe you're talking about corporate espionage, and that's illegal, my son."

"I'm not your son. I'm barely your grandson."

"You're my only grandson." His eyes flashed, and he reached up, his hand moving fast.

I reacted, catching his hand, and I held it.

He tried to yank it back.

I still held it.

"Let go, Grandson. Ro—" His teeth were clenching as he

spoke.

"*Don't.* Do not call me by that name."

"It's your given name. Your family na—"

"It's an embarrassment. That's what that name is." I had the upper hand here. "You hate this, right here, this hold because it shows how old you're getting. That *you're* the weak one here. I could break your hand. I could break your wrist. I could break all of your fingers. I could do *anything* to you in here, and no one would know. You don't keep cameras on when you're in the room. We've learned that lesson. But you sure like having them on when your *daughter* is in the room. Don't you?" I applied pressure, shifting my hold so I only needed to dig my thumb in, twist, and break three bones in his wrist.

Jesus, I wanted to so badly.

"You hurt me, and you'll know who I can hurt more."

My mom. I got his message, loud and clear.

I didn't let go, not yet. "What were you doing with Ramsay?"

His eyes trailed past me, to the door. "That's between Miss Williams and me."

I moved my hand again until all I needed was to twist. Just one twist and snap. "What were you doing with Ramsay?"

"That's not—" He cried out as I yanked his hand backward, kicking out his legs. He landed roughly on his knees.

This was the ultimate humiliation.

He'd make me pay for this, I had no doubt. I just didn't care because nothing would change after this. I was still going to live the life he chose for me, but the deal was me for my mom. I'd still offer that. He'd take it, and he'd have the power over me then.

"One last time, Grandpops, or look forward to only having the use of one hand for the next few months."

"Scout!" Ramsay was there. She rushed to my side, her hand going to the hand I was holding, and she began trying to pry my fingers off him.

"I thought you left."

She didn't respond, saying instead, "Let him go."

I tightened my hold. Another inch and the bones would shatter. I had enough force. "You don't know what he can do, Ramsay. You don't know what he *will* do."

She held firm, trying to get between my fingers and his hand, but she said softly to me, "You're wrong because I do. He's an abuser. He ruins lives and shatters souls because he *can*. He's that type of man. And you're wrong because I know he'll hurt you." A tear slipped down her cheek, but she was still working on my hand. "He'll take you away from me, and I'll never have you again. That's what he's going to do if you let him." She dropped her hands and stepped back. "You make the decision. Hurt him and give him something to weaponize against you, or walk away completely because you *can* still do that."

"I can't." The image of how my mom looked, when I walked through the kitchen and saw her there was burned in my memory. She'd been completely hollow. "He'll keep hurting my mom, and I can't keep letting him do that to her."

"Scout," Ramsay started.

I ignored her, not letting myself feel anything as I looked down at my grandfather. "Me for her. That's the only choice I'm giving you. I become your next puppet and she walks free. She gets to live how she wants, love who she wants, do anything she wants. You will completely withdraw from her life, having no influence over her at all, and that includes her money. She'll be able to have free access to her own money and all the money she's inherited and earned until this day. Me for her."

He didn't say anything, but the control was almost all gone. He'd snap. I'd seen him do it before. He'd roar. He'd throw things. He'd hurt things—sometimes people.

"Grandson," he almost whimpered, a sound I'd never heard from him before.

"Me for her. That's the deal."

"Or what? You'll break my arm and—" *Snap.*

Too late. I broke it.

Snap, snap.

There were the other two places.

A muffled scream left him.

I let him go, stepping back, and because I'd never get this again, I pulled Ramsay into my arms. My hand to the back of her head. She came right in, stepping to me. Her arms went around me as mine folded around her.

Finally.

Home.

She'd become it, and I'd never realized. I hadn't known.

I knew now, and it was too late.

She heaved out a sob, her body sagging into mine, holding on for dear life.

My grandfather was cradling his hand to his chest as he staggered to the couch. His eyes were daggers at me. An unnatural pallor came to his skin, but he lifted his head enough to say, "You for her?"

I started to answer.

He finished, "Or your mother?"

Ramsay stiffened in my arms.

A deep growl came from the middle of my chest. "What are you talking about?"

"It's why I came here to have a word with your girlfriend." He was starting to pant, but damn if he didn't stay to finish his threat. "I have influence over the Prestige family. I can either help them bury her or bury them. Your girlfriend or your mother." He reached over, pressing a button on the side table.

He stood, a little unsteady, as the door flung open. One of his men swept into the room. "Sir." He immediately went to my grandfather, who kept his glare on me. "You'll tell me your decision when you come to me. You have twenty-four hours."

84

RAMSAY

"What are you doing here?"

I stiffened before I stepped back from Scout because no way had I heard his accusing tone right. "Excuse me?"

He wasn't even looking at me. He was still glaring in the direction his psychotic grandfather went. He flung an arm out. "Why would you come up to a private suite? How could he get so close to you?"

Uh-huh. No way. "Are you blaming *me* for this?"

"No, but what the hell were you doing here? How'd he get you here?" He started pacing, his hands on his hips, and that was when I really took in his state, or the lack of his state. His hair was messily rumpled, like he'd been raking his hand through it on a non-stop basis. His sweats hung from his lean hips and he was wearing a ragged and torn T-shirt. I'd been in a flight-or-fight mode when he suddenly showed, then I was flooded with relief, then panic, and then horror as I heard everything.

"I came for the dance. A hotel employee just brought me up here. I thought Kira wanted us to show up in the penthouse first, so I went along with it. Once I realized this was *beyond* sketch, I was curious. That was your grandfather? He's diabolical."

He snorted, turning to pace the other way. "Tell me about it. My God! He had you here. Alone. What the fuck, Ramsay? You have no idea how bad of a person he is. What he could've done to you. He would've gotten away with it. He gets away with everything. Everything. And you—"

The anger was masking his fear. I got it then, and everything calmed in me. "Hey." I went to him, putting a hand to his arm, stopping him. "Hey," I said it more gently, reaching up, framing his face. "I'm fine." My thumb smoothed over his cheek, and his chest rose up in a ragged breath. His hand caught mine, and he held it in his, intertwining our fingers.

He was calming a little. "Jesus." He moved in, taking me into his arms. "Fuck. You're gorgeous."

I tried to smile, but I couldn't. A part of me felt at peace, being near him again, feeling his touch, but the other part was torn to pieces. He was leaving me. "Well, there's a dance that I helped plan. I figured I should enjoy it despite the fact that my date dumped me."

The corner of his mouth tugged up into a half-grin, but it didn't make it to his eyes. They were still wild, almost feral. He leaned down, letting his forehead rest on mine. "If he'd touched you or hurt you, I couldn't have lived with that. You have no idea."

"I heard it all, Scout. I do know."

He tensed, but he didn't move back. Thank goodness.

"You were going to leave?"

Tenser. He half-growled, but he never lifted his forehead. "I have to. Didn't you hear him? He's got my mom under this thumb. She's so brainwashed by him, and she keeps going back to try to earn his approval. It's sickening. He has so much control over her."

"And you? What would he do to you?"

He started to pull away.

"No." I dug in. "Stay."

He did, but his chest was a frozen wall. "You don't know these kind of people. You go into their world, and if you think you can get out unscathed, you're kidding yourself. They're not like your dad's killer and his family. That family's like kittens compared to mine."

"Why are you going now?"

He lifted his head, his gaze holding mine. He was haunted. "Because my mom showed up with bruises. He put actual hands on her."

He began to step back. My hands curled into fists, holding onto him. "So she can go to the police?"

"My grandfather owns the police. He owns the FBI. You don't get how much power he has. Think the illuminati. If they were real, he'd be a member. And my mom won't say anything. He's been brainwashing her since she was born. It's over. I can't let him keep hurting her."

"He said it was her or me."

A tenderness came over him, softening around his eyes, his mouth. His eyes were warm. His hand moved to cup the back of my head. "I won't let him hurt either of you."

I started shaking my head.

"Hey. Hey." He moved back in, his chest against mine. He framed both sides of my face. His thumbs smoothed out over my cheeks, lingering on my jaw. "I want to be with you tonight."

"No, Scout." Not just tonight. I knew that was what he meant.

"Yes." His thumbs moved over my cheeks again before one hand lifted, tucking some of my hair behind my ear. A single strand. "I didn't come here because I knew you were with him. Cohen mentioned the hotel, and I knew this was him. It's our family's hotel. He'd made his second move, like I said he would.

I got here, tore up to this floor. It's where he always stays at every Chelton, and then I heard your voice inside. I was terrified of what he could've done to you. Knew it then. Wanted to kick myself for not knowing it earlier, but I should've known. But you hated me, so I had to hate you back."

"What?" I whispered, confused. "What are you talking about?"

He cupped both sides of my face, bending down to me. His eyes so solemn, so grave, so serious, and all seeing inside of me.

I... I didn't know what was going on.

"I love you."

What?

He grinned, almost sad, but so beautifully. "I fell in love with you the first time I saw you. I just didn't know."

"What?" I couldn't talk. Was he...

"I didn't know I could love someone." He shook his head, his eyes raking over my face as if he needed to memorize every inch of me. "But I did. I *do*. You've told me you were broken, but I was too. I was broken before you. Feel like I've *only* been broken. Then you came here, and I didn't know what hit me. Still don't. You bulldozed over me. All of this is new to me, but I love you, Ramsay. Fucking completely. It's your fault. You made me fall for you."

A small laugh left me, but it hurt. "You're blaming me?"

He loved me?

My chest rose, filling with hope. With warmth.

With love.

I loved him too.

"Yeah. On that one, I am. If you hadn't hated me . . ." he teased, his eyes haunted.

Pain coursed through me. "I just got out of a bad situation. It's not my fault. It's yours."

"Mine?"

It was. It was his fault. I was deciding.

"I didn't—I didn't want you either, you know." A tear leaked out of me, sliding down my cheek, sliding to his thumb.

"What are you talking about?"

Thump.

Could I tell him?

Could I love him *more* if I told him?

It would make everything *more* messed up.

But he loved me too. As soon as he said those words, everything was cemented. I wouldn't have been able not to—"I love you too, you know."

He went still. His eyes now glittering. A whole new gentleness entering them. "Ramsay," he murmured, as if heartbroken. "I didn't know you loved me back."

"Yeah. I do. So it's all your fault actually."

My heart picked up.

Thump.

I looked down, my words whispered, "I love you too."

Thump.

He sighed, pulling me into his arms.

This was all so seriously messed up.

He held me, and I held him, and I didn't want to leave him again.

His voice was rough. "We got tonight."

I didn't want just tonight.

I wanted forever.

"Tonight," he said again. His head leaned down. His lips found mine, and it was different.

There was more feeling.

More love.

More warmth.

More tenderness.

More magic.

I'd fallen in love again.

And I was going to lose him.

I stood on my tiptoes, wound my arms around his neck, and I kissed him back harder.

His eyes flashed before he bent down, grabbed my legs under my ass, and turned, walking us out of the room, still kissing me.

To the elevator.

We kept kissing.

To the lobby.

He carried me out, his mouth never leaving mine, exploring me at the same time.

Someone yelled, "Get a room!" Then laughed. There was a whole bunch of laughing. Some cheering too. I heard a few female sighs.

To his vehicle.

He drove us out of there.

He thought he was going to save me, but I needed to figure out how to save him.

It was my turn.

85

SCOUT

"You love me, huh?" Ramsay asked, her voice raspy as I was moving inside her.

I ran my hand down her arm, needing more. Always needing more. Always knowing I would need more. It'd never be enough. I knew that now.

Figured it out too late.

I raked a hand through her hair, tilting her head back to see me better. I kept my rhythm, but I lifted so I could see her better. I liked having sex like this. I liked having sex like this with Ramsay, *only* Ramsay.

We were making love.

I knew my feelings, finally admitted them to myself. I needed to admit what this was too.

"You love me too."

She grinned, her eyes glossing as I went to the hilt and held there, grinding against her. She panted. "God, I love that." She lifted up, raking her hands down my back. Her nails dug in before she fell back with a gasp, arching her back. "Who's going to do this when you leave?"

"No one," the growl erupted from me, and I took hold of

both her wrists, pinning them above her head. It brought our bodies flush, and I held still inside her.

Her eyes lit up. "Don't like that?"

I just growled in response. "No one touches you. No one except me." I put her wrists together and freed one hand to move down and grip her hip. I used it as an anchor as I reared back and thrust inside, going long, deep, and slow. So slow.

She began panting again. "You can't go then. You don't want anyone else to have me then—"

"Enough," I clipped out. "No one touches you but me." I thrust in. "You got that?" And out. "No one. Ever." Inside. "No one looks at you. No one *thinks* about you." Out. "No one but me." My hand moved to her clit.

I moved over her, rubbing, and felt her exploding around me.

I ducked down, my lips grazing her shoulder. "You're *mine*, Williams. *Only* mine." Then I came on a deep groan.

I just collapsed beside her when a door slammed downstairs. "Scout! Scout!"

Ramsay tensed.

"It's my uncle." I smoothed a hand over her stomach before pushing up. "The fuck, though?"

Footsteps thundered upstairs, coming to my room.

I jumped up, prepared to meet my uncle.

Suddenly, he stopped. "Are you in there?"

I shared a glance with Ramsay, who'd drawn a blanket over her.

"Scout, are you in there? I'm not going to ask against before I—"

I wrenched open the door.

Ramsay yelped as something hit my side.

I grabbed it, using it to cover me before I moved so he could see me. "What do you want? Kinda busy."

He was glaring at me, his hands holding a letter in front of him before he took me in. He ripped the paper in half, and scathingly said, "Get dressed and get your ass downstairs." He turned, stalking off. "Ramsay too."

He was pacing in a tight circle when we got there, finding him in the kitchen.

Angel was leaning against one of the cupboards, his arms crossed over his shoulders. I tried to gauge his mood for a clue as to what was going on, but he only tipped his chin up to me. "Scout." His eyes slid over Ramsay, but nothing showed. Angel was like that. He killed at poker.

"What's going on?"

"Why am I getting papers delivered to me that state I broke my father's wrist?"

Ramsay stepped closer to me, her hand coming to my back.

"There are pictures and X-rays proving his wrist is broken, and you're a corroborating witness?"

"The fuck?"

My uncle ignored me. "Why is my father telling me that if I don't sign over the very few shares of the company that I have —and I cannot express enough how few of these shares are or that they were hidden by my brother for me—then he'll press charges against me. *What is going on?*"

"Shares?"

"What is going on, Scout?" Miles lost all control, shouting at the top of his lungs.

Angel's arms came undone, but he didn't move from the cupboard. "Brother." That was all he said, the one word.

Miles's eyes closed, and he drew in a long and deep breath, fighting for control. Before he opened them, he said, "I swear to God, Scout, if you don't start telling me what's going on, I'm going to—"

"He's being a dick!" I exploded. "What else do you want to know? He's a dick of the biggest dick proportions there are."

"Are you kidding me?" He opened his eyes. "Are you jerking

me around here?" He thrust one of the ripped pieces in my face. "Why are you a corroborating witness?"

"Because I did it."

Now Angel straightened from the cupboard, but he still didn't move away from it.

"Say again?" My uncle cocked his head to the side.

"I broke his wrist."

"Why the fuck would you do that? When did you see him?"

"Cohen called me," Angel said. "He told me about a conversation he had with Scout, that he told him about the new Chelton hotel being built up by Wembley Creek. They call it Dragon Abyss."

"The what?" Miles twisted around to his best friend. All blood drained from him.

It'd been the same reaction I had.

Angel, who spent the last fifteen years as a cop, wasn't fazed by anything. He was fazed now, but only a little. He raised an eyebrow. "Why do you think I came to find you tonight?"

"You could've told me this. You didn't say a word."

Angel lifted a shoulder, leaning back against the counter. "I beg to differ. I asked where Scout was, and you were already seeing red." He nodded toward the paper in my uncle's hands. "I figured you'd find out in a few more minutes, why should I be the one to break the news?"

Miles raked a hand over his face, muttering a curse under his breath. "Morons. I'm surrounded by morons." He asked Ramsay, "You have anything to share as well?"

Her fist balled my shirt up, pressing hard against me. "No."

He grunted. "Jesus. Scout. What is going on? I've had these shares for years. My brother hid them from our dad, and now this? If I don't give them to our father, he's going to press charges against me for something you did?"

"He's not going to do shit." Why was the room suddenly so small? My shoulders felt so heavy.

Ramsay moved even closer, her entire front plastered against my back. "Scout."

I moved a hand back, sliding it under her shirt, needing to feel her skin there. I told him everything.

"Oh, shit." Angel half cursed, half laughed when I was done, and this time, he moved from the counter. He went to stand behind my uncle.

Miles didn't move. For a full minute, he stared at me as if he couldn't comprehend what I just told him. The room was getting more and more tense. The pressure felt like it could snap at any moment.

I found myself holding a breath.

I think everyone was.

"Get away from me," a low growl came from my uncle, his head slightly down. He was talking to Angel.

"Like fuck I will." His response was just as low. "You're my brother. I'm not letting you do something stupid right now."

"Murder wouldn't be stupid in this case." Miles's nostrils flared. "It'd be justified."

Angel met my gaze over my uncle's shoulder. His eyes were grave. So were mine because we both knew Miles wasn't talking about my death.

"You can't tell me it wouldn't be." He kept on, not facing Angel, but everyone knew he was talking to him.

Angel was the detective here. He would also give his life for my uncle.

"Miles—"

"Don't!" He flung a hand toward me. "Don't fucking say a word. What were you thinking? You hurt him. You can't give him anything. Anything. He will use everything within his power to ruin whatever he needs to in order to get what he wants. My god, Scout, what were you thinking?"

"He was trying to protect me." Ramsay burst from my side.

I wrapped an arm around her waist, holding her back to me.

She strained against my hold. "Your father was threatening me. Scout wasn't thinking—"

"Of course he wasn't!" Miles muttered a curse, stepping back and running a hand over his face again. "*Lo siento*—I'm sorry. I'm sorry." He switched his gaze to me, stricken.

That was a punch.

"I've taken you in. You are like my son. Don't you get that? Why wouldn't you have called me? We could've—we could've done something. Planned something. I—"

"You know what he's doing to her." We both knew who I was talking about, my mother. "He's hurting her. He's going to always hurt her. He's going to always get away with it. If I go back, do what he wants, I'll make him promise to let her go. I'll—"

"You can't negotiate with him. You know that. He'll always win."

I exploded, the pressure snapping, "Why do you think I'm doing this?"

Ramsay was back to molding herself against me, turning to me. Her hand moved under my shirt, resting over my stomach. "There's no winning with him. I'm sorry, but I wasn't thinking. When I realized he had Ramsay in the room with him, I wasn't thinking straight." A strangled laugh erupted from me. "I wanted to hurt him. Just one fucking time. I wanted to get back at him, and he moved to strike me first. I got a shot, one time, to hurt him. I took it. I don't feel bad either. I'll never feel bad about making him feel pain, and I swear . . . I swear that, when I go in, I'll do everything in my power to destroy him. I will, Uncle. I will."

A different look came over him, making him look broken. "Scout." He came to me, a hand falling on my shoulder, and he kept it there. "I'm so sorry, Scout. So very sorry. I never should've let this go as long as it has. I—this has to stop."

An uncomfortable shiver went down my spine. I really didn't like what I was seeing, hearing from him, and I wasn't alone. Angel and I shared a look.

He moved a step closer. "Wanna clue us in, Brother? What are you planning on doing?"

A wholly alien look was on Miles's face as he turned to him, his hand falling from my shoulder. "I have to stop this. You know that—"

I sprang, wrapping my arms around his neck. He tried twisting out from my hold, but I held it in place. I didn't give him an inch to get away. As his body fell, mine went with it until we were on the ground. He tried twisting again, using his body to remove my hold, but I wrapped my legs around him and held him firm.

It didn't take long until he went limp.

"I'm guessing he's unconscious, right?" Angel had knelt with us, his expression unnerved.

I let him go, his body slumping farther down to the floor as I stood. "Yeah. He'll wake up in a bit, but you might want to handcuff him so he can't go and do something stupid." I reached for Ramsay's hand, twining our fingers.

"Where are you going?"

"We'll go to Ramsay's place. It's best if he doesn't see me before I go. Don't tell him where I am."

His gaze was heavy as he looked up at me, but he wasn't moving from my uncle's form. "Not liking that option either, Scout."

I didn't respond.

There was no point.

86

SCOUT

R amsay was gone when I woke the next morning. I felt her side of the bed. It was still warm, so she hadn't been gone long.

My phone beeped.

Mom: Don't do anything. I'm doing something on my end. You'll see.

A normal son might've put stock in that, but I was me. She was her. I knew my mom. She'd want to help. She'd plan and brainstorm and maybe even make a phone call, but in the end, she'd back down. The hold he had on her was too deep, too severe. There was no going back. I'd given up on getting my mom back a long time ago.

Miles: Where are you? Are you at Ramsay's?

Me: Yeah. Still here. I'm going to leave soon.

It was two seconds after I hit send that my phone lit up. He was calling me.

I answered, "Hey."

"Your plan is stupid. Everything is stupid, but I get it. I get why you think doing this is the only thing you can do, but listen to me. Your mom is blowing up my phone, urging me to make sure you don't reach out to him. Forget about what I want to do to him. Listen to your mom. I think she's for real this time. She's going to do something so you don't go back into the family. And if she doesn't, I will. I'm not going to let you go down this path. We both know how it'll end."

"It's Mom." A pit settled in my chest as I said that, ignoring the rest of what he said. "She's not going to do anything, and you know it."

He was quiet. He couldn't argue with that. "Still . . ." His voice was hoarse. "Come home. I want to spend time with my nephew while I can."

He knew the deal. When he got out, he was excommunicated. If I went in, it'd be the same thing. They'd threaten me about reaching out to him. He and I would go back to being strangers.

That pit just kept growing and growing. "Give me the morning with Ramsay unless her mom kicks me out."

"I can give her a call."

"No. I'm going to tell her what's going on. My other friends too. They deserve to know at this point. I'm leaving."

"You want me to be there when you do that?"

That meant a lot. A whole lot. "No, I can handle it, but thank you for the offer."

We hung up, and after using the bathroom, doing what I could to clean up, I made my way downstairs.

I stopped when I saw who was all there. "What the fuck?"

Ramsay was in the kitchen. Across the island were Clint, Trenton, and Alex. Rounding out the end of the island were Gem, Theresa, Alred, and just coming in through the main door was Kira.

Ramsay froze when she saw me, her eyes big. She had a piece of toast in her hand and dropped it. "You're leaving?"

The doorbell rang.

Kira rounded to answer it, and Cohen and Amalia were

there. Cohen tipped his chin up to me, giving me a tight grin. "Hey, man. You pulled your head out of your ass with Ramsay, huh?"

Amalia was fighting back tears, coming right to me. She threw her arms around me, her head pressing against my chest.

"Hey." I folded her in and she drew back, her face streaked with tears.

She said, "You can't go. You just can't."

"I—" I scowled at Cohen. "I was going to break that news myself."

"Sorry, man, but no, I'm not." He lost the tight grin, staring hard at me. "I overheard our uncles talking, and what the fuck, dude?" He was pissed. "I'm the one who called everyone. You can be pissed at me, I don't care. I'm pissed at you, but seriously, man. They need to know. They deserve that. Ramsay deserves that. You deserve that."

I wanted to glare at him, but he was right. Everything was fucked up.

"Save your breath. We already know." Clint was eating the toast Ramsay had dropped earlier. He waved it at me, grinning before taking another big bite.

"You know what?"

He gestured to Cohen with the toast. "He told us the basic points when he called us to come over. After that, sorry, but it was a whole phone tree happening. Word's out in the group."

Fucking hell.

Alex gave Clint an exasperated look before shaking his head. "It's not even like that either. We know. The three of us. Cohen told us enough to get our asses here, and then I called Miles. He told me the rest." His eyes narrowed at me. "I'm your best friend and I find out like this?"

"It's not like that."

"You have people here who care about you. I care about you. We should know about this shit."

"Also," Clint held up his last piece of toast. "It's cool how wealthy your family is, but we don't give a fuck. Just saying that."

"I might care." Trenton smirked.

Clint snorted. "He's the one who really doesn't care."

Alex spoke as if his brothers hadn't interrupted, "We'll do everything we can, anything we can, to help keep you here. You don't have to fight him on your own. I don't know what we can do to help, but we'll try."

Ramsay had come up to my side, her hand slipping in with mine. She leaned against me, tipping her head up and I saw *everything* in her eyes. I wasn't alone. She was trying to remind me of that.

Fuck. Damn. Shit.

I shook my head. "I was going to tell you all anyway." I caught sight of Kira and Ramsay's other group. "Or some of you."

Clint shoved back his seat, coming to stand by his cousin. He had a new piece of toast in one hand and threw his other arm around Ramsay's shoulders. "I got no problem figuring out some way to immobilize your grandpops."

Trenton stood too, holding a plate of eggs with one hand and shoveling them in with his other. "Me too," he said around the food before swallowing. "We'll put all our thinking caps on today and figure something out. You don't need to go anywhere."

I leveled Cohen with a look. "You told them about my mom?"

"Your mom? Just who your grandfather is and that he's making you return to the family, which means you'll leave here. That's all they know."

Alex had moved to stand by Cohen, who'd drawn Amalia away from me.

Clint's arm fell away from Ramsay as she moved into me, her front against mine.

Yeah, okay. Maybe I needed a minute, one fucking minute to process all of this.

It felt so good to hold her.

Alex spoke up, "I don't know the shit that's going on with your mom, but hearing who your family really is and knowing that kind of power and wealth tends to corrupt"—his eyes were on Ramsay as he spoke—"I can only guess the shit going down to make you return to that family. And now knowing that's probably the reason you ended things with my cousin, we're here, brother."

He held up his fist, and I met it with mine. "Appreciate it."

The doorbell rang.

I was looking down at Ramsay when Kira opened the door, saying, "Hello. Come in—what are you doing here, PJ? You're not one of Scout's inner circle."

"Neither are you. Who'd you suck to get an invite today?"

"Oh my God! I didn't—"

"She's with us!" Theresa held up a hand with a half-eaten doughnut in it.

Everyone looked at her. Even me.

"What?" Ramsay turned, but I kept her back against my chest. I hung my arms over the front of her, and she settled in, linking our hands.

"Yeah. We, uh, we kinda—" Theresa ducked down, swallowing the last of her donut. "We don't really know what all is going on because we're not in the Williams family tree, but boy, are we glad that we decided to drop in on Ramsay."

"What?" Ramsay stiffened in my arms.

Gem waved a hand, her head ducking a little. "Yeah. Sorry. We came here to see how you're doing, and well; the guys arrived at the same time and Alred hushed us, told us to play along. We're doing a catch-up with everything, but we're here for you too." The last statement was directed to me.

Alred was indignant. "I did not tell you to be quiet."

Theresa said, "You did, but it's not like we weren't going to *already* do that. From the grim faces, it was obvious something was up."

Clint started laughing.

Trenton flashed a crooked grin. "I dig that."

Alex cringed. "We thought you knew."

"Nope.

Kira made an exasperated sound, and stepped around, her hands on her hips. "And I'm here because we bonded at the dance. I asked where you"—she glanced toward Ramsay—"were, and Theresa didn't know, and honestly, we just started talking. That led to some mutual respect being acknowledged. Some apologies that were needed from the past. And—"

"And they danced the rest of the night," Gem spoke up.

Alred held up a hand, waving it. "Also, a manager guy came to complain about the glitter on my shirt, but Kira and Theresa had my back. It was beyond."

Gem was nodding. "True story."

"So, yeah. I invited her, but I didn't know we were walking into *this*."

Kira flipped some hair off her shoulder. "I needed to go home and make myself presentable, but I'm here. Consider me a part of this group. Teamwork, right?" She sent me a smile. "Kudos to you for being so wealthy. Is it Fritz Rothchelton? I know my dad's been sweating about a Rothchelton being in the area. Now we know who's the who, you know?" She tossed that all out as if she was informing us about the weather for the next few days and moved to join the donut group at the island, snagging one from a box there. "Also, hi, Cohen. You ditched me last night. Consider yourself my mortal enemy."

He grinned at her. "Until next Saturday night, right?"

She rolled her eyes and turned her back to him, huffing.

Theresa scowled, moving to stand in front of her, blocking Cohen's point of view. She lifted up a glass of orange juice and said before taking a sip, "We've shifted our alliance, so you know."

"For now." He didn't sound too worried.

Ramsay had been stiffening more and more in my arms until she'd had enough. "Okay! I mean, seriously. We have a real emergency here. We need to think of something to do to keep Scout here."

"A question." Trenton raised a finger. "Why don't you, like, not go?"

Ramsay was back to tensing against me.

I ran a hand down her arm, holding her firmly against me, more for me than her. "Because he's hurting someone else, and I'm going in to protect them."

Everyone got quiet again. Those eating ceased eating. All eyes returned to me.

Theresa lowered her orange juice. "Who are you protecting?"

"I can't tell you that."

Clint cursed. "Is it Ramsay? Did that motherfucker find out about her and threaten her or something? You're going in to protect my cousin?"

"Our cousin." Alex glared at him.

Clint rolled his eyes. "You know what I mean. When I'm heated, I sometimes don't speak triplet. Flay me."

Trenton snorted.

"Stop it." Ramsay slightly leaned forward from me. "We need to brainstorm ideas and do it quick."

"Right." Gem.

"Yeah." Theresa.

Alred nodded, finishing his donut.

Kira held up a hand. "I have an uncle who lives off the grid in Alaska. You could go there."

Ramsay growled. "Maybe something actually productive?"

Theresa asked, "You have an uncle who lives off the grid?"

Kira shrugged. "I figure every family has a black sheep, right? He's ours. He's also a conservative liberal, if you can figure that one out. I still haven't. He, like, mails us letters, but they're mostly filled with threats about World War Three, and to save the trees, he writes on leaves. The leaves are usually broken by the time we get them, so the threats are like, 'Save the—' and nothing. We don't know what we're supposed to save. One said 'take cover' but again, the rest of the leaf was in pieces so every now and then I look up and wonder what I'm supposed to take cover from, but anywho. That's my uncle. Maybe not such a solid idea."

Theresa and Gem were fighting back smiles.

Ramsay bit out, "You think?"

THE GENERAL THEME WAS BLACKMAIL.

Alred knew people who knew people who knew people, and he was convinced he could get some damning information on my grandfather. Considering he didn't know who to contact or what information he could get, it wasn't a solid idea.

Theresa offered to ask some of their relatives if they could dig up dirt on my grandfather too.

Gem didn't have a suggestion. She came over to hold Ramsay's hand at times when I wasn't holding her.

Clint suggested going to find that fraternity guy who knew my family and interrogate him about what he knew and see if there was anything there they could use.

Alex kept calling my uncle to see what he could do to help me. The conversation would end the same way, that Miles was doing what he could, but he'd have to get back to him. They'd hang up, and Alex would call a couple minutes later with the same request, but mixed with more impatience. I had to give my uncle credit. He always answered.

Trenton mulled it over before saying, "We could go to the golf course and infiltrate those cronies. Shit goes down on the golf course. Maybe we could plant listening devices in every hole."

As ideas went, I was thinking that had the most merit.

Kira had another idea, suggesting she get me a room on a yacht heading to the Mediterranean next week. Most of her ideas were helping me go somewhere else. She wasn't factoring in that my grandfather had a private jet. He could fly anywhere to get me.

After four hours of brainstorming and an early lunch, Ramsay tugged me to her bedroom. She held my hand. "I'll go public."

Hearing everyone trying to help meant more than I realized it would've, but I needed to end this. I shook my head, cupping her face. "With what?"

"He threatened me. I can say everything he said to me. I—"

"They'll call him for a comment, and it'll be laughed off. They'll spin it so you look like some teenager who's infatuated with me. You're not going to say anything. I can't let him hurt you anymore than he already has."

"But—"

I pulled her to me, kissing her forehead.

Her hands reached up, fisting my shirt. "It can't be over. Just like that."

I struggled with swallowing before pulling back enough to see her face. "This, all of this, everyone coming, this means a lot to me."

"Don't, Scout." She tried pulling away.

I held her close, a tenderness filling me that I never knew I could've felt in my life. "I'm glad I met you. I'm glad I got this time with you, with your cousins. You gave me something to hold on to when I'll need it. The world is hard. There's no color with him. No happiness. No love, and you gave that to me. I realized I loved you too late, but at least I realized it."

"Don't." Tears welled up on her eyelids. "You gave that back to me too. I never would've let myself open up to someone again, not after Max. Sometimes I wonder if my dad brought you to me, if he—"

I pulled her to me again, holding her. I smoothed a hand down her hair, her back. "I've been broken for so long that I didn't realize I *was* broken. You gave me life back."

"Shut up. Just shut up." She choked on a sob.

I chuckled lightly. "We're a pair, huh?"

"We're not broken anymore."

I brushed a thumb over her forehead, tucking a strand of hair back. "Yeah. Not anymore." We were both ignoring the inevitable. I'd leave and we'd go back to being two broken pieces. I didn't want that. Not for her. I wanted her to be whole.

How could I do that? What could I do? Anything?

Maybe I shouldn't have said anything, but no. No more secrets. Not between us.

I couldn't have that. I couldn't leave with things unsaid between us.

I'd always remember this—of telling her, of realizing, of holding her, of hearing her say the words. She loved me back. That was burned into my memory. I'd never forget that.

My grandfather would follow through with what he said. I needed to go to him today. I needed to somehow make a stand so he wouldn't hurt Ramsay and my mother.

It was time to go.

"Ramsay," I started to say right when there was a burst of footsteps stampeding up the stairs.

Cohen and Alex both burst through the door at the same

time. Cohen slightly ahead. A wildness in his eyes. "Dude! You need to come see this. Now!" He took off, sprinting downstairs just as fast as he'd come up.

Alex was in disbelief, shaking his head back and forth. "I can't—holy shit, man. Holy *shit*! Come and see this."

87

BREAKING NEWS

"We have breaking news, and it's quite incredible. The daughter of long-time CEO of Chelton Corp, Fritz Rothchelton, has come forward with allegations of long-term abuse at the hands of her father. From what our sources are saying, she's gone to the police after reportedly spending decades under the threat of blackmail, extortion, and there were even allegations of sexual exploitation."

"This is mind-blowing, Nadia. And these claims have credibility to them, I'm assuming?"

"Yes. We're being told that not only did she walk into the NYPD this morning with what can *only* be described as bombshells but also she had evidence in hand. Diaries. Email. Texts. She kept it all, and it's very, *very* damning to the man who runs an empire."

"So, in other words, this could be just the beginning."

"Yes, Dalton. This is most certainly not a good day for Fritz Rothchelton. This is very bad for him."

"We'll be back after the commercial break with more details in this developing story."

"BREAKING NEWS! Years of detailed accounts of abuse from the daughter of Fritz Rothchelton. More to come at the hour with this fast developing story."

"WE'RE NOT JUST TALKING about any wealthy man. We're talking about the man who's been at the helm of a complete global empire. Rothchelton University. Chelton Hotels. Carby's. The Fritz Movie Cinemas. That's just to name a few. This story broke just yesterday and more people have come forward with allegations of abuse, exploitation, extortion, intimidation, and sexual misconduct. The story broke with his daughter, but now we have thirty more individuals with their own separate allegations against him. Some pressing charges."

"So remarkable. I can't imagine what Chelton Corp is going to do. They have their hands in everything, it seems. Movie franchises. Food. I believe I read they have shares in a thousand companies? Many of them household name companies too."

"Considering that these 'crimes' occurred in different states, would the FBI have to be a part of this investigation?"

"I'm sure they're already involved since the Chelton Corp is a national and global brand. Some of the allegations regard corporate crimes. There's multiple jurisdictions involved here."

"Yes. We'll see what more news comes out tomorrow, Peter."

"POLICE INVESTIGATING fifty-plus counts of abuse against Friz Rothchelton."

"AT THE TOP of the hour, we have more developments from the downfall of Fritz Rothchelton. The board of Chelton Corp had an emergency meeting late last night. Fritz Rothchelton has been voted out of any shares in Chelton Corp, and his son, Roth VI, was voted in as the new CEO and will be taking over all of his grandfather's duties."

"Now, Roth VI, I'm guessing that's a family name?"

"I believe so. I'm told Roth was named after a founding grandfather, Roth Rothchelton, Sr. Fritz's oldest brother, who passed away last fall, was given the family namesake. Roth V."

"What a name, huh? I'm sure Roth VI is married, but to show up for a Tinder date and introduce yourself as Roth the VI Rothchelton." The newscaster was laughing.

———————

"IT'S BEEN two weeks since the first bombshell hit the news wave, but this is a story that just keeps on coming. Fritz Rothchelton's daughter states that she finally broke her silence because, and this is heartbreaking, to save her son from suffering at the hands of Fritz Rothchelton. Apparently, one of the most recent bouts of abuse, which turned physical, prompted her son to try to offer to take the place of his mother. Now, I'm not sure how that would've worked, but it sounds just awful. Doesn't it, Maria?"

"In these families where they are so powerful, so wealthy, they have resources that none of us normal folk would be able to comprehend, I'm sure there are dynamics that we wouldn't be able to understand. They almost live in their own worlds sometimes. I really believe that."

"Yes, it was said that the year before, she had shipped her son to live with his uncle, who was exiled from the family. It's being reported she wanted him to have a normal life, but Fritz wanted his only grandson in the family."

"Just so heartbreaking that the core of all of this was the story about a mother trying to save a son, or a son trying to save his mother."

"NADIA, I can't believe we're still learning new details about the downfall of Fritz Rothchelton. Tell us the latest."

"Well, the latest is a new connection between the Rothchelton scandal and a local family in Cedra Valley, Texas. Sources report that the youngest son of the Prestige family was in a prior romantic relationship with the girlfriend of Fritz Rothchelton's grandson."

"So the girlfriend of—"

"The *current* girlfriend of Rothchelton's grandson had previously been in a relationship with the youngest son of the Prestige family."

"This is interesting. I've heard of the Prestiges. They're also old money, but on a way, *way* smaller scale than the Rothcheltons."

"There were allegations and claims of abuse at his hand. Her father reportedly confronted the son to leave his daughter alone, and fearing for his life, the boyfriend murdered her father."

"Are you kidding me?" The other newscaster was horrified.

"The evidence was documented. We have to still use the word 'allegedly', but the abuse seems to be factual. There was a local investigation done, but no formal charges were brought forward with the murder."

"Prestige is currently facing a possible civil suit for a blog written about the relationship. It's been since taken down, and the civil suit is moving forward, but a judge has granted a restraining order against Prestige on the girl's behalf. There have been previous restraining orders filed against Prestige as well, and after her father's death, one was granted." The reporter waved a hand in the air, leaning back in his chair. "There've been some other incidents, one involving a fraternity party and a vehicle vandalism, but apparently that's all cannon fodder."

"Cannon fodder?! Who still talks like that? Cannon fodder. Tell me, Garrett, do you even know how to spell cannon fodder?" They were back to laughing.

———————

"A NEW INVESTIGATION *has been launched into the death of Brett Williams. New evidence and new sources have come forward."*

Cedra Valley Gazette

———————

"THE CEDRA VALLEY POLICE DEPARTMENT *has announced they plan to file formal charges in the death of Brett Williams. More details to come."*

Cedra Valley Gazette

88

RAMSAY

Holy Mother of God, it was almost Christmas. I was saying that because we were in church, and I was praying to Mother Mary so I wouldn't murder one of my cousins. I was stuck between Clint and Trenton. Alex was on the other side of Trenton, and Scout by his side. We'd come for Cohen, who'd come for Amalia because she was partaking in a Christmas choir program. I was getting tired of the up and down, but the Christmas songs were nice.

Since being in Pine River, and since everything that happened, I had started a new obsession with Christmas. I liked everything about it. The singing. The festivities. The snowmen. The gifts. The parties, but I luh-ved Christmas lights.

But I also really liked experiencing the holiday with my boyfriend.

Scout got here last because of a legal meeting he and Miles attended.

With the fallout from his mom's pressing charges, and then further doing one in-depth interview that aired on primetime, the shockwaves were significant. His grandfather was rumored to be holed up in Tuscany while his other uncle was now at the steering wheel and controlling everything. One part of him taking over was extending an olive branch to both Scout's mom and Miles. The one brother, who I hadn't met and didn't know if I ever would, was still running the show, but Miles had a few new roles to help with the Chelton Hotel in our area. Scout mentioned other responsibilites, but it was all in business speak.

I didn't speak business speak.

His mom, who'd I met on numerous occasions over the last two months, was planning on returning to the family business, but after an extended stay in a mental health facility. Her trauma was severe and very real, but Scout spoke to her daily so that was all very good news.

And I never could've imagined how his mom's move was going to affect my own life.

Max was being officially charged with the homicide of my father. The trial was set to start in the summer. My mom offered for us to go back for it, more to visit my dad's gravesite, but the trial was the other reason.

I'd need to testify. The lawyers had been clear about that, but I was offered to do it via Zoom so we'd see what I wanted to do when that time came.

My father's other family also stopped contesting his will. And our settlement came through against Max's family. All of that helped ease some of the financial burdens my mom had been shouldering. She wasn't working at the nursing home. She didn't even need to work anymore, but she enjoyed it so she'd been hired to manage a crafting store in Pine River. The owner approached my mom, offered her the job then and there. My mom was loving it so far. I couldn't pronounce the lady's name, so I never tried. My mom called her Mrs. Meemow.

Mrs. Meemow herself shortened it to Mrs. Meow and she was forever the cat lady to me.

She was intense, scary at times, but it was obvious she adored my mom so she was okay in my book.

As for my aunt, the divorce was still pending. I never found out what Clint did that day, and when he said it was best if I didn't know, I was taking it to heart. I'd learned my lesson after the fraternity battle, but he and I were still the trouble twins so we'd done enough other dumb stuff since.

I loved every bit of it.

But next time I was going to wait for Scout because it would've been a lot more fun sitting next to my boyfriend.

EPILOGUE
RAMSAY

My mom parked the car by the river, set downtown. We were here to meet Scout and he was getting out of his truck, coming around the back in his coat.

"Okay. Thanks for the ride." I began to reach for the door.

"Wait."

"What?"

She had a funny look on her face. "Just, you and him?"

I almost laughed. "Where is this coming from?"

She shrugged. "I don't know. I, after last night, I . . . I don't know."

Scout had a fight the previous night, and we'd all gone to it —even Amalia. It was the original fight he'd taken against a guy from Cedra Valley. They found out that Max's father had been the reason the fighter even reached out to Scout for a fight. He offered to sponsor him.

Or, more specifically that Max had been the one who suggested the fighter go against Scout Raiden and Max's dad looked into who Scout was, found out who his family really was, and *that* was the reason why the fight was first scheduled.

When the news broke later about Max's family and the connection to Scout Raiden's girlfriend, that fighter's team canceled the fight. They hadn't known and were pissed about being manipulated. But, a month later, they asked again with a new sponsor because it turned out that a fight against Scout Raiden would be good publicity. Scout agreed, and he'd annihilated the guy.

I'd been more nervous if I'd run into anyone I knew from my old town, but only a small group from Cedra Valley came. The fighter, his team, his family, and a few others. No one I knew, but I still made sure to stick with my group.

Now thinking about it, my mom had been quiet after the fight.

Once I realized none of my old frenemies were there, I'd been distracted for a whole other reason, Scout himself.

Watching him fight.

Watching him fight without his shirt.

Watching him without his shirt. Or, really, just watching my boyfriend. There was something about seeing his new tattoo of the Norse rune for freedom that made me want to jump him. He got it the day after his mom went to the police. I'd been salivating over him last night, the tattoo, *all* his tattoos, but it was hitting me that my mom had *also* seen him in a very violent manner.

"He's not like that, Mom. You don't need to worry about him."

"Oh. No, no, no." She waved that off. "I didn't know when you'd let another boy into your heart. After, you know, but he got in. I don't think he even knew he was doing it until he was there."

I almost laughed because it was so true. "It surprised me too."

"But you do. You love him."

I nodded. "I do."

"He's a good boyfriend. He has been. He's been thoughtful and kind. Not at all what I thought he'd be like as a boyfriend. You were having sex for so long."

"Mom." The back of my neck was heating up.

"I know. I didn't realize until later, but he's surprising me. That's it. And today, this is a very thoughtful thing to do for you."

I gave a shrug, squirming a little in my seat. "I've not seen any whales and we're in Oregon. It's one of their migrations."

"I know, but the boat ride on the river. It's a long river ride to the ocean, and then going farther out to whale watch is a kind thing to do."

"Once we get to the ocean, we're switching to a bigger boat."

"I know, but the whole thing has been nice. He brought over coffee and donuts this morning. You guys drove around looking at Christmas lights last night. The night before he took you to Pine River's Winter Fest. Now this today." Her eyes were shining. Her voice was hoarse. "I'm just happy for you, honey. That's what I'm trying to say."

I took her hand in mine and squeezed it. "Some of it is because he's finally free."

"I know." Her voice cracked. She covered it with her mouth. "To think about what he's been going through, and what he was going to take on for his mom, it just gets to me sometimes. I watched you after Max, and after we lost your father. I didn't know if you'd ever love again, but you do. You are. You're happy."

My heart skipped a little. "I'm getting there, Mom. I am. With Dad, I'm getting there."

"I know. I love you so much." She pulled me in for a hug before I got out, and I wasn't surprised when she stayed to watch us leave.

Scout waved as we walked down to the marina, my hand in his other one. "Your mom worried I'm trying to kidnap you or something?"

"No." I told him about the conversation.

His hand gripped mine tight. "She's right, though. I didn't know I could love until I fell in love with you, and now look at me. Taking you on a fucking whale watching date. I'm cheesy as fuck. I wouldn't recognize myself either."

I laughed, bumping my hip into his. "We can be cheesy together. We've earned it."

"I'm trying to make up for not taking you to Homecoming."

"There's still prom."

He groaned, until my elbow made contact with his stomach. "I mean, yeah. Prom. Can't wait."

We headed over to the docks and made our way to a boat. A guy was there, moving around, throwing a line back into the boat itself. He saw us and held up a hand. "Brawler, get in here."

I recognized him. Winslet. He was giant in person and even bigger in a coat and hat.

He tipped his chin up to us. "Nice seeing you again, Miss Scout's woman."

Scout snorted a laugh, holding his hand out and helping me into the boat. It wasn't a big one, but big enough for the river. Scout kept my hand in his, motioning toward Winslet, who was now pulling away from the dock. "This is Winnie's full-time job."

"Yep. Boxing don't pay the bills yet. Good old boating does." He gestured to some seats in the back and front. "I got a nice set-up if you want some drinks, something warm. There are blankets too. Get comfortable. We have a good haul in front of us."

He and Scout did the thing where their fists lightly touched before Scout was pulling me to the front. There was a small seating area, but he took us to the railing and put me in front of him. Both of his hands went around me, resting on the railing, as his body moved in behind me. A beat later, his chin came to my shoulder. "Cold?"

A shiver went through me. "Not from the cold."

I felt his grin into my skin as he nuzzled me before resting his chin on my collarbone. One of his hands went to my waist, slipping under my sweatshirt, pulling me better against him. "Winslet does tourist boat rides for a living. He knows the guys who do the whale watching. Normally we'd have to share a boat with a bunch of others, but not this time. He got me a deal."

I almost snorted. "Right. You. Like you're using a coupon for whale watching." After all the changes in his family, Scout admitted to me that his other uncle had shifted a bunch of the family finances. Everyone was now getting almost a fair share of everything. I didn't know the specifics, but I was figuring that made my boyfriend one very, *very* wealthy billionaire. And I was being modest in that guess.

He grunted out a laugh, his teeth nipping against my shoulder. "A deal's a deal. Don't knock it, and my family's finances are my family's finances. They aren't mine." His hand pressed against my stomach, flattening there. "I want to fight. That's all I want to do."

I leaned back against him, putting all my weight into him and tipped my head up, angling so I could see him. "What about me?"

"I'll do you *all* the time."

A tingle spread through me. "You know what I mean."

He looked down, his gaze finding mine and darkened. A whole different look came over them. A more somber one, almost endearing too. He touched the middle of my chin before letting his hand go back to the railing, holding me in place. "I want to be the best fighter I can be, and I want to be able to love you while I'm doing it."

A thrill went through me.

He added, his voice dipping low, "How's that for a plan for the future?"

That same thrill wrapped around my insides, warming me, sparking me. It made me feel alive. And I smiled, knowing I'd been given a gift from the universe. Or maybe my dad. Maybe it was him who brought love back into my life.

I turned around in his arms and wound my arms around his neck, my hand splaying over his neck. I pulled his mouth down and arched up to meet his lips. "That sounds amazing. That's how it sounds."

WE SAW A POD OF WHALES, which was my newest obsession after my renewed love for Christmas.

The first glimpse of the first whale and done. My heart thudded in my heart. I was gone, totally infatuated with all things whales now.

The boat captain said we were lucky because none had been spotted all week.

Maybe. Maybe not.

Or maybe it was my dad at work all over again.

Either way, no matter what would come in the future, I was happy. And I was grateful for that as well.

I also couldn't wait for Scout's next fight.

I had a feeling things were just going to get better and better.

For more stories like this

and to join my newsletter, head to
www.tijansbooks.com

If you enjoyed Pine River, please consider leaving a review.
They truly help so much!

Stay tuned for more stories to come!

RESOURCES

National Domestic Violence Hotline
1.800.799.7233

Love Is Respect
1.866.331.9474

Break The Cycle

Crisis Text Line
Text HOME to 741741

ACKNOWLEDGMENTS

Oh man. First, I started writing Pine River so long ago. I need to thank all of my readers who read the first few chapters and were so supportive for me to finish the book. I'd also like to thank my editors, my proofreaders, all of my beta readers, and Becca Hensley! Thank you to friends like Debra Anastasia, Rachel Van Dyken, and Helena Hunting who would check in on me regularly. I truly appreciate your support.

I wrote two drafts of Pine River. The first focused mostly on Ramsay and all of the horrible things that had happened to her, but when I went in for my second draft, the rest of Scout's own struggle really took hold as well.

There were so many layers in this book and it felt like this book, more than my others, demanded something more out of me. That's the only way I can explain it, but I do hope everyone enjoys Pine River!

HOCKEY WITH BENEFITS
CHAPTER ONE

I liked hockey. I already knew it, but by the third period, I *really* knew it.

The wine might've been a factor, or the two beers that my roommate bought me, but either way, I was having fun. I had a new appreciation for the sport.

I was also enjoying watching Cruz Styles, the team's star player, zip around the rink like he'd been born on skates and not with two normal feet. He wasn't the only one, though. They were all going so fast, like they were flying on ice. It was exhilarating to watch. It wasn't my first hockey game, but it was my first hockey game at Grant West. Everyone on campus had been raving about the new guy for a while now.

His looks didn't hurt either.

His picture was flashed on the jumbotron so many times over the night that I'd lost count. It was having an effect on the three girls in front of me, and also in my vagina. With the hockey mask on, you could still see his fierce dark blue eyes. His high cheekbones. With the mask off, he had a whole chiseled jawline that wasn't legal. I swear. And those cheekbones were set high and wide, giving the sides of his face an indented look, but it worked on him. Not to mention the messy dark hair on top of his head and how he had the look where he could rifle his hand through it, let it go and he still looked fucking hot. Comb that shit back, put him in a suit, and he'd be giving off 007 vibes.

The guy wasn't just pretty. He was sizzling hot, and right now, he was whipping down the ice, going left, through two defenders, creating an opening to the goal and *bam*–the puck was slapped–*denied*. The goalie thrust his leg out, and the puck went off it, going behind the net.

It was picked up by the other team and sent sailing to the other side of the rink.

Off Cruz went, but he'd be back in two seconds because that'd been the theme of the night.

Grant West was pushing hard the whole night, but Cruz was leading the charge. Over and over again.

I was half winded just watching them.

"Yo." Miles Gaynor moved next to me, his shoulder lightly bumping into mine. "You know Race Ryerson?"

"What?" I was fully in a drunk haze, and I was enjoying it.

Miles had first been a class friend. Then a party friend. Now he was kind of a roommate. A little skinny, floppy brown hair, but where it looked cute on him, and baby fresh cheeks, the guy was a looker. It'd been because of him that I was living in my own little space in the attic of a house where he and his cousin, a guy from the football team, and a couple other girls all lived as well. They were all chill, but I'd only met them twice and hanging out at the hockey game was the second time of those two instances. When my roommate from first semester left college to pursue a job in her family business, I hadn't wanted to stick around and see who else my college chose to be her replacement. Hence, Miles.

He nodded to my left. "He's been staring over here at you almost the whole time. Isn't he with someone?"

I frowned, but looked around, the edges of my vision blurring before I focused and saw the guy Miles was talking about. At my look, he diverted his head, but bent down to his girlfriend, who was cheering for the team.

There went my nice buzz.

Tasmin Shaw and Race Ryerson.

As he talked to her, she stopped cheering, her smile falling as she leaned forward, her eyes searching, searching, and finding me. I frowned, narrowing my eyes, but she only went still before raising a hand up and giving me a slight wave and smile with it.

I scowled, but she barely blinked at that.

Goddamn.

"What's the deal there?"

I jerked forward, my whole body going stiff. "Nothing."

"He's never been a creep before."

"He's not. His girlfriend is next to him. Tasmin Shaw."

"So?"

I shrugged. "Taz is probably just confused why I moved out of the dorms. She lived across from me, that's all." I was lying because while she wasn't from my hometown, she knew people who were, and I was guessing that she'd heard the gossip. Her boyfriend too.

My phone buzzed, and I glanced at the screen.

Kit: OMG! Your mom?! Are you okay?

Dad: Checking on you. Wanted to see how you're doing? I'm so sorry you're going through this. I know you like your space and you don't process like that, but I'm here if you want to talk. Any time, no matter what day or hour. Love you, honey.

Nope. Kit was a friend from back home. Panic burst in my chest, right before everyone and everything began to swim around me. Turning my phone off, I refused to deal with what I knew that text was about, what the gossip that Taz and her boyfriend had heard about me. It'd been the catalyst of why I came to the game tonight. What my mom did earlier, why I panicked, drove three hours home and three hours back wasn't going to be dealt with tonight.

I wanted more to drink, and the sooner the better.

"OH!" His eyes got big, and his shoulders went low. "I didn't even think about that. Good to know. Just thought it was weird, that's all."

I fixed him with a look. "Look. You don't have to do this."

My stomach was swirling, and I wasn't getting a good feeling here. Miles and I partied. Sometimes we shared a table at the library, but that'd been the extent of our friendship. I had rules with friends, no personal questions. There was a reason for it, and it was significant. I was usually able to handle that rule with friends because so far, I picked the party crowd. Deep meaningful conversations weren't the norm. It was mostly drinking, flirting, all that jazz. Sometimes there was a catty comment from another girl, and I had a few run-ins. It happened with me, not because I sought them out but because a guy was hitting on me, and the girl got jealous. Guys liked my face. It was round, but my chin somewhat gave me a heart-shaped face. They also liked how my hazel eyes looked combined with my long cinnamon dark hair. Plus, the fact that I was tiny, petite, but I had a rack and some ass. I also had sex appeal, and the reason for that is because I enjoyed sex. God. With my life, it'd become my coping mechanism, but guys could sense that from me and that's what they were only interested in from me. Beyond that, I wasn't the girl that got the guy.

I knew the deal. The guys knew the deal. It was the other girls who didn't.

I was fine with the deal, not that I partook. That's just what the guys wanted from me, but it gave me space sometimes with people. But what Miles was bordering on was something that felt like what a friend would do for someone.

I didn't want those types of friends. Or, to be more accurate, I couldn't have those types of friends.

"What?"

"You. Me. This." I gestured to the roommates, and the game. "I've got walls. I know this. You know this. They're there for a reason. You don't owe me anything. You don't have to be protective because a guy is looking my way."

He took a step back, his tone coming out cold. "Fine. I just know we watch out for each other at parties. Didn't think it was different here, but cool. Good to know. I won't watch out anymore."

Crap.

He had me because he was right. We did do that.

"Miles," I started.

"I'm out of here." He pushed his hands in his pockets and shouldered through the crowd.

Another roommate came over. Wade Kressup, Miles' cousin. His gaze slid to where Miles had just disappeared before he bent down to me. I was almost a whole foot below him. "Do I ask?"

The buzzer went off, signaling the end of the game, and I shook my head. "Nope."

I sighed, needing to refocus my thoughts. I was off today.

I turned my phone back on long enough to send a text to Miles.

Hey. Some stuff happened earlier today, and it was serious. I don't want to get into it, but it's no excuse. I'm sorry for being a bitch. Thank you for being you.

Everyone was heading out, but I stayed for a beat. I needed to get grounded. Too many emotions I was trying to ignore and thoughts I was trying not to think were creeping in. Add to all that, I'd been a bitch to a friend and yeah... I wasn't doing so well on being a decent human being here.

The whole day had gotten away from me.

My chest felt like it was being sucked out of me.

It took me a little bit before I realized Cruz was down on the ice. He was staring up at me and he half raised one of his gloves up. I gave him a small nod right back. Which, okay, I was down for what he was asking to do. Because that whole gesture was an invitation, but also crap, because that meant I'd have to turn my phone on.

"We're heading out." Wade was still there. The crowd was starting to disperse. I couldn't see where the other roommates were.

"I'm going to find my own way back. Thanks for inviting me out tonight."

He frowned a little but nodded. "Okay. Well. I'll catch up with the rest. See you later."

He headed off, and I went to the bathroom. When I was done, the crowd had lessened significantly. Still. I knew it would be a wait, but I couldn't bring myself to turn my phone back on. Because of that, I went over to the door that the players used and slid down to the floor.

I got comfortable.

I didn't have to wait long.

Fifteen minutes later, still sweaty from the game, Cruz Styles found me in the hallway. He'd changed into his Grant West hockey sweats and hoodie. He also had a ball cap pulled low over his forehead, and both his hands were inside his hoodie.

He tapped my foot with one of his and gave me one of those smiles I'd been seeing on the jumbotron all night. "Need a ride?"

"You're supposed to look intimidating for your team pictures."

He frowned but held out a hand.

I put mine in it, and he pulled me up. "Huh?"

"For your pictures." I motioned behind us to where there

was a six-foot mural picture of just him. He was in his hockey gear, holding his stick and smiling wide for the camera. "That doesn't strike fear in anyone. The opposing team comes through here. They look at that and want to be your friend."

"No, no, no. You got it all wrong." We turned for the door. "That smile gets under their skin. They've already come in hearing about me, and then they see that, and they get confused. Some guys want to wipe that smile off my face and others want to be my friend. Then I leave 'em all in the dust when I make the first goal and by then, wham. They're all sorts of fucked up."

I laughed because it wasn't true at all. Cruz was just being Cruz.

He opened the door and I stepped out, knowing which one was his truck and heading there. "You didn't shower?"

He went to the driver's side as I got in the passenger side, and he smirked my way. "What? And forget how hot and bothered I saw you were up in the stands? Figured we could shower together. You game?"

He sent me a smile as he started the engine, and I couldn't help but smile back because like Miles, Cruz knew the deal. No personal shit.

He knew the rules because he was my not-friend with benefits.

And he was right. Showers with him were the best.

Keep reading Hockey With Benefits here!

ALSO BY TIJAN

Broken and Screwed Series (YA/NA)

Jaded Series (YA/NA suspense)

Davy Harwood Series (paranormal)

Carter Reed Series (mafia)

The Insiders

Mafia Standalones:

Cole

Bennett Mafia

Jonah Bennett

Canary

Paranormal Standalones and Series:

Evil

Micaela's Big Bad

The Tracker

Davy Harwood Series (paranormal)

Young Adult Standalones:

Ryan's Bed

A Whole New Crowd

Brady Remington Landed Me in Jail

College Standalones:

Antistepbrother

Kian

Enemies

Contemporary Romances:

Bad Boy Brody

Home Tears

Fighter

Rockstar Romance Standalone:

Sustain

More books to come!